THE
BURIAL
PLOT

Elizabeth Macneal is the author of two *Sunday Times*-bestselling novels: *The Doll Factory*, which won the 2018 Caledonia Novel Award and has been adapted into a major TV series on Paramount+, and *Circus of Wonders*. Her work has been translated into twenty-nine languages. Born in Scotland, Elizabeth is also a potter and lives in Twickenham with her family. She can be found on Instagram @elizabethmacneal

ALSO BY ELIZABETH MACNEAL

The Doll Factory
Circus of Wonders

THE
BURIAL
PLOT

ELIZABETH MACNEAL

PICADOR

First published 2024 by Picador
an imprint of Pan Macmillan
The Smithson, 6 Briset Street, London ECIM 5NR
EU representative: Macmillan Publishers Ireland Ltd, 1st Floor,
The Liffey Trust Centre, 117–126 Sheriff Street Upper,
Dublin 1, DOI YC43
Associated companies throughout the world
www.panmacmillan.com

ISBN 978-1-5290-9095-6

1 3 5 7 9 8 6 4 2

A CIP catalogue record for this book is available from the British Library.

Typeset in Adobe Caslon Pro by
Palimpsest Book Production Ltd, Falkirk, Stirlingshire
Printed and bound by CPI Group (UK) Ltd, Croydon, CRO 4YY

Visit **www.picador.com** to read more about all our books
and to buy them. You will also find features, author interviews and
news of any author events, and you can sign up for e-newsletters
so that you're always first to hear about our new releases.

For my family,
Jonny, Arthur and Esme,
with all my love.

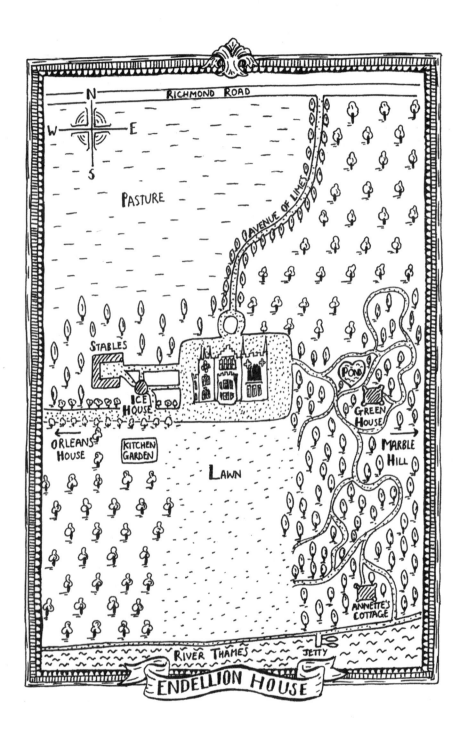

ENDELLION HOUSE

Killing Moths

It was close to nightfall and Bonnie was killing moths in the bedroom that had once belonged to Mr Moncrieff's dead wife. Mr Moncrieff detested the scent of cedar and camphor, and so the only way to be rid of them was by hand. Bonnie ground them against carpets and dressing tables, pulverized them against the rugs. It was a massacre, each insect obliterated in a small smear of white. When she opened the wardrobe, she saw that the moths had already eaten their way through the fur stoles. The fox brush looked like it had been peppered with shot.

It had been more than a year since Mrs Moncrieff had died and still the room hadn't been touched: there, in the corner, was a browning globe on a stand which creaked when Bonnie put her hand to it, and on the dressing table was a lace collar, unwashed and yellowing with age. Bonnie paused, palms smarting, and placed the collar against her throat as she had done each time she had stepped into this room. She regarded herself carefully. But today she felt absurd, such a fine garment layered on top of her linen maid's apron, like dressing a pig in a cravat. She dropped the collar hastily. The room seemed to hold its breath, as though Mrs Moncrieff was about to breeze in the door; as if she would snatch it back and slap her across the cheek.

Bonnie shook her head: Mrs Moncrieff was gone. It must

have been Mr Moncrieff's talk about the new cemetery that had dug its fingers into her, made her imagine ghosts. She stared out of the window at the vast stretch of distant pasture where the cemetery would be built. Soon that sloping, nettled land would sprout grand avenues, vaults, catacombs, a chapel in a Gothic style.

A moth rose up before her, pale as a bride. Bonnie gritted her teeth and resumed her work, opening cupboards and drawers and clapping out the moths, grinding them under her heels. She lifted the lid of an old mahogany chest, smacked a few creatures that fluttered out. There. Gone in an instant, turned to dust. She paused, looked closer. Bonnie already knew that there was nothing of worth in this chest, no necklaces or shell earrings. It was crammed with white silks in neat stacks. She should not linger. It was late and she still had to bathe Cissie and fetch her a chocolate, then warm Mr Moncrieff's sheets with a pan filled with hot coals. But what were a few seconds? She reached towards the stack of fabric, shook one out.

It was a nightgown. She thought of the yellowed rag that she wore to bed, darned and patched, sweat stains circling the armpits, rusty streaks where her menses had caught her unaware. She held this dress to the light. It was cold, as fresh and bright as new china. Frilling at the collar, tightly drawn sleeves, a big fat ribbon around the waist.

Who could resist such a thing? It was the decision of an instant. She balled the nightgown into a bundle, slammed shut the chest, half-ran into the hallway.

Annette would be in the kitchen, slicing tomorrow's bacon, old Manton by the fire, blacking Mr Moncrieff's boots. A stag eyed her from the wall, marbles glinting in its sockets, antlers shadowed. She dithered for a moment, then raced down the hallway, up the servants' stairs, to where her little room crouched in the eaves. She closed the door, unfurled the dress. There it was, clutched in her red, work-sore hands. Had Mrs Moncrieff – *Josephine* – worn this as she waited in bed for her husband each night? And as Josephine lay there, did she think about how everything outside the window – the woodland with its ice house and greenhouse; the copses where foxes sheltered; the jetty leaning into the Thames – was all hers?

Bonnie sat in her attic bedroom as the sun lowered, teasing the silk between her cracked fingers. She pulled it so tight that a thread snagged. She cursed. And then she laughed; it was her dress now, wasn't it, and couldn't she do what she wanted? It was nobody's but *hers*. She could trample through mud in it if she chose, torture it on the fire, and nobody would know.

The damp on the wall shone in the dusk. Her heart quivered. She thought of the wind-up toy that Crawford had once bought for her and buzzed against her neck. A machine that, once started, could not easily be stopped.

Part One

CLEMENT'S LANE, ST GILES, LONDON

1839

Wanted

'WANTED,' Rex boomed as he read from a broadsheet, his fingers leaving sweaty imprints on the paper. 'A respectable, steady, young girl as Dairy Woman. Must be well acquainted with making good butter.' He glanced at Bonnie. 'I can see her, sweating over a churn. Can't you, Crawford? A sweet little rosy-cheeked maid.'

They were sprawled around the garret they shared at the top of the Angler, summer heat thickening the air so that it felt as dense as gravy. There was Bonnie, twenty-one, as green and pretty as an apple, swinging her legs and picking the greasy meat from a chicken carcass. Crawford sat beside her, watching her with small flicks of his eyes, his fingers circling her ankle. Rex sat a little apart from them, shadowed by the eaves: he was a wide, brutish man with the heft of a prize-fighter. Sweat pearled on his forehead, his damp shirt abandoned on the floor, his task of weighing brass coffin plates briefly neglected.

'It's hot,' Bonnie said, barely paying attention to what Rex had said. Everything seemed to shy away from the heat. Even the men who gathered in the inn below for the rat-baiting sounded muted, lethargy stiffening their conversation. The wood-cuts Crawford had tacked to the walls – of a white turreted house and river views – curled at their edges. A wasp had expired against the glass, the gaps in the window plugged shut with scraps of linen. Still, the hot reek of the graveyards seeped through – Enon Chapel and the Green Ground, both bulging with the dead, no matter how much quicklime Rex heaped over the bodies to hasten their decay.

'I can see it,' Crawford said.

'See what?' Bonnie asked, turning the carcass over and prising out the soft sweet oysters.

'You as a dairy maid,' Crawford said, a little impatiently.

'Me?' Bonnie scoffed, licking the fat from her fingers. For a moment she imagined herself hunkered under a cow with a handful of udder, milk chiming against a pail. 'In heat like this, the milk'd curdle in seconds.'

Neither man spoke.

'And I detest cows. Their slow, stupid looks.' She glanced up from the chicken. 'Why are you staring at me?' She turned her chin from side to side, deliberately coquettish, enjoying Crawford's eyes on her.

'I'm not sure I'd call you either steady or respectable,' Crawford said, and she cuffed him, so he leaned forward and kissed her. Her head filled with the scent of him – peppermint and pipe smoke – and the taste of salt on his mouth. He sucked the chicken fat from her finger, holding her wrist tight.

'Beast,' she cried, and tried to wipe her hands on his green jacket, but he pushed himself out of the way, chuckling.

She watched to see if Rex flinched, ready to savour her triumph at being closer to Crawford than he was. But Rex shook the paper, cleared his throat. Crawford stilled.

'WANTED,' Rex continued. 'In a Gentleman's family at Endellion House, a short distance from Richmond, a single woman as LADY'S MAID for a young girl of sixteen years. She must be accustomed to the care of fabrics, a competent dressmaker, and a good hairdresser. A thoroughly honest, respectable, considerate—'

'Ah, but there's that damned respectability again,' Bonnie said, nudging Crawford with her toe, expecting him to grasp it, to tickle her. 'You might as well tolerate me here. I'll spend my days slowly roasting in this garret, being as devilishly unrespectable as possible. Won't I, Craw?'

But Crawford didn't smile. And as they both stared at her, she felt as though she were being cut up and weighed.

'What is it?' she asked. Rex looked away, but Crawford leaned forward again, his look so intent that it made the hairs on her arms prickle. Was this another of the small, careful tests he devised for her? She licked her lips, found them cracked and scabbed. He would dare her to take a bun from a distracted baker; he would hide from her in a crowd and watch her panic as she tried to find him. Little checks to see if she still loved him, if she was still entirely his own, if she still wanted to please him. Occasionally, these tests had become a way of drawing in money: Crawford would send her to coax gentlemen down an alley where he and Rex would be waiting to rob them. Each time she triumphed and he loved her for it. She raised her hand to scratch her wrists, her fingernails raking an insect bite.

'A *lady's maid*. You can't mean it. Richmond might as well be the moon,' she said, as airily as she could, glancing from one man to another, for any cue as to what she was supposed to say.

'Didn't you tell me you were a lady's maid when we first met?' Crawford asked, moving so close that she felt the whisper of his breath against her arm. '*To a fine house on a fine street in – in – in May-fer.*'

Rex guffawed; Bonnie winced, then forced herself to join in, laughter catching in her throat. 'What a dolt you must have thought me.'

'You might have been, though. A lady's maid. Mightn't you?'

Bonnie laughed again: it came out more as a cough. Rex's amusement died away, his mouth set. Both faces were closed tight against her, and she had the sense that they had discussed this, arranged it somehow: these two friends who had known each other for years before she met Crawford. But arranged what? Anger spiked through her: Rex was never tested as she was. Crawford's dog, a man had once called him, who would dance to his master's tune like a terrier on a hot plate. But Crawford accepted his loyalty without question. And what was it they now wanted from her? She couldn't fathom what the test was or how she might pass it. Agree that she wanted to be a lady's maid, and she might fail – it would seem she wanted a new life, away from Crawford; disagree, and she might fail – she would be disobeying some secret, opaque wish he had.

'I can see you with a pair of tongs, curling a little brat's ringlets,' Rex said.

'What is this?' she asked, swatting Crawford on the arm. She would have taken a pin to the room if she could, but it held, resisted, as unyielding as a leather balloon.

'What is what?' Crawford asked, coolly.

'Crawford could write you a fine character,' Rex said. 'Thoroughly honest, respectable, considerate—'

The back of her throat began to itch and when she spoke, she was surprised to find herself on the brink of tears. 'You want to—' *pathetic*, she scolded herself, as her voice snapped and she felt the miserable seep of self-pity. '– You want to get rid of me. You want to put me out there, like a cow to pasture.'

'Like a cow to pasture!' Crawford repeated, and smiled. 'My own sweet Bonnie? A *cow*? Even more entertaining than the thought of you as a lady's maid. You'd singe the poor girl's hair to cinders.'

There: the pin had found its place, and she might have heard the whistle as the room deflated, as Crawford reached for her hand and kissed it, and Rex discarded his newspaper and picked up another coffin plate and dusted soil from it. *Albert Smith*, it read, and she wondered what the man had looked like, who he had loved.

'And besides, get rid of you? Unendurable thought,' Crawford added. He hoisted Bonnie onto his lap and began to kiss the dip between her clavicles. 'Be without you for an instant? I'd rather die.' He lowered his voice, cutting Rex out. 'One day I will buy you a castle with ten turrets, and a parrot that asks for a dish of strawberries. You will have your own palazzo.'

'It's getting late,' Rex interrupted, standing suddenly, irritation creasing his brow.

It was true: outside, the crowd was growing restless, and Bonnie knew that soon they would process downstairs and the rat-baiting would begin. Rex had bought a new dog, a one-eyed fox terrier called Tiny, and he had staked five guineas on it. He hadn't fed it in two days so it would do his bidding and massacre the rats in a desperate fury.

Crawford ignored him, even when Rex crossed the floor. It was all fine, Bonnie told herself, as Crawford held her close against him, and she rested her head on his shoulder. He began to stroke her hair. She wanted to keep him there, pin him to her. Surely, she had imagined the oddness of earlier. There was no test, no secret kept quiet from her. But as they took the old wooden staircase to the inn below, she let herself tip forwards, let herself see the panic on Crawford's face as she fell, and he seized her round the waist, catching her.

'Good God!' he said. 'Are you hurt? What happened?'

'The heat,' she replied, her ankle stinging with pain. 'I – I must have stood too quickly.'

His expression was clear: worry, fear. Proof that he loved her, that he cared for her.

She felt the nudge of a familiar whine she had never given into, never expressed, though it squatted everywhere they went. *Why won't you marry me?* Their unknown children with his nose, her lips, a melding of them, not a seed blossoming on the sheets.

'Hurry *up*,' Rex insisted. 'If Bonnie can climb down the stairs without throwing a fainting fit.'

Bonnie accepted Crawford's arm. As she limped down each step, she found herself thinking about the advertisement again, wondering what it was about; if she had said the right thing, if she had passed whatever trial Crawford had devised for her.

Green Days

At the beginning, the trick with the gentlemen was Crawford's idea. But as time passed, it had wormed its way into Bonnie so subtly that she scarcely realized that it was her who had begun to notice which gentlemen were worth their while. At the briefest glance, she could discern which shirts were loose-fitting, cheap Penny Lane cotton; and which were chalked and stitched by a tailor, starched by a housemaid. Even as she entered the inn, the trap door to the ratting pit yawning below, she found herself measuring up fobs as gold or painted tin, taking in the cut of the gentlemen who wore them.

They pursued their ruse a few evenings a week, leaving the shabby quarters of St Giles for the wide streets of Mayfair and Kensington. There, she, Rex and Crawford would saunter from inn to inn. Whenever a man blocked Bonnie's way, whenever a hand slid down her side as though by accident, and whenever that hand wore a fat signet ring or was cuffed by a fine merino frock coat, Bonnie would nudge Crawford. 'Oh,' she would exclaim, nestling against the hand for just the briefest moment. She would turn and pretend to be flattered, delighted at the attention, when really her skin felt sticky and her waist ached from the pressure of his palm.

It took little time to reel them in, these hungry, sweating men with port-stained lips. When she saw she had them, she would nod at Crawford, and she would watch as he and Rex sloped out of the inn.

'How stifling it is!' she would exclaim to the gentleman. 'I need some air.' He would scarcely be able to stop himself, his fingers pawing at her as they left, his desire rising shamelessly. She would say, 'No, sir, not here!' and then, 'Just this way, sir,' and there, in the shadows of an alleyway, Crawford and Rex would be waiting.

It was easy to suppress her niggling unease as she led the men to the alleyways, to forget the harsh *thwack* of Rex's bat, and the way the gentlemen begged and gibbered as gold and watches were pulled from them with a conjuror's ease. These men, she told herself, would have pressed her head against the wall and forced themselves into her whether she'd offered it or not. She chose instead to remember the brimming thrill as she and Crawford raced through the streets afterwards, gold rattling, and how he would spin her round and kiss her and say, 'The way he thought he had you! And his face when he saw it was *you* who had *him*—' and she would know she had done what he wanted, and that, surely, counted for everything.

But that, of course, was not the only racket Crawford had. There was collecting the bets on the ratting, though he grumbled that the owner of the inn took a fat cut. Of some matters, Bonnie knew only snatches: the knocks that sometimes beat against the door in the middle of the night, the weeks he would spend away from her. She could always tell he was leaving by his clothes: his green velvet jacket brushed down, his hair slicked back, shoes oiled.

'Where are you going?' Bonnie would ask, and she would

see Rex's head angled with the same question. But Crawford would tap his nose and she would have no choice but to wait until he returned, clutching a blowsy bunch of roses or hyacinths, hanging his head in an exaggerated show of contrition. When she crossed her arms, he would pull her onto his lap. 'Come now,' he would say. 'Don't I love you? You wouldn't love me if I was a little lapdog, if you knew everything about me, if you could drag me everywhere on a silken lead. You wouldn't love me if you owned me.'

'Is that so?' Bonnie would say. 'Is that so?'

And then there were the burial grounds. The Green Ground and Enon Chapel were small, privately owned squares of land. They were as foul and packed as any of the graveyards of central London, and Crawford managed them both, cramming in more and more bodies, fudging the burial notes and creaming off the profit. The fact was simply this, he explained: the city was over-flowing with the dead and there was no ground left for burials. And wherever there was a problem, there was money in a solution. Money, he'd add, that lined a hundred pockets before it touched his own.

'It's leftover's from another man's plate,' Crawford once said with something close to fury, his glass making circles of condensation on the table. 'The owner of the ground's making a fortune. Fifteen shillings a burial, and fifty interments a week.' But Bonnie knew perfectly well that Crawford only registered thirty-five of those burials with the owners. Bodies were buried in sham ceremonies and exhumed, the coffins sold for firewood, the corpses thrown either into a burying pit or the vault under Enon Chapel, then slaked with quicklime. The cleaned bones were sold to a man in Liverpool who ground them down for fertiliser. Mourners must have known how it was: how couldn't they? But they had no other choice.

Crawford brought home pamphlets about grave-digging and *mephitic odours* and studied them late into the night, and sometimes Bonnie would sift through them the next day, keen to share his interest. When the broadsheets carried articles about the construction of a new cemetery at Highgate and its aim to be a *convincing token of a nation's progress in civilization and the arts* as Kensal Green and West Norwood had been, he had scrunched them up and hurled them across the room. 'If I owned land like it, bodies would tumble in like coins, not be laid out in wide, pretty spaces.' But later, when Bonnie unfurled the papers and studied the neat designs – a large turning circle, carefully dotted trees, numbered sections with arcing paths – she wondered if it was simply being cut out of things that angered him. If it was the idea that in this same city, men were sleeping in beds draped with silk and profiting from a grand cemetery, and here he was with his stinking pit, scheming and hoping, skimming off profits that were rightfully another man's.

The reek of Crawford's burial grounds seemed to slip under her skin. She began to find herself raising her wrist to her nose and sniffing, wondering if she stank of it too. She had always loved summer for its greenery and bursting flowers, but she hated it here. It was a season of bluebottles swelling against the windowpanes, of air so thin that she could scarcely light a candle, of a stench as dense as soup.

Every time she passed the grounds, she would try to turn away, but one afternoon she had found her gaze drawn back to it. There, rising from the soil, she had glimpsed an arm, faintly tattooed with the outline of a mermaid. That night, sleep eluded her. Crawford's body was hot against her own, but all she could picture was that arm. Carefully, she dropped her hand over the bed frame, let it hang, slack: still her fingers twitched. She could no more picture herself out of the world than she could imagine the moon pinched out, the buildings crumpled and turned to wasteland. A woman's laughter rose from the street below. Everyone was simply trying to live, to make their way through this life. The dust, glinting in the air, as though it too was alive and sparkling. It felt so unjust, so *vulgar*, that a person could simply stop existing. All these people she had known who had died: where had they gone? The elders from her church when she was younger, her brother's friend who'd fallen into a stream when drunk, her own mother.

She had run between their graves as a child, careering over the raised bumps of grass, spires of Ely in the distance. She had fitted her fingers to the engravings on her family's headstone and found her mother's name: *Jane Fairchild.* Laundress. She had died when Bonnie was too young to recall her in anything but snatched fragments: the smell of the coke fire, the handkerchiefs and collars that hung across the kitchen like streamers, the hand that smacked her away from the rows of glowing irons.

Her mother had taken in laundry from Highwell, a vast stone mansion around which the entire village revolved and fawned. Her brother had worked in the grounds as a stable boy and, as Bonnie grew older, he had often let her ride the horses when the family was away. He had told her she was a natural, that she had *the horsemanship of the finest gentleman*, as she galloped up and down the avenues, sitting astride like a man. In those moments, she could believe she had become one of the Highwell family, but when Sunday came, the illusion swiftly dissolved. The Highwells had the pew at the front of the church and Bonnie watched as they processed in regally, little girls in their starched white pinafores, ladies dressed in velvet and silk. Bonnie itched in her darned woollen cape, her entire body craned towards them, aching with the desire to sit in that pew beside them, to make heads turn as she walked out.

'But you are special,' Bonnie's sister had said when Bonnie confided this. 'You'll outdo all of us. You'll be mistress of the rectory. Isn't that enough?'

It was a fact that Bonnie had been told for as long as she could remember: one day she would become the rector's wife. Every afternoon, while her sisters scrubbed soiled Highwell undergarments, continuing the work her mother had done, and her father weeded the Highwell flowerbeds, and her brothers shovelled Highwell dung, she walked to the rectory and took her seat with the rector in his library. A bead of white spittle sat at the edge of his mouth, saliva rasping with each breath.

He did not touch her. That was deliberate: he would not touch her until they were married. Was he not an honest man, a Christian? She was ten, eleven, twelve, thirteen, fourteen, fidgeting in her darned frock. Each afternoon he schooled her, teaching her to read, to write, to eat politely, to pray modestly, to bottle fruit and attend to the accounts of the house, to check the work of the maids. One day, he would dictate his sermons to her and she would record them for posterity. One day, she would run his household. He had raised her, had he not? He had set her aside from her peers, from her own family, taught her to use words she had never encountered before, to write with the hand of a lady. She did not return from the gardens of Highwell stinking of soil and mulch and horse shit. She did not have the traces of the Highwell girls' laundry grime bedded under her fingernails. The rector had made her *special*, built her mind. He was moulding a wife, just like God had crafted Eve from Adam's rib.

I knew you would be my wife the moment I christened you, and you turned your big blue eyes towards me. It was a sign from God. I knew you were special then: that was when I fell in love with you.

Lucky thing, that four-week-old baby, crying at the shock of the cold water, trickled on her forehead. Opportunities spread themselves open like books, like flowers. Her father delighted in it. He was a garden labourer, a drudge, and here was a *rector* who would have his daughter. Baskets of apples and pies and meat arrived from the rectory. In exchange, he sent the rector cuts of bacon, hacked from the carcasses of Bonnie's beloved pigs, which the rector ordered to be cut and fried into titbits and which she refused to eat. 'Your sentimentality does you credit,' the rector said, cramming lardons into his mouth as her pen hovered above the page. 'You will make a wonderful mother.'

'I hope my children will not end up on your plate, Reverend, basted in butter,' she had replied, and he had looked at her with quick annoyance.

Yes, she remembered that there was bacon sent as a gift. Bacon wrapped in paper, carried by a little girl in a blue dress with cleaned hands and a scrubbed face. Looking back, Bonnie recalled only a single, tremulous thought: that she would postpone the marriage as long as she could. An age was bargained over, reluctantly agreed: twenty. So old it felt unattainable. A time that would surely never arrive.

The winters passed and Bonnie met each with mounting dread: fifteen, sixteen, seventeen, eighteen, nineteen. Each day, she skirted her mother's grave on the way to the rectory. *If my mother were alive*, she told herself, *she would not allow it*. But the days ticked on. A date was set. Bonnie's life was a piece of flotsam, tugged downstream: she was helpless to put a stop to what her father and the rector had put in motion. She endured the laughter of the village women as they measured her for her wedding trousseau and jabbed her with pins, *just a small prick*.

A week before the wedding, she and the rector were sitting in the library.

'Might I cover your hand with mine?' he asked.

She could feel his gaze as though he meant to burn her up.

He didn't wait for a reply but slipped his meaty palm over hers, the liver spots quivering.

Cover. It made her think of a stallion covering a mare. The rector, pale as a grub, his cock a little boyish thing, flapping against her backside. Despite herself, she laughed, then flushed and cleared her throat.

And as she watched their hands, she realized that that small white hand was her own, that she had mastery over it. She slipped her palm free, watched the dart of his frown. Her mother was not going to burst out of her grave and save her. Her father would never understand. She had only herself.

That evening, she listened more intently to everything the rector said. Her mind swelled with all he had taught her: her fine script, the recipes for home medicines, matters both learned and practical. *London.* Wasn't that where girls went to find work?

When the rector excused himself for a moment, she listened to the faint swish of him pissing in the neighbouring room and helped herself to two silver candlesticks, tucking them into her shawl. Then, when he returned, she pleaded a headache and rushed home, out to the lanes where the trees were stretching their fingers higher and higher.

She escaped that night, hitching a ride on a donkey cart to Ely, selling the candlesticks to a rag-and-bone man, and then buying a ticket for a London coach. It was breathless, how quickly it was all done. All the while, she trembled at her own daring and trepidation, her new life unfolding with each beat of the horses' hooves. *London. London. London.*

Bonnie expected, somehow, that London would soon become

familiar to her too, that she would tune herself to its streets, its alleys. But when she arrived, she found buildings so tall she could see only a scrap of sky, a pulsing tide of people moving with a certainty that cowed her. The reek of it, yellow and choking, smoke and decay and rot. Scorned out of house after house. A governess? No experience? No recommendation? Then: a lady's maid? No experience? No recommendation? Then: a housemaid? No experience? No recommendation?

Frightened nights spent in doorways, under bridges, afraid to sleep. Soon even the rectory began to tug at her: the hot meals and fires, the view of the churchyard with its neat mounded graves. Generations of her family, each new name added to the stone.

But then a woman with smooth, pearly teeth seized her hand on a street near a tall cathedral. She could give Bonnie a bed for the night and a hot pie if she was a good girl, and Bonnie ignored the metallic taste flooding her mouth. Her establishment was called Mrs Pennyweather's, the woman said, and she often took in destitute girls. Bonnie thought only of hot crumbling pastry, and when she was given the pie, she shovelled it in so fast she scalded herself. 'We check our lodgers' clothes for fleas,' the woman explained after Bonnie had taken off her shoes, leading her into a room with a small iron bedframe, a stained mattress. 'You'll take them off here and put on this nightgown while we inspect them. I'll be back to collect them presently.' She shut the door behind her.

Bonnie's tongue began to work the blister on the roof of her mouth, prising off the skin. Because she knew what place this was, what trick she had walked into, as blithe and dim as a country sheep; she saw the narrow window with its single bar. The room seemed to shrink, the rotting ceiling pressing down on her, but Bonnie gritted her teeth. There must be a way out. She ran to the chair in the corner and edged it against the window, aware of each small scuff of the chair legs, the tap of the frame. The bar was loose. Thank heaven, the bar was loose. She rocked the metal gently, each second a hammer in her ears, until, finally, it broke off in her hand. And then, gracelessly, like a worm blinded by the light, she shimmied through that narrow window, landing awkwardly in the street. It didn't matter she had left her shoes behind. She began to run, hair slapping her back, euphoria pulsing through her. There was no God, she thought, and the idea lifted her. There was no God! She was alone in this world and she wouldn't sink without fighting. She had escaped the rector. She had escaped Mrs Pennyweather. Bonnie laughed as she thought of the woman barging into the room, finding her gone. She laughed until she realized that tears were edging from her eyes, and she was standing alone in a street she did not know, in a city she did not know, and it was growing dark.

Ahead of her was an inn, lit with burning lamps. Bonnie hurried towards it, stockings soaked to her knees, a small cut on her foot. There was an empty booth by the fire and she sat there quietly, no money to buy a drink or scrap, hoping merely to heat up her bones before anyone shooed her out. It was ludicrous that she was already hungry again.

A man found her there, slid into the seat opposite her, a glass of steaming brandy in his hand. She would not be a fool, Bonnie thought; she would not make the same mistake again. But how intensely he had stared, a slight smile on his face, like she was a priceless artefact – a rare orchid, a fine silver locket. He was more handsome than anyone she had ever seen before, but his was a beauty so unattainable that it both stirred and repelled her. His eyes, almost black; his hair brown.

'Who are you?' he asked.

Who was she?

'What sort of question is that?' she replied, with more conviction than she felt.

'Well?'

'I – I'm a lady's maid.'

'Where?'

She scarcely knew London, felt only that she wanted to impress him. 'To a fine house on a fine street in – in –' she tried to think of a wealthy area, adding, hopefully, 'May-fer.'

He kept looking at her. It was only when she noticed a teardrop-shaped scar under his lip that her chest began to stir. It made his handsomeness feel less oppressive. Later, he would tell her all sorts of stories about where he had got it: that he had caught it on the edge of a golden egg, that the Queen's coachman had licked him with his whip. But just then, she had simply wanted to sit closer to him, to study that tiny blemish and press it under her thumb, to know a small piece of his history. There was so much she wanted to know about him.

'Liar.'

'What?'

'You aren't a lady's maid.'

And then, suddenly, he stood up and vanished. Gone. Bonnie stumbled to her feet, searched the patrons for him, sifting through face after face. Something like grief crashed down on her. Why had she lied to him and so patently? She felt sure she had missed a chance – but a chance for what? They had barely spoken.

The evening was wretched. Bonnie stole an empty glass and nursed the dregs, to give the impression she had paid for it. Her joints would not warm up, no matter how pinked and rosy her skin grew from the fire's heat. Gradually, she became glad he was gone. The truth was, he had frightened her. She had been drawn towards him so powerfully that she felt she would destroy herself, like standing beside a deep well and being overcome by the urge to fall.

Later, just as the inn was closing, the man returned. He was holding a pair of pink silk slippers with slender ribbons – the sort of thing that might belong to one of the Highwell daughters. Wordlessly, he passed them to her, and as Bonnie reached forwards, his hand caught her wrist. His finger pressed against her pulse point. They had stood there, frozen, neither moving for ten seconds or more. Just her pulse thrumming against his fingers, so fast that he must have guessed she longed for him.

Later, in his garret, he went about it wordlessly, stripping her down until she lay naked on the bed, and she felt so entirely surrendered, as if her body had no choice but to yield to his. It was all new to her and the roughness of it shocked her – the violence of his thrusting, his teeth biting into her shoulder. But she found it was what she wanted, more than anything she'd ever desired before.

In the morning, she was woken by a banging at the door. A man shouldered his way in, glared at her, and Bonnie covered herself quickly.

'It's only Rex,' the man said.

'You bastard, Crawford,' Rex said. 'You shut me out last night. You locked the door.'

Crawford.

'I had company.'

Rex scowled.

'Come now,' Crawford said. 'Come now. Be a saint and buy me a pastry. I feel like I haven't eaten for days. Here's a coin.'

When Rex had gone, Crawford fucked her again,

dispassionately this time, as though she meant nothing to him. Afterwards she turned to face the wall, afraid she would cry.

'Won't your mistress want you home?' he asked.

'What mistress?'

'In *May-fer*.'

'Oh, very good.' She felt desperate and suddenly furious. 'You don't know anything about me.'

He leaned closer. 'Tell me, then.'

She obeyed him. It was all she had. Her whole life spilled out: her father and his flowers, the rector and the days learning her letters in the library, how she had chafed against the future these men had mapped out for her. Crawford listened, his thumb moving over hers, the inn creaking underneath them. As she spoke, he tightened his grip on her hand, as though she was worth something, as though she was precious. When she finished, he was silent, staring at her in the same way he had looked at her the night before.

'You know exactly what it's like,' he whispered.

'What?'

He balled his fist. 'What it is to be raised in education alone. To be scorned as low, but to know you're better than any of them. Always, to feel out of place.'

She squeezed his hand. 'Yes,' she said, then louder, '*yes*.'

'I should have seen it in you,' he said, pulling her back towards him on the bed, the covers still on her. He tucked her head against his chest, kissed her crown.

There was a sound on the stairs. Crawford glanced at the door. 'Rex will be back soon, and how cross he'll be to discover you're still here. Won't it be fun?'

They shared a smile, two conspirators.

Bonnie tried to echo the commanding way he had spoken, but her voice was tentative. 'Tell me – about yourself.'

'You don't want to hear any of that,' he said, lifting back the sheet so she lay naked before him. Her ribcage rose and fell. He bit her earlobe, her lip. 'I was dropped here, last night, by a bird, and what a blessing that is.'

And Bonnie knew two things then. That his past was sealed against her. And that she was entirely his, and she would do anything he asked of her.

Tiny

The rat pit was set into the earth floor and lit by a circle of candles. A rickety staircase led back to the inn above it. Bonnie watched as a boy spread chalk over the ground of the pit so the rats would show against it. She did not look at the box in the corner, but she knew that a hundred rats were trapped inside, scrabbling and scratching against the wood, their pink, human-like fingers grasping for escape. She shuddered. The stink of them was suffocating: that particular animal scent of piss and shit, and above it, spilled beer and thick pipe smoke.

'Ah sir. What can I do for you?' Crawford asked, opening his pouch to take a bet from a man with clipped ginger whiskers.

'What do you say, then?' the stranger asked Bonnie.

She glanced at him briefly: gold fob watch, silk waistcoat, almost certainly tailored. 'To what?'

'Will the dog kill a hundred of them in ten minutes?'

'Easy,' she replied, without thinking.

'Well then. I'll trust the girl. A guinea she'll do it.'

'Will you now?' Crawford said, frowning at Bonnie. She touched his arm in apology but he shook her off. 'A guinea. A guinea! Well, sir. The odds are against you, so perhaps a lower bet might be more prudent, loath though I am to undermine—'

'But the winnings might be high. I could triple it.'

'Indeed, sir,' Crawford said. 'Indeed you could.'

She heard the clink of metal, coin bitten between teeth, another exasperated sigh from Crawford.

Bonnie settled onto their bench and watched Crawford out of the corner of her eye. She had simply spoken thoughtlessly; he would forgive her. Anyone could see it was hardly malicious. And Tiny might lose. Already, Crawford must have made back any loss she had caused him. He was in his element, dark hair curled around his ears, coins chiming against his purse, cheeks pink with the heat of it all. *Three shillings she won't do it, two then, one! Three shillings the dog won't be wounded and turned upon!* The benches were packed: foreheads glassy with sweat, mustachios wilting, wet rings blooming on shirts. A few women sat among them, paste jewels clipped to their ears and linked on cheap chains. There was no chatter, just the creak of benches as the crowd jiggled their legs in anticipation, the whining of the dog, the faint screeching of the rats as they clawed against their box.

Crawford sat down next to Bonnie. Rex nodded back at him, lifting the heavy wooden box as easily as if it contained nothing but air, and placing it into the pit. The crowd stilled, the benches tilting as everyone pressed forwards. He pulled the lid free, leapt back, rats writhing over each other, butting against the edge of the pit, nowhere to go. A man handed Rex the dog, and it foamed and barked, wriggling in his arms. Crawford raised his hand, the watch clutched in his fist. Rex dropped the terrier; a roar beat through the crowd. Even if Bonnie had not heard it – the scream of injured rats, the manic fury of the terrier as it snapped and tossed them in the air – she would have felt it in the crackle of Crawford's body as he leaned forwards, his fingers clicking. But even through the blur of sounds and screams, she felt the unmistakeable bristle of being watched, as though someone was reaching out and running their fingers through her hair, down her cheek. She shifted in her seat. Across the room the ginger-haired man fixed his eyes on hers. She recalled the rector so abruptly she might still have been sitting in his library: the sickly scent of beeswax, the drawn shutters, the hot shift of his leg. Her quill, creaking on the page as he spoke.

Twelfth verse. Let us see if the vine flourish, whether the tender grape appear, and the pomegranates bud forth –

Stop. Lighter. Press lighter. What has this bird ever done to you?

The man did not look away even when she stared right back at him. His fob shone in the candlelight. How cavalierly he had handed over a guinea, as though his pockets were full of them. She tugged Crawford's sleeve. They would run laughing through the streets tonight: they would weigh the watch in their palms, and the gentleman would return home embarrassed, beaten, forlorn. How pleased Crawford would be; how delighted with her.

'Him,' she hissed.

Crawford did not reply. His eyes were fixed on the pit. The muscles in his neck were tight as he craned forwards, his fingers absently shredding a piece of paper. Tiny tossed more rats and Bonnie winced at the crunch of skulls, the snap of necks.

She nudged him, harder this time. 'Craw.'

'What is it? I'm—'

'*Him.* Don't look.' She spoke quietly, knowing she was observed. 'The gentleman who placed the bet. With red hair. He'll be easy.'

A pause. 'You're sure? But here? He'd know where to find us.'

She spoke with more conviction than she felt. 'I'm sure. He'll be too humiliated. And that way, you can reclaim the three guineas I lost you, and more besides.'

'Well.' He squeezed her knee. 'My little terrier.'

A cry went up, a groan. Crawford leapt to his feet. 'Eight minutes, twenty seconds!' he declared, tapping his watch. 'A hundred rats in less than ten minutes!'

The pit was stained, bloodied. A few tiny ribcages still stammered and fluttered. Rex began to sift through the rodents to see if they were all dead and Bonnie saw how neatly, how slyly he broke the necks of those still breathing, dispatching them as cleanly as his dog had. He lifted the terrier, exalted, decorating her neck with a silver collar. 'A little champion!' he declared.

As Bonnie rose to leave, she still felt the gentleman's eyes on her. She noticed that he waited for her to climb the steps ahead of him. As she passed him, he brushed his hand against her fingertips, so lightly she might have missed it.

'Barbaric,' he whispered. 'Isn't it?'

Bonnie kept her head down and smiled.

Barbaric

The trick was not to seem too interested. Bonnie leaned on the sticky counter, ordered an ale. It was warm, the glass grimy, but she drank it so fast that her throat burned. She could sense the needling of the gentleman's gaze as he stood apart from the crowd. Crawford handed her a second glass and she dabbed the sweat on her forehead.

'*Him*,' Crawford hissed to Rex. 'There, find him in the mirror. Don't let him see you. There are winnings that are rightfully mine in that waistcoat pocket.'

'Not here?' Rex asked, shaking his head. 'Never here. We leave to find them—'

'That vagabond's not escaping with a penny of my takings,' Crawford said, holding up a finger to silence Rex. 'It was Bonnie's idea and—'

'Of course,' he interrupted bitterly. He let out a short laugh. 'Of course it was.'

'Oh, Rexie,' Crawford said. 'Your jealousy does you a discredit.'

He spoke glibly, laughing, but he moved his arm around Bonnie. Rex's face soured, and Bonnie saw how their situations were exchanged: before it had been Rex, crowing over the advertisement and her confusion. She kissed Crawford's cheek, held Rex's eye. They were like a pair of plants tilted towards the sun, with no room for both to flourish.

Crawford glanced at the gentleman's reflection in the mirror. 'He's dying for you, Bonnie. He's *desperate*. I'll wager you're the prettiest thing he's ever seen.'

He looked at her, appraising, and she knew it excited him to see other men desire her so forcefully; other men that he knew she despised.

'Nod when you need us.'

Crawford and Rex walked away and the red-headed man moved in as easily as a hooked trout. Bonnie's dress clung to her, a slim line of sweat working its way down her back.

He stood beside her, his breath sweet with pipe smoke, the little gold chain glinting tantalizingly in the lamplight. She took a long glug from her glass and waited for him to speak. Crawford had bought her a sherry this time, dry enough to knock a gasp from her.

'You reside near here?' he asked.

An abrupt, stilted beginning. 'Oh no. In this pit? I should think not.' She looked at him. His eyebrows and whiskers were neat, speckled with grey, his chin purpling with the rash from a cut-throat. An invisible hand would have soaped his jowls that morning, scraped the ginger dregs of stubble into a bowl. 'Yourself, sir?'

'Hyde Park.' He puffed out his chest, and she saw that was all he had wanted: to be asked the same question in return, to peacock. 'The big new terrace on the north side. Polygon Street. It's a glorious spot. You might even know it. Ours is the biggest house in the street – it has these magnificent Grecian pillars. Gilding on the ceilings. No expense spared.'

Bonnie watched the way his nose twitched as he spoke, the wide pores stretching and compressing. She kept her voice bland. 'How fortunate you are.'

'Fortune doesn't come into it,' he said with a derogatory wave of his hand. He trailed his finger down her arm. The nails were stained with tobacco. 'But forgive me. I mustn't deprive your – *husband* – of your charms.' He stretched out the word, gesturing at Crawford, who'd found himself a seat at a booth.

'You must mean my brother.'

The man smiled a yellow grin. '*Brother*. Indeed. Well. I should wonder that he brings a girl as fine as you to a place like this. I have a daughter around your age and I would be horrified to see her here.'

Already, he had nudged himself closer, his thigh resting against her dress. The air caught in her lungs. She drank down the sherry. 'As fine as me?'

'Well.' The man looked uncomfortable. 'You're – you're no wretch.'

The lie curdled. She knew it was better that he saw her as low and pitiful: he'd do things to her that he'd never dream of doing to a girl like his daughter. She was a worthless thing to be had and discarded, serving her function as cleanly as the maids who scrubbed out his pisspot. And yet, she wanted him to see her differently. 'My brother and I had a different life once. Different prospects. We had a fine house in Sussex, but it was lost to us when my father married again.'

'A shame,' he said, his eyes glazed. She could hear the breath snagging in his nostrils. The time was now, surely.

She glanced over to where Crawford had been sitting at the booth. He was gone. His glass was still on the table. He and Rex must already be waiting in the alleyway. As she pressed herself closer to the gentleman, she almost stumbled. His face was blurred, meaty. She had drunk too much. How had she let it happen? The oddness of the day began to needle her: the strange silence when Rex had read the advertisement, the careful way Crawford had watched her. She had to see this through, to have it done with. All she had to do was bring the man outside.

'I need some air,' she said quickly. 'It's hot.'

'Isn't it,' the man agreed. She led the way and he linked his fingers through hers.

Outside, the flies were ferocious, as fat as bumblebees, settling on Bonnie, buzzing about her face. The crowd had thinned and it was deserted in the alley, the gas lamp stuttering. She turned and he bore down on her straight away, so suddenly she could scarcely breathe: his mouth covering hers, his hands pulling at her waist, sinking into her buttocks, grappling with the fabric.

'Wait,' she said, wrenching free, and he paused, panting. 'Not here. Not—'

She looked around. A rat was dragging something across the path, a bone of some type, skinned of meat. Soon, it would be over with, her job done. Rex would be waiting down the passage, Crawford crouched in an alcove nearby, ready to box in his victim, to swing a bat into his chest and rob him of his coat, his fob, the guineas in his purse. She walked down the alley, turning towards the narrower passage, trying not to stagger, her feet scarcely obeying her. The sherry had been the mistake. Too much, too fast, and the day so hot.

'Wicked,' the man whispered. He was panting, already reaching for his shirt, untucking it. 'Wicked, wicked wretch of a girl.'

She turned the corner, her heart pounding. It was dark, unlit by lamps, and at first she thought she must be mistaken.

The passage was empty.

She stared wildly about her, at the wall and its ghostly shapes: the drainpipe, the heaps of old potato peelings, a rusted tangle of old metal.

'Wait,' she tried to say. 'I just – I—'

She put up her hands as though they were simply making conversation, as though his wide shoulders were not already hemming her in and she wasn't taking small steps backwards – steps that she knew led nowhere.

The sherry and ale thickened in her, as though she was swimming through something dense and syrupy, and she raised a hand to her face.

'Please. I – I don't want to.'

Like the plaintive bleat of a child.

She could smell the sweet stench of his breath. *Barbaric* he had said, when they had walked up the stairs, and the word spun in her mind. *Barbaric*. She felt like she had as a child, the dark fear that swamped her when she paddled in the deep mill stream, her brothers daring her to swim out further and further. Her hands, sculling her away from the banks, contrary to every instinct. Wet slippery things brushed against her legs. Monsters with clacking jaws, the ghost of her brother's drowned friend. How frantically she'd kick her legs. 'The river creatures enjoy the taste of little girls,' her brothers whispered from the edge. 'Just like our Reverend.' And it had driven a terror through her so sharp and fast she thought she might have died.

The man lunged for her, stronger than she could believe, spinning her round, seizing her thighs so sharply she cried out. She felt the hard brick against her chest, slimy from pots emptied from the shuttered windows above. She strained for the sound of hurrying footsteps, for Crawford's cry as he burst down the alley and ripped the man off her. But she knew that there was nobody to save her. It was coming as swift and sure as sleep. Already he was wrestling with her skirts.

'I'll shout,' she tried, desperate, but her voice was so quiet it was almost a whisper.

'No, you won't.'

And she realized that he was right. It would be worse to shout and have nobody hear her: just another penniless girl in an alley – mattering so little.

'Be a good girl,' he hissed.

The rector, leaning over her. The rasp as he sucked spit into the corner of his mouth. *Good girl.* His hand over hers, guiding the quill. The slow horror of it, his cold fingers. *To have and to hold. To love and to cherish.*

The man's face grated against her cheek, pinning her there. She could not breathe. She reached below her, scrabbled. She grazed something hard – she fumbled for it. It was simply a stick, a child's plaything like her brothers might once have used to fight one another. What was it she intended? It was laughable, surely, but what else did she have? Because as she stood there, a single certainty beat through her: that she had not yielded to the rector or Mrs Pennyweather, and she would not again. All those men in all those inns who had tried to help themselves to small parts of her, who had not cared what she wanted. And when she wrenched herself around and raised the stick and the man chuckled and reached to snatch it from her, she let him; and he stumbled backwards because he anticipated resistance. He was about to catch himself, about to stand upright, when she saw her chance. Her mind was bright and unclouded, glorious—

He was off-balance when she knocked him, hard in the chest. He fell fast, no time to shoot out a hand, and his head collided with the sharp edge of a brick. A wet crack of bone, like hands clapped together.

And there he was, lying at Bonnie's feet, his arm at a jaunty angle. His blood pooling darkly on the ground, his mouth a little open, a caught fish in mid-gasp.

The Green Ground

The world tipped, cracked open. And yet, she was still there. Those were her own fingers gripping the wall, the joints white. It was her breath, stuttering in and out of her throat, her own hair that straggled in front of her face. Her own shoes, dampening with blood from the man at her feet.

How long did Bonnie stand there? How long was it until she heard running footsteps and Crawford and Rex tore round the corner? She saw what she had done in the shock of Crawford's mouth, the way Rex took a step backwards. It was only when Crawford's arms were around her that she allowed herself to crumple.

I killed him. I killed him.

He gripped her shoulders, put his face close to hers. 'Listen to me.'

I killed him—

'He's dead. He's—'

Crawford shook her. 'Bonnie. Bonnie. Listen to me.'

'But—'

'You didn't mean to. I know that. But it doesn't matter—'

'He—'

'What matters,' he said, his voice calmer than she could have imagined. 'What matters is what we do next. We'll arrange it, Rex and I. We will see it tidied away.'

Bonnie let him lead her back to the inn, up the stairs, into the garret. He sat her on the bed, held her hand. The bedframe was trembling, creaking.

'Stay here,' he said, and kissed her.

She did not move from the bed. The room was exactly as it had been that afternoon. The woodcuts of that fine house lifting slightly from the walls, the chicken carcass on the table, crawling with flies. The newspaper, crumpled on the floor. It was as if Bonnie could simply step back a few hours and have it all undone, the evening unpicked like a row of bad stitches, the gentleman revived and brought back to life.

She did not need to ask what they would do, where they would take him. Quicklime, the Green Ground. He would be gone, vanished, pinched out, as though he had never been to the Angler at all, as though he had never drawn breath.

Rex and Crawford returned some time later. She heard them on the stairs and then they were in the room again, Crawford pacing back and forth, Rex standing to the side, not looking at her.

'He – he attacked me. If I tell them what happened then—'

'Tell who?' Crawford demanded. 'Who exactly are you going to tell?'

She gestured vaguely.

'Tell the jailor? Tell the hangman?'

Her hand was over her mouth, that cloying aftertaste of sherry on her tongue. Crawford's expression softened and he sat beside her, his arm around her shoulders. 'It's my fault. If I hadn't left to use the pot—'

She bunched her dress between her fists. The fabric was damp and slimy from where she had been pressed against the wall.

'You'll make it go away, won't you? You won't let it happen? The – the—'

Hangman. Her mouth refused to form the word.

Crawford shifted. 'He was a *gentleman*, Bonnie.'

'I know.'

'You think his family won't look for him? They'll come sniffing around, and how many people saw you talking to him? How many people saw you leave together?' He added, more gently but with the same urgency, 'He's gone at least. Rex and I have seen to that. But – but if we were seen. If *you* were seen then—'

She nodded.

'You understand me, don't you?' Crawford asked, stroking her arm. 'You understand why you can't stay here?'

Rex scuffed the newspaper with his foot.

The advertisement.

'They'll never hire me,' she said, gripping Crawford's hand so tightly she saw him flinch. 'When I came to London I tried—'

'You're a different person now, Bonnie. Think of all you've learned. It's not like before. You're not a green country girl any longer. I know you can do it. You were educated before, but now you're resourceful. You're clever.'

He touched her chin with his fingers, raised her face so that she looked at him.

'You can do this, Bonnie. It's just for a while, a place to hide, away from here.'

There was nothing for it. Nowhere else to go.

Crawford pulled out a chair and settled at the table, shoving the chicken to one side. Rex handed him a sheet of crisp paper, a pen and ink, a stub of sealing wax. Bonnie stood beside him and watched as the words formed on the page.

Dear Madam, he wrote. *I write to heartily commend Bonnie Fairchild to your service as lady's maid –*

Part Two

TWICKENHAM

For the Housekeeper,
Endellion House, Twickenham

Dear Madam,

I write to heartily commend Bonnie Fairchild to your service as lady's maid. It has not been easy, I confess, to find servants who are not wicked, wanton or impertinent, and it is both my delight to find none of these faults in Miss Fairchild, and also my eternal regret that she must leave my service due to her desire to live closer to her brother.

I have kept house at Brinwick for nigh on three-and-twenty years, and have had the satisfaction of moulding Miss Fairchild into the accomplished, honest, civil and industrious maid she has become. There are many maids with half her charm who might gaze for hours upon their reflection in a fire-iron or shovel; who pout at the door handles, and make pretty faces at the mirrors they ought to be cleaning, and ultimately – though I shudder to mention it – I find that this wantonness leads to the destruction of the peace of a family. You will find Miss Fairchild as chaste as day, as hard-working as a mule, and I can think of no more agreeable influence on a gentleman's young daughter.

If I have been a little over-particular, pray forgive me – it is with no modicum of pride that I confess I have run Brinwick with the precision of an Officer. And Miss Fairchild, I am delighted to say, ranks amongst the finest of her breed.

If you have any further enquiries, please do not hesitate to contact me.

Your obedient Servant,

Agnes Trimble, Brinwick Hall, Sussex

Dreamscapes

By the time Bonnie was halfway down the drive to Endellion, she was out of breath, a stone caught in her shoe. She should have stopped at the coaching inn for a drink, but she had kept her head down, afraid of being seen or remembered. Now her mouth was dry, a small pain quivering at the back of her skull. The shade from the avenue of limes was the only respite, their branches meeting overhead as though to shield her from view. On her right, a few cows grazed acres of sloping pasture, nettles and brambles bleached and wilting in the heat. On the left, narrow paths forked into thick woodland.

A slight bend in the avenue and Endellion was before her, as ornate and crenelated as a child's drawing of a castle. For the first time since she'd climbed off the cart, Bonnie stopped, shielding her eyes against its white stucco glare. She had expected another Highwell with its exacting Palladian symmetry, but this house might have been cut out of card. Pinnacles rose like small church spires, two turrets and a battlement placed seemingly at random against its sides. Bonnie wiped a damp strand of hair from her forehead, leaned against a tree trunk. All these crenelations and fortifications should have been imposing, but there was something so exaggerated and playful about the house that it looked more like a magnified doll's house. It seemed to Bonnie that she might unhook the entire front wall and tuck herself inside. Nobody would find her or know what she'd done. There, she might be a new girl again, fresh, unboxed, her shoes scoured clean of blood, the shaky feeling in her legs simply buffed away.

A plump pheasant ambled into her path, so tame she might have wrung its neck, and she sidestepped it, walked on. Her skin was speckled with grime and she scrubbed her cheeks, her forehead. Her footsteps raised little clouds of dust but the wind soon covered them. She was leaving no trail. Hurrying, almost running. Once she'd crossed the turning circle, she didn't pause but marched right up to the bell, the rope clanging in her hand. She realised her mistake too late: she should have gone round the back to the servants' entrance. But already, she could hear footsteps, the slide of the bolt. She would not run; she was equal to this. Her words were ready, prepared. She had repeated them a thousand times in the cart, and she didn't falter when the door swung open and a gangling man with blue eyes stared at her in surprise.

'Good afternoon. I'm here about the position,' she said, her words tumbling into each other. Her voice was scratchy with thirst and didn't sound like her own.

'The position?'

The man was holding a crate containing a red hat and a small silver box.

'I was expecting the auctioneer—' He stopped. 'No matter.' Then, 'What position?'

'The – the position. I saw the advertisement. For a lady's maid. For a girl—'

'My daughter. Yes.' He peered behind her. 'You see, I didn't advertise. At least not yet. Since my wife – since – well.'

Bonnie stared at him. She could scarcely untangle what he was saying.

'But you are in need of a lady's maid?'

46

His eyes flicked to the box containing the hat, then back up again. 'It is – not straightforward. But if you write to the house-keeper at Orleans House—'

The marble tiles behind him seemed to stir, their lines shifting like the veins on the flank of a horse. Bonnie put out a hand to steady herself. It was already unravelling, all going wrong.

'Oh dear,' he said. He placed the box on the floor inside the door, his movements clumsy. 'You seem unwell.'

'I just.' Her legs felt flimsy, a buckle to her knees. 'I've – I must have walked too far—'

'These days are relentless. I keep the shutters closed all after-noon. You can't possibly leave here until you've had something to drink or eat. Annette will fetch you a jug of apple juice before you go on your way.'

On your way.

All of Bonnie's prepared speech fell away – *it is with great regret I must leave Brinwick after years of loyal service* –

She tried to recall what he had said, how it had come to this: how, after journeying for five hours, her hopes rising with each turn of the wheels, it was already over.

'Oh, but she's away, fetching Cissie from Little Marble Hill. I've some lemonade in my study. Please, if you'd care to follow me.'

She found herself trailing the man mutely. Her throat felt leaden with thirst. At least she was inside the house. She had an image of herself clinging to the banisters, being dragged out by her feet, her head knocking against the tiles with the same *crack* as the gentleman's had made against the brick. *Murderess,* her shoes whispered as she crossed the floor. *Murderess* –

She had to stop thinking like this. She unfurled her fingers, tried to look around her. But it was so dark inside after the blinding brightness of the white house, the parched lawns. The hall was narrow, gloomy, a single candle flickering in a red-glassed lantern, casting the staircase in a pinkish light. It made her hands look parboiled. Bonnie blinked, stumbling on an uneven step. The walls looked panelled but when she moved closer, she saw it was just flat plaster painted in trompe l'oeil, as though the house was part of a stage set, fragile and easily dismantled. Everywhere, there were figures or animals. A cherub, peeping above the skirting board, another hiding behind a shutter. Peacocks and a field mouse in the stained-glass windows, a few cracked ancestral portraits.

It was so dark that it was only when they were on the first floor, low arched doors leading off the landing, that Bonnie noticed the mourning. Black crape hung from the lanterns like the limbs of a gigantic spider. Desiccated wreaths of laurel were heaped above each doorway. When the gentleman beckoned her across the threshold of his study, she had to duck under a loop of black ribbon.

All this mourning must be for his wife. Bonnie had guessed it in the quick way he had mentioned her, the small flash of pain that crossed his brow. She wondered how she had died; if it had been frighteningly fast like the red-haired man's; or slow and wasting. It was alarming to think how quickly everything could change. This time yesterday, the gentleman had been alive, attending to his correspondence, perhaps, or swirling a glass of claret in his hands, no idea how little time he had left.

'Here,' the man said, handing her a tumbler. She accepted it tentatively. Lemon pith floated on the surface. 'It isn't poisonous.'

'No,' Bonnie said, struggling not to gulp it down. She could have drunk the whole jug. 'Of course not.'

'Well,' he said, and fidgeted with his earlobe. 'Well.'

He wanted her to leave.

She took half a step inside the room.

Blue light filtered through the stained glass. The study was surprisingly modest, but perhaps it was just the drifts of clutter that made it feel smaller than it was, books the size of flagstones scattered across the floor. The wide desk – spanning half the room – was heaped with drawings and torn scraps of paper.

What would he do if she refused to leave? He did not look like he wanted to take command of the situation: surely his desires would usually be predicted and then met because of his position. A household, fluttering about him. But eventually, she supposed there would be servants called, raised voices. He would evict her. But if she just, well, *paused*, what would he do? She could already sense his discomfort, the way he kept glancing at the door as though willing her out of it. She stared instead at the sugar that had gathered at the bottom of her glass, resisting the urge to dip in a finger and scoop it out.

'The – the position,' he said. 'We are without a housekeeper too. Perhaps, if you want to be considered, you might write to the housekeeper at Orleans House, as I mentioned. She knows about—' he wafted his hand vaguely. 'Such matters. I'd recommend you write to her.'

No lady's maid, no housekeeper. She began to notice the thick dust, the desk unpolished and ringed with the imprint of wet glasses. There was a gap where a sideboard might once have been.

'I'd recommend it,' he repeated, more firmly this time.

Soon the man would break with civility and usher her out, and that arched door would slam shut behind her. She bound her hands, trying to keep the desperation from her mouth. She would have begged him if it would have made a difference, flung herself at his feet. Her fingers reached for her throat again, circling it, as though expecting to find a rope already chafing the skin. The red-headed man would not have returned home the evening before. His servants or wife would have raised the alarm. Perhaps they were all waiting for him to breeze through the door and explain his absence. Perhaps Peelers were already crawling over the alleyway, the inn reverberating with the shriek of rattles and whistles.

'You presumably know Orleans House,' the man continued, a slight stammer to his voice. 'I'm sure she will welcome your application.'

Think, Bonnie told herself. *Think*. She needed Crawford here. She needed him to tell her what to say and it would be exactly, precisely right. If she could only delay her departure, something might occur to her.

'You are a draughtsman? An artist?' she asked, a little desperately, glancing at his papers.

He shook his head. 'An architect.' He added, 'I studied at the Royal Academy.'

'What have you built? Did you build this house?' She took another step inside the room. He didn't seem to notice.

'Here? No – I – I am afraid to say I've scarcely pursued my profession. In a – a serious way.'

Was that why there was no housekeeper, no lady's maid? Because he had no profession, no income? But he was a *gentleman*; surely he did not need to rely on a trade? 'These are all your own drawings?'

She turned her head to try to look at the papers but she could not make sense of them. Tightly ruled lines crossed every page, tiny circles nestled together like honeycomb. His script was so minuscule it was indecipherable. She saw, then, other drawings – sketches in charcoal – of strangely lit chambers with urns and broken columns. On each page the same shape returned: a crenelated house with no windows. She picked one up.

'Give me that,' he said, snatching it. But the flare of temper was followed abruptly by embarrassed politeness. He held up his hands. 'Forgive me. Please.'

He stood so still and it was only then that Bonnie began to

notice him: his alert, almost startled expression, his dark tousled hair, the heaviness under his eyes. His shoulders were narrow but his restlessness lent him a curious strength, his feet tapping the floor, his hands reaching for a pen. He rapped it against the paper. 'It is a mausoleum. A sepulchral chamber. It will be as large as a cottage.'

'Will be?'

He gave a derisory scoff, as though he expected her to find him absurd. 'Well. I should say, might have been. I'll never build it.'

Bonnie leaned over his desk and this time he did not shield his work, though a heat pinked his cheeks. It was not only that he had sketched the same building hundreds of times, each version very slightly different, but it was the structure itself. She could not reconcile this wide, marble-floored burial chamber with the vault at Enon Chapel and its heaps of rotting bodies, skulls still half-covered with hair.

Desperation emboldened her. 'Is this for your wife?'

His shoulders wilted, any defensiveness gone. 'My wife?'

'I just thought—'

He pressed his hand to the page. 'I suppose – I hoped she might have rested here.'

'But why won't you build it?'

The gentleman paused, regarding her carefully.

'It's a piece of madness, I know. It will never be done. She's already buried in the churchyard.'

Bonnie waited. He seemed the sort of person who spoke anxiously into pauses, who was unpractised in conversation.

'But – it was a – a difficult time. It was too much for me. She would have wanted something grander than what she has.'

'But why can't you?' Bonnie insisted.

'It's nothing. It's just a – a dreamscape.' He reached for the pristine drawing and crumpled it up.

Before she could stop herself, Bonnie cried out, 'No!' and stepped forward as though to wrest the paper from him. She drew herself back, holding up her palms in silent apology. Perhaps she should lead him away from discussing his dead wife, a matter that clearly gave him pain. But time was passing and he had still not ushered her from his house, and the idea seemed so bright, so shining, that she found herself saying, 'You could build a whole cemetery here. A beautiful cemetery, like the ones they've built in London. I read about them all. Kensal Green and West Norwood and a new one at Highgate.'

'A *cemetery*?'

'It could be for her. For your wife. Besides, there's a fortune to be made. You could build it on all that empty pasture.'

He did not move, the balled-up paper still in his hand. A small vein on his temple flexed. Surely she had overstepped herself. She was always speaking too loudly, too quickly, Crawford drawing her back. Who was she to speak like this to a gentleman? Who was she to speak of cemeteries to a grieving man?

'A fortune,' he repeated. 'A mausoleum for her.' He turned to Bonnie and looked at her fully, his gaze surprised, almost tender. His blue eyes, she noticed, were long-lashed, the irises fringed with gold. There was a whiteness to his cheeks, a softness to his hands, that spoke of a life of subterranean study. He seemed to recollect himself, uncreasing the paper and smoothing it out on the desk once more. 'I – please. I should have offered you something to eat. Are you hungry? Annette will be home imminently.'

'I can wait,' she said, hope lifting her voice into a question.

'You see – I can see you are educated. You want, surely, a position as a governess, not a lady's maid. My daughter already takes her lessons with the other children at Little Marble Hill.'

'Please,' Bonnie said. 'I – I want nothing more than this

position. It is with great regret I must leave Brinwick after years
of loyal service—'

'My daughter is a little sensitive. A little – troubled,' he
barrelled on, scarcely looking at her.

'Oh?'

'You will have to take care with her.'

Bonnie thought she must have misheard him. He knew
nothing about her. He had not even asked to see her written
character. If Crawford were here, he'd slap his leg, incredulous.
'What a fool,' he'd say. 'What a dupe!'

'*Will?*' she repeated, so quietly she wondered if he had heard
her.

'If – if you will accept. I am sure we can find a place for you
here. There are only a few things you must know.'

'Please,' she said, lifting her chin. The stammer had returned
to her legs, a brightness close to biliousness spreading through
her. She would polish this room until it gleamed, wipe grime
from the windows, tidy the books, oil the desk.

'The first is the situation we find ourselves in,' he continued.
He sat in his chair, worrying a loose splinter. 'As you have
surmised, my wife died recently. But Cissie – my daughter, that
is – has found great pain and grief in her passing.'

He glanced behind him, and it was only then that she noticed
there was a large bright square in the wallpaper where a painting
must once have hung.

'The second matter is – the position is precarious. *My* position is precarious. It is part of the reason the household is so
depleted, though we sorely need more help.'

He continued, speaking fast, doubling back on himself. There
were a few men who managed the gardens the best they could,
and a stable boy, but they all lodged in Twickenham; there
was, as he had expressed, no housekeeper. Bonnie's duties might

be more – *lowly* than she was used to. The roles weren't as sharply defined as in a more expansive house. She would be required to do the work of a housemaid too. He paused, fidgeting with his cuffs, turning over a pair of gold calipers in his hand. These were lean times. Things had not been – easy – his wife's – no; *their* finances had been – excessive – he had made some poor decisions; and the house was suffering – he was sure she understood, but the fact was he could not say how long Endellion would remain in his possession, if he would have to give it up. His mouth twitched downwards, and then he spoke even faster than before. The post might not be forever, but he was determined to reward loyalty wherever he could. Manton the butler had been in his family's employ for forty-five years, Annette, who was a maid and cook, for fifteen years.

Bonnie nodded along, scarcely taking it in. Her mind was racing ahead. She imagined herself in the kitchen of this house, helping Annette stew apples, laughing over the demands of this gentleman's pretty, tyrannical daughter. She would walk down these narrow hallways, flinging the shutters wide to let the sun stream in, and below her the avenue of limes would stretch towards the road, pasture on one side, woodland on the other. How safe she might feel.

She heard footsteps on the stairs, loud and echoing, and then the door was thrown open. A girl stood on the threshold, her pale hair unravelling from under her bonnet, a leather-bound book clutched in her arms. 'Oh!' she exclaimed when she saw Bonnie.

'If you'll allow me a moment, Cissie,' the gentleman said, standing. 'Perhaps you might run and ask Annette to bring us tea and a dish of strawberries. And then, when you're back, I will show you a treasure I found for you to paste into your

54

book.' He smiled at the girl. It transformed him, all that heaviness lifted away.

The door closed behind her. 'Cissie, my daughter,' he said, as though it was not clear. He coughed. 'What was I saying? Yes. Annette and Manton. They have offered this house years of service. Of loyalty.' He laid his hands palm-up on the desk and Bonnie glimpsed the insides of his wrists. They were as pale as milk, the veins arcing in neat, thin lines. Robin's egg, she thought; lilac. A sight so vulnerable she had to glance away.

'Deceit,' he said, 'is unforgiveable in this household. It is the one thing I will not tolerate.'

Bonnie fidgeted. The edge of her forged letter of recommendation cut into her hand. The red-headed man, his blood so black in the darkness. She would be good, she told herself. She would be new, different.

'Is that understood?'

He waited.

'Yes,' she said hurriedly. 'Yes, of course, sir.'

She thanked him, backed towards the door. The headache began once more, stabbing her brow.

'Annette, the housemaid, will explain everything you need to know. You will meet my daughter properly tomorrow.'

Just before she opened the door, Bonnie glanced back, her eyes resting on the fresh square of wallpaper above the mantelpiece. His eyes followed hers, and a redness spread up his throat.

She stepped into the hallway alone. She brushed one of the painted cherubs with her fingertips.

She had done it. Bonnie Fairchild, lady's maid.

Lady's maid.

Above her, the red-glassed lantern spun and winked.

Brawn

'As things stand, it'll be me roasted for dinner,' Annette said as they walked into the kitchen. The maid took a spoon and prodded a pig's head that was boiling on the stove. It bobbed back up, its snout seeming to reach for air. 'And tea! Who drinks tea in weather like this?'

'Hot drinks are cooling,' Manton, the butler, said without looking up from his ledger.

'Nonsense.'

The stove was roaring and Bonnie could already feel sweat prickling her collar. Two half-plucked geese hung from the ceiling. Bloody chicken livers were browning on the table, the floors stacked with heaped baskets of limp herbs, a sack labelled *lemons*.

'Oh, but you must forgive me,' the butler said, taking in Bonnie for the first time. He stood. 'I had no idea we were expecting company.' He had a face that seemed instantly familiar, and Bonnie wondered with a flare of dread if they'd met before.

'This is Cissie's new lady's maid,' Annette said. 'Bonnie Fairchild.'

'Her new lady's maid?' Manton frowned slightly. 'Mr Moncrieff said nothing to me of this. If he had—' The man's eyes flicked to his ledger and Bonnie saw long columns of numbers, a few lines of looping script. *Madeira, three bottles.*

Gravy boat: two, one ornamented with a leaping trout. Then he shook his head, brightened. 'But that is no concern of yours. You will be welcome. This house is too big for the pair of us, and I'm certain Annette is tired of my company.'

'I wouldn't mind discussing something other than boot blacking and engines,' Annette said, ducking out of Manton's way as though she expected him to swat her.

'See what I must contend with.' He raised his hands in mock surrender. 'By the end of the week, Miss Fairchild, you are sure to find yourself riveted by flywheels and pistons.'

'I will devote myself to it,' Bonnie replied, and when he smiled back at her, the knot in her chest began to loosen.

'You had better not,' Annette said, leading Bonnie through to a small scullery set apart from the kitchen, a stone sink and copper tub beside the high window. In the half-light, Bonnie saw that there was something beatific about Annette: her full lips, her thick black hair, gleaming with oil. What would Crawford think if he met her?

'We do laundry here on a Wednesday,' Annette explained. 'You will find the buckets and brushes here.' It was strange being shown the house in this way, like peering into a body and seeing how the guts all functioned. Annette began opening and closing cupboards, each filled with a disorientating array of brooms, cloths, pails, mops, each allotted a precise task. How was she ever to learn what implement to use? And Annette moved so swiftly through it all, bustling her into the housemaid's closet, the cellar with its wine bottles and locked gun cabinet, the silver room with rows of tarnished platters and knives.

'Of course Mr Moncrieff will sell all of this soon,' Annette whispered, pausing beside the silverware. 'Manton's weighing and valuing every piece.'

Bonnie kept her own voice still and quiet. 'And how long do

you think it will be until Mr Moncrieff is forced to sell the house?'

'Manton says it might be soon. Months.'

'Months!' Bonnie repeated. 'And do you know where you will go?'

'Mr Moncrieff says he'll find me a position when the time comes. Though I'm used to our easy way here, and I know housekeepers can be exacting—' She shrugged.

'Are they indeed,' Bonnie said, recalling the endless rows of tall houses she had called upon when she first arrived in London, each interview shorter and more finite than the one before it. 'And there's no chance of him keeping the house?'

Annette shrugged again, then said with a knowing look, 'It's all because of *his wife* of course.'

'Oh?' Bonnie asked.

Annette's eyes glittered. 'She was terribly extravagant. All of the painted walls and the stained glass and the arched doors were her doing. She liked the *theatricality* of it, to be surrounded by the unusual. She bought all sorts of fripperies. Mr Moncrieff is selling Cardinal Wolsey's hat this afternoon.'

'His actual hat?'

'And a lock of Mary Tudor's hair.'

'But what would anyone want with such things?'

'Mrs Moncrieff liked to touch the past,' Annette said, forgetting to whisper. 'She liked relics and they cost her a pretty penny too. She'd have bought the pimple off Jesus's nose if it was for sale.'

'Annette,' Manton's voice from the kitchen. 'I need hardly remind you whose house this is.'

'Manton's been here so long you'd think he'd have sealed himself to the chairs.'

'I heard that.'

'Did you indeed?'

Bonnie followed Annette back into the kitchen. It struck her as curious that anybody would want to touch the past. All the things she would cut out of herself if she could: all those times she'd shucked her skin and started afresh. But it was all still there, biting at her: the grazes on her wrist from the gentleman's fingernails, the smell of beeswax which always hooked her back into the rector's library.

'I'll show you the rooms upstairs and then I'll finish this damned brawn,' Annette said, wiping her hands on her apron.

This time they did not take the staircase with its cameo-set recesses, but Annette led Bonnie to a smaller door disguised in the coving. The steps were narrow, the pine grimy and worn. Lowly stairs for lowly servants; Annette climbed them quickly, leading her onto a landing where the grand stair emerged. She pointed out Cissie's bedroom door, Mr Moncrieff's, the chamber that had been his wife's. The rest of the house was narrow and winding, rooms heaped on rooms with no apparent sense of order, as though one era was scribbling out another, the past nothing more than a ghostly echo. Cherubs and goddesses burst from walls and ceilings, fireplaces ornate and jagged like the tombs of cathedrals. Most of the rooms were half empty, gaps on the walls where furniture and paintings must have been sold. Annette pointed out a dining room, a drawing room, a library, a round room, a little parlour, all bathed in a reddish stained-glass glow, and Bonnie followed her, bewildered, entranced. What sort of person had Mrs Moncrieff been to create this oddity of a house? There was an undeniable romanticism to it, a desire to press oneself into the fabric of a building, to be *remembered*. Of course such a woman would not have desired a modest churchyard burial, a small headstone.

All the while, Annette chattered, and Bonnie struggled to

take it all in. 'The friezes and ceilings are papier-mâché so you must clean them as such,' she said. Or, 'The fireplace is carved wood, so do not treat it like marble.'

And how, Bonnie wondered, was she to clean marble or wood or anything at all? Which of the brushes, which of the ointments she had seen in a hundred neat jars? Her mob cap kept slipping across her ears, her apron pinched too tight. *Yes,* Bonnie said. And, *Of course,* and *I see,* but it would not be long, surely, until she was discovered.

A door clicked open and Mr Moncrieff nodded at them, said, 'Very good, very good.' He was so tall he had to bow his head through the arched door. He had a dog with him, huge and grey, dressed in a velvet cap, a short cloak tied to its collar.

'Don't you look like a dandy, my sweet hound,' Annette said, rubbing its ears.

'Cissie dressed him just now,' Mr Moncrieff explained, shrugging. 'Poor Zephyr.'

Bonnie leaned to stroke its fur, but the dog nosed her crotch, its tongue licking her hand.

'Zephyr!' Mr Moncrieff scolded, and she could see the mortification on his face as he led the dog away, hurrying down the stairs, the dog's claws clicking, black crape twisting in a sudden breeze from the door.

'All this mourning,' Bonnie whispered to Annette. 'Did she die very recently?'

'Oh no. She drowned a year and a half ago.' Annette lowered her voice. 'Lots of folk think she did away with herself.'

'A suicide?'

Annette looked gratified at Bonnie's shock. 'That's what they say, though Mr Moncrieff quieted it. They'd never have buried her in the churchyard as a *suicide*. But he likes to keep the mourning in place. He likes to remind himself of his guilt, I think, even though everyone can see how wretched it makes him.'

'But it wasn't his fault!'

'He was never very attentive to her.' Annette led her up another set of narrow steps, spiralled like a shell.

'Do you know why she did it?' Bonnie asked.

Annette turned round so abruptly that Bonnie almost fell backwards. 'She died for love.' Her whisper was hot, her eyes unblinking, and Bonnie glanced away. The housemaid had not seen death, had almost certainly been kept apart from anything surrounding her mistress's drowning. It was all just a bright, thrilling story to her. 'She had a lover. We all knew. They used to leave each other letters in Mrs Moncrieff's greenhouse, though we never saw him. She was going to run away with him. She asked her maid to pack her trunk, but Mr Moncrieff found the girl and demanded to know what was happening. We were all frightened half to death. There was a terrible row and the next morning, Cissie found Mrs Moncrieff in the pond.'

'Cissie did?' Bonnie felt it squarely in her chest. She thought of her own mother, the quiet absence that had filled her life. 'She found her mother dead?'

'Isn't that horrible?' Annette said, in a voice which implied the opposite. 'Endellion has always been full of dalliances. King George II bought this house for one of his mistresses, Caroline Moncrieff. Imagine, being given this. As a *gift*.'

But Bonnie was still thinking about Cissie: imagining her dragging her mother's body from the pond, the girl's shock and fear. *Sensitive*, Mr Moncrieff had called her. *A little troubled*. It was no wonder.

Annette opened a door at the top of the stairs. 'This is where you'll sleep,' she said. 'And here's your bedding.'

Bonnie stepped inside. The window was clover-shaped, the

mantelpiece small and plain. Two brass beds were fitted under the eaves, a china bowl and jug on the floor beside them, a pot under the bed. The sun was sinking and it set fire to the walls, to the white, worn mattresses.

'Will you sleep in the other bed?'

'Lawks no,' Annette replied, and Bonnie smiled to herself. This small space would be all hers. 'Manton allows me to live in a little cottage in the grounds, provided I don't admit any *gentleman visitors*.' She laughed. 'Wouldn't it be a lark to be married? It's the aim of every girl, surely. But I want to visit Paris and Rome. I wish Mr Moncrieff would travel like the other households along the river. The owner of Orleans House brings all his staff when he leaves for France. Imagine!'

Annette sat on one of the beds, springs creaking. She lay back with her arms spread out. 'I've been desperate for Mr Moncrieff to hire another maid. We could take a rowing boat one Sunday after church. We're given every Sunday afternoon off, you know. We could float down past all of the grand houses. Ham House and Radnor and Pope's Lodge. They're as pretty as a picture. Look, you can see the river from up here.'

Annette stood and pointed at the brown Thames snaking past the window, the view uninterrupted by wide lawns. A few boats bobbed along it.

'Where's the greenhouse?' Bonnie asked, standing beside her.

'There,' Annette said, waving her hand vaguely at the woodland. 'Though I never go there.' She turned to Bonnie. 'Oh, do say we can take a boat on Sunday, if it isn't raining.'

'I'd like that,' Bonnie replied, smiling, and she found she was undone by the unguardedness of Annette, her quick gossiping confidence. But so, too, did she long to be alone: she wanted to sink into the day, to convince herself it had all been real. 'Will the pig—'

'The pig!' Annette exclaimed. 'She'll have boiled all over the stove, unless Manton's caught her.' She paused in the doorway. 'I'll bring you a slice of ham and some bread for dinner, if you want to rest after your journey.'

And with that, Bonnie was left alone in the room. In *her* room. She must have the finest view in the house, she thought, hurrying back to the window and prising it open. The breeze was hot. Between the gaps in the battlements, she could see for miles: acres of woodland and distant church spires, the Thames, brown and sluggish. And all around, Mr Moncrieff's gardens, tangled and unclipped: the sun-bleached lawn reaching the river, a round brick hut, serpentine paths threading through woodland. In the other direction, towards the road, it had seemed so much flatter and plainer: the long drive and the pasture that she'd suggested for the cemetery.

All this land. This house, this room – Bonnie clenched her fists, her breath catching. She had done it, hidden herself here. She thought of the bed she had shared with her three sisters, the garret in the Angler with Rex asleep on heaped clothing on the floor. *Our beloved Great Dane, snoring at our feet,* Crawford had once said with a laugh. *What?* he'd said, when Rex had scowled. *I said beloved.*

Bonnie reached out a hand and began to touch the room as though to mark it, pinging the jug, running her palm along the bedframe, up and down the marked walls. Soon the mattress would be indented with her shape, the china pot chiming with her piss. Her fingernails and dropped hairs would fall through the gaps in the floorboards, as though the whole house was breathing her in, swallowing her up.

A laugh broke from her throat and she took the sheet and threw it around herself like a cape, winding it tighter and tighter as she waltzed around the room, as she leapt onto the bed and sprung forwards, clumsy, tumbling across the floorboards. She did not care if anyone heard. She gazed down over acres of countryside and pinched a spire between her fingertips, flattened a patch of woodland with her palm.

And she knew, as she fell back on the bed, that she could not let this slip away. She felt as though time had stopped, this whole house dipped in aspic. Who would trace her from that sour passage in St Giles to this bright room? Crawford had been right: she would stay hidden here. This paper house with its papier-mâché ceilings, its painted plaster walls, its fireplaces carved of wood not stone. She and this house: they were both playing at being something else. But if it slipped away; if she found herself being packed up with the bureaus and dressing tables, what then? A crowd at hanging day, jeering, impatient to see the sharp catch of her body, the flail of her legs. She gritted her teeth, her forehead resting against the wall. If this house would keep her safe, she would guard it in turn. What other choice did she have?

The Heart-Shaped Pond

As the sun lowered and Endellion quietened, Bonnie paced up and down her attic room. Silence except for the rustle of her skirts, the faint creak of the floors. Underneath it, if she strained to listen, mice clicked in the walls, the bricks of the house groaning as they cooled after the heat of the day, like an old man snapping his joints by the fire.

The black sky was the same sky that had watched her the night before, the moon hooked like a scythe. It glinted as if to say, *I know*. There might be men, even now, tracing the road she had travelled, picking up the crumbs she had dropped. They might be fanning across the grounds. What if someone had seen her? What if they had seen Crawford and Rex carrying the body to the graveyard? It felt implausible that her hands could have snuffed somebody out, removed them from the earth.

Crawford would know what was happening. She missed him with a sudden ache. If he was here, he would hold her, kiss her, reassure her she was safe. But he was miles away: almost certainly asleep in his garret, his body curled in that familiar comma shape. The old candle would still be on the bedside, the pictures on the wall. Was it better to be there and know everything; or here, just waiting, oblivious?

She had to stretch her legs properly and shake off the thoughts that clung to her. The woodland was a thick mass outside her window. Somewhere within it was the greenhouse Annette had mentioned, where Mrs Moncrieff had received all those letters. An illicit place. Bonnie rocked on her heels, bound herself tightly with her arms. *She had a lover.* The sense of shared wrongness was somehow comforting, and Bonnie moved towards the door. She wanted to find the greenhouse. If anyone saw her, she would say the heat had made her restless.

It was surprising how quickly she had forgotten her way through the house, how narrow and winding the hallways were. Doors were hidden in covings. It was black without a candle, her footsteps stumbling. Through one room, back again. She passed paintings where all she could make out was the white teardrops on fruit, the catchpoint of an eye. When, at last, she found herself on the landing where the three bedrooms lay, she could hear the faint fall of Mr Moncrieff's breath. The walls were thinner than she had realized.

She found the servants' stairs, and then finally, she was in the kitchen. The geese were laid out on the table, their skin stippled and plucked, feathers bursting from a sack beside them, Manton's snores rising from his quarters. Something flickered in the corner – Bonnie put her hand to her heart, gasped. But it was only Zephyr, lifting his head from his spot beside the stove, his chops brown and bloody. A bowl of liver gleamed silver in the moonlight.

She unlatched the door, stepping outside into the cool darkness. She was wearing nothing but her worn nightdress, her feet bare, but the grass was soft and dewy. An owl called from the trees, the hedgerows rustling with small creatures, dark shapes she couldn't make out. It had been so long since she had smelled air so fresh and earthy.

Highwell had gardens that were almost military in their axial lines, their formal geometry. But she had never liked them, preferred places where things straggled free. Here, she walked among unpruned rose bushes, down winding paths that snaked back on themselves. By the wall, two dead citrus trees were still wrapped in fleece for the winter like shrouded bodies.

Bonnie stopped. There, disguised in a carpet of green algae, was the pond where Mrs Moncrieff must have drowned. It was heart-shaped, fringed with weeds, surprisingly small. She could have walked around it in twenty paces. Bonnie dipped her toe in the water, gasped. How cold it was, even in this hot summer. It would have been winter when Mrs Moncrieff drowned. What had possessed her to wade in, the silt slipping between her toes, the icy water closing over her head? What desperation had led her to do it? Bonnie could picture it all so clearly, a wintry sun rising to show her hair, fanned against the water, her pale hand outstretched. The cry Cissie must have made, how Mr Moncrieff would have heard it and run downstairs, the shame that would gnaw at him for things he had said to her when they had argued the night before. The guilt that made him heap his house with black, to leave the dark ribbons and foliage to gather dust for more than a year after her death, to draw endless sketches of the grand mausoleum he had failed to give her. If Bonnie could only understand him and his wife better, she might convince him to build the cemetery, and then he might keep Endellion.

On Bonnie walked, wincing at the crack of twigs, searching for the greenhouse. She passed a pavilion and the round building she now saw was an ice house. The grounds were enormous, far larger than she expected of a house the size of Endellion. She might have fitted the whole of Soho into this space, packed in houses and garrets, inns and churches. If Crawford saw it, he would be beside himself with fury that a man had let this opportunity go to waste: all he might have done with land like it!

At last, she noticed a twist of ornate black iron, almost hidden by a straggling hawthorn and brambles. She pressed forwards, thorns scoring her arms. The greenhouse. It was a surprise to realize that she was back at the pond. She must have walked straight past this building. But she had expected a different place: an ostentatious structure, set apart from any foliage, bursting with exotic fruits and ferns, orchid stems bowing against the mass of their buds. But this was so secret, so hidden. Bonnie put her weight against the French doors, the swollen wood juddering open. There was glass underfoot, broken panes above. She picked her way forward gingerly.

A humid reek rose up and Bonnie put her hand to her nose, almost gagged. All around her, fruits were scattered on the floor, some rotting, some dried to husks. She picked one up, dislodging a cloud of minuscule flies. Scaled skin, brown leaves almost like palm. A pineapple: it couldn't be. But they were everywhere, decaying on the ground. *Fripperies*, Annette had called Mrs Moncrieff's purchases. Their finances had been *excessive*, Mr Moncrieff had said.

Bonnie surveyed the ruins, the dried skins of long-dead fruit. It seemed a shame to leave a scene so disordered. As a child she had always enjoyed the task of making a rough patch of earth beautiful. She would forget anything except the feel of the soil under her fingertips, not even recognizing the ache in her thighs until her sisters called her in for supper.

Memories swelled in her as she began to brush the soil and broken glass into a pile. That earthy, homely scent. She'd often assisted her father with potting tulips or wrapping bulbs in paper for the winter. He could not read and nor could anyone else in her family, and so he would hand her the head botanist's planting plans. It had given her a small thrill that she could decipher the pages and instruct him: yellow climbing roses and lilac against the walled garden, banks of lavender down by the lake, violets and forget-me-knots at the front of the borders. 'I'm sure the rector will give you a small patch in his garden that you can tend,' he had told her, and she had grown quiet, that cloud growing between her and her father once more.

Bonnie hummed as she worked, imagining Mrs Moncrieff in here too: the ghostly smudge of her, nurturing her plants. Bonnie wondered if the master would mind that she was tending to this place, if she might even be allowed to grow flowers which she might arrange on his tables. The agitation she had felt in her bedroom began to fade. She found a flowering orchid in the mulch and potted it, a few dried snail shells cracking as she tamped down the soil around it. She wrapped the orchid stem around a stick she found by the door. There was so much to rescue, so much to rake in and discard. She stacked terracotta planters, spiders dashing about blindly, woodlice curling into tight balls. As she worked, the hours slipped away from her, the moon inching across the sky. The light turned pale blue.

Bonnie had just lifted the largest planter, wet soil clinging to her nightgown, when she saw a tiny scrap of paper nestling below it. The page was yellowed and torn, the ink a little faded and blotted, and in the dim light she could make out only the first word.

Josephine –

Bonnie peered closer. The name was written in a clear script, less blemished than the rest of the writing. *Josephine*. A French name, charming and exotic. It sounded like the name of the person who might have turned a house into a piece of theatre, who might have had lavish tastes.

A flash of movement behind her; Bonnie turned and saw a fox, streaking across the lawn. Soon the household would rise, Annette hurrying in from her cottage, fetching water to boil on the stove. Bonnie moved towards the French doors but she was too hasty to be gone and she knocked one of the empty pots, sending it plummeting to the ground. It cracked like a gunshot. Shards pattered over the tiles and she ran – ran all the way across the lawns and into the scullery and up the pine stairs, her chest heaving. There was her bed, covers cast aside.

She struck a Lucifer, the candle listing to the side. A stink of sulphur filled the room. The note crackled as she unfurled it and pressed it flat.

Josephine –

Then below it, fainter.

I hunger for you, crave –

Bonnie swallowed, her throat dry. Such a simple line, its longing so naked. The paper torn there as though what was desired was beyond expression. What had Mrs Moncrieff thought as she read it? How could it have led her to abandon everything, to cast herself into nothingness? This house was hers. Bonnie felt her whisper in every arched window, every inch of painted walls, as though she had just sailed out of every room.

The candle guttered and spat. Bonnie held the note above the flame, ready to catch the edge. She should burn it, she told herself; she should pinch this thing out. Mr Moncrieff's words rang in her ears. *Deceit is unforgiveable in this household.* But was it deceitful to keep this small memento of a woman who had gone? When the edge caught and blackened, Bonnie gasped, blew on the note, flinching at the burn on her palm.

I hunger for you, cr – it said now, the edges charred, and Bonnie tucked it under her mattress. She lay there, her heart galloping, dawn beginning to split open the room. She began to move her hand across her thighs like Crawford used to do, drawing back as he did, forcing herself to wait, until she was sick with wanting and pressed herself there, hard, the shock of it almost making her cry out, and she thought, *Josephine –*

Curd Soap

The next morning, Bonnie hovered outside Cissie's door, shifting her weight from foot to foot. Annette had mentioned to Bonnie twice that she should go upstairs and prepare Cissie for the day, until Bonnie hadn't been able to defer it any longer. She felt she might as well have been asked to build one of Mr Moncrieff's mausoleums as prepare a girl's toilette. But when a quiet voice called, 'Who's that? Outside my door?' Bonnie found herself opening her door and stepping inside.

Cissie was sitting at a desk by the window, tightly wrapped in a quilt. A large book lay open in front of her, a brush and china dish of glue next to it. As she turned towards Bonnie, something inside Bonnie's chest twisted: despite the glimpse Bonnie had had of Cissie the day before, she had still imagined a cold, queenly girl, like the Highwell daughters. But Cissie looked hunched and small and hapless, her covers pulled about her. So *young*.

'I – I am Bonnie Fairchild,' she said. 'We met yesterday. Your father will have explained.' She moved towards Cissie, then stopped, almost tripping. Cissie's ungainliness made her feel clumsy in turn. What was she meant to say? It was imperative that the child warmed to her. 'Is that a scrap-book?' she attempted. The pages in front of Cissie were papered with letters and clippings of hearts and cupids.

Cissie slammed it shut. 'It is not a scrap-book.'

'Sorry—' Bonnie said, holding out her hands. 'I didn't mean—'

The girl held her chin high. 'It is full of letters from the man I will marry.'

She stared at Bonnie as though daring her to defy her, so Bonnie kept her expression steady. 'That sounds very special.' The idea of this girl, so soft, so unmoulded, marrying anyone – Bonnie had an image of her, lying still and pale on the bed, a knifing between her legs, a heavy body huffing on top of her. She winced. 'There will be time enough for that, I'm sure. An endless merry-go-round of suitors. But who is this particular gentleman?'

'Lord Duggan,' Cissie said, carefully prising open the book and returning to her place.

'A Lord! I see.'

Cissie dipped her brush in the glue. It slurped like a tongue. Bonnie inched closer. The letters were written in what must have been Cissie's careful hand, the *i*'s dotted with hearts. The book was bulging, the pages crinkled with dried glue. The single-minded focus it took to make such a thing: Bonnie thought of Mr Moncrieff and his endless mausoleums, the nervous energy that also thrummed through him. 'He writes to me,' Cissie said airily, without a shadow of humour. 'He is so full of love that he might die!'

'How desperately romantic,' Bonnie said, echoing her tone. 'Now, would you like to dress?'

Cissie shifted in her chair, then glanced towards the bed, her cheeks hot. 'I—' she began, her voice breaking as though she might cry. 'I'm sorry. I'm so sorry.'

'Whatever for?' Bonnie walked to the bed. The sheets were streaked with fresh blood.

'No matter,' Bonnie said brightly, stripping the bed. 'We'll have you out of your nightgown in a moment, too. I'll bring a bucket of hot water and we can fill the bath.'

She worked quickly, bundling up the sheets and hurrying downstairs to the kitchen. The water boiled and hissed on the stove. She could do this, she thought, a lightness in her step; this was the sort of work she could manage.

The bucket was heavy, water slopping against her chest, her arms aching by the time she'd climbed two floors. Back in Cissie's bedroom, she helped the child out of her gown. She looked as pale as a grub as she crouched in the tub, more of a little girl than a woman. Bonnie handed her a flannel and Cissie dipped it in the bowl, cleaned her armpits, shielding her body as far as she could. Bonnie snuck quick glances: the girl's little rosy breasts, scarcely more than swollen nipples; the small coil of hair between her legs, rusted with blood. The water ran orange down her thighs, puddling in the tub.

'I saw a man in the grounds this morning. He was hiding in the trees.' Cissie spoke abruptly, and Bonnie's hand stilled as she reached for the flannel.

'Was it just one man? Did he look like—'

How to say it? How to voice what she feared most?

Like he was there to find Bonnie, to take her away.

'There was nobody else,' Cissie replied. 'He was wearing a green jacket. He was the most handsome man I ever saw.'

Bonnie let out a breath, grasping the flannel once more, wringing it against Cissie's neck. Crawford had been here. If only she'd seen him. She would have stayed outside all night if she'd known. The relief she would feel just to have his arms around her, his cheek against hers. And what if he had come because there was something he needed to tell her about the gentleman and the search for her; what if it was urgent?

'It was so early I wondered at first if he was a ghost.' Cissie's voice rose in excitement. 'I read a novel about a hero who was poisoned by a girl's jealous father, and the hero's ghost waited each day until she died and she could join him. Isn't that romantic?'

'It would be nicer if she hadn't needed to die too,' Bonnie replied. 'But did the man – did you see, did he stay for long?'

Cissie shook her head, then glanced at the window. 'I saw you last night, running through the grounds. I thought you might be a ghost too.' She turned to stare at Bonnie. 'I see everything.'

Was it a threat, Bonnie wondered, reaching for a piece of linen to dry the girl with. But Cissie had spoken so simply, it seemed more a statement of fact. All night, she had thought she was alone but Cissie had been sitting at her window, wide-eyed, watching her. 'You ought to have been asleep.'

'I can't.' Cissie picked a scab on her hand. It must have hurt but she didn't flinch. She glanced down. 'Not for more than a year. I just *can't.*'

Josephine hung there in the silence, just as she did in each room of the house. Bonnie could have let it slip past them both, but she saw the hopeful way Cissie looked at her, as if desperate to bring her mother back into the light.

'It must have been very painful,' Bonnie said carefully. 'I lost my mother too, but I hardly remember her. I always thought that if she'd lived, she might have protected me better.' She hoped that Cissie might offer a confidence of her own, even say more about Josephine. But the girl was silent. Bonnie edged forwards, wondering if she was taking it too far. 'Your father told me a little about your mother. You must miss her.'

Cissie's eyes, Bonnie noticed, were a sharp, clean green. 'There are things I wish – things like, that she had loved my Papa fully.'

Bonnie swallowed, shying away from Cissie's gaze by busying

herself with tidying a brush on the dressing table. Could she also have known about her mother's lover? 'But perhaps there was affection there,' Bonnie suggested. 'Your father certainly wishes to honour her now.'

'But they were never like in my books. That's love. When you'd die for each other. When you'd bury yourself away and never speak to another soul. That's—'

'It sounds like your books,' Bonnie said gently, 'have a very breathless sort of love. And surely, you cannot wish your father had died too?'

'No,' she said at last. 'No.' Cissie fell quiet. Bonnie rubbed the girl's arms with the cloth and followed her instructions as to where the belt was kept. She looped it around Cissie's hips, securing the napkin with a pin.

'Do you suppose Papa will find another wife soon?' Cissie asked at last.

'Your Papa?' Bonnie patted down one of Cissie's dresses. 'It wouldn't be my place to say.'

'They're already swarming around him.'

'Who are?'

'I call them the seals. They're from the houses near here. Strawberry Hill and Marble Hill and York House.'

'Why seals?'

'Because of their sleek hair and skin. And the way they throw themselves before him as though they're begging for a fish. Seals with sharp claws, digging them into poor Papa.'

'Seals!' Bonnie exclaimed, almost laughing. She pictured an oily-faced woman with fingernails filed to claws, slicing her talons into Mr Moncrieff's pale skin, the fat as yellow as pheasant lard.

'I hate them all. Papa says if he marries again, everything will still pass to me, but what if he changes his mind?'

'I'm sure he'll honour his word,' Bonnie replied. 'But it's little wonder you can't sleep with all these worries.'

'Sorry,' she said, wrinkling her nose. 'Sorry.'

'No matter,' Bonnie said, 'but put this on, before you grow cold.' She reached for a shift, lifting it over Cissie's head and teasing her arms through the sleeves. A soft ringlet tumbled from the back of Cissie's neck, light brown where the sun had not lightened it. Tenderness swelled in Bonnie, a feeling she had not had since she dressed her little brothers. That uncomplicated, ferocious love: their legs so plump and dimpled, their sweet bellies so round.

'There we are,' Bonnie said, and Cissie looked at her and smiled.

It had been so long since Bonnie had encountered that particular intimacy that can spring up between women, that conviction of being kindred, as melding as any love affair. She found herself humming as she carried the rusty bathing water back downstairs, Cissie's bloodstained nightgown and bedclothes bundled under her arm. She shielded them from Manton but he didn't seem to notice, barely looking up as his pencil scratched at the accounts.

In the scullery, sunlight rained down on her, a deep sense of peace settling in her bones. It felt like years since she had found such a small pocket of joy, so long since she had done a thing alone and succeeded at it. Cissie liked her. And so, too, had Bonnie crept further under the skin of the household, hooking herself to it. She boiled more water, scrubbed the sheets as she did her own stained drawers. The stains faded to pale amber but that was as spotless as she'd ever got them. She was about to take the bedclothes outside to dry when Annette walked in.

'Lawks,' she said. 'Did you use salt and lemon juice? Is the water *hot*?' She paused, eyeing Bonnie. It was enough to make Bonnie's shoulders sag, and she felt washed out by that familiar feeling of hopelessness, that she could do nothing without help, without Crawford.

'Don't look at me like that,' Annette said, touching Bonnie's sleeve. 'Listen, leave these to me. You can bring Cissie to her lessons at Little Marble Hill instead.' She took the sheets back to the sink. 'What was the name of your last house?'

'Brinwick Hall,' Bonnie murmured.

'I should wonder how it's run,' Annette replied. 'I should wonder you worked there at all, with bedclothes cleaned like this!'

It was said lightly, but Bonnie's belly began to churn. Everything looked suddenly dull: the fat-spattered pans hanging from the ceiling, the brawn in its coat of jelly.

She hoped that Manton hadn't overheard them, but later in the day, Bonnie found a booklet slipped under her door. A small note was affixed to it, reading only, *In case it is of use. C. Manton.* Bonnie turned it over. *Household Management*, it read. She flicked through the pages. *Furs, Feathers and Woollens. Treatment of Jewels and Epaulettes. Restoring Whiteness to Scorched Linens.*

She took it all in greedily: the pastes she would need to make, their ingredients as obscure as spells. Dried fowl's dung, bullock's gall and curd soap. The different brushes and cloths for each task, each one illustrated. She would study this, learn every page.

But as she read, Annette's words clung to her.

I should wonder you worked there at all.

She had almost given herself away. She stared out the window, searching the grounds for Crawford. There was no sign of him. The booklet might help, but only he would know what to say, how to smooth over everything with Annette. Only he would know what was happening in St Giles.

She thought of men's feet pounding up the stairs, seizing her from this small room, dragging her across the gravel. And the last thing she would see as she was hauled down the avenue would be Mr Moncrieff, his shock as he saw her for what she was, the wrongness he had invited into his house.

Pipe Smoke

Time slipped by. The heat of August split open at last and September arrived with its smell of rot and ripeness. Each morning, Bonnie would find a way of asking Cissie the question that had burned in her head as she lay in her attic bedroom, unable to sleep.

Has the ghost in the green jacket visited? Have you seen him?

Cissie would be sitting by the window writing herself another secret letter from Lord Duggan, always ferociously guarded, slipped out of sight when Bonnie neared her. And each time Cissie would give a slight shake of her head. *No.* Or, *not today.* It would puncture something in Bonnie. Crawford loved her, she knew that, and yet she felt forgotten, unwanted. Perhaps, as time had passed, he'd grown appalled by what she'd done. The alleyway, the spread of blood.

Crawford would come, Bonnie told herself. He *would.* For weeks, she had even avoided Annette's promised boating trip, afraid he'd come and she'd miss him. But as another Sunday came and went and there was still no sign of him, she gave in at last.

To Bonnie's surprise, she found herself looking forward to it. The day was clear and bright when she walked to Annette's cottage, the hamper of meats knocking against her leg. She and

Annette strolled arm-in-arm to the jetty, Manton waiting with the boat already unmoored. He leaned back as Annette rowed, pointing out the great houses they drifted past, the luminaries that had lived on the river's banks. Alexander Pope, Horace Walpole, Lady Mary Wortley Montagu, Henry Fielding, William Turner.

'Twickenham has more chaises than Versailles,' he said. 'There's nowhere on earth I'd rather live. On days like this I fancy I can see Pope's ghost, skimming along the river.'

'Manton's been here since the third century B.C.,' Annette said.

'Why would I live anywhere else? Though I suppose I could always leave service altogether. There's my mother's old house in Hampshire.'

'Don't talk nonsense,' Annette replied. 'You were made to be a butler. I imagine you were born already dressed in a tiny green livery, doffing your cap.'

And as the down drifted low on the air, Bonnie smiled. She understood why Manton had not left the house, why he had bedded himself in for almost fifty years. Her knees were reddened, her palms cracking, but she wore them like small victories: signs that she had made herself necessary, that she was taking good care of Endellion. She did not mind that the work was supposedly beneath her station. Bonnie scrubbed and polished until the whole house glowed. Suddenly, she caught her reflection everywhere, in shining gilt frames and grates, in door handles and fire irons, just a little whisk of movement as she breezed past. She dusted old cobwebs from the stained glass, burnished pheasants and shepherdesses and blue panes until they gleamed. She pounded rosins and melted wax, she squeezed limes and bruised bulbs of garlic, Annette staring at her in bewilderment, soon running out of tasks to allot her. Manton took to calling her *the Whirlwind*. With the passing of the summer heat, Bonnie threw open the shutters, the hallways filled with light. Everything felt fresh, as though the house had died and been brought back to life.

Sometimes, when she worked late in the greenhouse, gradually uncovering the red tiles and planting seeds; every flower or weed seemed peculiarly single to Endellion, new and surprising. The perfect geometry of a dandelion clock; a foxglove made of little pink thimbles, just the right size for her finger. She was alive, she thought. Nobody had found her. The house had wrapped its arms around her, kept her safe. At the edges of her vision, she felt a light presence. Her hands, working the soil that Josephine had once tended. Two women, their heads bowed over pots and raised beds, coaxing life into seeds and bulbs.

And then, returning late, earth in her hair, she would glimpse a small strip of light under Mr Moncrieff's study door. This room and Josephine's bedroom were the only rooms she was forbidden from entering and cleaning. If she pressed her ear to the wood, she could hear the whisper of his pencil, the wet sound of a pen being dipped in ink, papers rustling like cloth. She imagined him frowning as he drew another mausoleum where his dead wife would never rest. Always, he whispered to himself, and Bonnie could not catch a word.

It was only when she heard the floorboards creak and his bedroom door close that Bonnie would let herself into Josephine's chamber. Its arsenic-green walls would glow in the light of her candle, and she would peek under the shrouds laid over the furniture. She uncovered a Japanned card table, a French chaise in unblemished pink silk, a globe. The bed, unmade, the blankets coverless. Sitting at the dressing table mirror, hands trembling, Bonnie would pin tortoiseshell brooches to her plain apron, hold up her hair with a fragment of conch, almost transparent against the candle's flame.

'I want you,' she would whisper to her reflection. 'Crave—'

One sunny afternoon in late September, Bonnie decided to walk to Little Marble Hill to collect Cissie. By the time she arrived, storm clouds were massing overhead, grey and swollen.

'Bonnie,' Cissie cried, hurtling down the steps when she saw her. She threw her arms around Bonnie's neck. The bruised circles under her eyes had gone, a new plumpness to her cheeks. *You've been as good for her as a month's stay in Bath*, the house-keeper had said to Bonnie.

'Tell me what you learned today,' Bonnie asked, and Cissie unravelled everything as they walked: the Latin translations, the pianoforte class, how Emmeline had shown her how to fold paper flowers. But all the way, as the rain began spotting the path and they quickened their pace, she kept her scrap-book pressed against her.

'Why don't you let me carry it?' Bonnie asked, but Cissie drew her mouth tight. Bonnie tried again. 'If this is the man you'll marry, surely you'd like me to know him? Surely you'd like me to see what he writes to you?'

Cissie shook her head, removing her shawl and wrapping the scrap-book in it, guarding it from the rain and – Bonnie couldn't help feeling – her, too.

A low rumble, and the skies split open. Cissie shrieked, ducking for shelter under an oak tree, the canopy shielding her. Within minutes the downpour was torrential, and it infected Bonnie with a restlessness, with the elation of things knocked off-kilter. She clasped Cissie's hand and ran towards the lawn.

She half expected the girl to resist, but Cissie propped her scrap-book carefully against the tree, still tightly wrapped in its shawl, and allowed herself to be led. Bonnie grinned at her, emboldened.

'Isn't this wonderful?' Bonnie cried, arms held up, rain sluicing down her cheeks.

At first, Cissie moved stiffly, eyes flitting from side to side, but then she tipped back her head, her lips cracking into a smile. They spun in circles, hands clasped, mouths hinged wide, Cissie's laugh breaking from deep within her. Their dresses gummed them, their bonnets sagging, and at last when the rain petered out, it was Bonnie who broke away first, Cissie who still spun and spun, arms out.

'You'll give yourself a chill,' Bonnie said, slipping her arm around Cissie's shoulders. Her skin was goosefleshed. 'And you're *cold*.'

Cissie pushed her away. 'I want to stay here always. I want to keep dancing.'

But when Bonnie set off towards the house, Cissie retrieved her scrap-book and followed, skipping a little. All the way through the woodland, flowers drooped with rain, but Bonnie still snapped a rose from its stem and held it out. A spider was nesting inside. 'Sent from Lord Duggan,' she said solemnly, and Cissie accepted the bloom, inhaling its scent deeply, her wet hair falling in tendrils about her cheeks.

'What a generous soul he is,' Cissie said, with such serious-ness that Bonnie wondered if she knew it was all make-believe and there was no Lord Duggan at all.

They burst back into the house, dripping a trail of water up the stairs. Before Cissie saw Mr Moncrieff for tea, Bonnie dressed her in a dry frock. Cissie's arms and belly were rosy with cold. Then they both hurried towards Mr Moncrieff's study door.

'Papa, did you see the rain?' Cissie exclaimed. 'We were caught in it, and I didn't care a jot.' The door slammed shut behind her. Bonnie paused in the hallway, her own dress still sodden. She caught the low rumble of Mr Moncrieff's voice, quick hiccups of laughter. Minutes ticked past and still Bonnie didn't move. She was a maid; her place was downstairs in the kitchen and scullery. And yet, she felt the same as she did when she used to pass the tall brick houses in Mayfair: that she might breeze up to one of the shiny doors and find it swinging open, just for her.

That was all she saw of Mr Moncrieff most days: a small fragment of him as the door closed behind Cissie. And so it was as a surprise to Bonnie that he came across her three days later when Cissie was at her lessons. Bonnie was returning from Twickenham village, her basket full of new lace for Cissie's pink bonnet, even though the trim was only a season old and barely worn. The towpath was quiet, just a few artists sketching on the banks. Hooves sounded behind her; a voice called her name. She turned, her heart skipping, but of course it was not Crawford. It was only Mr Moncrieff, dismounting, leading his horse alongside her. His cheeks were pink, his hair blown over his eyes.

'Well,' he said. And then, 'Have you been far?'

She nodded at the basket. 'Cissie wanted a new ribbon for her bonnet.' She added in case he thought her profligate, 'I asked Manton.'

'Ah.' He wound the rein around his wrist. His pace was quick and she had to lengthen her strides to keep up. 'You should know that if – if she asks for any trinkets like that then I am happy to oblige. And what is a ribbon?'

'Indeed, sir,' Bonnie replied. It had cost the same as a week of her wages. 'If you want to ride, please don't feel the need to walk with me.'

He dismissed her. 'No,' he said. 'It's nice to – to walk. To have company.'

'Oh. Yes. Of course.'

They kept walking. They passed another artist, Mr Moncrieff glancing at his easel. A set of woodcuts were laid out on the ground. Marble Hill with its fine Palladian symmetry. York House with its shuttered windows in the French style. He paused, his horse nudging a dandelion on the path.

'There it is. My house. My house, for now, I should say.'

He pointed at the picture, each spiked turret and battlement carefully copied. Bonnie leaned closer, her breath catching. She was sure she had seen this woodcut before.

'But that is Endellion,' she blurted out.

'Of course it is,' Mr Moncrieff said with a short laugh. 'What other house might it be? There's no other place like it, I'd wager.'

It was the same picture that Crawford had pinned to the walls of their garret. She was certain of it. How hadn't she noticed the resemblance before? And if Crawford knew Endellion, why hadn't he mentioned it? Her stomach turned; the horse moved on, Mr Moncrieff waiting for her. She began to walk quickly, her dress hissing against her legs, the harrumph of Mr Moncrieff's mare behind them. Occasionally, Mr Moncrieff would speak, pointing out the architectural features of the houses they walked past: cusp-pointed windows, an onion-domed pavilion in the Indian style. But Bonnie only half listened, her mind lingering on the woodcuts. It was probably nothing, she thought; pictures like it were sold over most of London. And could she be sure it was the same house? But Mr Moncrieff had said it himself: there was no place like it.

As they walked closer to Eel Pie Island, the grand villas gave way to a crowded riverbank, the air thickening with smoke, with the cries and shouts of glue-boilers and tanners, glassmakers and brewers. Dilapidated barges were strung along the river, one crammed with grubby grey chickens, a child picking the fleabites on his leg. Mr Moncrieff steered her inland, down a cobbled lane, past a church.

'Kentish ragstone,' he said. And then, quieter, 'Though I do not often walk this way.'

The church had a small graveyard apportioned to it. Bonnie peered over the wall. The grass was neatly clipped, the graves modest and well-tended, a little like the churchyard Bonnie's mother was buried in. An elm tree was so hunched it looked wounded.

'It is pretty enough, sir. There are worse places to be laid to rest.'

Mr Moncrieff's mouth pressed downwards. He seemed lit by something close to anger when he turned to Bonnie. 'But it isn't what she would have wanted. She'd have wanted to be *commemorated*. She wanted fine things. Why doesn't anybody understand?'

'I didn't mean—' Bonnie broke off. 'I didn't know Mrs Moncrieff. Please, forgive me.'

He buried his chin in his collar, quickening his pace, his horse clipping alongside him, as though he wanted to put as much space between himself and the churchyard as possible. His arms sliced the air. Soon they had re-joined the towpath.

Bonnie fell back. It was hopeless: she could not get the cut of him at all. She said again, 'I can take another path, sir, if you'd like to walk alone—'

'No,' he said. 'No. Please. I have – I expressed myself badly. It isn't easy to think about her in that way.'

Were they just to walk like this, hurrying down the river in silence? But he seemed to be on the brink of speaking, as though there was something he wanted to say: twice, he glanced up at her, opened his mouth, closed it again.

At last, he spoke, so quietly that Bonnie had to press closer to hear him. 'Of course you did not know her. You must think me – well, mad.'

'No, sir—'

He turned to look at her, his expression so plaintive that Bonnie almost flinched. 'Perhaps nobody understands why I care so much. She's gone, isn't she? There's no undoing it. Why does it matter where she's buried? And our marriage was hardly – well.'

This time, Bonnie did not try to offer a false condolence, to smooth over matters like a maid might be expected to do. She simply waited.

'But she had – extremes. I see them in Cissie too sometimes. The way she will swerve from joy to despair. The way she thinks the answer is in *things*. It alarms me.'

Bonnie spoke cautiously. 'Cissie seems quite – quite lovely to me. And just because one woman followed one path, does not mean another will do the same.'

'Oh, she *is* lovely, isn't she?' Mr Moncrieff replied, smiling despite himself. 'And so was her mother. Tremendously exciting, in her way. It was difficult not to be pulled along by her.'

What was Bonnie meant to say to such a quick easy confidence, and to her – a mere maid? Perhaps there were many people who spoke as freely as this, but she could think only of Crawford, the way he held himself back, and how she had simply grown used to it: *I was dropped here, last night, by a bird, and what a blessing that is.* He had woodcuts of Endellion on his wall and she did not know why. How little she knew about him, really; and how ill-equipped it made her with Mr Moncrieff's bursts of honesty.

'People think she ruined me. But the truth is, I ruined myself. These great houses—' He waved his hand as they passed Orleans.

'The owners like to think that they sprang out of nowhere, that they're sealed places of retirement and retreat. But they never are. They're built out of plantations or tin mines or the toil and misery of others. Endellion was a gift to my great-grandmother but rent from tenanted farmers kept the house thriving, their labour given for free. I was supposed to evict the older labourers and bring in fresh young bucks. I was supposed to raise rents. But I didn't. I gave them the cottages. It was a fool's mistake, and yet I cannot bring myself to regret it.'

They were approaching Endellion, the house so white and misshapen. Mr Moncrieff spoke on, his voice high with agitation. It seemed to Bonnie as though he was circling something: that all of this had, in fact, been nearing a point that still evaded him.

'I thank God my father was not alive to see it. He could be a miserly old curmudgeon when he wanted to be, but he was practical. Endellion flourished under him. It might be a Gothic mousetrap of a house, but my whole life is baked into its bricks. And now, it's a husk, and it breaks my heart that I will see it gone.'

Instead of cutting across the wide lawn that ran to the river, he steered Bonnie the long way to the house, down the snaking paths to the greenhouse. Trees entwined over their heads until they were almost entirely shadowed: almonds and hornbeams, a myrtle. He stopped suddenly, his horse colliding with him. 'But you say, I might recover the house yet. I might amend the mistakes I made.'

Bonnie tilted her head. 'I don't understand.'

'I've been hoping I might speak to you about it. What you said in my study. It lingered with me. I've found myself unable to forget it.'

'You mean, sir – the cemetery?'

He nodded. 'I want to understand more.'

She knew only what she had read in the articles that Crawford had discarded on the floor of the inn, or picked up in snippets from his conversation. 'I know – I know, sir, that ground is worth more to house the dead than the living. Fifty times more, even.'

Mr Moncrieff grimaced.

Bonnie saw that this was not the way to convince him: even if his financials were a consideration, he was not like Crawford, stirred by profit. She recalled the wide carriageways on the sketch of Highgate, the small circles of trees, the words underneath. *Haven, instructive,* all the things that had drawn her in. 'It could be a soothing, enriching place. It could be a place of beauty.' The Green Ground came back to her, the man's arm with its inked mermaid. 'Have you seen the burial grounds of London? I can hardly describe them. They are so full that some days, it feels like the dead are burying the living. There's nowhere left for bodies. Think what a thing it must be to die and know you would be picked apart; to have a loved one perish and know they weren't safe. It could be different here.'

'But to trade in the dead – to profit from it. It is so *murky*. To be a profiteer of corpses. To bring that here, to Endellion—'

'Sir,' she said, a sudden warmth in her voice. 'It would be your chance to build something of your own. To leave your mark. Those – those mausoleums on your desk,' she spoke more carefully, his earlier flare of temper still fresh, but he was watching her earnestly. 'It would be a monument to – to your wife. But more than that, it would be a monument to anyone who came to rest there.'

'I don't know,' Mr Moncrieff said, chewing his bottom lip. His lips were surprisingly girlish, carved in two fat sweeps. 'Leave my mark,' he echoed. 'Have you ever wanted anything so strongly that you can't think of anything else?'

'What do you mean?' Bonnie asked, frowning.

'You must have something that you want.'

Nobody had ever asked her such a thing. She laughed, expecting him to forget the question, but he kept looking at her. 'Well,' he said. 'What is it?'

Bonnie thought of all the things she had wanted as a child: to be one of the Highwell girls standing at the front of the chapel, her hair neatly groomed, every head turned towards her. She thought of her days spent with her father in the gardens, the small pleasure of watching things grow, knowing it was her hand that had coaxed up hellebores and irises. And then she thought of that tattooed arm rising from the soil.

She glanced at Mr Moncrieff, and it was only then that she realized how much she wanted to see the cemetery built, to have it made like the etchings of Highgate. And more than that, she wanted to stay in this house. 'Perhaps not as strongly as – as that. But I want to see this cemetery. I want to help plant its garden. I want it to be a beautiful place, filled with flowers and life.' He watched her, his head on one side, chest rising and falling.

'I see,' he said slowly. 'I wish I could. I wish I could build it. But – I just don't know.'

A cloud passed over the sun, masking his expression. There was something awkward about the way he clutched his arms and she felt sure she had pressed too hard and upset him.

'Sir,' she began, about to try and make amends, when she stopped. She caught the scent of pipe smoke in the air. Faint, peppery. She inhaled sharply. She would have known that smell anywhere. Crawford's tobacco. She glanced behind her. Something flickered on the path where the rhododendrons were thickest. Her heart began to hammer, a biliousness in her stomach. She thought of the way he would hold her, desire rooting hard and fast within her. He had come back to her; he had missed her. He would tell her what was happening with the red-headed man. Soon she would *know*.

Mr Moncrieff took a step towards her and for an awful second, Bonnie thought he was about to kiss her, his hand reaching forwards as though to cup her chin. Of course he did not. It was just a leaf that he pulled from her hair, that he crumpled in his hand and let fall to the ground. Her chest swelled, almost painful. She wondered if Crawford had seen and her elation turned to something metallic, bloody; something closer to panic.

Arsenic

Bonnie watched Mr Moncrieff leave, his stride long and sloping, his head a little bowed. He vanished around the side of the house, in the direction of the stables. Only then did Bonnie move closer to the greenhouse, its frame shielding her from view. She would wait for Crawford to find her. She touched her throat, felt the flutter of her pulse. The scent of pipe smoke reached her, stronger now. Soon she would bend his head towards her mouth, feel the press of his arm around her waist.

'Crawford?' she whispered, moving towards the bushes where she had last seen movement. It was a sick feeling, that anticipation, a disquiet that was almost unpleasant. And then she stifled a shriek; she was seized from the side, arms bundled round her.

'Crawford!' she cried. 'Crawford.'

He kissed her neck in short playful pecks. There was no trace of jealousy in him. 'I missed you.'

She grinned. 'Did you?'

He drew back, and his beauty was so striking that it made her feel unworthy, almost appalled. 'He'll be a while in the stables. Won't you invite me in?'

At first, she didn't think he was serious, but before she could stop him, he had set off through the woodland, taking the path to the house, cutting across the lawn.

'Wait,' she said. 'If they find you—'

'Why ever not?' he said, without looking back. 'The butler's in town. I watched him leave. And that maid is collecting the girl from school.'

'But what if any of them come back—' she began, but he was already several strides ahead of her, reaching the kitchen door before she did. Against the small windows at the rear of the house, he looked like a giant, peeping into a Lilliputian mansion. He turned the handle and ducked inside.

'Well,' he said, picking up a bowl of mashed salmon from the kitchen table and dipping in a finger. 'Well, I see you want for little here.'

His eyes flicked over the cabinets, the stove, the chairs, as though marking them as his, and Bonnie thought how odd it was seeing him in this house where she'd begun a new life. He moved towards the stairs.

'Crawford,' she whispered, following him, pulling on his arm. 'We shouldn't. You can't. If I'm caught—'

'What are you afraid of?' he asked, shrugging her off. 'We're never caught, are we?' He grinned at her, and then turned and climbed the stairs, confidently.

What would Manton say if he returned? How would she explain it to Mr Moncrieff? Excuses raced through her head, each as flimsy as the one before. Crawford was already in the entrance hall, his footsteps chiming on the chequerboard tiles, making no secret of himself. He touched everything he saw, as Bonnie had once done in her room: the grandfather clock, the polished side table, the harpsichord, wonder written on his face, a twisted edge to his mouth. He pressed an ivory key and the note sang out.

'Yes,' he said at last, not whispering, not making himself small or quiet. 'This is something. To live here.'

'Let's go outside,' Bonnie urged him, sidling up to him, hoping that she might win him over, nuzzling his cheek. 'I've missed you. I—'

But he pulled away as though he had not even noticed her, craning his neck to look all around him, taking the grand stairs two at a time. She had no choice but to trail him, the cameo portraits eyeing her, the red stained-glass lantern casting a warning across the floor. Each footstep seemed to rattle through the house. Never had the walls seemed flimsier, the doors so brittle. Crawford passed Mr Moncrieff's study, taking the hallway to the landing with the three bedroom doors leading off it – Mr Moncrieff's, Cissie's, Josephine's – and it was Josephine's room he moved towards, her door that he opened. Bonnie slipped in behind him, shutting it quietly, panic spreading up her arms, pounding in her ears.

'What are you doing?' she hissed. 'Please. We can't—'

'Look at you,' he said, reaching for her. 'Such a frightened mouse! What's to say we can't be here? I thought you'd missed me.'

'But—'

He dipped his lips to the hollow of her throat and she pushed him away, her fear its own pulse.

'What if someone finds us?'

'They won't,' he murmured. 'And we'll hear them, won't we?'

'Then they'll hear us first.'

'Look at you, with your neat little cap.' He said it in an admiring way, as though it excited him. 'How different you look.'

'Crawford,' she said, her mouth dry, the question sawing at her. 'Crawford, are they looking for me?'

He paused. 'No. You're safe here. Nobody's even come to the inn.' But his left eyelid flickered.

'Are you sure? You'd tell me if they were, wouldn't you? You would?'

'Listen, Bonnie,' Crawford said, almost exasperated. 'He died, we dealt with him. It's gone, forgotten. You aren't going to hang for this.'

It felt like a knot unravelling in her chest. Nobody was hunting her down. She watched Crawford as he pulled the sheet off the wardrobe, running his palms up and down the polished mahogany. 'This is fine,' he said. 'Isn't it?'

'You know this house, don't you?'

'What?' He spun around.

'Your woodcuts on the wall. They were of this house.'

He scoffed. 'This house is famous, Bonnie. It's a famous Gothic bauble of a place. I bought those woodcuts from a man on the Strand. But I never thought I'd enter it, walk through its rooms.' He touched the edge of the bed, the dressing table. 'You can imagine my surprise when I realized it was the same place as the advertisement.' He turned to her. 'Do you ever come in here?'

'Sometimes,' she admitted.

'Show me what you do.'

The relief about the red-headed man had made her bold. She took a seat at the dressing table, opened the drawers. The brooches glinted back at her and she weighed one in her hand, then cautiously, carefully, she pinned it to her apron.

'My!' Crawford exclaimed. 'One day, in your palazzo, you'll have a room filled with charms like this. I'll make sure of it.'

She raised her chin, stared herself down. He ran his hands down her sides, gently cupped one breast, finding the nipple, rubbing it between his fingers. Her desire sparked, hot as flint.

'Take something,' he whispered.

She drew back. 'What?'

'You could have anything here. Choose it.'

'I can't.'

'They're worthless scraps. Don't you think he'd have sold them if they were worth something?'

There was truth in that; hadn't Mr Moncrieff already sold the cardinal's hat and the lock of hair? But this room had the feeling of being sealed off, untouched. There were no gaps against the walls, no spaces where paintings had once hung.

Crawford pinged a green gemstone with his finger. 'Paste,' he said.

Bonnie felt queasy, undone. She was a good, loyal servant; and yet – there was that delicious tug, that intoxication. Nobody would know. When Crawford slid the tortoiseshell brooch from her apron and she felt it land heavily in her pocket, she did not take it out again.

'You could bring these things to me,' he whispered. 'They won't be worth much to a gentleman like *him*, but to us—'

'Maybe,' she said.

'Maybe? How you like to toy with me.'

But she knew, as he did, that she would do as he asked, that she had already felt that tug towards him, like being dragged underwater.

He stood up suddenly and her desire cooled, nowhere to go. He pulled the dust sheet from the bed, then crouched down and peered underneath it. 'Is this her? His wife?'

Bonnie gasped: for a moment she thought he'd found a dead body under the bed – Josephine, slowly decaying, her skin purpling, flies nesting in her flesh. But of course it was just the painting that had once hung in Mr Moncrieff's study, hexagonal and neatly framed. Crawford dragged it into the light.

Josephine's hair was dark and spun in ornate ringlets, her cheeks tinged with the lightest dusting of rouge. But for all that, she did not look vain; there was something about the tilt of her chin that made her look clever, commanding. The word,

Bonnie thought, was *imperious*: the exact look that Bonnie had expected of Cissie before she met her. Bonnie peered closer, studying the painting: the brightness of her cheekbone, a fresh-water pearl clipped to her ear. Mr Moncrieff's lips would have moved across her cheek, found her mouth. He would have taken her in this room, on this bed, his breath sharp and quick—

'Do you suppose he did it?' Crawford asked.

'Did what?'

'Killed her.'

Bonnie almost laughed. It seemed outlandish, implausible.

'I've heard he's a brute. That he has a ferocious temper.'

'Who told you that?'

Crawford shrugged. 'It's what people say in the inns around here. You can learn a lot.'

It was true that there was something unfathomable about Mr Moncrieff, something about him that had unnerved Bonnie. His obsessions consumed him, his endless drawing of that mausoleum. Could that mania tip towards control, towards violence? 'He's strange,' she said slowly. 'Annette – the housemaid – she said his wife had a lover.'

'Really,' Crawford widened his eyes. 'Tell me.'

'She told me that they used to leave letters for each other in the greenhouse. I found a scrap of one.'

'What did it say?'

'Very little.'

He leaned forwards. 'What if he'd found those letters? He'd have been furious, surely?'

Bonnie met his eye. 'Annette said they had an argument on the night she died. Mrs Moncrieff was going to run away.'

'Really? He'd have been humiliated, wouldn't he? And for a man with a temper—'

'It's too awful,' Bonnie said, shaking her head. 'I can't believe it.' Mr Moncrieff, a murderer. But then, hadn't she done the same? It only took an instant, when time hung by a thread, for a body to fall and break. What frightened her most was the understanding that anyone might do it. Anyone, given the right circumstances, the right amount of fear, might empty the world of another person. Remorse could eat at him like it ate at her: it could make him cling tight to a memory of her, to keep their house draped in mourning more than a year after her death, to try and make amends in whatever way he could.

'They say he's handsome.'

'Mr Moncrieff?' She shook her head. 'He's as lanky as a spider.'

Crawford smiled, and she knew she had said the right thing. 'And the girl?'

'Cissie,' Bonnie said. She felt the curdling of betrayal, but she knew the way to please Crawford. 'She – she has an imaginary lover called Lord Duggan. He writes her these strange letters.'

Crawford flinched. 'Like what? Who is he?'

'Oh, he isn't real. The letters are foolish. Just some girl's whimsy. She writes them herself, pretending to be this – made up Lord.'

'Have you read them?'

'She won't show me. I've tried. And the more she hides them, the more I'm desperate to see them. I don't know why, when they'll just be a piece of nonsense.'

'How strange.' He laughed suddenly, and Bonnie was struck again by how much she'd missed him, how golden it was to be in his presence. He walked away from the painting, back to the dressing table with its drawers of jewellery. 'I could find a position here. I could be in this house with you.'

'There aren't any positions.' Bonnie said it too quickly and she saw the surprise on his face, so she added, 'Mr Moncrieff's almost bankrupt. He can't afford anyone else.' She pulled back her shoulders. 'I told him to build a cemetery on some of the land he has here. I told him that was the way to save himself from ruin.'

'Why?' She was surprised to find not pleasure in his voice, but anger. 'Why are you trying to save him? If he's ruined, let him be a fool. People should receive what they deserve.'

'But I need to stay here, Crawford. If the house is sold, then where will I hide? And then perhaps, if he has more money, you could join me here and—'

'What sort of cemetery?'

'Like Highgate and Kensal Green.'

'What do you know of that?' His words were sharp, possessive.

'I – I read an article,' she said. 'One you discarded.'

'I see,' Crawford said, his eyes darting around the room, not settling. 'I see.'

He brightened suddenly, and Bonnie exhaled: she hadn't upset him after all.

'My love,' he said. 'Come here.'

And when he slipped his hands around her waist again, she let him; she let him push her backwards onto the bed, and she reached for him with a hunger. Crawford was here at last. As she felt his hands on her hips, her thighs, she was struck by a new appreciation of what a fragile thing it was to be alive: how easily disrupted the line was between living and dead, between here and not here. His head, bowed against hers; the heat of his fingers as they moved across her waist, the life that raced through him. She wanted to cling to him, to remember this always. She wanted to feel the bruise of him inside her. They were in Josephine's bed. And Bonnie was her, Mrs Moncrieff, as his hands ruched up her dress and pulled roughly at her drawers, and he pressed her onto her belly. She heard the clinking of his belt, his breath hot and fast, and—

A creaking on the stairs – she kicked Crawford off her, pushing him onto the floor behind the bed. In an instant, she had leapt up and smoothed her dress, just as the door opened. There was Mr Moncrieff, staring at her. The room was rumpled, the bedclothes tousled, covers missing from most of the furniture. Her crime must have been written all over her: her flushed cheeks, her hair straggling loose, her cap gone. And what had he heard?

'I was tidying—' she began. 'There were moths—'

'What is this?' Mr Moncrieff demanded, a small vein twitching at the corner of his eye. Heat rose from him, and it struck Bonnie how tall he was, how easily he could overpower her. 'Who said you could come in here?' His voice grew louder, a twist to his mouth like he had been punched. He took in the painting on the floor. 'Her portrait! Who said you could take it out? Who did?'

For the first time, Bonnie could picture it fully: his hands holding Josephine under, the beat of his fury as he watched her drown.

'Why?' he asked again, but suddenly his voice cracked, a redness gathering in his eyes.

'I—' Bonnie began. She glanced round the room. The edge of Crawford's boot was peeping out from the end of the bed. She stepped towards the door, towards Mr Moncrieff, trying to block it from view. If Crawford was discovered here, she would be cast out. She would have nowhere to go. A heaviness gathered in her chest, a sawing in her throat. She could not look at Mr Moncrieff. 'I'm – I'm sorry,' she said. 'I knew I shouldn't be in here, but I – I thought I would air it. It smelled stale and there were moths, and—'

She shifted her weight to the other foot. She could see a little more of Crawford's leg now. Had he moved? She began to wonder if he was doing it on purpose, if he was enjoying the thrill of it.

Mr Moncrieff rubbed his cheek. 'It was just a fright, that's all. To hear someone in here after all this time. Just – just put the painting away, please. And the sheets back. And leave this room alone.'

It was only when the door clicked shut that Bonnie allowed herself to breathe, hand held to her heart to calm the panic that still lingered.

'What a fool,' Crawford said, clambering to his feet. 'How didn't he see me?'

Bonnie's palm was still on her chest. 'Don't,' she said. 'Please don't. If he'd found you—'

'They aren't special, you know. The Moncrieffs. They're no better than you or me.'

'I know. It's just – you can't stay here. You have to go.'

'Fine,' Crawford snapped.

Misery bit at her, that it should end so sourly. 'You must understand.'

He paused, weighing up what to say next. And then he kissed her cheek. 'We weren't caught. There's no need to fret. Now, I'll be on my way.'

They walked silently down the hallway, Bonnie first, Crawford following when she beckoned him on. They took the wooden staircase to the kitchen, the room as quiet as they had left it. Manton and Annette had not returned. When she shut the door behind Crawford, Bonnie leaned against it, panting. She wanted the day scrubbed clean and to resume her duties as normal.

All afternoon, the brooch weighed in her pocket. She told

herself she would return it to Josephine's room when everyone was asleep. But when night fell, she lay in bed and felt a little shard of her old self like a splinter under the skin. She slid the brooch under the mattress.

Last Night I Dreamed Of You

It was like it had always been: the more Bonnie did something she knew to be wrong, the more it dulled the dishonesty. It felt almost like the first stirrings of desire, or drinking too much and finding the whole world so shimmering and entertaining. Knowing that the feeling would pass only made it headier.

Every few days, she hurried out to meet Crawford beside the greenhouse, a new piece of jewellery in her pocket. Even though she knew they were all paste, she always chose the trinkets that looked cheapest: coral or conch or tortoiseshell. And Crawford had been right: Mrs Moncrieff was dead. What use could a dead woman have for treasures such as these, and surely if Cissie wanted them she would already have claimed them?

Nobody noticed. Not even Cissie, who had begun to sleep better at night. Nobody saw her, tiptoeing down the cold spiral stair when the house breathed in and out with gentle snoring, Josephine's bedroom door closing behind her, Zephyr nosing her for affection. As the night deepened, she would sit at Josephine's mirror and press a necklace against the dip between her collarbones, a bracelet across her wrist. The thrill was as hot as wine. Each day she would wonder what she would slip into her pocket next.

There were some days when it felt petty and childish, when she wondered why Crawford would bother with something so small, or why she would risk so much. But then, when the next morning broke and she saw Crawford in that patch of rhododendrons, he would hold the little piece to the light and grip it in his fist like a trophy. *Mine*, his face would say, and he would kiss her on the forehead, and she would bury herself in that peppermint scent of him, his velvet jacket soft against her cheek.

If she had finished her chores for the morning, they would walk briefly down to the river, or he would press her against one of the trees and kiss her; if she hadn't, she would hurry back to the house, dew dampening her shoes. She always worked harder on those days, scrubbing the floors until her palms cracked and bled, until even Manton tried to coax her down to the servants' room for a piece of ham or cheese.

But every time that she crossed that green lawn, as the trees unleaved and September passed into October, she would feel a little less wrong, a little less wicked, until she had almost convinced herself that these trinkets belonged to her as much as anyone else.

One night, instead of opening Mrs Moncrieff's door, Bonnie moved towards Cissie's bedroom. The decision was instinctive. The light on the landing was low and shivering. If she pressed an ear to the door, she could hear the whisper of Cissie's breath. How thin the wood seemed, as if only a curtain separated each inhabitant from the other. The house had felt so strong when she first arrived, but each day she discovered another piece of theatrics or small frailty: a carved screen loosening at its edges, a ceiling rose bubbling and flaking, a fake door painted into the woodwork. It had always been this way, she told herself: the house could not have sensed her little thefts, was not crumbling under the shame of her betrayals.

The hinges creaked; Bonnie made a note to oil them in the morning.

Cissie's hair was spread against her pillow, her lips parted. It was a sight so unguarded that it hit Bonnie with a feeling close to love. Bonnie watched her for a short time, then slipped her hand under the pillow, prising the scrap-book out from under Cissie's head.

Cissie's curtains were drawn back, the moon full and bright. Bonnie cracked open the book, angling the pages towards the faint light. They whispered as she turned them. Bonnie swallowed. Why was she doing this? To understand the girl or because she hated being shut out from a secret?

Bonnie opened the scrap-book near the end. There was Cissie's neat hand.

My dear mousekin,

Last night I dreamed of you. You fill each of my dreams. Your long ringleted hair, your eyes that twinkle like distant stars on the black horizon! One day, when we are wed at last, I will watch over you and keep you safe – I will be your protector, your one true Lord Duggan!

Disappointment swamped Bonnie. There was nothing exciting or intriguing here. It was all sickly convention, all ringing clichés. Was this really what Cissie wanted? To be patronized, protected? All of the romances Cissie read were like this. Bonnie had once picked a book off her shelves and yawned her way through the opening pages. A sea of pale heroines who convalesced for weeks, fainting on the sight of a hero, their hearts hammering at the touch of a finger grazing their arms.

She leafed through the scrap-book, the paper crackling with pasted flowers and cherubs and arrows. Hackneyed phrases filled each page.

My own to cherish and fuss over, to gaze at each evening in wonder and love –

Oh, your sweet pale hand, delicate as a swan's feather –

In my dreams, I saw a butterfly rest its gentle wings on your blushing cheek –

Bonnie shuffled back to the beginning, about to give up. She wanted only to see how it began. But here, the handwriting was different, the paper thicker. The first letter was pasted in carefully.

My dear heart,

You know nothing of me and my torments, but I can be silent no longer. I glimpsed you at the Marble Hill ball. I was transfixed by your elegance and the astonishment of your beauty. I thought then that if you were to reach for me I would die. I tell you only this: I need you. I want you. I know, somehow, that you will reply. That, bewildered though you will be, desire stirs in you too. You cannot be satisfied with what you have. I know it. Your heart aches for more. If you leave your letter here, I will find it.

I cannot tell you my real name for fear of exposure. Like you, I am married, and like you, it was never for love. A love that, only now, do I feel the pain of its absence, what I might have cherished. Take pity, I beg, on a poor, wretched soul.

I will sign this, merely, a concocted name,

Lord Duggan

The book shook in her hands. *Like you, I am married, and like you, it was never for love.*

She turned the pages, reading each letter desperately, hungrily. She had to be certain she was not mistaken. *My heart* soon became *My own sweet Josephine* which became *Mousekin* which became *my dearest, most darling Mousekin.* Rendezvous were arranged, assignations alluded to, escapes proposed (*There is an hotel in Paris where we will be happy, and our whole worlds will be each other. What scraps are left for you at that ghastly mansion? You need only breathe your agreement and I will have it all arranged – the coach, the steamer, the hotel!*). The letters might have been cloying, but they were grounded in events, in meetings, in *reality*. Sometimes, the saccharine gave way, spiked with the realness of love: with jealousy, with small needling recriminations, with hurt and pain.

She turned the page and saw a letter with a piece torn out of it.

I must tell you how fervently –

It broke off. Bonnie's lips moved over the sentence as it would have continued. *I want you, crave –*

And then, it began again: *your mouth against mine.*

How had Cissie found these letters? And what had compelled her to imitate and continue a story her mother had started, to put herself at the centre of it? A coal shifted in the grate and Bonnie shivered. And if Cissie had found them, perhaps Mr Moncrieff had too. How much more wounding it would be to read these mounting betrayals than hear about an abstract lover. He would be licked into a fervour, a passion, a fury: had he lost control then?

'What are you doing?'

Bonnie jumped, her hand on her throat.

'Cissie,' she said, slamming shut the book. 'I thought you were asleep. I thought—'

Cissie was staring straight ahead, her eyes black in the moon-light. 'You read my book,' she said, her voice a single, dull note.

'I – I did. Yes. I'm sorry.'

'Did you see the letters he wrote to me?'

'Yes.'

The girl didn't seem angry, just confused from being woken. Bonnie sat on the bed beside her and lit a candle. 'You found those letters, didn't you? The ones at the beginning. They were written to your mother.'

Cissie's gaze flitted from the book to the window. She fidgeted with her fingernails. 'Is it – is it very strange of me? That now he writes to me too?'

Bonnie reached for her hand, wondering if she was pressing Cissie too far, forcing an intimacy that was still new and brittle. 'It must have been a terrible fright, discovering her. I would not think anything strange if it helped you adjust to that.'

Cissie's eyes were unblinking, glassy. 'When she died it was like – it was like I could become her. I thought she wouldn't be dead if he kept writing to her. To me, maybe.'

'Oh, Cissie,' Bonnie said. 'What a thing for you to shoulder.'

As Cissie settled against her and her eyes began to close, a feeling of peace passed over Bonnie. Cissie's breathing steadied. Bonnie blew out the candle. The final thing she saw before the room was cast into blackness were the words, *Last night I dreamed of you*, and she blinked, unsettled, feeling her way across the room, back into the hallway, and upstairs to where her bed waited for her.

Mary's Son

Mr Moncrieff wanted to see Bonnie in his study at three o'clock that afternoon. Manton told her over bread and jam in the morning.

'Why?' Bonnie asked, her hand slipping as she poured water into Cissie's beef tea. 'Did he say why?' There was no jewellery in her pocket but still her apron felt heavy.

'I'm afraid not,' Manton replied as he blackened Mr Moncrieff's riding boots.

'Did he seem – cross? Did he say if anything was amiss?'

'Cross? I shouldn't say so.' He drew a cloth over the toe of the boot. 'And he's asked Annette to see to the moths in Mrs Moncrieff's room this evening, but the dust gives her an awful cough. I thought you might do it. He hates the smell of camphor so it must be done by hand.'

'Of course,' she said, but she was hardly paying attention. She stirred the tea, a thin skim of fat on the surface. Had Cissie told Mr Moncrieff that she'd entered her room the night before? Or worse, had he noticed the missing jewellery, seen her sneaking out of Josephine's room? *Deceit is unforgiveable in this household.*

All morning, her tasks never seemed to fall into place. She darned Cissie's jacket wrong, the stitches ugly. She spilled the pisspot over the rug, found herself scrubbing the fire irons with glass paste. Time sauntered, stretched, and it felt like hours until midday, when she knew Crawford would be waiting by the greenhouse for her. She was there before him, pacing up and down.

'There you are,' she said, and he held out his arms and tucked her into them.

'What's wrong?' He took a step back from her, and she remembered how he had turned to her one night in the garret and whispered, *You're like a girl made of glass, Bonnie. I can read everything about you, turn you in my fingers like a small crystal sphere.*

'Mr Moncrieff wants to see me.'

'Why?'

'I don't know.' She began walking, following the shaded grass path down to the river, skirting Annette's cottage. He hurried to keep up. 'I don't know. He might have found me out. He might have noticed the jewellery's missing. He might be casting me out. What will I do then, Crawford? If they're looking for me—'

'They aren't. Haven't I told you?'

'But what if—'

Crawford shrugged, lighting his pipe and tucking it into his teeth. 'It will be nothing.'

'How do you know? What if it isn't?'

'You'll see,' he said. 'He doesn't know. You could steal the nose off his face and he'd be none the wiser.'

It calmed her a little, to see how unruffled Crawford was.

'Look at him,' Crawford said, pulling Bonnie into the woodlands, to where the grounds of Endellion ended and the public thoroughfare began. Through the trees, Bonnie saw Mr Moncrieff on his horse. His gun was slung over his shoulder, a brace of pheasants dangling from one hand. 'He thinks he's so important. Lording it above everyone. The gentleman with his big gun.'

'I don't think that's how he is—' She stopped, but it was too late.

'Oh?' Crawford asked, putting his mouth close to her ear. 'Tell me then, how is he?'

'Stop it, Craw,' she said, nudging him away, but a racket had started up in her ribcage.

'You'd ride him, wouldn't you, given the chance? You'd ride him like he's riding his mare now.' He made an obscene braying sound, and he bounced on his heels. 'Tell me you wouldn't.'

'No,' she snapped. 'You know that's not true.'

He was watching her carefully, assessing her, his eyes flicking over her like a blade against the skin. Her heart thumped. He pulled her close, his mouth against her ear. 'You would.'

'Stop it,' she repeated, almost tearful, pushing him away. But he was smiling, and he reached for her all the same, rolling his hips against hers.

'You need me in the house to stop you from giving in. You need me there, or he'll have his wicked way with you. Perhaps that's why he wants to see you, all alone. The pair of you.' But Crawford was not looking at her at all. When she followed his eyes, they were fixed on Mr Moncrieff, watching him as his horse retreated, its hooves throwing up clods of earth, its breath billowing in the autumn air like smoke.

'Is't you?'

Bonnie startled. An old woman stood before them, a basket of coal slung over her back, her knees turned inwards with the weight of it. 'Mary's son? Lord, it is! I saw you a few days ago and it scared the wits out of me. I told myself, it's been twenty years since I saw you and I wasn't sure I'd know you, but here you are. I'm still there, on the barges. But I—'

Crawford took a step backwards, a flush in his cheeks, already steering Bonnie away. 'I think you must be mistaken—'

'Crawford, it's you! As I live and breathe.'

'You're mistaken,' he said again, more loudly, and he pushed Bonnie forwards, snatching her arm and linking it through his. He hurried her away, back towards the pond and greenhouse, twigs snapping underfoot. Bonnie had to half-run to keep up with him, his fingers digging into the inside of her elbow.

'Who was that?' she demanded. 'How did she know you?'

'It was nobody,' Crawford said through gritted teeth. 'She must have been mad, confusing me with another man.'

Bonnie wrenched her arm free, stopping suddenly. 'No, Crawford.' She was panting. He turned to face her and she glared back at him. 'She knew your name. You used to live near here, didn't you? You said you'd never seen the house before but it's not true. I knew it. Those woodcuts.'

Crawford shook his head slightly, a vein pulsing in his temple. Bonnie didn't think he was going to answer her. He would refuse her his past, again.

'Don't you *dare* lie to me, Crawford. Don't you dare shut me out again.'

'Stop it,' he said, his hands rising to his face, his mouth twisted. 'Why do you care so much?'

'You know everything about me.' Her voice cracked. 'And this is my life too. I'm here because of – of you. And I don't know why. You're supposed to love me.'

'Of course I love you!' He reached for her but she flinched away, holding up her hand to stop him. Then he said, suddenly, 'Fine. I grew up on the barges by Eel Pie Island.'

Bonnie stared at him. 'Where? How?' It did not make any sense. His fine education, his green velvet jacket. And then, that midden with its reek of smoke and tanneries and chickens, that she had passed with Mr Moncrieff. It did not seem like it could possibly contain Crawford. And not only that, but to have lived on the *barges*: their tarpaulin roofs, the sides cobbled together from scraps of metal and wood, the child who had picked his fleabites. 'You? *There?*'

'This is why I didn't tell you,' he said, all fight drained from him. 'Because I knew how you'd see me. How it would change everything. You'd think I was dirty and poor.'

He sat down heavily on the grass and hugged himself with his arms, making himself small.

Bonnie reached for his hand and began to stroke his thumb. 'But my family was poor too—'

'Not like mine,' he said. 'Not always hungry. Not living on scraps. You had food. A pig to eat each winter. We had nothing.' He rubbed his eyes. 'My mother died because we couldn't afford medicine. It clings to you. Being poor in that way. It sticks to you like tar. You can't ever forget it.'

'You could have told me. You could have trusted that it wouldn't have made any difference to me.'

He began shredding the grass in thick tufts. 'I wanted to make myself new. You of all people should understand that. I wanted to see myself like you saw me.'

'It wouldn't have changed anything.'

'But it would have!' he said, angrily. Tears began to break from the edge of his eyes, and he turned his face away from her. Endellion shone in the daylight behind them. Bonnie hovered her hand over his, hardly daring to interrupt him. All those times she had longed to understand more about him and here he was, opening himself up at last. 'And every day, when I was a boy, I passed this house, and the ache set up here.' He thumped his chest. 'I wanted to be part of it. I couldn't believe it when Rex read that advertisement. And there was the name. *Endellion.* It was like you were meant to come here. I knew that this was the place to keep you safe.'

'But your education—'

'I had to work so hard to stay hidden and undiscovered.'

'But how—'

'Just stop it,' he said, gouging his eyes with his fists. 'Please. I don't want to talk about it any more.' He half-smiled at her, tears in his eyes. 'One day, I'll buy my Bonnie her palazzo. I will, I swear it.' He pulled her close to him, tighter than he'd ever held her before, an embrace that was desperate, clinging. 'I love you, Bonnie. You know that, don't you? You know it, here.' He put his hand on his chest.

'Of course I do. But—'

'I *said* I don't want to talk any more.' She watched how easily his face slipped back into its old expression, the pain gone from his brow, the amused curl settling back on his mouth. He dusted the grass from his lap, said, 'You'd better go. They'll miss you.'

'I can't go, not when—'

'Not when, what?' he asked, as though she had imagined the conversation.

She wanted to pocket the way he had held her, the soft way he had spoken to her, but already it had the haziness of a daydream. When she was halfway across the lawn, she glanced back at him. He was staring at the house with narrowed eyes, kicking a rotten tree stump, grinding the wood down until it was nothing but pulp. It should have warmed her that he had confided in her. And yet, she was left with a strange feeling of dissatisfaction, that what he had told her had only just skimmed the surface.

The unease of a thing half-finished clung to her as she let herself into the house. Her day seemed incomplete, nothing fully accomplished. She helped Annette fold a sheet, then went to Cissie's bedroom to tidy her after her morning lessons with Little Marble Hill's governess. When Bonnie raised her hand to knock, she wondered if things would be askew here too: if Cissie would cringe away from her, or flare at her for reading her scrap-book. But the girl greeted her warmly, showed her a Latin translation she had completed, a small cushion she was beginning to embroider with a fleur-de-lis.

'It isn't any good,' Cissie said, but still she raised her eyes hopefully to Bonnie, waiting for her approval.

'But the way you've mastered these French knots,' Bonnie exclaimed. 'And I think that shade of green is exactly right for ivy.'

The girl sat back, gratified. 'I worked twice as fast as Emmeline. Look at my thumb.'

'But Cissie!' The tip was swollen and bloodied, peppered with pinpricks. 'Doesn't it hurt?'

'No. Not a bit.'

She must have been lying. But when Bonnie dabbed it with salted water, Cissie barely flinched, her gaze curious rather than pained.

'Papa says I'm to come with you to see him,' she said, flexing her thumb.

Bonnie had almost forgotten about Mr Moncrieff, and now she remembered, she felt even more acutely that she was losing her hold on things, that everything was tipping just out of reach. At least Cissie would be there too: surely Mr Moncrieff wouldn't accuse her in front of his own daughter.

'Is there time for you to curl my hair? Mama liked hers done that way.'

That unsettling echo: a girl trying to become her dead mother.

But Bonnie nodded and smiled. 'I'll make you look as fine as any London belle,' she said.

Bonnie heated the tongs in the coals and wrapped them in paper. Cissie sat upright, her hair sprayed with water. Soon Mr

Moncrieff would call for them. Soon he would explain what it was that he wanted to speak to Bonnie about. But her mind was filled with new frustrations: why, when Bonnie had unburdened herself so readily and so fully to Crawford, couldn't he trust her with his whole story? It made her feel naked, a little foolish. Cissie's damp hair smoked and hissed, the scent of scorched feathers filling the room.

The Burial Plot

'I asked Annette to arrange tea,' Mr Moncrieff said, fiddling with his teacup, papers scattering in the breeze from the window. He did not look angry, but there was something weighing on him: she saw it in the way his fingers agitated the calipers, as he glanced at the door and then back at his desk.

'It should be steeped by now,' he said, lifting the teapot, but Bonnie moved forward and took the handle from him, poured. It was better, she thought, to reinstate the natural order of things, not to be served tea by her master in his study.

'What is it, Papa?' Cissie asked.

'Sit, sit. I'll tell you. There, move the papers, yes – just so. Zephyr, back, no.' He pushed the dog away from his desk.

'But why have you called us?' Cissie asked, hopping from foot to foot. 'Are you taking us somewhere? To London?'

Bonnie took a step back, hoping Mr Moncrieff would forget about her.

He stood up clumsily, and to her surprise, he was looking straight at her. He beckoned her forwards, then reached for the handle of his teacup, lifted it, replaced it without drinking. 'Bonnie,' he said. 'It's easier, perhaps, if I show you.'

'Yes, sir?'

His eyes didn't move from hers. She thought of what Crawford had called him. *Handsome.* There was animation in him, certainly, warmth: the anxious turn of his smile, the creases around his eyes. He rustled through his papers, stabbing his finger on one page. 'There, see. I've been drawing it the best I can.'

Spread before her was what looked like a village, observed from above. It was so precise, so exact. At first Bonnie could not make sense of it: just lines and loops and small squares. She peered closer to read the careful labels. *Chapel. Vault. Catacombs.* She glanced up at Mr Moncrieff. Her eyes widened.

'It is—'

'Yes,' he said.

'What is it, Papa?' Cissie asked, but her father didn't answer her.

For all Bonnie had urged him, she realized she had never expected to be taken seriously. She took the sheet from him. A wide drive led from a gate set on Richmond Road to a turning circle in front of a chapel. There, with a lash-fine nib, Mr Moncrieff had drawn the building as though the lid had been taken off it: ante-room, altar, tiny side doors. She pictured mourners the size of ants filing into the pews, eight black horses waiting on the gravel outside, ostrich feathers trembling in the breeze. With her finger, she followed meandering paths as though a tiny procession of mourners was already walking them, passing broad colonnades and catacombs with their neat honeycomb rectangles, turning into a wide pathway labelled *Egyptian Avenue*. And then, they might take one of the narrowing lines to the plot allotted to them: what peace they might feel, assured that the person they had loved would be safe, undisturbed.

'These are mere ideas,' Mr Moncrieff said, scrunching up his face, but Bonnie found she did not want to speak, not yet. Her mind hummed over all she had said to this gentleman; how he had listened to her and drawn it so carefully. This little rectangle of a chapel might become a great stone edifice because of her; a thousand bodies might rest in this pasture because of her.

'I haven't included any trees or shrubbery,' Mr Moncrieff said, hastily. 'We will employ a horticulturalist, a man of botany, of course, and I have an old acquaintance in mind. But I thought perhaps, I know you said you have an interest in gardens, just like Cissie's mother did. And I'm sure you are far more experienced than me in such matters and might want to try—'

Bonnie's chest felt tight. She began to see the plan with a new layer: the cypresses studding the drives, the cherry trees that would weep blossom over the graves. The first hint of violets every spring, fringing the paths as mourners walked along them.

'What *is* it, Papa?' Cissie demanded again. 'Tell me!'

'I hope to make the most beautiful garden in the world.' He placed more drawings in front of Bonnie and Cissie, scrabbling through the pile. These were sketched elevations, the chapel as it would really be seen. Gargoyles and arched windows; and a vast avenue, flanked by obelisks. Wide steps descended to catacombs.

'A garden?' Cissie asked.

'Well, a cemetery,' Mr Moncrieff corrected. 'Look, Cissie. It would be where the pasture is, out there, walled off from our grounds. There are rival cemeteries like it, but this will be more unusual than any of them, just as this house is far from neat Palladian proportions.' His voice rose, his words tumbling into each other. 'It will be Gothic, not neoclassical, but there will be an Egyptian influence. There will be a section, too, for paupers' graves. Countless generations will stroll through here. It will be a school of instruction in architecture, in sculpture, in landscape-gardening, in arboriculture, botany.' He turned to Cissie, reached for her hand. 'And what would you say, sweet girl, if

– what would you say, if this was where your mother rested at last?'

He drew his thumb over a square on the plan, spanning at least twelve of the brick graves. Josephine's burial plot. He slid another drawing over it, an elevation just like one of the many hundred mausoleums Bonnie had seen on his desk before. It was an ornate but diminutive house, a little like a folly. Its arched roof was supported by pillars, the top crenelated just like Endellion. Cissie touched the little door as though pushing it open.

'This is for Mama?'

'It's the sort of memorial that befits her, don't you think? You can help me lay the final stone.' He pressed his daughter's hand. 'Would you like that?'

The girl nodded slowly, her new curls bobbing. 'She would want to be at Endellion, I think.'

Mr Moncrieff smiled. 'But that isn't all, Cissie. Through this, everything would be assured. You will always be able to live here. Endellion will be yours to inherit one day. This . . .' He took in his desk with a broad sweep of his hand. 'This will restore us.'

Cissie only sniffed and rubbed her nose. Bonnie started to move back towards the door. She should leave them to this private moment. Perhaps Mr Moncrieff sensed her discomfort because he turned to her and asked her, with the same unguarded pride as Cissie showing her embroidery, 'Well? You haven't said what you think?'

Bonnie stammered. 'It is more than I could have imagined.'

He smiled, laughed. His pen danced in his hand. 'Good. I'm glad. You see, I knew I could draw the plans. But how, I thought, do I turn these pieces of paper into an *actual* cemetery? I am hardly a practical man and I knew that I needed a business mind. I needed someone who might know what steps I must take, how I would have this thing approved, constructed. I needed a person who knew about,' he cast Bonnie a sly look, '*profit*. I couldn't possibly have navigated any of it without the good chance that was thrown my way. I could scarcely believe it! You know, of course, who I mean.'

Bonnie shook her head.

'A *certain* man who—' He nodded at her playfully, as though evoking a shared understanding. 'A certain man who helped establish Highgate.' He smiled. 'First of all, I should thank you, for pestering me until I began to see just how magnificent this cemetery could be. And *this man* . . .' He wagged his finger. 'He explained how you told him about your idea, and then he felt compelled to write to me, to express what a splendid idea it was. How it could save the house, and also be in the public benefit. A place of beauty and commemoration. And when he offered his services, it felt like a moment of such serendipity. What's needed here is not a director or an MP, but a man who's been *involved*. Who's seen it all, who's rolled up his sleeves.'

'I don't know anyone who helped establish Highgate—' she began, but it was already dawning on her, slower than it should have.

'Your brother,' he said, finally, clapping his hands. 'Your brother, of course! He'll be assisting me with all my business affairs, to help see this through. He sent me some of the wood-cuts he had drawn of Endellion itself, and I was pleased to see he is a fine draughtsman, as fine as the artists that sketch on the riverbank.'

Crawford. Of course. Crawford.

Bonnie cleared her throat, but her breath felt trapped, like a fishbone was stuck there.

'He has probably already told you that he'll be joining us

tomorrow. Now, I hope he won't mind that I've put him down-stairs, in the room adjoining Manton's.' He pulled a face. 'The right order of these things is always difficult to assess, but as we have no spare bedrooms, the decision was made for me. But he will be welcome. What a merry party we will make!'

'Yes,' Cissie said. 'And now we will be rich and you needn't marry any of those awful seals.'

'You are a silly goose,' Mr Moncrieff said, shaking his head.

'Might I send to London for a bonnet from Trimble's?'

'I don't see why not,' Mr Moncrieff said. 'Even if matters are not *quite* assured yet.'

'Oh, thank you, Papa!'

But their conversation washed over Bonnie. She gripped the edge of the desk. Crawford would be coming; Crawford would be here. It was all she had wanted, to have Crawford so close, to walk through these hallways beside him, his smile flashing like sunlight on a blade. But the brief flicker of excitement died in her belly. Crawford had done all this without telling her, penning letters to Mr Moncrieff, working his way into the house. When she had seen him that morning, he must have known why Mr Moncrieff was calling her to his study, and he had kept it to himself. And why? To have her wrong-footed, to show that he was the one in control? As a *surprise*?

When Bonnie left the room, Cissie's arm linked through hers, she felt as though an invisible hand was reaching out and shaking a snow-globe, flakes like ash storming around a lonely house. She did not know what she had begun and how it would end.

Part Three

Tripe

'He's put me to sleep down here with the rats,' Crawford complained, shouldering his way into the kitchen, a bag slung over his back. He was wearing a new green coat with gold buttons and he took it off, slumping in Manton's chair by the fire. 'I am managing his affairs, am I not?'

'But your *sister* is a maid,' Bonnie replied. 'You're hardly a gentleman, sleeping in a curtained bed, if your sister scrubs the pisspots.'

A cough from the corner of the room; she had not noticed Manton by the sideboard. Bonnie's cheeks glowed. 'This is – this is my brother,' she said. 'Crawford Fairchild.'

'Mr Fairchild,' he said, walking over and extending a hand. Crawford stood, shook it gruffly. Manton's smile did not reach his eyes. 'I understand you are here to *assist* Mr Moncrieff on some private business?'

The rebuke, unmissable: a careful reminder of Crawford's station. Crawford held Manton's gaze for a little too long.

'Annette has prepared dinner for us. In the meantime, your sister can show you your quarters. You will find them quite spacious, I'm sure.'

That afternoon, Bonnie had made Crawford's bed, tucking in the sheets, pounding air into the pillow, imagining his body settling here. She had placed a late-blooming dahlia in a vase on the dresser, thinking how pretty it looked. She had pictured him lying there, waiting for the house to settle before he sneaked upstairs to her. Their stifled laughter, their secret whispers to each other: together they would watch dawn creep across the walls, hear the first pheasants bickering on the lawn.

From the kitchen, she had heard Annette singing as she chopped up white slabs of tripe, milk bubbling on the stove. Soon, Manton's deep baritone had joined in, and a sense of wholeness had filled Bonnie. She and Crawford would be together again, and there would be no Rex, no reek of the Green Ground, no bluebottles knocking against the windows.

But then, hours later, Crawford walked into the room beside her, arms held outwards. His fingertips grazed each wall. 'It's little more than a coffin. If I suffocate in the night, you might name Mr Moncrieff as my assailant.'

Bonnie wondered whether she should mock him out of it or sympathize; it was always so hard to know. She felt suddenly tired of anticipating every need and mood of Crawford's, always appeasing, always soothing.

Instead, she said nothing and began unpacking his bag, shaking out his coats. The bedcovers lay unwrinkled, as smooth as paper. He had not thrown her down on them, their laughter muffled; he had not touched her at all.

The bell rang for dinner and they filed through to the kitchen, still not speaking. It was late October and the nights were drawing in earlier. For the first time, Annette had lit candles. Manton was at his usual place at the head, a place laid for Annette at one side of him, places for Bonnie and Crawford on the other. But Crawford lifted his place setting and laid it opposite Manton, at the other end of the table. Manton's eyes widened for an instant, but he lowered his head, murmured grace.

Annette heaped each plate with fried tripe. It glistened in the candlelight. Bonnie took a mouthful, the meat yielding, elastic, like eating nothing at all. Nobody spoke. There was only the sound of food sifting in mouths; the glug of Annette swallowing. Upstairs, the floorboards creaked.

Finally, Manton addressed Crawford. 'Mr Moncrieff tells me you will advise him on a private speculation. If you're able to divulge it, what exactly is the nature of your work?'

'Cemeteries. He will build one.'

Manton's knuckles whitened on his knife. '*Cemeteries?* And build one where?'

Bonnie concentrated on sliding her blade through the tripe. It broke the skin easily, the white flesh as pale as a maggot.

'My sister has not told you? But that is why I am here,' Crawford exclaimed. 'And with it, Mr Moncrieff will reverse his fortunes.'

Manton cleared his throat. 'I must have misunderstood. I thought you were saying, he would construct a cemetery on the grounds at Endellion.'

'But that is exactly what I am saying,' Crawford said, with some relish.

'You can't possibly be in earnest? What about the noxious odours?' Manton asked. 'It is well known that graveyards are hotbeds of pestilential infection. To build such a thing here is hazardous not only to ourselves but to our neighbours.'

Crawford laughed. 'Perhaps you will be out each night, warding off spirits with a pair of bells, garlic bulbs slung around your neck.'

The room fell silent. The meat churned in Bonnie's mouth, too peppery. Manton put down his cutlery.

'It will not be at all like that,' Bonnie attempted. 'This cemetery will be—'

'Profitable,' Crawford interrupted. 'Without it, you'll be plying your trade as a waterman in less than a year.'

'I trust I have more qualities to recommend me,' Manton said coldly.

'But the miasma,' Annette chimed in. 'We will sicken, surely.'

'I've never heard such nonsense!' Crawford said, laughing.

Bonnie watched Crawford reach for Annette's arm and pat it. Bonnie's fork stopped halfway to her mouth. She became aware of the way Crawford's chair was angled towards Annette's, how Annette, in turn, had leaned her body in Crawford's direction, her shoulders held back. Her lips looked full and wet in the candlelight, her cheeks so rosy that Bonnie wondered if she had pinched them.

'Come,' Crawford said, and he smiled at Annette. 'You cannot possibly think that.'

Annette looked at Manton, then back at Crawford. 'Perhaps,' she began cautiously. 'If it really will stop Endellion being sold and all of us cast out, a cemetery would not be the worst thing.'

'Precisely!' Crawford beamed. 'My sister suggested it to Mr Moncrieff, but it was my idea.'

Bonnie scowled. *Sister. Brother.* How bland and sexless those words were. He had cut her out of his past like an ulcer, reshaping himself into somebody eligible. She glanced up at Annette, saw her fingers trembling on the cutlery, and Bonnie hated her with a venom that shocked her: hated her and her round blinking eyes, her pretty tight mouth.

'This will not be like the private burying grounds in St Giles and Soho,' Crawford continued. 'Those are despicable, dangerous places, nothing more than death pits run by charlatans. They should be immediately and forever closed. I should have nothing to do with a place like that.'

'Is that so?' Bonnie asked, meeting his eye. 'I wonder who might be involved in such a venture.'

Crawford shook his head very slightly. 'But enough of that talk!' he said, bright now, spreading his hands across the table. 'I've heard that this house was a gift from the King to his mistress, that it was a place of *assignations*. With such pretty girls in his care, Mr Moncrieff must, surely, have a special fondness for one of you?'

Silence again. Crawford must have seen how he'd misjudged it because he blanched. Annette's smile tightened, Manton trembling. The butler stood, balled up his napkin. 'Such idle chit-chat like that can ruin a girl,' he said, each syllable enunciated carefully. 'I trust you will not bring Annette and Bonnie into disrepute again.'

He left, slamming shut the door behind him, and a chill settled on the room. Annette pushed her cabbage around the plate. Bonnie took a sip of wine. It was vinegary, acidic. And then Crawford leaned back and laughed.

'What an old stickler.'

Bonnie expected Annette to defend Manton, but she merely shifted in her chair. Her hands were almost touching Crawford's. There was a fingernail's distance between them.

'Is the wine collection fine?' Crawford asked.

'Oh, Manton would never allow it,' Annette replied. 'He keeps a list. We have only what is left from upstairs before it sours.'

'How generous of Mr Moncrieff to offer you his dregs,' Crawford said. 'But what if we were to take a bottle from the back and replace it with the empty bottle. Would he ever know?'

The girl laughed behind her hand, her eyes so round, like a deer trapped at night. 'I – I don't know.'

'Think of how hard you work, and they just give you scraps. Don't you deserve it?'

'I – I've never thought of it like that.'

Crawford moved his hand closer to hers. And then Annette sprung to her feet, her face glowing, and Bonnie saw how desperate she was to impress him.

ELIZABETH MACNEAL

At the cellar door, Annette turned to look back at Crawford as though willing him to join her. Bonnie stood quickly.

'I'll come with you, Annette.'

The air was damp and musty, Annette's candle casting long shadows.

'You never told me about your brother,' Annette whispered. 'He is a fine man, is he not?'

'He will hear us,' Bonnie said coldly. 'And you shouldn't roll over to men like that. You should guard yourself better.'

'*Roll over*,' Annette said, laughing. 'I didn't know you were such a prig.'

'Humiliate yourself, then,' Bonnie replied. 'I shan't stop you.'

It was impossible to read Annette's face in the darkness, but Bonnie saw how her grip on the bottle tightened. 'I was only making light,' Annette replied, pushing past her.

Bonnie watched her go, the cellar wall cold against her back. The slow drip from the ceiling cooled her forehead. How easily won Annette was; how hollow! When Bonnie had first arrived in the house, she'd cherished their friendship, but she began to wonder if Annette would have given herself to anyone. The way she'd shown all her cards, begging for any sort of intimacy, regardless of who it came from. *I've been desperate for Mr Moncrieff to hire another maid.* Like an oyster, hinged open, revealing its soft insides. And now that friendship counted for nothing; Bonnie could have crumpled it in her fist.

Upstairs again, Annette held the bottle of wine above her head like a military conquest. Bonnie saw Crawford's face break into a smile. Annette had proved herself compliant, another dog skipping about his ankles, and there was nothing Bonnie could do to stop it.

That night, Bonnie lay in bed, listening intently, wondering if Crawford would come. She balled up her pillow, threw it across the room, scorned herself. Of course he would not. There were no muffled footsteps on the stairs, no doors opening. It was silent except the trees rustling, a sole bird hooting into the night. Teetering on the brink of sleep, lurid images filling her mind: Crawford slipping Annette's lip between his, biting down on it. *You mustn't tell my sister—*

She must have drifted off, because she was woken by the door opening, Crawford sitting on her narrow bed. She pushed him away, pressing herself against the wall so no part of her would touch him.

'You're cross,' he whispered.

'Leave me alone.'

'If I did, you wouldn't like it.'

She hated that what he said was true, and she bit hard on her cheek. 'I thought you'd have gone to Annette.'

'It's too cold,' he said. 'I wouldn't venture all the way to her cottage.'

Bonnie pushed him again, harder this time, and he laughed. 'Poor jealous Bonnie.'

'I'm not.'

'I should be wounded by such a suggestion.'

She waited.

'She's a dullard. As dim as a cow. You can't *seriously* suppose I'd like her? Over a firework like you?'

Bonnie still did not move.

'Let me under your eiderdown. I'm half frozen. My toes might drop off. Why isn't your fire lit?'

Bonnie didn't oblige, but she didn't refuse either, and he lifted the edge of her cover and slipped underneath.

'You should be in one of the big beds downstairs, with all

those hangings. We both should be. Not tucked away in a cellar and a garret as though we don't matter.'

'I like it here.'

He leaned closer to her, pulled her head to rest on his shoulder. She lay stiff. His fingers traced patterns on her arms, her ribs. 'Aren't you glad I'm here?'

'Hmph.'

'I missed you. I came, didn't I? Rex was furious I left him behind. He's being a baby about the whole thing.'

'Is he really?' she asked, then cursed herself for betraying interest.

'Now. If I'm to beg your forgiveness, I really think I might need a little help.' He kissed her cheek but she pulled away. 'Because I'm *terribly* repentant.'

'You're mocking me.'

'The mere suggestion.' He clutched his chest. 'Won't you give this poor wretch just the tiniest sliver of hope? A little guidance on how I might address you?'

'What are you talking about?'

'I need fine words, for a fine lady. I know just the gentleman who has an artillery of sweet words. What sort of things do Cissie's letters say? From Lord – Lord whoever he was.'

'Duggan.' Crawford waited for her to continue, but she set her jaw.

'You *are* cross,' he said. 'It's worse than I imagined. Perhaps Lord Duggan will give me some idea how I might pay my respects to a fair lady. Might beg her forgiveness, prostrate myself at her feet.'

'You're making fun,' she said, but she was beginning to ease, a smile twitching the corners of her mouth.

'Lord Duggan is *always* sincere, I assure you.' He paused, his lips against her cheek. 'Well? Tell me, at least, what does he call her?'

She could never resist a chance to entertain him. Quietly, she said, 'He calls her *Mousekin*.'

'Mousekin! Well, I shall bow to his greater experience in matters of the heart. *Dearest mousekin*. But what am I supposed to say next? He will use the right romantic language, I'm certain of it. The man might woo a thousand duchesses.'

Bonnie spoke into the darkness, mischief beating through her. '*Last night I dreamed of you. You fill each of my dreams. Your long ringleted hair, your eyes that twinkle like distant stars on the black horizon*—'

'Stop!' Crawford exclaimed. 'I believe I have the cut of the man!' He began to kiss Bonnie, his voice muffled between the pecks. 'I must ask, how does my poor trembling little mousekin fare this evening? Might she admit a lowly suitor, desperately, *wildly* repentant—' He moved his hand below her navel.

She pushed him off, horrified. 'Crawford! That is – foul.'

'Well? Where else might your mousekin be?'

'No!' she declared, rolling onto her side, away from him. This time, she was smiling when she kicked him away, and he flung himself backwards in exaggerated grief, half-sprawled on the floor. He began to crawl back into the bed as though the task were impossible, the blanket flailing around him. He began to laugh, and despite herself, she did, too, until they were both shaking, lying there, clutching their ribs. It was just as she had imagined it: Crawford at Endellion. Annette and the evening melted away, and Bonnie simply thought: He is mine and I am his. That is all there is to it.

The W.L.C.C.

When Crawford told Bonnie that he would be discussing the cemetery in Mr Moncrieff's study the next morning, she waited until she heard a knock and the whine of the study door. She hurried to the kitchen, gathering a seedcake and a pot of tea, then carried the tray upstairs. Outside the door, she paused. Crawford had not asked her to come and Mr Moncrieff had not requested tea, but wasn't the cemetery *hers* too? She would only lay out the cups and plates. She would hardly linger. Inside, she caught raised voices, though not angry: she knocked and pushed her way in.

Crawford was standing to his full height, grimacing, Mr Moncrieff sitting at his desk, his hair falling in front of his eyes.

'You can't be serious,' Crawford exclaimed. 'You can't be, sir. You—'

He broke off when he saw Bonnie and she moved slowly, the china clinking as she lifted the pot and poured a long stream of tea.

'I'm sorry to interrupt,' she said, hoping they would carry on.

'Bonnie, you must hear this,' Crawford said. 'You must hear this *madness*.'

Mr Moncrieff didn't seem to mind. He steepled his fingers. 'Tell me why it's mad.'

'He wants to sell the land to a prospector. He's been offered

134

six thousand pounds. Six thousand! The prospector would laugh himself senseless. It would be like netting a whale with a petticoat.'

'They'd build it all for me. They'll take care of everything. I wouldn't need to take any risks—'

'Any risks! You're right there. There'd be none at all, and no reward either. Forgive me if I speak too plainly, but six thousand pounds will see you through a couple of years, no more. And then you'll still have to sell Endellion.' Crawford began pacing. 'No! I can't allow it. It's madness. It's madness and foolishness.'

Bonnie busied herself with the milk jug, watching Crawford out of the corner of her eye. The muscles in his throat were strained, his fingers rapping the desk; it was an agitation that seemed genuine. What had he said to her? *Why are you trying to save him? If he's ruined, let him be a fool.* And yet, here he was doing the same as she had.

'You must not sell it. Allow me to explain this plainly,' Crawford continued. He snatched a pen, began scrawling on a sheet of paper. 'Here. Twenty acres. Yes?'

'Yes,' Mr Moncrieff agreed.

'That is ample space for thirty thousand graves. Each grave will contain, on average, three bodies. Let's say – sold at the lowest figure of two pounds per burial, that will yield one hundred and eighty thousand pounds. And a vault or catacomb will cost—'

'Twenty guineas?'

'Twenty guineas? A hundred pounds at least! That's their price at Highgate. Let's say there are two thousand of these. That is an additional two hundred thousand pounds. So here, we are being conservative.' Crawford shook his head. 'The building and maintenance work will cost seventy thousand pounds, but that will principally be raised through shares. That leaves you with—' Crawford circled a figure, his pen snapping through the paper – 'a profit of three hundred and ten thousand pounds. Not all of that will be yours: much will go to the investors. But I would say a substantial portion will be, depending on the share you agree with the board.'

Mr Moncrieff stared at the sum, his teeth gnawing the inside of his cheek. Bonnie did too. The zeros, sprawling, like a row of wide eyes.

'And you'd consider accepting a charlatan's offer of six thousand pounds.'

Bonnie could not keep her eyes off the paper. Thirty thousand graves. Ninety thousand bodies. More, with the vaults and catacombs. All those lives, snuffed out, decaying underground. She thought again of the red-headed man. The flesh would have slipped from his bones; perhaps he had already been sold to the fertilizer manufacturer and ground to dust. Were his family, his daughter, still hoping he might come home? Were they watching the door each day, fingers jabbing at embroidery hoops, at anything at all to keep their minds still?

'Three hundred and ten thousand pounds,' Mr Moncrieff repeated.

'And you think the prospectors will allow your plans to be executed if they buy the land outright? Before you know it, the cemetery will be neo-classical, your sketches scrapped. They will bring in a new architect.'

'But are you sure we can do this? It's a risk.'

'Listen,' Crawford said, placing his palms on the desk and shifting his weight onto them. 'Without risk, you gain nothing. I know what I'm doing. *I* will guide you, make sure you meet the right people, hire the right labourers. I will make it a success.'

Mr Moncrieff let out a breath. 'Very well,' he said at last. 'You have convinced me.'

Crawford slammed the desk in relief. 'Now we must begin work. We will denounce that fraud and his *pitiful* offer.' He took a new sheet of writing paper, positioning it in front of Mr Moncrieff. 'But he can wait, stewing in his own putrid hope. First, we must incorporate a joint stock company. All of the other cemeteries have such a body, and that way we can raise capital on a vast scale. Shares, we will sell at the standard rate of twenty-five pounds each. We will call ourselves the West London Cemetery Company. The W.L.C.C. What you must realize, is that cemeteries are a murky business within parliament. Many MPs are major investors or directors of rival cemetery companies, and they will vote down a new company if they think it will affect theirs. It helps that we are so far out of London, that there is no proximity and the competition that comes with that. But you will still need to whisper in the right ears, perhaps even line a few pockets. You will need to go to London, to charm them, to dazzle them with the returns you will make them. They will agree, because there is money to be made, as long as they themselves are cut a sizeable piece of it.'

Mr Moncrieff nodded, barely blinking. He watched Crawford as though he could not believe he was real; as though Crawford held the answer to everything. 'And you will accompany me?'

Bonnie saw Crawford was about to agree, when Mr Moncrieff added, 'They will know you, I'm sure, from Highgate. These gentlemen and MPs will be familiar to you. That will help. The introductions will already have been made.'

Crawford faltered. 'It would be best,' he said, slowly. 'For you to go alone. For them to see *you* as the spearhead. It is your land, after all. Better to remove any association between this cemetery and a rival.'

Mr Moncrieff spun his pen in his hand. 'But—'

'Oh, I will help prepare you. When it's approved then we

– *you* – will hold a celebration for any potential investors. An occasion to show off the fine setting. A ball perhaps. No, a *shoot*. They will see your land to its most glorious advantage. And they will be fired up, hungry – their blood will rise and they will part with hundreds of pounds!'

It was astonishing to see Crawford like this: how, beneath his excitement, he was so composed, so articulate. Where had he learned so much? As he spoke, he held his hands a little apart as though clutching an invisible sphere: it was the way he always stood when he was devising a plan, when pieces were falling into place and he was in control. He seemed to have forgotten all about Bonnie as she waited beside the door, the empty tray clutched in her hand. He barrelled on, confident, unwavering, dictating letters with the eagerness of a composer. It was impossible to imagine that this man had spent his childhood on those grimed barges by Eel Pie Island. So many simply repeated the lives of their parents. Patterns passing from father to son and mother to daughter. But he had escaped his old life; she had too. They were the same.

He spoke on and on, referencing Père Lachaise as a Parisian model, and Carden's campaigns about the burial provision in London. Crawford paused at the end of each sentence, waiting for Mr Moncrieff's pen to catch up.

It must be admitted that the burial of the dead in the midst of large and populous cities and towns is extremely dangerous and injurious to the health of the inhabitants –

The proposed cemetery is strikingly eligible as a place of sepulture, being on the summit of rising ground and surrounded by land both picturesque and romantic. It benefits from ready access from public roads –

The plan, already devised by me, combines landscape beauty with economy, architectural interest with picturesque effect –

Finally, he finished speaking, and Mr Moncrieff blotted the page, smiled. 'I would be quite adrift without you,' he said.

Crawford stepped forward, placed his hand on Mr Moncrieff's shoulder. 'I have been preparing for an opportunity like this for some time.'

They both seemed to notice Bonnie then, and she said quickly, 'Forgive me. I can gather the teacups if you've finished—'

But Mr Moncrieff held out his hand. 'Stay. Please. It was your idea first of all, wasn't it? If you wanted, you could sit here and sketch your planting plans. You have an hour before Cissie returns from her lessons, perhaps longer.'

'Now?' she asked. 'Here?' Outside the door, she could hear the shushing of Annette's broom. There was paper on his desk, three pens. She might sit here for a whole hour in this crammed, haphazard room, the heat of the fire against her back, her mind filled with plants and trees. 'But I have chores—'

Mr Moncrieff waved his hand and began to clear a space at his desk. She hardly dared move. And then she recalled Crawford and darted forward quickly, out of fear he would say something to dismiss her, to cut her out.

Crawford cleared his throat but she ignored it; finally she heard the creak of a chair as he settled at the side table behind them.

Mr Moncrieff handed her a sheet of paper on which he had traced the outline of the cemetery in broad strokes. A long carriageway, branching into narrower paths, the sweep of the turning circle around the chapel. Catacombs and avenues.

The pen was cold in her hand. She held it above the page, did not move. A bead of ink gathered at the nib.

She could feel Mr Moncrieff watching her, a sympathy to his look. He bit his lip as though wondering if he ought to speak.

'It can be difficult to know where to begin,' he said at last, speaking so quietly it was almost a whisper. He drew his finger over the paper, his hand brushing against hers. 'I tend to start in the middle. Why not here? With the turning circle. Which trees would you plant around it? It's just ideas for now. No purchases have been made, no labourers enlisted. This is just a dream. A notion. There's a freedom in that, isn't there? You can make mistakes. There's plenty more paper.'

This time, Bonnie pressed the pen against the page. The line of ink was uneven. Mr Moncrieff smiled slightly, his head on one side. A round circle. She added another six beside it, neatly spaced. *Cypress*, she labelled them. The clock ticked like a tongue in a mouth.

'There,' Mr Moncrieff whispered, his eyes meeting hers. 'Now you've begun.'

The room was silent as they worked side by side, though Crawford tapped his watch, sighed, and she tried to ignore the rustle of his fidgeting. But soon she forgot even him. The day fell away. Just the scrape of pen on paper. Circles and labels bloomed into flowers: the bright yellow of primroses, the droop of hellebores, and behind them, fringes of light woodland. The names of plants came back to her, the thick scent of the flowerbeds her father had planted. Bonnie felt like an architect, a God, a twist of her pen indicating a tree, a shrub. She knew a trained botanist would be employed and his pencil would score out her own ideas, but for now she could believe this garden would be dug and planted. And in doing so, she realized she was writing over Enon Chapel and the Green Ground, unravelling that cavalier violence towards the dead. Its stinking pits and rotting vaults, the way bodies were flung about like sacks of meat. These plans were a thing of careful study: every person had their own set place. Every plant had a small space of soil allotted.

It was Crawford who broke the peace at last. 'I'm ravenous. It must be time to eat. It's as quiet as a tomb in here.'

Bonnie gathered the cups of cold tea, sliding her drawing onto Mr Moncrieff's pile. She could tell by the way he levered himself out of his chair that he wanted to discuss it with her, but Crawford gripped her arm, steering her away. She bobbed her curtsey, and it was only when she reached for the tea tray that she saw Crawford's hand slide out, quick as a pickpocket.

Lying on the corner of Mr Moncrieff's desk were his prized calipers, gold and shining. It was the work of an instant, Crawford's fingers nudging the edge of them so they dropped from the table. He caught them swiftly and they seemed to glide into his pocket.

Everything Is Happening Exactly As It Should

It was so petty, as though Crawford were nothing more than a cheap pickpocket, a cutpurse working the crowds in the hope of a shilling or two. Bonnie followed Crawford up the stairs to her attic, a fire raging in her chest. She wanted to reach out and seize hold of his coat, to make him understand what he had done. All those earrings and bracelets and brooches that she had passed him, little talismans of another life he could not have, and what was it for? His impulse was like a hunger, hands reaching out and snatching. And to have taken those calipers when they would certainly be missed.

It was only when they were inside her attic room that she turned on him. 'Give them back to me *now*.'

'What are you talking about?'

But she spoke over him, her voice a low hiss. 'I saw you. I saw what you took. He'll notice, you know, and then what will we do? This isn't like the trinkets. I never thought you were such a fool.'

Fool. The word, spat out, cooling like fat between them. She liked seeing him flinch, feeling the power in the word, and she said it again, watching as the blow landed once more. 'You're a fool, Crawford.'

'You don't know anything, Bonnie.'

He took out the calipers, spinning them in his hands like a taunt.

'You have to put them back.' Her voice, high now, breaking. 'He'll notice. And after everything we've done to find positions in this house—' She swallowed. 'My situation is different from yours. I'm wanted for—' her voice tripped on the word. '*Murder*. I killed a man, Crawford. I killed a man!'

'Calm down, Bonnie. You're not on stage on Drury Lane. I've told you, nobody's looking for you.'

'But what if someone remembers something. What if—' She rubbed her neck.

'You stole the trinkets easily enough and you weren't caught.' He smiled at her, shaking his head. 'Don't you see, Bonnie? Everything is happening exactly as it should.'

His calm only sparked her confusion, her disarray. She would have shaken him if she had not feared him; that cold smile. She reached for the calipers again, snatching them from his hand. A tussle; the hot thump of rage. Crawford seized her by the arms, and she let out a cry, felt herself pushed back against the bed, wrists pinned above her head. He plucked the calipers from her fingers with distressing ease.

'Everything is happening as it should,' he whispered again, his voice humid and close. The bedframe was jutting into her back. 'Don't you see that, Bonnie Bee?'

But she did not see, and she squirmed, writhed, thrashed her head from side to side.

'How? What do you mean how it *should*?' She snatched her arms free. 'You're keeping things from me. I know you are, Crawford. You always are.'

He rolled off her and lay against the mattress, breathing hard. 'Don't act so wounded.'

'Tell me, Crawford. Tell me what's happening.'

Bonnie caught the whine in her voice and she stopped herself. That was not the way to get anything from Crawford. She had to tread gently, wheedle it out of him, flatter him. There were so many things slightly out of joint, and he had explained them away with excuses that now felt flimsy. His education. Why he'd give everything up to come to Endellion. Why he suddenly wanted to help Mr Moncrieff when he'd called him a murderer, a fool.

She reached for his hand, squeezed it. His eyes glinted, so dark she could not see the pupils. She kept her voice calm. 'I wondered – the way you spoke to Mr Moncrieff. All you knew about cemeteries. Where did you learn it all?'

'Not such a fool, am I?'

She did not look at him. 'I spoke in anger.'

He cradled his head with his hands. 'It's easy to learn things if you charm the right people.'

'Which people?'

'It took some work, I'll admit. But then I found an article about Highgate. It credited the men in the middle, those who oiled the whole machine.' He enjoyed sharing this, she could tell: his voice rose with pride. 'One of the men had an unusual surname. I'd seen it on a shopfront. I made enquiries, and the owner gave me the address of his cousin. Those in the middle are so easily flattered, so easily won, such dupes! Just a little praise, and they'll tell you everything they know. He wrote me pages and pages about his work at Highgate, in exchange for nothing at all. He told me the committees we must appease. The permission required. The mechanics of it all.' He rubbed his fingers across Bonnie's knuckles. 'Wasn't that clever of me?'

'And then you wrote to Mr Moncrieff,' Bonnie continued. 'You knew this house, of course.' Suddenly, she recalled the evening before the rat-baiting, the looks that had passed between Crawford and Rex, her own disquiet. 'You always intended me to be here, didn't you? It was *this* house. Rex made up that advertisement, didn't he? Mr Moncrieff said he hadn't advertised and I thought it was *him* who was confused. But—'

'Rex? You think Rex made that up?' Crawford stared at the ceiling, the beginnings of a grin on his lips. She took a breath, her jaw tightening. It was her life; it wasn't a puzzle to assemble. 'Rex has the brains of a prizefighter. I wrote it. Of course, we didn't think you'd come. Not *really*. But then – well, there was the gentleman and it all seemed so neat, so perfectly done.'

So perfectly done. Bonnie turned to face the wall, her lip trembling. The guilt that ate at her, the fear; and that was *perfectly done* – but Crawford was still speaking. 'I knew you'd be safe here. I knew you'd trick your way in past Mr Moncrieff. And it was for the best, wasn't it? Nobody's found you, have they? If I hadn't known about this place, you might have been hanged.'

'But why did you want me here?' she asked again.

A fly circled the ceiling. The window rattled.

Silence; he stared ahead.

'Crawford?' she whispered, gritting her teeth. She would not raise her voice. She would not lose control. 'Why did you need me to come here? Why this house?'

Perhaps he sensed that even now she was drawing herself back from him, tired of being left in the cold. Perhaps he knew he needed to give her something more, to bind her closer, to offer her the power of confidence.

'You know that I lived nearby as a boy.' His voice was halting. 'That was all true – that we lived like – like rats. My mother and I had nothing. And then, when I was five or six, she brought me here, to Endellion. It looked like a castle. A white palace. The windows were so low I could see inside without even standing on tiptoes. I saw perfect little scenes. Of – fires in grates and rooms stacked with books.'

He seemed lost, his eyes almost closed. 'And what then?' Bonnie prompted. 'Did you go inside?'

He nodded. 'We sat in the kitchen, and the tables were heaped with vegetables and a roasted chicken, and they let me eat two slices of cherry cake.' He smiled. 'My mother said there was someone she needed to talk to, and when she returned, she told me that I was to have a gentleman's education. They sent us off with more food. It was like a –' he traced shapes in the air, 'it was like something from a fairytale. Our fortunes reversed with the click of a finger. It wasn't ordinary. I knew it wasn't ordinary. I knew that there was something I was missing.'

He spoke to the ceiling, to the little patch of mould that bloomed there, and Bonnie didn't interrupt him.

'I had a smart green uniform and my own pen. If only you'd seen me then! I liked to keep the inkwell filled to the brim and my shoes so shiny that I hated the walk to school. I'd dance around the puddles. But it still didn't make sense. Every day when I sat at my desk I thought: *Why*. Why, why, why. Why would I receive all this for nothing? Everything had to be bartered or earned. And then it occurred to me. I was fatherless, or so I'd thought, but of course I wasn't. Everyone had a father. It was obvious that mine lived at Endellion. When I asked my mother, she denied nothing, said only she'd made him own his responsibilities. She wouldn't tell me anything more than that, except to say I should be grateful. But when I heard that, it was – I wish I could tell you how that lit me up. For the first time in my life, I felt alive. Important.'

'The old Mr Moncrieff?' Bonnie asked. 'But how did your mother know him?'

'She used to work here, as a girl. And you know how it is. Maids sent away in disgrace. Perhaps she made him realize how wretched her life had grown and his mood changed towards her. This was when Endellion was in its heyday. He had money. Perhaps she threatened him and he silenced her. I don't know. But she got me my education, my means of raising myself in the world.' He grinned. 'She was a resourceful woman.'

'But that means Mr Moncrieff is your *brother*?'

Bonnie tried to summon the resemblance between them, the whisper of the one in the other: both tall, both dark-haired, both nearing forty. But beyond that, she couldn't find the confluence. Mr Moncrieff was so angular, his handsomeness almost furtive. Crawford was disarming, his features muscular and perfect.

Crawford didn't stop talking. 'I watched him all the time. My – my *brother*. I came to think he was me. That it was me riding horses, or playing with a hoop, or running through the gardens. That this thin veil separated our lives and I could just step into his house and become him.' He laughed, gently. 'It sounds mad, doesn't it?'

'No. It doesn't at all,' Bonnie replied, thinking of the Highwell girls.

'I loved to think of the house as mine in those days. To think I had this secret. But then my mother sickened. It was – it was a growth. We could see it in her chest, egg-sized. But the doctor said that it would be cured by a rest by the sea. She had no money left. I begged her to let me ask at the house. To ask *here*. She refused, but I went anyway. Old Mr Moncrieff was still alive then. My *father* was still alive then, I suppose I should say. I rang the bell and when he refused to see me, I waited until he went out riding. It was hours. I was freezing, standing by the trees. I just kept having these horrible thoughts – of my mother weakening, sickening and dying when I was gone. Of arriving too late. Like I was living in some kind of penny fiction.'

Crawford's teeth were clenched, the words coming out in short, sharp gusts.

'He would not know me. He said I was mad. That he had never even heard of my mother. That if I didn't move from the path in front of him, he would ride his horse right over me.'

'No,' Bonnie said, her mouth falling open. 'That's – *monstrous*.'

A *curmudgeon*, Mr Moncrieff had called his father. A practical man. Bonnie pictured a smaller Crawford standing beside the stables, his face raised in supplication to the man that towered over him. All he had needed was a little money; all he had needed was an acknowledgement of the truth of his life. She burned for him; she pulled Crawford closer to her, but he nudged her away, curling up like a child.

'What did you say then?'

'What could I say?' Crawford demanded. 'What could I possibly have said to him? I left, like the coward I was. I wish – when I think of it now, I wish I'd thrown him from the horse, whipped him. I wish I'd cut his throat.' His hands tightened into fists. 'And then, when I was leaving, I peered through the window, and I saw the boy at his studies. He was about my age, perhaps a little younger, his head lowered over his books, and I thought about how I studied my books in a dank pit. After that, I hated this house just as much as I longed for it.'

His eyes were bruised and heavy. He clung to Bonnie then, his breath shallow and tight.

'I'm sorry, Crawford. That's all so awful.'

'It wasn't your fault. It was them. It was *him*.'

Crawford sat up on the bed. He stood, surveying the gardens. It was a brisk autumn day, dew glinting on the lawns, the Thames smoking in the mist.

But more questions still tugged at her, and she did not know how to ask them, not when he had already shared so much. She looked up at him. 'But you're here now, aren't you? You're in the house.'

'Yes,' he said, gripping the edge of the window, his gaze flitting over the woodland.

'I wondered.' Her words were cautious, tentative. 'I wondered why you wanted me here too. Why you made up the advertisement.'

'I don't really know.' He held out his hands. 'That's the truth. Life just felt so – *stagnant*. Every day I stared at the woodcuts of Endellion on my wall. It was here, and there I was, stuck in a stinking garret in St Giles. All I was doing was skimming profit from another man. Every so often, I'd come here and just walk through the grounds. I drank in the inns nearby.'

'That's where you went,' Bonnie said. 'Those days when you just disappeared.'

He did not turn his head. 'Word passes easily over ales. I heard about Mrs Moncrieff's death and the departure of most of the staff. Everyone was full of talk about how the house was being auctioned off bit by bit, and there was no housekeeper, and his daughter didn't even have a lady's maid. And I thought – if you were only here, something might happen.'

'What do you mean, *something*?'

'I don't know. I thought an idea might occur to me. At first I thought it would be enough for me just to come here, just to know you were inside. But then when I visited you and we went to Mrs Moncrieff's bedroom, I knew I needed more. It wasn't enough just to take the trinkets. I needed to live here too. I hated not having a plan. It all felt so – so *pointless*. It took me a while to realize how we'd do it.'

'How we'd do what?'

He turned to Bonnie, the curtains catching in a breeze, the cold air making her shiver. His eyes narrowed. He held his hands aloft, the invisible sphere clasped between them. 'One day, we'll have all of this.'

'What do you mean?'

'We'll own it all.' He spoke clearly, his fingers linking with hers.

'I don't understand.'

'Bonnie,' he said, gently. 'Bonnie. *Think.*'

She shook her head.

'Every household on the river knows that Mr Moncrieff is in want of a wife.'

Vertigo washed over her. She had to grip the edge of the bed to steady herself. Mr Moncrieff's hand brushing hers as he showed her how to begin drawing her plans. The way he had sought her out on the towpath, the kind, interested way he looked at her. She had wondered why he did not always treat her like a maid, his confidence open and brimming. But mainly, she thought of how little Crawford had seemed to mind the intimate way he spoke to her, looked at her. *You'd ride him. He's handsome, is he not?* And how, usually, Crawford's mind was sharp with imagined betrayals: how carefully she had to tread if she spoke to anyone who was not a ruddy gentleman, not some part of their game.

'Mr Moncrieff?' she whispered. Her mouth was dry. 'I couldn't. He wouldn't—'

'You *could*,' he whispered. 'If anyone could. You're pretty enough. Any fool can see that he desires you. He treats you so differently from Annette.'

'Even if he does,' she said slowly, 'it doesn't mean anything. I'm a *maid.*'

'That's where you have to think carefully. Where you have to change the way he sees you. You have to put yourself in his way. Haven't we been doing that our whole lives, fitting ourselves to new situations?' He gestured around him, an edge to his voice. 'Don't we deserve it? All that his father snatched away from me. Why should he enjoy all that splendour when you're stuck up here in the eaves and I'm in the cellar? What right does he have?'

The girls at Highwell; the rector who had expected her gratitude. Bonnie swallowed. 'But you said, didn't you, that he killed his wife? That he killed Josephine. And you want me to try—'

'Oh, Bonnie. You're hardly spotless. Two murderers together.' He leaned closer to her, his breath whispering against her neck.

'But what about you? If I'm his wife, what do you gain?'

'You'll raise me with you. My *sister*. He's so oblivious and trusting, he'd let us do anything we wanted, spend his money however we chose. I could live here too. At night, you could visit me.' His hand caressed her arm but she nudged him away. Under the mattress was the nightgown she had stolen. Josephine's nightgown. What would Mr Moncrieff think if he saw her in it? Her own body filling the space where his wife's had once been; tight against her ribcage, transparent against her thighs.

Bonnie stood, walked to the window. The trees stirred. There was the ice house, the distant edge of a summerhouse, the wild tangled paths, the thick avenue of limes. A house of illicit love, of assignations. Caroline Moncrieff, the King's mistress. Josephine and her lover. She touched the iron bedframe as she had done the first time she entered this room. *Mine,* she thought. The greenhouse with its rusted pipes, the wide gleaming staircase. That blue and red light spilling across the floor, the diamond-shaped panes, rooms glued to rooms. It could be theirs. She could walk down the avenues and groves, the hallways and gallery, mistress of it all.

Part Four

The Gentleman

The next morning dawned chill and white, the first cold day of the year. Bonnie drew out Cissie's stockings and woollen chemise, an extra petticoat. She kept her ears pricked for Mr Moncrieff's footsteps, the click of his door, the patter of Zephyr's claws. Twice the fire spat and she jumped; the fabrics in the closet shushed against each other like hot, angry breath. Cissie's fingernails snapped as she bit them. Bonnie imagined Mr Moncrieff sitting at his desk and finding his calipers missing, turning over his papers, casting books to the floor as he searched for them; then hurrying down the hallway and demanding to know why she had taken them. But there was no sound of him. She sighed, raked through Cissie's dresses. The night before, she had felt herself on the trembling cusp of something new, the world cast into a dizzying array of colours. But this was all the same, all so ordinary. She could not let it be so. She would have to put herself in Mr Moncrieff's way.

'I don't like that gown,' Cissie said. 'Emmeline said the sleeves are outmoded.'

Bonnie returned it to the wardrobe. All morning, Cissie had been fretful: deep bruises puffed under her eyes, her right thumb blackened with ink. 'You didn't sleep last night, did you?'

Cissie jiggled her leg, her dressing table chattering. 'I can't stop thinking about how – how cold she must have been.'

Josephine and her winter drowning; of course.

'After it happened, they made me stay in bed. They gave me bitter teas to drink. You won't let them do it again, will you?'

'Who did?'

'The doctors.'

Bonnie placed a hand on Cissie's forehead. She was possessed by the sudden urge to kiss the crown of her head, like she once had kissed her younger brothers. 'I'll try. But you must try to sleep at night. Promise you'll try?'

'Promise.'

Bonnie returned to the dresses. They were mostly pink or quilted paisley. Towards the back she found a navy blue dress that Cissie had never worn before. It was the same colour as her own, though the fabric was heavy silk where hers was worsted; and the sleeves were trimmed with Binche lace, where her hems were beginning to unravel. 'What about this gown?'

Cissie looked up. 'Mama used to wear one like it.'

'Should I put it away?'

Cissie twisted her mouth. 'No. No. I want to wear it.'

When Bonnie tied the final clasp, Cissie touched the sleeves, the tight waist. She looked from herself to Bonnie. 'But you're also dressed just like me!'

Bonnie tried to look incredulous. But she wondered, as they sat side by side, if the same might occur to Mr Moncrieff, Bonnie echoing Cissie, who was echoing Josephine, a chain of women, all reaching out a hand and feeling the graze of their fingertips.

By eleven o'clock, Mr Moncrieff was still in his study. Bonnie tried to keep busy, working in the rooms nearest to him, so that she might rush out and encounter him if he left for his ride. If he had missed the calipers, he gave no indication of it. In the library opposite his study, she emptied the grate and laid a fire, leaving Cissie's linen shifts to be scoured later. Everywhere, she was surrounded by that hallowed stained-glass light, by mantelpieces built to resemble cathedrals, as though the house was dressing up as a church. Bonnie dusted a still-life painting, so detailed that she felt she might bite into the peach, feel its fuzz against her cheek. None of it was real. She heard a creak, paused. It was only Manton and Annette, clearing breakfast, discussing how they might possibly manage the planned shoot with such a small staff. Annette suggested serving sausages in pastry; Manton said devilled eggs. Annette's voice was high and singsong; how had Bonnie never realized how irksome it was? Her loathing for the maid was as sharp as a piece of glass in the skin. Bonnie drummed her fingers on the wooden screen, a patch of sky glowering down at her. Soon they were gone. Bonnie tiptoed across the hallway to Mr Moncrieff's study and listened. He was bound to come out soon. He liked a morning ride, after all. The mourning crape on the banisters lifted in the breeze.

And then, when she was just about to give up and take Cissie's linens to the kitchen, she heard the snap of Mr Moncrieff's door, creaking on the stairs. Bonnie spat on her hand and smoothed her hair, pinched colour into her cheeks. The front door slammed, footsteps on the gravel. She would need to be fast. She careered down the staircase, then hurried in the opposite direction from Mr Moncrieff, towards the pond and greenhouse. Soon she would collide with him. As she slowed to a saunter, she pulled off her apron and mob cap, balling them under a bush. There he was, rounding the corner. She had to find some reason for being here. Roses climbed the walls, brown and flaking in the cold. She pulled at one, though it was hard to twist the stems without a knife, and the petals fell off. She heard his footsteps, nearing her.

'Oh, you shouldn't occupy yourself with that. I'll ask one of the Smithson boys to deadhead them,' Mr Moncrieff said.

Bonnie pretended to jump. 'You surprised me!'

She wondered if his heart hammered as hers did.

'I should have announced myself better.'

They stood there, Mr Moncrieff's hands tucked into his pockets, Bonnie fiddling with the roses, a thorn cutting her finger. She would wait for him to speak. She took him in in small glances, so unlike Crawford, his *brother*: Mr Moncrieff's coat was untailored, unravelling at the cuffs, and he had cuts on his lips where he had bitten them. Ink stained his shirt. He might have been slender, but there was strength in his height, his broad shoulders. She wondered how he had done it: how fragile Josephine must have felt in that moment before she died. Had he regretted it immediately, as Bonnie had? How senseless it must all have appeared. This woman he had desired enough to marry; to have a child with. This woman who had known everything about him: whether his thighs were pale and hairless, the shape of the thick muscles flanking his hips. She coloured, severing the rose stem, a thorn slicing into her thumb.

'Heavens! You're bleeding,' Mr Moncrieff said. 'Here, take this.'

He pressed a handkerchief into her palm. She allowed her thumb to graze his hand and then flinched, as though it was him who had done it. He flushed, kicked the gravel into small mounds.

'I wondered.' He cleared his throat. 'I'm afraid I can't find my calipers. I wondered if, perhaps, you saw where I put them yesterday. They were on my desk, weren't they? They're always on my desk.'

'I don't remember.' Bonnie raised her finger to her mouth and sucked. That sweet taste of iron. She managed to look quizzical, surprised even.

'Nobody would have taken them,' he said, though his voice rose as though it was a question.

'Of course not, sir.'

'No matter. No matter.'

Bonnie let herself exhale. Was this all it would amount to? All her worry, and the calipers were already forgotten.

He put his hands into his pockets, took them out again. 'I'm preparing for my trip to London, to line up the parliamentary motion for our cemetery company. Your brother is proving intractable. I can't convince him to accompany me, though he'd be able to introduce me to everyone from Highgate.' He sighed. 'I don't suppose—'

'I'm afraid I hold very little sway over him.'

'Ah. Then.' He held out his hands, a gesture of helplessness.

'You will be more than equal to it, sir.'

He pulled a face. 'I don't know. I don't fit naturally into that world.'

'But you're the one with the power, you know. You can make all these men rich. They'll fawn about you, too.' She found she enjoyed it, this gentle flattery, like coaxing a shy bud to unfurl.

'Well. We shall see.' He smiled. 'Your brother has proved very resourceful. I can't think how I'd do without him. Like you, he is clearly well educated.'

'We were fortunate in our schooling.' She knew the question that Mr Moncrieff wanted to ask: *how?*; and she knew how she would answer him, how she would shift herself very slightly in his eyes. She took a breath. 'Our story, sir, is not a happy one.'

'Oh?' he said. 'I'm sorry to hear it.'

She began to walk towards the greenhouse and she was

pleased that he joined her. With each step, their hands skimmed past each other's.

'My brother and I had a different life once. Different prospects. We had a fine house in Sussex but it was lost to us after our father remarried. In fact, it was not wholly dissimilar from this.' She glanced behind her at Endellion, and the windows winked back at her.

'How awful,' Mr Moncrieff said, a note of genuine sorrow in his voice.

For a moment, she was hooked back to the last time she had recited this speech: the Angler, the red-headed man slipping his hand around her waist, the stench of his breath. She squeezed shut her eyes, blinked. She could do better. She could believe in this story, turn it into a half-truth: she could write herself a new past. In this story, the red-headed man would not exist at all. She could un-kill him, place him back in his grand house near Hyde Park like a little wind-up toy.

'The house was a lovely russet brick. Honeysuckle climbed the walls. I had my own room and my own dog, a terrier called Bertie. My brother and I shared a governess, and we delighted in her classes. And then,' she lowered her voice, surprised to feel the prick of tears, 'my mother died of consumption. We missed her terribly, but my father soon remarried. At first we liked his wife. She seemed doting and agreeable. But it changed when she bore him a son. He became everything to her and we were nothing more than a nuisance. When my father died a few years later, we discovered that his new wife had convinced him to alter his will, his entire estate and income falling entirely to my half-brother. In short, Crawford and I were cast out, destitute, with no option but to enter service.'

It was a foolish story, even she could see it, as tired as Cissie's romances. She looked up coyly, half-expecting to see Mr

Moncrieff wagging his finger at her. *What a fine performance.* But his face was pale, distraught. 'But that is an outrage! Did you consult lawyers?'

'The will was clear,' Bonnie replied sadly. 'You must know how these matters stand.'

'And your half-brother! Perhaps when he comes of age he will realize the cruelty, the *wrong* that was done to the pair of you.'

'It is generous of you to say, but I think it would cause us more pain to hope and be disappointed.'

'That is why I have left my estate to my daughter, not a wife, if I ever remarry.'

'Oh?' Bonnie asked, stumbling slightly on a patch of weeds. She had a faint recollection of Cissie saying something of this nature, but the details were indistinct. 'But what if Cissie then casts *her* out?'

'I've guarded against that too,' Mr Moncrieff said. 'A wife would receive a generous allowance each year.'

'That is good of you.'

Bonnie twisted the rose stem between her fingers. Their plan might not even work, and if it did, Mr Moncrieff was hardly infirm and about to die. But if the worst happened, wouldn't she still have what she wanted? What *Crawford* wanted too? A rise in the world, far greater than she had ever imagined. The allowance might furnish them both. Still, a part of her decided to bind the information close, not to tell Crawford for now.

'There's your brother!' Mr Moncrieff declared. 'Mr Fairchild!'

Crawford was walking across the lawn, a stick in his hand. He raised his arm in salute. The look he flashed Bonnie was so quick that only she would have caught it. *Bravo*, it said. *Bravo.*

'The labourers have arrived and started work. Won't you join me?' he asked, and together they took the lime avenue to the pasture.

As they approached, Bonnie could see figures bent over the earth, scythes hacking at the weeds and tall grasses. The proposed area was fenced off with canes. It was strange to see it already looking so different: real marks in the soil, not pen lines on a page, so much larger than she had remembered the pasture. Twenty acres. In a year, if they had their way, the hillock would be transformed, crowned with a chapel, the ground spanned by gravel paths and rustling trees.

'There's nothing wrong with beginning before we have approval,' Mr Moncrieff said. 'Your brother seems so sure it will be granted.'

'He's always so sure of everything,' Bonnie replied, nudging Crawford. His hands found hers briefly, and squeezed.

Calipers

The next morning, Mr Moncrieff summoned the household to his study.

'Perhaps he wants to offer us a few days to visit our families at Christmas,' Annette whispered.

But Bonnie knew different. She knew it when the four of them filed in and Mr Moncrieff stayed seated, his mouth tight. They stood before him. Her, Crawford, Annette and Manton.

'There is no easy way to say this.' Mr Moncrieff's gaze flicked to each of them in turn. He picked up a piece of paper and began twisting it absently in his hands. 'I've noticed – a few things have disappeared. Gone missing. My calipers, that I never move from this study. Cissie's silver brooch. And today, I visited Mrs Moncrieff's bedroom and found most of her jewellery missing.'

Annette gasped theatrically and clasped her throat. Bonnie stared at the floor, trying to keep her cheeks from flushing. Manton gave a small shake of his head. It was only Crawford who began to fidget, rolling a piece of lint between his fingers and cricking his neck. He looked guilty; he looked like a man concealing a crime. Bonnie tried to nudge him, to step in front of him, to shield him from Mr Moncrieff's gaze.

'If it had been one item, I would have blamed my carelessness. But this – this suggests a pattern. This suggests,' he took a breath, '*theft*. My wife's jewellery was – it was highly valuable. I could not bring myself to sell it. It would have been worth hundreds of pounds.'

Bonnie inhaled sharply through her nose. *Hundreds of pounds?* It explained Crawford's new coat, his blackened shoes. *Paste*, he had called it. *Worthless scraps.* Winter sun flickered through the red glass and made the whole room seem flimsy. She should never have taken the jewellery. Her fists whitened, a high humming setting up in her ear. And now Crawford had been so carelessly grasping and got them caught.

'I hate matters like this,' Mr Moncrieff continued. 'I can assure you that I will not be pursuing any recriminations. I merely ask that the perpetrator step forward, and we will deal with it between ourselves. Trust is how I have always run my house.'

'If I may,' Manton said, and they all turned to stare at him. Annette blinked. 'I have been in your service for more than forty-five years, before you were even born. Annette has been in your family's service since she was fourteen. We have had no difficulty with Bonnie since she arrived three months ago, and she has worked tirelessly.' He cleared his throat. 'This is a new problem. And I feel it would be remiss of me to fail to direct attention to the newest member of your household, who has been here less than a week.'

Bonnie stared at the floor, her heart galloping.

Manton continued. 'It is, I confess, not a matter I hoped to raise with you in this way. I wish to separate what I feel about Mr Fairchild from his sister, Miss Fairchild, who has proved herself to be a dutiful and hardworking servant. But I have been – uncomfortable – with Mr Fairchild since he entered your employ. I have found him to be disruptive, even conniving. I do not mean to criticize your judgement.' He bowed his head.

'What I mean to say is this: I do not believe Mr Fairchild to be a man of honour.'

Silence fell. Annette sucked on her teeth. Bonnie waited for Mr Moncrieff to speak; she waited for the swing of the axe.

'Sir, might I speak?' Crawford spoke in a tentative, fawning tone that Bonnie had never heard before. 'Might I address this accusation?'

Mr Moncrieff nodded as if to say, *please.*

'What I would like to say gives me no pleasure. Such aspersions are – I find them intensely damaging and painful, especially when—' He broke off, rubbed hard at his eye. 'I find it interesting that Mr Manton has been the first to level accusations. The first – when – perhaps it is best, if you follow me. Because I have been at a loss to know how to raise a matter so grave, when I am so new to this household, and Mr Manton so clearly a trusted servant of many decades—'

'What can you mean?' Mr Moncrieff said. 'Talk plainly.'

'Please, sir,' Crawford said. 'Just – it's best if I show you.'

They followed Crawford and Mr Moncrieff. Annette tried to mouth something at Bonnie but she ignored her, a clamminess in her hands, a roiling in her stomach. Down the grand staircase, down the servants' pine steps, into the kitchen. Crawford paused, then led them through the silver room to Manton's quarters.

'If we may, Manton?' Mr Moncrieff asked. 'If you would permit us to enter?'

'I am concealing nothing,' Manton replied, nodding gravely.

His room was as neat as Bonnie would have expected, a bedspread tucked in at each corner of the mattress, a tapestried Bible verse hanging opposite the window. Books lined the walls, the gilding flaking from the spines. *Household Management. The Modern Butler.*

Crawford moved forwards slowly, as though pained.

'It was Bonnie who told me about it. She was fetching fresh coals to warm Miss Cissie's sheets, and afterwards she interrupted Manton in Miss Cissie's bedroom. She was surprised to find him there at all, and so flustered, and it was this that aroused her first suspicions—'

Bonnie's cheeks burned.

'What nonsense!' Manton burst out. 'Bonnie will correct him, I am sure of it—'

Bonnie could feel his gaze, boring into her. She was silent, her breath echoing in her head. The seconds were weighted with Manton's expectation that she would speak up, defend him. She watched a small bewildered spider scurrying to and fro on the boards, first one way, then the other. She crushed it under her shoe.

'It is – a – lie,' Manton said, weaker now. 'It is not true.'

'I – I confess I did not want to believe it either,' Crawford continued.

'How dare you—' the butler burst out.

'Manton,' Mr Moncrieff said, a pleading in his eyes. 'I allowed you the chance to speak, and now Crawford must have the same privilege.'

'We ought to have come to you straight away,' Crawford said. 'But – I – I thought I would confirm my suspicions first. I heard the scrape of a board and when I went in afterwards—'

With a showman's flourish, Crawford bent to his knee, levered up a loose floorboard. Bonnie did not need to peer over Mr Moncrieff's shoulder to know what she would see: a few of Mrs Moncrieff's trinkets, Cissie's brooch, the calipers.

Annette scratched her scalp, flakes of skin catching the light. Bonnie wanted to be outside in the gardens; she wanted to be anywhere but here. The air was tight and close. *Say something,* a voice hissed, but she batted it away. Because if Manton was not the thief, who was it? Crawford had implicated her along- side him; she was a part of it too. She watched as he placed the trinkets on the floor and stood shakily.

'This is an outrage,' Manton said, his hand trembling. 'Mr Moncrieff, you must see at once the appalling crime that has occurred here.'

Mr Moncrieff did not look at him. He stared at the skeleton trees drawn like fingers against the window. 'I just – I want to understand, how these items came to be in your possession.'

'They've entered this room, *my* private quarters, and hidden them here!' Manton declared. 'These – these – *bastards!*' The curse word, incongruous on his polished tongue. 'They've had me for a fool. And if you can't see it, you're the biggest fool of all.'

'I want to discuss this with you privately,' Mr Moncrieff said. 'If you'd care to follow me. You have been in my service for—'

Manton gaped. 'You don't believe me,' he said.

'Please, Manton, of course you must stay,' Mr Moncrieff said, reaching out to pat Manton's shoulder, but he flinched away. 'There is no doubt in my mind. Endellion could scarcely exist without you. We have the shoot coming up and you will be sorely needed. As you yourself said, you have been in this house since before I was born, and my father and I have always been delighted with your work. I simply want to understand—'

'You don't believe me,' Manton repeated. 'You will excuse me, but you will not believe me. Suspicion will always stick to me.'

'Manton, we can resolve this amicably,' Mr Moncrieff said, a small flare of desperation in his voice.

'I will not endure this,' the butler said calmly. 'I will not endure any suspicion attached to my name. I am nearly seventy years old. I have seen enough in this household to satisfy me that I could not stay on with the new staff you have hired.'

Mr Moncrieff raised his hand to his throat, fluttered it there. 'Mr Fairchild's services have, in such a short time, become invaluable to me. Without him, I stand no chance of reversing my fortunes. He has become a trusted *partner* in business. I'm sure we can find a way of living agreeably together, a way—'

'You have my apologies,' Manton interrupted. 'And I have cause to believe that you will rue the day I left, when you handed your house over to this band of thieves.'

'Please—'

'I will be gone by this evening.'

A strange coolness settled on them, a sense of things knocked out of joint. Mr Moncrieff coughed and said, 'Back to your duties, the rest of you,' and they all filed away, leaving Manton in the room, facing the small window.

The house fell silent that afternoon, as though it was shrinking back in disgust at what Bonnie had done, or rather had not done; as though it could sense Crawford's grip tightening. Annette did not sing as she cooked dinner. Cissie was peevish and cold after her walk back from Little Marble Hill and would talk of nothing but Lord Duggan. Towards the evening, Bonnie saw Crawford enter Mr Moncrieff's study and then reappear, a grin twitching the edge of his mouth.

'Until a butler can be found, we have a new footman,' he whispered to Bonnie as he passed her in the hallway.

'No,' she said bitterly. 'You wouldn't.'

'I don't understand why you and Rex always fight like dogs,' Crawford said, taking the grand stairs to the entrance hall. Bonnie stayed where she was, Cissie's bonnet in her hand.

'He's a brute. You've said so yourself,' she hissed.

But Crawford only smiled as he sauntered down the stairs.

Bonnie narrowed her eyes. Now he had his beloved companion, and he might click his fingers and see anything done.

Bonnie saw Manton later, crossing the lawn. It was sunset, the sky as red as camellias. This time he had two large leather bags with him and his Sunday topper on. Just as he was about to turn the corner of the drive, he looked back once, raising his hat. For a horrifying moment she thought he had seen her and was saluting her, and she shrank back against the wall. But he wasn't; it was the house itself he was acknowledging. A flicker; a blackbird sang. And when she looked out the window again, he was gone, swallowed up by the garden, lost to the avenue of limes.

Mink

But in the days that followed Manton's departure, Bonnie found that the sting eased. Each morning, when she walked into the kitchen, Manton's empty chair was by the stove, its arms burnished auburn through decades of use. She would glance away, Cissie's pisspot slopping in her arms, and continue to the scullery to drain the pale liquid into the sink. And when she heard the hoofbeats of Mr Moncrieff returning from his morning ride, she would make herself consider all the tasks she had to do to clean up after him and his daughter, to make his life easy. His boots that needed scrubbing and blacking. His bathwater that would be grey and grimed. How must Crawford feel to see it? To be cast aside and scorned; to have his mother languish and die because she had no money, when this house flourished a short walk away.

She began to see that it had been necessary for Crawford to clear the way for them, to remove any obstacles that might stand in her path on the way to becoming Mr Moncrieff's wife. Everywhere, she would make sure to anticipate Mr Moncrieff. She would make light of it. *Why, sir, it surely isn't you again?*, or, brightly, *I should begin to think you're following me, sir*, watching as the redness spread to his ears, and he would smile.

And why shouldn't she raise herself? The world was full of such convenient arrangements, the means by which one party would slither up a few rungs. *The second Mrs Moncrieff*. It was what she wanted.

A week after Manton left, Bonnie approached Mr Moncrieff.

'The laurels are as dry as a bone,' she said. 'If you like, I can replace them with fresh cuttings, or—'

She let the suggestion hang: the removal, at last, of the final vestiges of his wife.

He paused, his shoulders hunched forwards.

'I think,' she continued carefully, 'that Cissie – she has trouble sleeping. She is plagued by thoughts of her mother. The crape – I wonder if it's too much of a reminder.'

It was true, she told herself; there was no deceit in her words.

'Take it down,' he said at last. 'Take it all down. Almost two years have passed. It is enough.'

'Certainly, sir.'

'Do you think we need a doctor?'

'Oh no, I feel sure it will pass soon.'

He exhaled. 'Compared to last year – that was a desperate time. She wouldn't attend lessons for a whole month. I think this year she is perhaps just a little subdued. In fact, I thought a change of situation might do her good and she could accompany me to London next week.' Mr Moncrieff looked at Bonnie, his gaze so clear and open. 'I must credit you with her recovery. She seems so fond of you.'

'As I am of her.'

He smiled. 'Good. That is as I hoped.'

And later, when Bonnie stood on a ladder and clouds of dust billowed from the mourning crape, a thrill ran through her. Had he agreed to have the crape and laurel removed because of his desire for her? It was a small yielding, a making space. She swept away the last of their dust and carried armfuls of dried laurels into the gardens, watching as the stable boy heaped them on a bonfire and they spat and crackled like fireworks.

On the morning that Mr Moncrieff was due to leave for his appointments in London, Bonnie dressed Cissie in her finest silk. Outside the window, she heard Crawford's voice, low and commanding, briefing Mr Moncrieff again on what to say, who to address, enquiries he should invite or avoid. Mr Moncrieff spoke more quietly, his voice lifting with questions. She could picture the furrow of his brow, the way he would scrunch up his eyes. Lately, he had seemed restless, scarcely able to answer a letter or decide on an architrave or vaulting without summoning Crawford. Every question had become a doubt. It was as though the more Crawford advised him, the smaller Mr Moncrieff became, like a fly leached by a spider.

'What will they be like, in London?' Cissie asked.

'What do you mean?' Bonnie asked, turning away from the window. She dabbed a cloth in milk and began wiping Cissie's kid-skin shoes. 'They're no different from you. We'd better hurry, hadn't we, or your father will be late?'

Her eyes were drawn back to the window, eager to see Mr Moncrieff before he left, to imprint herself on him. He had not requested any evening gowns for Cissie but that did not mean he wouldn't have plans himself. Perhaps there would be a dinner, ladies positioning themselves beside him. She and Crawford had transformed him into an enticing prospect, the cemetery marking him out as a rich man; a man to be won.

Bonnie pushed Cissie's feet into the slippers, then sat at a level with her.

'Listen, Cissie. There will be seals in London, just like there are here.' She touched Cissie's arm. 'You must guard against them carefully.'

Cissie nodded, but she was busy fiddling with a french knot on her gown. 'What if I don't look right? In the city? I might be laughed at.'

'*You*, laughed at? I should think not. And if they do, it's only because they are jealous of Lord Duggan. They know how utterly you've promised yourselves to each other, what a fine match it will be.'

Cissie reached for Bonnie's hand. 'But I'll miss you.'

'The Pawleys' maid will do your hair even better than I do, I'm certain. I'd better take more care or you'll be angling for a new Parisian lady's maid.'

'Never,' Cissie said, shaking her head violently. 'Never.'

Bonnie squeezed her hand in return, smiled. The feeling that passed through her was different from conquest or triumph. It was a heat, burrowing down inside her; a reciprocation.

'I'll miss you too,' she said. 'Now, come. Your father will be sick with impatience.'

By the time they were outside, Mr Moncrieff was already settled in the carriage, tapping out his nerves on his knee. Rex stood by the door, his eyes downcast, the buttons of his livery straining across his chest. *Like a black pudding bursting out of its skin*, Crawford had said earlier, handing him his hat to hold. Rex had flung it back.

Rex's mouth was set in a grimace, and Bonnie moved past him, helping Cissie up the steps. At the last second, the girl turned to Bonnie and thrust something into her hands.

'It's for you,' she blurted out.

It was a small flower, crafted from delicate folds of paper, each petal turned into the next.

'Oh, it's beautiful,' Bonnie said, cradling it in her palm.

A cry, a crack of the whip, and they were off, rolling down the drive, and it was only then that Bonnie realized that she had not thanked Cissie. She stared at the careful little flower, wondering over the girl making it secretly. A gift for her. She would press it between the folds of a book, treasure it.

'So they are gone,' Crawford said, emerging from the house, clapping Rex on the shoulder. He smiled, and Bonnie saw that he already had a decanter in his hand.

Crawford had sent Annette home for the afternoon and evening, *if you do not tell Mr Moncrieff*, and the house was oddly quiet when they stepped inside.

'Well, Bonnie Moncrieff,' Crawford said, his hand resting on her hip. 'What do you say to our new kingdom?'

She laughed, and he pulled her up the stairs and into the drawing room, spinning her by the hands. The room blurred, the fire in the grate a quick flash of yellow.

'My sweet Bonnie Moncrieff,' he cried, and he caught her as she almost fell. He pressed the decanter to her lips. 'Here.'

She was about to hold up her hand to stop him but the port was already glugging out. She had no choice but to drink or it would splash over the rug. It was sweet, gritty. The drink coursed through her, cocooning her. She gasped, wiped a hand across her chin.

'All this is ours,' Crawford said, sprawling on the sofa and propping his feet on the ottoman. His soles were dirty, Bonnie noted, the mud already smearing the fabric. 'Or it damned well should be.'

She watched as he surveyed the gardens through the window, his eyes heavy with desire for it all. He leaned back, tracing the outline of the ceiling moulding with his finger. A fleur-de-lis. 'When you're queen of this place, we could do this every day. Just you and me and hours and hours of time. A life of easy entertainment.'

The door opened, Rex shouldering his way in. He had removed his jacket; a mink stole was wrapped around his neck, its legs and claws hanging flat and limp. 'Look what I found. Such a pretty little thing.' He jerked its head.

'That's Mrs Moncrieff's,' Bonnie said. 'Mr Moncrieff will know if you've been in her room.'

'And?' he said, settling into the armchair beside them. He reached for the decanter, spilled some on the fur. Bonnie tried to sink back into the warm fuzziness that had enveloped her before.

'We missed you terribly, Rex,' Crawford said. 'Thank God you're here.'

'Did you?' Rex eyed him, sardonic but still hopeful. 'You know, I won't always come when you call.'

Crawford put two fingers into his mouth, whistled. 'And yet, here you are.' He laughed. 'Now, no need to sulk. I did, you know. Miss you.'

The afternoon unravelled, time slipping away. There was more wine brought from the cellar, and then the joint of ham Annette had roasted for Mr Moncrieff's return. But the wine seemed to snag on Bonnie's mood. She lay back on the sofa and stared instead at the papier-mâché ceiling, concentrating on each swirl, each gilded flower.

Mrs Moncrieff, Crawford kept calling her, and every time he did, he moved closer to her, his hand resting on her knee, her arm, her waist. It should have made her feel bright and desired, but instead a dull worry thrummed at the back of her head, like a moth trapped in her skull. The whole notion seemed suddenly absurd. Mr Moncrieff would never marry her; it was nothing more than a schoolboy plot.

'She's going to make us both rich,' Crawford said to Rex. 'How could he resist a girl as pretty and clever as her? Soon it will just be us in this house.' He put his mouth close to her ear. 'I've never loved a girl like you, Bonnie Fairchild. And it frightens me.'

He had a glass of whisky in one hand and a lit cigar in the other, and the glowing end kept drifting towards the sofa. He took a gulp of whisky and leaned closer to her. His breath brushed her cheek, as humid as the air in the greenhouse. It made her think of Mr Moncrieff, how he had asked her what she wanted and lifted the leaf from her hair, and she felt the stirrings of something close to sadness.

'Where does he keep his gun, then?' Crawford whispered.

She pretended she hadn't heard him.

'Where?' he asked, his foot teasing her leg. 'I just want to hold it. It's mine by rights, isn't it? Everything here is mine by rights.' He swooped his hand in a low arc, his drink spilling on the floor. Bonnie bent over, ready to mop it up, but Crawford caught hold of her dress, his grip rough, yanking her back. She cried out.

'You aren't a damned maid,' he hissed. 'Do you hear me? We were made to own houses like this. It's people like Mr Moncrieff who are the real thieves, who've robbed us of what's ours, and nobody says a damned thing. Nobody stops them.' He held her tight, his mouth a hair's breadth from her lips. Fear passed through her: fear that was close to desire. The thickness of his arms, how his heart ticked when she laid her head against his chest, how he had chosen her when he'd discarded a thousand other girls. 'Where's the damned gun?' he whispered.

This time when Crawford tilted the glass against her lip, Bonnie pushed him away. The room was in disarray: empty bottles rolling on their sides, the logs half-falling from the grate and filling the room with smoke. Rex had wrapped himself in one of the wall tapestries and was parading up and down. Worry edged up and down her, imagining Mr Moncrieff returning now: him and Cissie leaving early from London, walking in to find them like this. All their careful work, unpicked in an instant. Everything lying in ruins.

Crawford lurched to his feet. 'I'm going to find the gun,' he announced, his words slurring. 'I'll find it.'

Bonnie sat still on the sofa. The door slammed behind Crawford. And she realized that there was no turning back: that they were like a great weight on a hill, and they were only gathering momentum, plunging further and further down. There was wine splashed on the walls, singe marks on the rug. This house she had promised to protect. Once, she had wanted nothing more than to carve a small, contented space for herself. And now, she, Crawford and Rex were perched on its carcass like wasps, rubbing their legs in glee, taking bites out of it, gnawing it apart.

Christmas

November passed into December. The trip to London had been a success, a flurry of letters arriving from MPs offering their support for the cemetery, full of subtle insinuations of what they might expect in return. The matter would be debated in Parliament, but until then, they could do nothing but stall the more expensive building work until they received approval. Each day, the post cart drove up to the house, and each day Mr Moncrieff shook his head and they all fell back to their work. Snow sugared the grounds, just a light sifting that the wind soon stirred from the trees. When the pond froze, Annette and Bonnie broke up the slabs of ice with an axe and carried them to the ice house, the brick walls reverberating with that thick *crack crack crack*. They did not speak. Bonnie watched Annette's body arcing with each blow of the axe; the strength in it, her wide hips, her breasts that pressed against her coat. *Fecund*, that was the word for her. Bonnie looked down at her own slim hips and kicked a wedge of ice, watching as it split and shattered.

But for all that, Christmas seemed to draw them all together, flattening their differences. Mr Moncrieff helped them saw down great heaps of yew and pine and holly and heft it back to the house, the scent of resin filling every room. It was too early for decorations, but Cissie insisted on it, walking from room to room and instructing where things might go. Paper chains swung from dado rails. Bunches of mistletoe now hung where mourning had once been, Josephine tidied away.

'I'm going to embroider Papa a handkerchief for Christmas,' Cissie announced one afternoon. It was three weeks before Christmas and she and Bonnie were in Richmond to buy oranges for Annette's mincemeat. Cissie lingered beside a shop window, stuffed with frothy bonnets and neat gloves, calfskin volumes of Sir Walter Scott. 'Mama used to take me here each year,' she said wistfully. 'She would let me have anything I pleased.'

'Your father would like the handkerchief,' Bonnie said, drawing her away. 'You might embroider Zephyr on it.'

Cissie smiled and agreed; they dawdled through the town, down to the towpath. The river was half-frozen, swans squalling, and as they walked back to Endellion, Cissie threw questions at Bonnie. It was a game she liked to play called, *would you still love me if?* What a thing it must be, Bonnie thought, to feel you could ask for affection so brazenly.

'Would you still love me if,' Cissie asked, 'I had yellow toes and you had to wash them each morning?'

'Of course,' Bonnie replied, her arm linked through Cissie's, their footsteps chiming on the icy path. 'Though I might try to trim them.'

'Would you still love me if I had a beak big enough to eat you?'

Bonnie paused. 'What an odd question! Would you be a bird or just have a beak?'

'Just a beak,' Cissie confirmed.

Though now Bonnie thought about it, there was something graceless and fledgling-like about Cissie: perhaps it was how she swung her limbs in an exaggerated way, her feet hitting the path too heavily, her hair frizzing from the edge of her bonnet like down. She was a pup yet to grow into its paws. 'As long as you didn't actually eat me,' Bonnie replied. 'I should think so.'

Cissie darted her mouth towards Bonnie's coat, bit hard on the wool, and Bonnie laughed and pushed her away.

'Is that the post cart?' Cissie asked, pointing to a coach in front of the house. Steam billowed from the horse's nostrils. 'Do you think it might be about the cemetery?'

'Let's see,' Bonnie said, hurrying across the lawn. She took the letter from the boy. She could tell immediately that it was something important from the thick dappled paper and the crest pressed into the wax.

She threw open the main door, Cissie fussing around her. Their excitement must have caught in the air because soon Crawford and Rex were there, calling for Mr Moncrieff. He emerged from his study, his shadow magnified by the low lantern. 'What is it?' he asked, hurrying down the stairs. 'Do you think—'

'I don't know,' Bonnie said, holding it out to him.

His hand shook as he took it from her, his paperknife snagging against the seal.

'It is—' he began.

Bonnie saw how Crawford strained to read the letter, and she too was on tiptoes, Cissie repeating, *What does it say, Papa, what does it say?* But Mr Moncrieff shielded it from all of them, his eyes ricocheting from line to line. He bit his lip and crumpled the letter into a ball.

'Well?' Crawford asked.

He exhaled slowly and said, 'I believe – I believe permission has been granted. For the cemetery company and the use of these grounds.'

'Papa!' Cissie exclaimed.

Bonnie leaned forwards as Crawford thumped Mr Moncrieff's

back, then rang the bell for Annette. 'Bring the finest champagne,' he instructed her, his chest puffed out.

Bonnie thought Mr Moncrieff would mind Crawford giving orders, but he didn't seem to notice. He looked a little stunned, almost uncomfortable, as though his limbs were suddenly too big for him. 'I don't think I truly believed it until now,' he said quietly. 'My plans will be built. Josephine will have her fine mausoleum. And it was your idea.'

It took Bonnie a moment to realize he was addressing her. He stepped forwards and reached for her hand. The instant their fingers met, he seemed to reconsider it, plunging his fists into his pockets. He gave a small shake of his head. 'It was all because of you, Bonnie. You began all this.'

She shifted, her skin goosefleshed. She did not know how to answer such raw gratitude.

'Champagne!' Crawford clapped his hands and the hubbub returned to the room once more, Cissie springing up and down on the balls of her feet, Mr Moncrieff shying away from any congratulations. 'And now we must begin real preparations for the shoot,' Crawford said. He led Mr Moncrieff to a chair. 'There is not a moment to spare. There is so much to be done! So much to begin.'

'Yes,' Mr Moncrieff said, and Bonnie saw how cleanly he met Crawford's gaze, the tremor gone from his hands. 'I thought, rather than a shoot, we might use the pack from Ham. A hunt. I shouldn't think they'd mind holding one of their Saturday meets on our land, and we can spill across to Marble Hill or Orleans if needed.'

Crawford glanced at Bonnie. He gave a quick shake of his head, his smile stopping short of his eyes. 'A hunt? Oh no. Sir, I think a shoot—'

'No,' Mr Moncrieff interrupted, gentle but firm. 'I've given this some thought. A hunt is the way to show off the land. I can't help finding the rattle of guns to be incongruous, distasteful even, when our cemetery is all about peace and beauty.'

There was a pause; Crawford cleared his throat. But Moncrieff kept speaking, a new conviction and urgency in his voice. 'We will hold it in February. The first Saturday. We need to hold it soon in order to secure our shareholders, but it also allows us enough time to prepare. The neighbouring houses must all be invited. The company of directors will want to attend too, of course. I'm sure that they will have people of influence to invite. I will write to them at once, inform them.'

He stood, his fingers agitating his waistcoat buttons.

'I will assist you,' Crawford said, but Mr Moncrieff waved him back.

'No need.' He stood, his heels clipping across the tiles, Cissie following him. 'No need.'

Crawford's shoulders sagged as though the air had been let out of him. He reached for the letter that Mr Moncrieff had left on the table, frowning as he read.

'It says here,' Crawford called after him, a catch in his voice. 'It names the company of directors.'

'Yes,' Mr Moncrieff said, pausing on the stairs. 'There is me, of course. Joseph Eland trained at Kew and Cambridge Botanic Gardens. He's an old friend from my university days. And then there are two MPs, including the gentleman who represents Richmond, and two men of industry.'

The paper rustled in Crawford's grip. Mr Moncrieff's study door slammed shut behind him and Cissie. It had not even occurred to Mr Moncrieff to include Crawford as a director. For just a moment, Crawford's face changed: his chin raised in supplication, his mouth twisted in raw anguish.

'Crawford,' Bonnie whispered, touching his arm. 'That was rotten. That was—'

'Please don't.' He brushed her away. 'I'm just a maid's brother, aren't I? Just a wretch who grew up on the barges. Soon he'll have no use for me and I'll be cast out.'

'Don't say that.'

'But it's true. For as long as we're here, in *service*, that's how they see us.' He turned to her. 'Shouldn't you chase after that brat? Wipe her nose? Empty the shit from her pot?'

Bonnie took a step back. 'This isn't *my* fault. You needn't snap at me.'

'No,' he said, softening. He took her hand. 'It isn't you at all.'

That night, she crept downstairs to his cellar room. He had moved into Manton's quarters, put Rex in the smaller room he'd once slept in. He held out his arms and she collapsed into them. Relief flooded her, that everything between them seemed to have slipped back into its usual groove. She loved him fearfully, ferociously; she felt like a jug filled to the brim.

'My love,' she said, kissing his cheeks, his forehead, his shoulders, in little tight pecks, until he laughed. He moved onto his side and she wrapped her arms around him, sliding her palms over the wide stones of his shoulder blades. She loved this part of him more than anything else. When she saw him dressing in the morning and they lifted and parted, she could not look away. *Blades.* The word, too, seemed to fit. The perfect unison of them. She burrowed against him. His heartbeat echoed in her own ears, welding her to him. One heart, the size of a fist, beating for both of them.

'We're the same, Bonnie,' he whispered. 'We understand each other. Nobody else can.'

Bonnie nodded. Crawford, who kept himself so distant from others, wanted *her*. Trusted her. Annette faded to a pinprick.

'We'll have this house, won't we?' she whispered. 'It will be ours, as it should be.'

'Yes,' Crawford breathed.

'And Mr Moncrieff?' she asked.

Crawford kissed her on the mouth. 'We needn't think about him at all.'

There were only two weeks until Christmas, but labourers flocked from as far afield as Hounslow and Kingston to assist in digging the foundations of the cemetery. When Bonnie walked to the pasture one morning, she found the nettles and brambles were all cleared away, a huge bonfire smoking. The ground was nothing but bare earth, men bent over as they rammed and compacted the pathways that were marked with string and canes. Mr Moncrieff saw her, saluted. He was alone.

'Is my brother here?' Bonnie asked.

Mr Moncrieff shifted. 'He hasn't been here for a few days. He says he has other letters to write but I think perhaps – I think his interest is not as it once was.'

Bonnie watched him. 'Why do you think that might be?'

'I couldn't say.'

How couldn't he see how badly he had treated Crawford? Declaring him invaluable one instant, then cutting him out of the directorship the next. She knew Crawford: how quickly he would withdraw if he wasn't valued or celebrated.

Mr Moncrieff shifted from one foot to the other. 'But might I show you what we have done? It is all still early, of course, but it all looks so changed. And I can *see* it.'

They walked through the muddy field, Mr Moncrieff's voice rising as he pointed out the progress they had made. 'There will be pathways, here, dozens of them, snaking in lines so that each grave can be reached. Those men are digging earthworks for the walls. More than half a mile of them! Stretching all around the perimeter.'

Mud gummed to Bonnie's boots and flicked up her cloak, but she did not care. Her breath was tight in her lungs: all the potential that lurked in this grey earth, just waiting to be layered with cypresses and cherry trees, with ornately carved stones and towering mausoleums. 'This is where the chapel will be built,' Mr Moncrieff said, holding out his arms, and she thought how the ground under their feet would soon be covered with paved stone and arched windows, with neat pews and a pulpit. A vault would be dug beneath it, the dead stacked neatly.

'It's all starting to feel so solid,' she said.

'Isn't it? Just wait until it progresses.'

'I've only ever seen small things being built. My father once built us a summerhouse.' The reminder was careful, though it seemed offhand: *I am not as low as I appear.*

'Did you ride as a girl?'

'A little. My brother and I had our own horses. Why?'

'I thought,' he said quietly, not looking at her. 'I thought that – this might seem out of place. I might be – it might be too much.'

'What is it?' She leaned forward.

'I thought – perhaps you might like to join us on the hunt. I'm sure Cissie will have a spare habit you can borrow. It would just be a small acknowledgement – a small way of expressing my gratitude for all you've done. If you hadn't suggested the cemetery and cajoled me into drawing it, then none of this would exist.'

'I would like that,' Bonnie said. 'I would like that very much.' She was filled with the sudden urge to find Crawford and tell him about the invitation. But she composed herself, walked as close to Mr Moncrieff as she could. Every time they swung their arms, she could feel the breeze of his hand as it passed hers.

'It's going to be extraordinary,' Mr Moncrieff said. 'We will make it so.'

'She would be pleased, wouldn't she?'

She watched him carefully for any flicker of guilt. Silence; and then —

'I think so. Yes.'

Mr Moncrieff looked at Bonnie, his head tilted, and there was so much eagerness in his eyes, so much belief and hope, that she had to glance away. She should eke out this moment, she knew, find a way to corral and guide it into something bigger, but for once she just wanted to *be*. To stand in this cemetery and imagine all that Mr Moncrieff would build, all that she had suggested.

On Christmas Day, they played parlour games, Mr Moncrieff drawing out a bowl of brandy-soaked raisins. He took a taper from the fire.

'Are you ready?' he asked.

'Hurry up, Papa!' Cissie cried.

He lit the bowl, the fire blue and shining. They shrieked as they fought to pick out as many raisins as they could, the heat scorching their fingers. Annette and Rex quickly sat back, nursing their burned hands, and even Crawford shook his thumb and laughed, bowing his defeat. But Cissie did not stop: she calmly scooped her hands through the flames, plucking out each black, shrivelled raisin, until there were none left.

'Your hands must be made of metal,' Annette exclaimed.

But Bonnie saw the blisters already forming on Cissie's palms, her fingers pink and swollen.

'It's just a case of forgetting the pain,' Cissie said. 'Just – putting it from your mind. But I triumphed, didn't I? I *won*.' She turned to her father. 'What do I win, Papa?'

'Eternal glory,' Mr Moncrieff replied.

'But I can't wear *that* on a walk with Emmeline.'

Mr Moncrieff tousled her hair, as Bonnie overheard Annette whispering to Rex, 'That was Manton's favourite game. He was the only one who could rival her.'

Was there bitterness in Annette's voice? Crawford must have heard her too, because Bonnie saw how carefully he drew her into the circle, touching her arm. Annette smiled, pressing herself closer to Crawford. *Fool*, Bonnie thought, as she sucked her burned finger. *Fool.*

'Now for my gifts to you all,' Mr Moncrieff announced, clapping his hands.

He hurried away, returning with a tray laden with brightly wrapped boxes. He handed them out shyly: lace collars and cuffs for Annette, a hat with a feather for Crawford, a work basket for Rex. They smiled and thanked him, the men shaking his hand, Annette kissing his cheek. And then it was Bonnie's turn. Mr Moncrieff's hair had fallen in front of his eyes. He thrust the gift at her, so fast she almost dropped it.

It was smaller than the other gifts. Bonnie peeled back the paper slowly.

'Hurry up,' Annette said. 'I want to *see*.'

'It's just a small thing,' he said, hastily, but his voice lifted in anticipation.

Silence fell. A brooch tumbled onto her lap. It was silver, set with a shining ammonite.

'Oh!' Annette exclaimed.

'That's—' Crawford began, but stopped.

Bonnie could feel embarrassment radiating from Mr Moncrieff. It was too much, far too much, and he must have realized it too. Annette picked at her lace cuffs, frowning. Bonnie could have put him at ease. She could have said something to diffuse the atmosphere, but she decided to let his discomfort curdle a little longer. She had seen in Crawford how powerful silence could be: its pressure unravelling a person, making them misstep.

'I'd be ruined if it wasn't for the cemetery,' Mr Moncrieff said quickly. 'If it wasn't for you.'

'It's beautiful,' she said, pinning it against her chest. She had fastened so many of Josephine's brooches to her dress and Mr Moncrieff had had no idea. 'My father once gave me a brooch just like it, when Crawford and I were children.'

'It's – it's really just a small gesture,' he said again. 'Nothing much.'

The others had embraced him after receiving their gifts. It was expected, the right thing to do. Mr Moncrieff stood, his hands awkward at his side, and she picked her way across the scattered paper towards him. Nobody spoke; she heard the bob of his throat as he swallowed. He meant to kiss her cheek, but she turned too quickly, and his lips brushed her ear instead.

'Oh!' he exclaimed, stumbling back, a heat spreading up his neck. 'I apologize. I—'

She clasped her ear. She could feel her lobe burning, could still feel the warm trace of his lips, their surprising softness.

'Close,' Crawford whispered when she sat down. 'So close.'

Bonnie shook her head to silence him. But for all that, she knew he was right. She could feel the line tightening, a stillness in the air. She just had to draw back, make Mr Moncrieff come to her. He had to believe it was all his own idea.

The Hunt

Six weeks passed and finally the day of the hunt neared. The kitchens became a storm of cooking and baking, the air glittering with tossed flour, the floor tacky with spilled fat. Servants were lent from neighbouring houses, and downstairs grew full of noise, of scoldings and laughter. Chicken livers were boiled and mashed into pâtés, pristine salmon tartlets brushed with egg, snipe encased in golden rissoles.

The night before the hunt, Bonnie sat in the kitchen peeling two hundred quail eggs, scooping them cleanly from their speckled shells. Upstairs, she could hear the creak of the floor-boards as Mr Moncrieff paced back and forth. She could picture his agitation, the way he would be pulling on his buttons, twisting them until the thread snapped. Bonnie had a quick urge to go to him: to take his hands and raise them to her mouth and kiss them. To calm him like she would calm a horse, a child in distress. Her fingers paused on the spoon, the egg she was holding sent tumbling to the ground. The yolk bled over the tiles. Even the thought was a betrayal, was it not? A border crossed into another country. A fluttering began in her breast-bone, as though tiny wings were beating against her chest. The next day seemed to grow teeth, to snarl at her. Across the room, Crawford caught her eye, and she glanced quickly away.

But when she stepped into Cissie's riding habit on the

following morning, a coolness swept over her. She held back her shoulders as Annette lifted the skirt over her hips, the maid's mouth tight and small. She did not speak, but her fingernails grazed Bonnie's skin, leaving a narrow scratch across Bonnie's stomach.

'But why are *you* joining them—' Annette burst out at last, but Bonnie cut her off.

'Thank you, Annette,' she said with the grandeur of a lady, and the maid shrank back, straightening her cap. 'That will be all.'

When Bonnie tried to walk, the gown was leaden, the neat black hat obscuring her vision. She felt ornamental, waterlogged, her feet stirring the fabric like paddles. Her reflection wavered in the looking glass.

She simply had to believe in her own artifice, to believe in the girl in the navy riding habit, wearing a pert little hat, her hair swept back.

Bonnie Moncrieff, she mouthed at the mirror, and the girl in the fine gown smiled back at her.

She could already hear chatter and laughter drifting up the staircase. The company of directors had arrived. She wished Cissie was beside her but Cissie had been agitated, scarcely able to attend her lessons: twice the doctor had been called. Josephine's name had been whispered in hallways; Mr Moncrieff had checked on her several times a day, sat with her as the sun lowered each afternoon. But it was only Bonnie who had been able to make a difference, Bonnie who had swept into her bedroom and insisted Cissie join her for a walk. She had stared at Cissie's pale cheeks, the way she held her hand against her forehead in a gesture of wan weakness. 'This isn't you,' Bonnie had said, shaking off the covers. 'Starving yourself won't help. You have more resolve than this. I know you do.' And Cissie had stood mutely and followed Bonnie into the cold winter air. Together, they had found old conkers, feathers, a blackbird's discarded nest, and Cissie had gathered them in a basket, her footsteps lighter. Mr Moncrieff had rushed out to join them when he saw them from his study, and he had smiled at Bonnie, thanked her quietly.

But for all that, no wheedling would make Cissie join the hunt, and so Bonnie had no choice but to enter the room alone. She steeled herself, a hand on the banister. One step, then another, the light so low and pink. Her fingers sweated in her lace gloves, the fabric stretched so tight they felt like the porcelain hands of a doll.

She sidled into the drawing room. A sea of red coats, of slicked-back hair, a wall of laughter. Glasses of port glinted like little vials of blood. If she were Crawford, she would know how to ensure she was drawn into the crowd, to ingratiate herself. But *the Highgate man* was hiding in a public house in Richmond for the day, afraid he would be exposed. She wished, suddenly, that she had not come; that she was down in the kitchen pouring drinks or wiping flour from the table, that all of this was the distant hubbub of another sphere.

Mr Moncrieff moved through the crowd towards her and she held herself back, waiting for a flicker of approval as he took in her fine riding habit. But his eyes landed on her only briefly. 'Well,' he said, and cleared his throat. He looked as awkward as a schoolboy, his hair neatly combed. 'Come, there is a gentleman you must meet.' He steered her across the room, introducing her to a slight man with greying whiskers. 'Mr Eland. He's been charged with landscaping the cemetery. I hope you won't mind, but I've taken the liberty of showing him your plans.' He paused, watching her anxiously. 'He says there is much to admire.'

'Did he?' Bonnie asked, flushing. 'Did he really?' But when she glanced back at Mr Moncrieff, she found he was already gone, drawn into another conversation.

'Your plans interested me,' Mr Eland said, taking a sip of wine. 'Especially your use of evergreens. In my mind, they are best suited to the solemnity, to the unchanging aspect of a cemetery, don't you think?'

It took her a moment to adjust to this short eager man. 'That's why I chose them,' she said at last. 'So in winter there will always be colour, like a little flash of hope.'

'Monkey puzzles are also a favourite of mine. And I've found that there is a certain class of American evergreens that flourishes with surprising luxuriance in this part of England. I am excited to introduce them to Endellion.' He leaned closer. 'But tell me, where did you acquire your horticultural knowledge? When Mr Moncrieff mentioned you had drawn plans, I'm ashamed to say I expected mere scribblings. There is much to amend, of course, but they are full of ideas that I hope to incorporate.'

'My father tended the gardens – I mean,' she coughed. 'He had an interest in gardens. We had our own land.' A momentary lapse: but what did Mr Eland know of her past, either real or invented? She listened carefully as he spoke, and in turn he talked to her as though he expected her to understand him. She found herself telling him about the greenhouse she had revived, the orchids and ferns she had planted there.

'I have my own hothouse in Kensington. You ought to visit. I'll mention it to Mr Moncrieff.'

'Oh, I'd like that very much,' she said.

Other directors jostled Mr Eland, insisted he introduce them to Bonnie. Annette and Rex often appeared with decanters, and the men kept talking as though their glasses were magically refilling with port. Bonnie supposed that was how it was for gentlemen like them: clean clothes perpetually in their closets, fresh meals arriving on their tables, their mess wiped up, whisked away. It should have made Bonnie feel important that they had noticed her; no longer the invisible maid, shrinking into the wainscoting. But she was in disguise, that was all. This dress was not her. She might as well have been Zephyr, dressed up on Bonnie's first day at Endellion, the velvet cap perched forlornly over his ears.

The men blurred into each other and she struggled to differentiate them: there was an MP, yellow-toothed, surprisingly short, who spoke in gasping hyperboles. Everything was *astonishing*, his hopes *almighty*; the site was *utterly triumphant*, his gestures so extravagant he almost toppled another gentleman's wine. A second MP – this one gaunt, laconic – imparted information that *ought to stay confidential* that he had heard the Duke of Haveringham had already reserved six plots; that over forty thousand pounds' worth of shares had been sold.

'Forty thousand pounds,' Bonnie repeated, wondering if Mr Moncrieff had been told.

'Hush,' he said, and placed a finger on his lips. He winked. 'I didn't breathe a word.'

Bonnie was glad when the crowd began to move outside. Shouts, cries; the yap of hounds. Glossy horses were led forward by footmen, some owned by the local houses, others ridden all the way from London or hired from nearby inns. Red coats shone in the morning sun. A groom she did not know handed Cissie's horse, Boudicca, to Bonnie, and she accepted the reins, climbed the mounting block. As a girl, she had always ridden the mares with a gentleman's saddle, her legs astride their backs. But this gleaming side-saddle was new to her, its pommel like a leering tongue: she glanced at the other ladies, tried to position her legs as they had, but she felt like she was on the brink of tumbling to the ground. She dug her buttocks in more firmly, settled back. 'Good girl,' she said to Boudicca. 'Good girl. You won't buck me off, will you?'

She had never been to a hunt before, though they had thundered past her enough times: horns blowing, the villagers waving handkerchiefs to cheer them on. She tried to look at ease, tried to hide the fact her collar was too tight and she longed to undo a button. The horse shifted under her. And where was Mr Moncrieff? She glimpsed him in a crowd of other gentlemen, seemingly at ease, taking a swig from his flask. Of all the ways she had imagined the day disintegrating – a fall, an accident – Mr Moncrieff was always there, aware of her, watching. She had not counted on his indifference. She might as well have stayed inside for all the attention he had paid her. And why had she thought it would be otherwise? *Stupid*, she rebuked herself, sitting higher in the saddle. *Stupid.*

The horn sounded and the hounds set off at once, chattering, noses to the ground, desperate to find the scent. Other riders began to stir, slowly at first, just keeping level with the pack. Bonnie nudged her whip against the horse's flank and to her relief, Boudicca moved as she commanded, a walk that soon became a trot. She could do this, she thought, those days at Highwell returning to her: hair unravelling, the wind so sharp, the sting of small flies hitting her cheeks. They headed into the woodlands, past the pond and the greenhouse. The gentle pace made it easy for Bonnie to find her balance, to realize that she ought to sit with her weight in the middle of the saddle rather than listing towards the right. The hounds doubled back; the horses did too.

'The pack's useless,' she heard a gentleman say. 'I heard that more hounds have been mashed on the roads than they've killed foxes this season. We might as well try to catch a vixen with a fishing line.'

And Bonnie found she was relieved. If there was no chase, there would be no risk of falling, no humiliation. The day would peter into disappointment. That night, she and Crawford would lick their wounds together, and he would whisper into her hair that he knew she had tried, that sometimes a plan simply did not work.

The horn blew again, a long high note. Bonnie startled, almost dropping her whip. The hounds had caught a scent. All was activity, fury. Some of the riders scattered to find a different line, all pressing, pushing, urging their horses into a gallop, racing down the grassy serpentine paths behind the hounds, eager to see a flash of rust streaking across the lawns. Bonnie found she didn't need to urge Boudicca on, that she was already breaking from a trot to a canter, and Bonnie gripped the reins, the pommel held tight between her legs. A new determination took hold: that she would make Mr Moncrieff notice her. She would ride alongside him. She would not let the day slip away.

She saw him ahead of her, his horsemanship deft, quick. She pressed Boudicca into a gallop, almost slipping in the side-saddle, but she caught herself, let out a cry of delight. It was not so different from riding astride. Sweat started to grease Boudicca's hide.

The hounds scrambled under the fence to Marble Hill; no choice but to follow them, over the top. Boudicca leaped forwards, stumbled, and Bonnie lurched, clinging to the pommel. She had not fallen. The earth was dry, frosted, bone-breaking, the horse's hooves a hard staccato beat; she drew closer to Mr Moncrieff, Boudicca falling into the same pattern as his own mare. He had seen her, Bonnie was sure of it. She need only draw abreast with him. She would show him how able she was, how accomplished: how she could ride just as well as any of the other ladies.

The horn sounded again, the hounds doubling back towards the grounds of Endellion, and as the breeze rushed past her, the chimneys of Ham House smoking across the river, Bonnie found herself smiling, settling into the rhythm of Boudicca's canter, daring to edge her back into a gallop.

She lost Mr Moncrieff briefly; glimpsed him again, closer this time. She could tell by the way he strained forward just how much he wanted this day to go well, and it echoed like a drumbeat in her own chest. Forty thousand pounds' worth of shares! And that was before the day was begun. She wished she had seen his face when he'd been told, that he had turned to her and they had shared the moment together.

She saw the fox suddenly, streaking across the lawns of Endellion.

'There!' she cried. 'There it is!'

And Mr Moncrieff turned and saw her. She drew her horse level with him, skimming a low hedge, the rush of wind freeing her.

'It's magnificent, isn't it? Endellion, in this sun!'

He nodded, and the relief of being able to talk to him crashed over her. His face too broke into a smile, his cheeks rosy with exertion. He loped slightly when he walked, but on horseback he might have been a different man: his body fitted to the mare, his thighs strained tight, his hair whipping around his ears. His cravat had loosened a little and she saw a slender strip of muscle reaching from the back of his neck to his hairline; she wanted to touch it. She leaned closer to Boudicca, feeling the horse's ribcage heaving against her leg.

This time, he did not draw ahead; this time, they rode side by side, and elation sung through her. She rode wildly, faster than she'd ever dared before, bracing herself as she vaulted low hedges, whacking her foot on a branch. The pain, easily swallowed, regaining her rhythm. It was as though the fox had known that Endellion was the right place for the hunt to end, drawing the day into a neat circle. The spires of Richmond shone in the distance, a cow drinking at the river's edge, the dappled beige and brown of hounds flying past.

'There!' she cried.

She saw it in a flash: the dirty white tip of the fox's brush, darting into thick woodland near the greenhouse, pack scrambling after it. The fox would be sheltering in the trees, perhaps under a tangle of brambles, too thorny for the hounds to enter without tearing their faces and paws. If it had gone to ground, they would send in terriers to flush it out, and it might bolt into the open, quickly outpaced by the pack, a clean kill they could all watch.

Bonnie waited on the lawn, drawing her horse back. She could see that others were catching up with them – the tall MP, flushed and sweating – and soon they would all mass together. Behind her was the house; before her was the narrow path that led to the river.

'Come,' she said to Boudicca suddenly, urging her forwards. She felt sure that Mr Moncrieff would follow and sure enough, she heard the stirring of his horse behind her, the hard crump of hooves on the grass, the rapid snorting of its nostrils. Her chest thundered, a metallic taste in her throat. On she went, not daring to glance back, not until she arrived at a copse near Annette's cottage. She slipped from her horse, and he too leapt from his mare.

They stood there, facing each other, neither moving. His arms were slack at his sides as though he did not know what to do with them, all his ease in the saddle gone. She was still out of breath, and he was too, his chest heaving. What was she to say to him? It was best, surely, that she left him to find a way to fill this pause; but the silence clamoured, roared. All that might be said or left unspoken.

He cleared his throat. 'I – I would often walk here when I was feeling wretched. I – I sometimes felt that I was a poor custodian of Endellion. That I should have looked after it better.'

Bonnie's knees felt shaky after the ride.

'But doesn't everything vanish in the end?' he continued, looking everywhere but at her. 'One day this house will fall, leaving no trace. But for now it matters, doesn't it? To us at least.' He raked his hand through his hair. 'What am I saying? I'm just – I just—' He looked at her at last. The gold circles in his eyes caught the light. 'I just find I'm so unsure of myself. So uncertain of what to do. What is right.'

The riding habit was so tight, so hot. Sweat gathered at the back of her neck. What was she to say to such disarming honesty? She took a step towards him, just the slightest shuffle. He was close enough, now, that she could have reached out and touched his chest. She could see the glimmer of heat on his brow, a small port stain on the edge of his bottom lip. His dark hair was streaked with a few strands of grey.

'I—' she began.

His hand was shaking as he placed it on the small of her back, drawing her closer to him. She felt the pressure of his thumb, his fingers moving so slightly against her.

'Bonnie,' he murmured, his eyes half-shut. His chest rose and fell. 'Bonnie. If you knew—'

Her head clouded. This was everything she had wanted: it was why she had led him away from the other gentlemen. And yet, it felt all wrong, one of Crawford's schemes that had run away from him. She thought of the gentlemen at the inns; of

Crawford's mother, fleeing the house as her belly swelled, destitute. She could not do it any longer. She stepped back abruptly. He raised his hand to his mouth.

'My God,' he murmured. 'Bonnie, forgive me. I didn't mean—'

She could not look at him.

'Please, Bonnie, I can't have been thinking—'

Bonnie could not meet his eye. He was already categorizing it as a mistake, an error. *She* was an error. A choke in her throat, her thoughts tangled. It was all lost, she thought: she had shamed him. It was the worst thing she might have done. And when she spoke, she found her words were sharp-edged, furious. 'I am not a wretch to use as you please!' she burst out.

He flinched, aghast, his cheeks inflamed with sudden heat.

'No,' he said, a break in his voice. 'I would never—'

He did not get to do this. To make gentlemanly amends, to tidy her out of sight. Everything would be changed now, unpicked. Every tender look and touch. The closeness that had sprung up between them, his excitement as he showed her the cemetery, hands held wide. *This is where the chapel will be built.*

'I cannot stay here. I – I should leave.' Her words tumbled out, and it was only then that she saw the truth in them, how wild everything had grown, the ground slipping away from her. How she no longer wanted to be part of any of this.

'You can't,' Mr Moncrieff said. His voice creaked and she saw that his eyes were filling with tears. 'I won't ruin this too.' Above them, the trees clattered in the breeze. 'Bonnie. I – I will marry you, then.'

The sky seemed to swing down towards her. *Marry.* Her hands fell to her sides. *Marry.*

'I will be a better husband to you, I swear it,' he said.

The shape of Josephine, faint, at the edge of her eyes. This woman who had drowned; who Crawford said Mr Moncrieff had killed. 'Bonnie. I will. If you will accept me.'

Her head ached. She raised her fingers to her brow. She was meant to accept. He was waiting for her to accept. And she did, a small nod, almost imperceptible. He reached for her hands, clutched them. A cheer went up. Bonnie thought at first that it was for her and Mr Moncrieff, that others had followed them and understood what had happened. But as they stumbled onto the lawns, the horn sounded, longer this time, and there was the huntsman, grasping the limp red body. The roar went up again, louder, the hounds whining and yapping.

'Bravo!' Mr Moncrieff shouted, and his eyes were wet and shining as he kissed Bonnie's hand. 'Bravo!'

The fox was too mutilated to stuff whole. The huntsman hacked off the tail and tossed the body amongst the hounds, and Bonnie had the perverse thought that if she had not led Mr Moncrieff into that copse, if she had not leapt from Boudicca, the fox would still be sheltering in a deep tunnel, its heart still beating, its brain ticking with fear, the dogs pawing uselessly at the entrance.

Mr Moncrieff kissed her on the cheek and she knew she should say something, should lean towards him. They were all playing a part, weren't they, him a gallant hero, rescuing her from a life of drudgery, restoring her to the place he thought she had fallen from? He would be a *better* husband; through her, he would make amends for what had happened to Josephine. And she and Crawford had designed all this, plotted it as carefully as one of Mr Moncrieff's architectural plans. So why, then, did she feel so taken aback, so frightened?

The trees on the horizon were still, stripped of leaves, and Bonnie had to stare at them for fear she might be sick.

Part Five

What God Hath Joined Together

It was the poppies that Bonnie noticed first. Blood-red and blowsy, hanging from the entrance of the chapel. She had only cream in her bouquet: pale roses and tightly furled ranunculi that she had grown from bulbs.

If she stared intently at the poppies, she could almost forget Crawford's thigh shifting against her own, his soft smell of pipe smoke and peppermint. The cart jolted; the bells pealed. He moved his foot against her pink slipper. And in an instant, she was transported back to that very first evening at the Angler. He had appeared in the doorway, shaking the rain from his oilcloth coat, a pair of silk slippers in his hand. He had searched the room for her and when his eyes found hers, it was as though a bright light were shining on her alone.

But there was no undoing matters now. Mr Moncrieff – *Aubrey*, he now insisted on being called – would be waiting in that small stone chapel, the stained glass slicing vivid colours across his new coat. Would he also be thinking of another time? Of Josephine, lingering in the porch, readying herself for the moment the wooden door was thrust open?

It had felt as though Josephine had been there, too, when they'd told Cissie. 'Mama,' she'd whispered, tentatively, as though seeing if the word could be applied to Bonnie. *Mama*; it had felt to Bonnie like putting on a warm and familiar coat. She'd reached out and kissed the top of Cissie's head. The girl had closed her eyes, squeezed Bonnie's hand.

'Will I do as a seal?' Bonnie had asked.

'Oh but you aren't a seal at all. You are a different species altogether.' Cissie had taken her father's hand. 'Might we ride to Hampton, the three of us, one afternoon? I think I feel so much better in myself now.'

'There will be a new mistress of Endellion,' Aubrey had told the rest of the household. His phrasing was as stilted as his delivery. A heat had passed through her. A new mistress, layered over the woman who came before her. She'd watched Aubrey's hands, seeing if she could imagine him snapping, losing control. It seemed both impossible and frighteningly plausible: perhaps he too understood how easy a thing murder could be given the right circumstances, the right anger, the right fear.

'A new mistress?' Annette had repeated, and then when Aubrey had gestured at Bonnie, she'd blinked, shaken her head slightly. Rex, his mouth set, had given nothing away, but Crawford had rushed forwards and pumped Aubrey's hand. '*Brother*,' he had said. 'If I may be so bold.' Perhaps only Bonnie had realized how squarely the word had landed, the punch in Crawford's voice as he had said it. And he'd turned to Bonnie, nodded, as though certain that his plans could only ever be pristinely executed.

'When you are married, we will go to Rome and Venice,' Cissie had said, later in the evening. 'Papa will take us, will you not? Oh, say it will be so.'

'First the cemetery must be finished,' Aubrey had replied. 'And then, why shouldn't we?' Sprawled in his chair, he had told Bonnie about the sights he wanted to show her. The Venetian Gothic architecture with its Byzantine and Islamic influence, the city shaped by its position as a trading port and all the cultures that passed through its waters. He would take her to the Basilica San Marco, and then onwards to Rome where —

'My brother must accompany us. He's always wanted to see Italy,' she had replied, and Aubrey had nodded in a way that seemed uncertain.

'And the Campanile!' Cissie added. 'We can climb it, see for miles.'

The cemetery seemed to keep time as the months ticked past, and spring and early summer shone out. She began to recall not the date a certain thing happened, but when it was according to how far the building work had progressed. When Aubrey had spoken about Bonnie's new room, she recalled only the sight of the clay tile drains being sealed in the soil. He had explained that the house had not been built for family life, and as she knew there were few bedrooms: he had no choice but to offer her Josephine's old room. A quiet had fallen over them, the only sound the scrape of the labourers' shovels against the earth, the pipes gradually heaped with soil.

She had told Aubrey she didn't mind, but later, she had let herself into Josephine's room. Every crevice was full of her. Was it here that Josephine had read the letters she'd found in the greenhouse? She might have fallen back against the bed, her blood hot. There might have been grass in her hair, leaves snagged in her collar: a sharp memory of another snatched liaison. And always, she would have been unaware of what lay in wait for her, how it would all end.

On the day Bonnie was measured for her trousseau, the first trees were planted on the edges of the paths. Mr Eland had laughed as she bent her back against the spade, the labourers watching her with puzzlement. Taurian pines, he had explained, grow rapidly and narrowly; they wouldn't occupy space that might be used for graves.

He'd stopped, pointing at the carriage that raced down the drive. 'Who is that?' And Bonnie had suddenly recalled her appointment with the scamstresses. She'd hurried back to Endellion, greeting the women who'd been sent all the way from Mayfair. They had stared at her, their mouths open. There was mud under her fingernails, on her chin. Her hair was unbrushed, grimed. They had smoothed their skirts, gathered themselves, brought out books of fine fabrics. Bonnie had leafed through them and chosen carefully, sparingly, not wanting to evoke Josephine and her excesses. But still, these dresses and fabrics were so much finer than the trousseau that she had abandoned at the rector's house. That had all been sensible cottons in colours dark enough to leach into her skin, high necks, tight wrists. But at Endellion, she was offered fine flowered silks and paisley lawn, one decorated with strawberries, another with tiny flying hummingbirds.

Crawford was raised alongside her, dressed in new velvet waistcoats, crisp cream cravats. After all, a girl like her could not have a brother in darned trousers, a yellowed shirt, could she? His position was assured. He would stay in the house.

'It's exactly as we wanted,' she'd said to him later, as he'd spun in the mirror, plunging his hands into his pockets.

He'd looked at her strangely. '*Wanted?* It's what we deserve.'

'Crawford,' she tried, as they neared the chapel. She kept her gaze fixed on the ribbons streaming from the horses' manes. 'I don't know. If I can.'

'Not now,' he snapped.

'Please,' she said, though she was not sure what she was asking for. To flee this place, to have him bundle her off like a captive? To take his hand and run? Her voice cracked. 'I can't do it.'

'Don't be absurd.'

'I can't.'

He gripped her arm. 'How do you think I feel in all this, Bonnie? You think this doesn't torment me too? The thought of you and him, tonight.' He ground his fists into his eyes. 'It makes me sick.'

'Then why—' The carriage stopped; ribbons flapped against her legs. She could not move.

'No,' he whispered, a resolve in his voice. 'If you don't marry him, how else can you ever be safe? As long as you're a maid, they could find you, hang you. But a *lady*. It's unthinkable. And don't we deserve all this?' He gestured behind him, at Endellion and its pocket-sized turrets and crenelations. The dirt from the cemetery was under her fingernails. The house was embedded in her. 'You'll do it, won't you?'

She didn't answer, but when he helped her up, she found that her feet were propelling her forwards: there were the steps of the carriage, the path. There was the tiny chapel with its shining poppies, and Aubrey inside.

Crawford gripped her arm and the door swung open. Aubrey had his back to them, as was proper. Cissie sat in the front row, her joy almost evanescent. Annette did not look up. Rex seemed as bewildered as if he'd been delivered to a distant moon; he was still squeezed into his footman's uniform.

In little more than four steps, Bonnie and Crawford reached the top of the aisle. Aubrey turned and took her hand, and she found herself passed from lover to husband.

'There you are,' Aubrey said.

Prayers were read, vows taken. Words fell from her lips, so faint that the rector laughed and asked her to speak louder. *For richer, for poorer – I promise to be faithful until death parts us –* but her mind was elsewhere, like a glass about to fall.

All those tricks they had played on those gentlemen, Crawford and Rex stepping from the shadows, a bat in Rex's hands. The way the red-headed man's skull had cracked against the brick. Crawford, pulling her onto his lap, the way he would whisper, *You wouldn't love me if you owned me.* And she knew that he loved her ferociously, passionately: she knew it deep in her bones. And he was right. She was safe now, wasn't she? Nobody would find her here. Nobody would dare accuse her. And before she knew it, the rector was binding her hands with Aubrey's, and it was all wrong; it was Crawford she wanted, not his brother.

The air was close and stale. It reeked of damp, mildewed stone. In no time at all, she and Aubrey were walking down the aisle, the door beaming open. Crawford shook Aubrey's hand on the way out, his face failing to find a smile. There was no turning back now. Aubrey climbed into the carriage and her face was white. Rooks bickered in the trees.

'Two magpies for luck,' Cissie cried. 'Isn't this a fine ending?'

And Bonnie knew that if they had been in one of Cissie's romances, the story would have ended there. Aubrey raising his hand in triumph, the couple disappearing off in the carriage. A maid who had made a fairy-tale match, a gentleman who had found himself a clever wife who his daughter adored. *The End,* the book would have said, and there would be no more pages.

'A fine ending?' Aubrey said, chucking Cissie under the chin. 'But this is only just the beginning.'

Later, Cissie stood at the top of the stairs gripping the newel post. 'Hurry,' she said. 'Just wait until you see what I've done.'

It was dusk, quiet in the house. The day had slipped away. There had been a wedding breakfast, a neatly trussed capon impaled on the carving tray. Aubrey's knife had sawed through the white flesh, the thighs cracked loose. There had been toasts, speeches, his hand drifting towards Bonnie's and raising it to his lips.

Cissie paused at Josephine's door. 'Are you ready?' She gripped the handle, flung open the door. 'Here!'

Bonnie stepped inside. The whole room looked like a giant boiled sweet. The arsenic green walls had been covered with pink wallpaper, a lurid trace of the paint still peeping through. New sheets and hangings had been made up for the bed in magenta chintz, the furniture rearranged as though to trick her into believing that it was not the same space. Not the same window, staring down over the pond where Josephine had drowned; not the same fireplace that she must have warmed herself against. Not the same bed – Bonnie touched her forehead.

'Well? Do you like it? I chose it all. Papa let me order all the fabric myself from Piccadilly. They sent me booklets with pictures like they used to send to Mama, and I arranged it all on credit. I wanted it to look like a room a princess might live in.'

Even the sconces were covered in pink glass. Such gaudiness. It looked like the houses Bonnie had hurried past on Jermyn Street: plush sofas visible through the front windows, women leaning from the balconies in dresses so low she could see crescents of nipple. Of course Cissie did not grasp this associ-ation, but Bonnie caught the resemblance between Cissie and her mother: they would steep everything in romanticism, every room a piece of theatrics.

Cissie sat on the bed. She bounced experimentally. 'One day this will be me.'

'You could decorate your room differently now, I'm sure.'

'No. I mean, one day I will be married to Lord Duggan.'

She has no idea, Bonnie thought. None at all. Cissie was so young, her slim body and its workings entirely alien to her. If she had ever seen dogs or cows rutting in the lanes and fields, she showed no sign of recognizing that humans were just the same.

'Should I leave you?' Cissie asked. 'I should, I know. Papa said I wasn't to linger.' She added, 'Mama,' and Bonnie kissed her on the cheek.

When the door closed behind Cissie, Bonnie found she was glad to be alone. She could sit and look out of the window. The view was different from her old attic, set into the front not the back of the house. It took in the cemetery in the distance, its high walls now finished, the half-built chapel peeping out above. She was mistress of all this: every tree, every bower, every long stretch of lawn. *Hers.* She might walk among it as Josephine once had. She might command labourers to fell trees, to build grottos. She might, if she chose, have each room carefully rebuilt, new turrets added, the house turned even more lopsided under her hand. But she knew, too, that she would not. That she wanted to preserve the echo of the woman who had walked the halls before her.

A knock on the door. Bonnie's stomach turned. But it was only Annette, there to help her undress. Annette was frowning, her lips pinched. She moved across the floor stiffly, flinching as she took in each new object. The silk-covered stool, the shining bottles of perfume. It was difficult to believe that this was the same woman who had rowed down the Thames with Bonnie, who had linked an arm through hers as they ambled through the grounds.

Bonnie pulled back her shoulders, the wine loosening her.

'Thank you, Annette,' she said coolly.

'That chair you're sitting on,' Annette said. 'It's just been covered in fabric. It's all *hers* you know. She's still here.'

Bonnie folded her hands. She would not rise to it. 'Begin with my cuffs, please.'

'Did you know he laid her out in here? On this bed, after she drowned. We had to take the mattress and dry it in the scullery. It took days, even with the fire roaring.'

Annette was standing so close, her fingers reaching for Bonnie's sleeve, and suddenly Bonnie seized her wrist. The maid recoiled. 'What happened to her?'

Annette stared at Bonnie, a small twitch of fear in her cheek. 'She drowned, Bonnie. I told you—'

'Did she? Or did—'

She broke off, but she needed to know, to understand exactly what had happened that night. She had to understand the man she had married. Annette bowed her head, fiddling with the clasps at the back of Bonnie's neck, edging the dress over Bonnie's shoulders.

'What happened to her?' Bonnie asked again. 'They argued and she drowned. Come. Don't be so naive.'

Annette's voice was cold. 'I should not have thoughts like those. Not when you are so newly wed.'

'We both know, Annette, that you are hardly discreet—'

'I should be asking you, *Miss*, how the calipers came to be in Manton's possession.'

Bonnie sat back, the two women regarding each other carefully. Annette's jaw was clenched tight.

'That will be all, Annette,' Bonnie said. 'If I were you, I would watch my tongue.'

'Undress yourself, duchess.'

And with that, the girl released the gown, her footsteps striking the boards. The door slammed shut behind her. Bonnie was left all alone, still in her stays and petticoat. She thought they would be easy to remove herself, but these seemed laced in a different way to her old underclothes, as though worked by a spider: all eyes and ribbon and hooks. She craned in the mirror, struggling to see.

Nothing for it but to leave them on; to sit at her dressing table, her flesh stippling in the breeze from the window. Aubrey would have to help her. She ran her fingers over the new perfumes that Cissie had bought, the glass chiming. She unstoppered one. The liquid pooled on her wrists, a floral reek.

A creak sounded from the corner of the room. She turned suddenly, as though caught with her hands in the silver.

'Crawford?' she whispered, then laughed at herself. For a moment, she'd thought that Crawford had hidden himself in the wardrobe. From there, he would press his eye to a gap in the wood and watch them, check she wasn't enjoying herself. But still, she found herself opening the closet door, then crouching on the floor and searching under the bed. Her new frocks danced on their hooks. The portrait of Josephine was gone. There was nobody there. Of course there was nobody there. It was mad to think Crawford would do such a thing. It was just the house, complaining in the wind as it often did.

Bonnie sat on the bed, wondering how Aubrey ought to find her. He would come soon. She should pretend she had not expected him. She lifted the covers and tucked herself inside, her petticoat creasing underneath her. The candle flattened as she blew it out, the sweet smell of smoke filling the room.

At last she heard the tell-tale squeak of a floorboard in the hall, the door being nudged open. No words between them. She could see the grey shape of him in the moonlight, the springs of the mattress creaking as he sat down on the edge of the bed.

He was breathing hard, like an animal in a dark barn. She did not know how he expected her, how she was to offer herself. Compliant, uncomprehending, desirous? His hand grazed her side, her leg, and she shivered, sat up.

'What is that—'

'The stays,' she said, miserably. 'I couldn't – I didn't know—'

He laughed, the stiffness cracking between them. She smiled, leaned her head against his shoulder.

'Here,' he said, and even though there was no candle, his fingers were deft, the hands of a man who had undressed a woman before. She reached for him, pulled him closer, and she could sense his relief and gratitude.

It was tender then, gentler than she imagined, her cues dropped so subtly he did not even notice that she was the one in command. She did not know why she had dreaded it. The steady rhythm, his chest hot against hers. He bowed his forehead so that they were nose-to-nose, and she felt a flicker of enjoyment, of reciprocation, a lightening within her. She turned her head away, snuffed it out. She was Crawford's, she told herself. She was his alone. She was simply confused because they were brothers; one man overlapping into the other. It was Crawford above her, she told herself: Crawford who was working himself to a faster pitch, close now. She expected him to pull his body free of hers, to groan as he spent himself against the sheets or her belly, to collapse against her – but he didn't. He pressed himself deeper, let out a sound that was half-animal.

She lay there as he kissed her cheek, as he smiled into the blackness.

'I'm sorry,' he said, but she didn't know what he was apologizing for. Her heart hammered in her ears. She shifted, and his seed did too: a warm stickiness between her thighs. How had she not anticipated it? They were married and she was young. It was natural, expected that he would father a child, just as he had before.

And as she moved her hand to her belly, a familiar longing struck her: for a small creature to hold against her chest, for an unquenchable love that rose to meet her own.

He fell asleep swiftly and Bonnie waited until his snores became deeper, steadier. Carefully, she lifted Aubrey's arm, slipped out from under him, put on a nightgown. He murmured, turned onto his side. She waited. His breath fell back into a steady pattern.

The door barely creaked as she opened it. If he asked her where she had gone, she would say she was hungry. Across the hall now, the ghostly shapes of the cameos on the stairs, ducking through the arched wooden doorways. Then down the servant flight into the kitchen, through the silver room to Manton's old quarters. Crawford's door was ajar.

'I knew you'd come,' he whispered. He reached for her arm, pulled her beside him. He leaned closer. 'Was he like a new-born deer, limbs flailing? Was his cock as small as a sprat?'

She could have agreed and made up all sorts of things, but she felt caught between the men, strung up on a line. Instead, she said, 'I missed you.'

'Tell me about what happened,' Crawford said, and his voice was impassive, a little cold. 'Every grisly, sordid detail.'

Bonnie winced. She knew she could not win: that he hated what she had done and telling him about it would only make it worse. But to deny him – 'Come here,' she said, and when he turned to face the wall, she said, 'It was your idea. You suggested all this. You can't hate me for it.'

'You're right,' he said. 'It was all me.'

There was something possessive about the way he said it,

almost bitter. Then he reached for her and kissed her hard, her lip pulled so tight between his teeth that she cried out. His strength had always frightened her just as much as it aroused her, and in a single movement, he had pushed her onto her front, drawn her hips up to meet his cock abruptly, roughly. She heard the ripping of fabric; her nightgown, torn. It was a conquest, a claiming of spoils. There was no tenderness as he rammed himself inside her. And this too was easy, in its way: to be told what she wanted, to be arranged like this. She loved him; she wanted him, didn't she? She had chosen this, hadn't she? He hammered at her body and he did not wait for her, but pulled himself out, spent himself over her back, her hips still gripped in his hands.

She thought he would hold her then, kiss her, whisper something in her ear. Make amends for the brutality of it. But when he collapsed on top of her and she reached for his hand, he flinched away. She had the sense that she had failed in some crucial way, that Crawford had expected something different from her. More cruelty towards Aubrey, more disgust, more ridicule. She slipped her hand under her belly and imagined a baby already rooting there, tiny fingers unfurling, flexing against her.

Hothouse

Bonnie woke alone. Sloping golden light, a high window. The pattern of the room took a while to settle. And then she saw Crawford's jacket by the door and the night came back to her. She threw herself to her feet, cursed. Why had he left her to sleep? Aubrey might already be awake, wondering where she had gone.

In the kitchen, she found Rex, sitting at the table with a plate of bacon.

'Is it late?'

'He isn't awake yet,' Rex replied. 'The disgraced duchess is safe.' He laughed. 'What a triumph you've proved. What a pearl.'

She glanced around her. 'Don't talk like that. The walls are thin. Annette might hear.'

'*Don't talk like that.*' He mocked her, his cockney vowels softening. 'You've always been one step above me, with your words and your voice and *Crawford.*'

'I didn't hate you until you hated me.'

But Rex wasn't listening. 'You've shown your worth. Crawford caught the mark of you that day you blew into the Angler. I can't fault him that.'

Bonnie drew herself back. How dare he speak to her like that, as though she was nothing more than a prize, a puppet to be yanked about? 'And you?' she demanded. 'The way you eat

216

up any scraps he casts you. If you could hear the way he scorns you when you aren't here. His *beloved great Dane*.'

Rex lowered his head over his bacon, shovelling in a rasher. The fat cracked and spilled from his mouth.

She took the stairs. In the entrance hall, she saw that the sun was high. Panic edged through her. Rex had lied: it must be nine o'clock, maybe even ten. Silver clinked in the breakfast room, the sound of a knife drawn across china. Cissie's and Aubrey's voices were faint. She hurried up to her bedroom, pulled on a simple dress, washed her face quickly. All the while, she prepared her lie, the silky excuse she would make, so that when she bustled into the dining room, it might slip off her tongue easily.

It was all me, Crawford had said the night before, but that was not true. It had been her who had carefully guided Aubrey from interest to desire to love to marriage. Her insides felt bruised from the way Crawford had used her, the cold slam of his body against hers. And after that, he had left her to sleep late. Annette might have found her there. Aubrey or Cissie might have seen her sneaking upstairs. For the first time, Bonnie wondered if it had been a threat, a careful flexing of his power over her, because she had refused to scorn Aubrey. He could unravel her life in an instant.

'Where were you?' Aubrey asked when she took a seat beside him at breakfast. He kissed her hand. 'I woke and found my love had fled.'

His tone was light; she smoothed the hair from her face. She ought to have brushed it. 'I woke early and took a walk. It was beautiful by the river. I could barely tear myself away from it.'

'You could have woken me,' Aubrey replied. 'I'd have liked to join you.'

'Oh nonsense,' she said, waving her hand. 'I thought you must need to sleep.'

'Did you see the ducklings?' Cissie asked.

'All six of them.'

'How puzzling,' Annette said, lifting the tea service onto the table. 'The doors were locked when I arrived. But I will clean the mud from your gown if you need it.' She eyed its immaculate folds.

Bonnie swallowed, reached for the teapot. The instinct to serve herself had not faded. But she bound her hands, took a piece of cold toast and spread it with jam. Annette poured her a cup, bending so close to Bonnie that she could catch the low scent of her underarms.

'Can I tell you a secret?' Cissie asked.

'Please!' Bonnie said, taking a quick gulp of tea, the heat scalding her mouth. 'Do tell.'

Cissie bounded over and whispered in Bonnie's ear, 'Papa is taking us to London as a surprise.'

'Cissie!' Aubrey exclaimed, laughing. 'That isn't how surprises work. But don't tell her anything else.'

'Isn't it wonderful?' Cissie asked. 'We're staying in a *hotel* in Mayfair, and I needn't go to my lessons. There's a shop where Mama used to buy me these magnificent boxes of candied ginger. One was rolled in a thin sheet of silver and you could *eat* it. Papa said we might visit it. But there is another surprise in London, and I shan't say a word.' She mimed sewing shut her mouth.

'Don't you dare!' Aubrey said, shaking his head.

'But London, Aubrey. What a treat,' Bonnie said with forced brightness.

It had been almost a year since Bonnie had fled the city, black thoughts of gibbets and nooses ringing in her head, the endless memory of a man falling again and again, that crack of bone on brick that she heard everywhere she went. But as Cissie helped her pack a small trunk and Rex lugged it down to the waiting carriage, she let her hands idle on the banister. Her feet were encased in green slippers. Who would suspect her now, dressed like this, a fresh bonnet on her head? She was not the same Bonnie Fairchild who had fled here. When she stepped onto the gravel, the coachman tipped his cap at her.

Crawford was waiting by the carriage door and she found she could not bring herself to face him. His eyes bore into her but she nudged past him, allowing Aubrey to help her up the steps. Cissie was already inside, staring out of the window.

'We'll look after the house admirably,' Crawford said. Bonnie glared at the drive ahead, an ache in her jaw.

Aubrey smiled and said, 'Very good.'

As the coachman stirred the horses, Bonnie remembered the day when she, Rex and Crawford had stood on the gravel and waved the carriage away. But this time, it was Annette, Rex and Crawford, standing a shoulder's width apart, their hands raised in farewell. Bonnie craned out of the window to watch them vanish. Just before the lime trees hid them from view, she saw Crawford duck away, and she imagined him walking to the sideboard in the drawing room, returning with a decanter of port.

'So they are gone,' he would say to Annette, and she would smile a crocodile grin.

It was astonishing how fast the journey in the carriage was compared to the vegetable cart she'd hitched a ride on from Covent Garden almost a year ago. The horses worked hard, the coachman urging them on, as they passed the countryside of Kew and Fulham. Dairy cows cropped the turf, sunlight splintering through the glass. With each turn of the wheels, more distance was pitted between her and Crawford. She opened the window and the air was fresh and sweet, the tightness in her chest uncoiling.

'Will you tell me the surprise?' she asked Aubrey.

'I should think not.'

'Not even a clue?'

'Not one.'

'But I hate surprises.' She nestled closer to him. 'I always like to know what's happening.'

'Then I pity you, for you have never appreciated the joy of anticipation, or had a good surprise.'

'And you suppose yours to be good, then?'

'Oh, indeed.'

His confidence surprised her, delighted her; that he felt he knew her so thoroughly.

'Cissie, you'll make yourself unwell if you keep reading,' Aubrey said. 'Can't you put that book away?'

'I need to know what will happen to Eleonor Tredegar,' Cissie said.

'She'll die, won't she?' Bonnie asked. 'Don't they always die?'

Bonnie leaned over and read a paragraph.

She limped on, ragged, pitiless, until she fell to the ground. And just as the last thread of life was wrenched from her grasp, she spoke the words that nobody would hear, 'I love you, Edmund de Beauvoir. But with your love, you have slain me. You have murdered me indeed.' And with that, she was gone, her angel wings sprouting from her back, her —

'There. She dies,' Bonnie said, wrinkling her nose. 'Though if I were her, I wouldn't have expired on that deserted road. I'd have hunted down Edmund de Beauvoir and made him sorry.'

'You're making light of it.' Cissie crossed her arms, pouted. 'It's very *serious*.'

'Oh, forgive me,' Bonnie said, and she reached out and clasped Cissie's hand.

They passed the rest of the journey in silence, Cissie sleeping with her mouth open. After two hours, the carriage drew to a halt at a grand house in Chelsea. A tall black door opened.

'Where are we?' Bonnie asked, but Aubrey just held up his hands in mock-confusion.

'I couldn't possibly say.'

Mr Eland breezed through the door, flapping away the footman and opening the carriage for them. 'At last!' he exclaimed, helping Bonnie from the carriage. 'Your husband has insisted I keep this quiet, a quality which I must confess is not in my nature. Now, come. Here, Margaret will take your cloaks, and oh – Cissie! Is that a new frock I spy? And a peacock feather in your hair? You look the very picture of your mother. I can see you've inherited her love of interesting things.'

On he chattered, leading them through his house, offering them glasses of ginger water. A tall marble staircase stretched up several floors, an oval window cut into the ceiling. It was so sedate and symmetrical compared to Endellion, each door framed by small pilasters. 'But you don't want to waste your time in here,' he said, showing them into a drawing room and library. The French doors to the garden were already flung open.

'Now,' Mr Eland said. 'Oh, Aubrey, take her hand and show her.'

Bonnie smiled, allowing Aubrey to lead her outside. Before them stood a vast glass chapel, almost the same height as the house. Wrought iron beams crisscrossed the roof. Palms were pressed against its windows, the panes steamed up. 'This is yours?' Bonnie asked him. 'This is all yours?' She took a step back, struggling to take it in. What a thing it must be to own such a place, to be able to walk down its paths each day and tend its borders.

'I have a terrible weakness for plants, as you know. Now, I have something to show you.' Mr Eland took her arm. 'It's a new plant I've acquired. A *Dionaea muscipula*. Through here. My glass chapel, as I call it, is not at its finest in July, I must admit. It's too hot.' The doors were swollen in the humidity and he had to lean his shoulder against them. Great pipes clicked under the floors. 'And I must wage a daily battle against rust.'

Cissie fanned herself, swatting at a fly, but Bonnie barely noticed. They walked slowly down a central path and he pointed out hibiscus he had brought back from the Indies; cuttings he had made of banana trees in Kew. They ducked under low, wet fronds. 'We have pineapples, just like Mrs Moncrieff used to grow. The late Mrs Moncrieff, I should say. That was all she wanted. Hundreds and hundreds of pineapples, heaped at all of her parties. Once, she had them all hollowed out and little candles placed inside them so they glowed like lanterns.'

He didn't seem to mind discussing her, and Bonnie found it refreshing to hear her name spoken so casually and openly. She wondered if Mr Eland had heard the rumours about Aubrey and her drowning, and if he had, what he made of them.

'Mr Eland is something of an expert in the grand houses of Sussex,' Aubrey said to Bonnie. 'I shared your terrible story. Cast from a home that was rightfully yours.'

Bonnie's heart quickened. 'Oh, you did—'

Mr Eland peered closer. 'What was the house called? It was in Sussex, wasn't it?'

'It wasn't that grand,' she said, waving her hand. 'You wouldn't know it. But these plants, sir, you must tell me where—'

'What was the name? I know many of the houses in that region. I've advised on so many gardens there.'

Her mind raced. 'Brinwick Hall.'

'I recall hearing the name spoken,' Aubrey said, frowning. 'Though I can't think where.' She cursed herself: she ought to have thought up a new name, not given the house where she'd supposedly worked before Endellion.

'I will look it up later,' Mr Eland said.

Bonnie's mouth was dry. 'There's no need—'

'What was it like?'

Bonnie tried to remember what she had told Aubrey. 'It was a – a lovely russet brick. Pink clematis climbed the walls.'

'I thought it was honeysuckle,' Aubrey said, and Bonnie's heart thumped.

'Both,' she said, too hastily. 'And jasmine too.'

She was glad when they moved on, when Mr Eland pointed at a rubbery spined plant, shaped a little like an open bellows. 'This is my beloved *Dionaea muscipula*,' he said. 'John Ellis named it, more commonly, *Venus's flytrap*. I bought it from a botanist who found it in the wetlands of South Carolina.' He took a pair of tweezers and prised open the lips of the flytrap. A large beetle was flattened inside, oozing liquid. 'The creature is enticed by the sweet scent, but when it brushes the cilia – the hairs – the plant snaps shut. Then, it's stuck, digested slowly by the plant. What a fate. To find yourself trapped, lured in by a sweetness that was nothing more than a sham.' He ran his fingers along the stem. 'A carnivorous plant. I couldn't believe it when I heard about it.'

Bonnie peered closer, hovering her fingers over the leaf. The jaws clamped shut, so suddenly that she flinched.

'Don't!' Cissie cried, smacking her hand away. 'What if it bites you?'

'I think even a plant as remarkable as this will struggle to digest Mrs Moncrieff,' Mr Eland said.

Bonnie forced a smile. The sun beat down on them. The error about honeysuckle was minor, a forgiveable slip. She was safe. And why should they suspect anything? It was Annette's comment about the hem of her dress that had shaken her, she thought. The maid was a loose thread that could not be cut away. When the others congregated around a small fountain, Bonnie strolled off by herself and Aubrey followed her.

'I wonder,' she said, 'if – if Annette is happy in our house.'

'What do you mean?'

Bonnie coloured. 'If – if she might prefer a different residence, with more opportunities to travel abroad.'

'If you mean getting rid of her, I'm afraid – that isn't how I manage things. She's been loyal, in service with us since she was fourteen. I couldn't.'

'I didn't mean that,' Bonnie said, hastily. 'I just thought she seemed a little – subdued lately. That was all.' She forced a laugh. 'Move her on! Unthinkable.'

'Our marriage must have jarred her. You two were such friends.'

Were, thought Bonnie.

'And if she's taking a while to adjust, it might be because – well, it must be strange having a new mistress at Endellion. I expected Cissie to struggle with the idea of a new mother, but she's coped admirably.' He added hastily, 'But that is largely due to you. And last January she weathered another anniversary. I only hope next year is easier still.'

'It must have been dreadful for her.'

Aubrey nodded, but didn't say more. They walked on, Aubrey's hand in the small of her back. It was companionable, almost chaste, his body warm against hers. She inhaled the hot, dank smell of vegetable mulch. How inviting it was, so unlike the rot of bodies. Flowers floated in a pond, their petals uncoiled like little pink pudenda. Golden carp drifted beneath the water, breaking the surface with gasping mouths.

'I did tell you,' Aubrey said, nudging her.

'Tell me what?'

'That you would like this surprise.'

She made a *hmph* sound.

'And does your husband have your permission for more surprises?'

'I will consider it,' she said.

My husband, Bonnie thought, and she found she liked the homeliness of it, its gentle consonants. *My husband*. It suited him too: his worn coat, the slope to his shoulders, the angular lines of his cheekbones and chin that only appeared handsome when she had studied them for some time.

'And we really will visit Italy?' she asked Aubrey. 'The three of us?'

'Certainly. But I thought your brother wished to join us too.'

She paused to touch some bananas, still green in their bunch. She faltered. 'Oh, yes. Of course. I should think so.'

As they walked past the dripping palms, one brushing her bonnet, Bonnie placed her hand on Aubrey's arm. He smelled soft, of fresh soap. A thought glimmered before her, treacherous: that they would return home and find Crawford's room empty, his belongings gone. Just – absent. No fissures, cracking through the dome of this small, careful world. No threats. Just – gone.

Alms

Aubrey had business affairs to attend to, an MP who had requested his company in Parliament. There was a rival concern, Aubrey had heard; he needed to learn more.

'I'm sure you won't miss me at all,' he said as the carriage trotted down High Street Kensington, stucco buildings flashing past. His voice lifted slightly. 'Will you?'

'Oh, not even a little bit,' Bonnie replied.

'Well, *I* will miss you, Papa,' Cissie said, snuggling against her father.

It was difficult to believe that she was the same girl who had been stricken with grief only a few months ago, hunched over in bed as she endlessly pasted concocted letters into her scrapbook. As Cissie raised her hand against a low slant of afternoon sun, she seemed to teeter on the brink between girl and woman: her skin was so pink and soft, her lips plump and arched like her father's. But she still bore the artless signs of a child. Her movements were abrupt and ungainly, her laughter so quick and guffawing. Bonnie wished Cissie might stay like this forever, stilled in time: that she would never learn the careful tricks designed to snag and snare, to turn herself into an object at balls.

'It's a rotten business,' Aubrey continued. 'Our cemetery is, beyond all doubt, in the public interest. But these MPs will block anything if it doesn't line their pockets. I hope to God

226

Parliament cleans itself up soon. It must, surely. We're a civilized country, are we not?'

He shook his head and settled back against the cushions. He seemed so different from the subdued gentleman Bonnie had met on her first day, as if he had grown into himself at last, his gangling limbs suddenly fitting him, a sureness to each movement. He whacked the ceiling. 'This way, Stimes. Take the King's Private Road.'

The carriage veered sharply into Hyde Park. It was as green as Twickenham, fig trees studding the avenue. They slowed against a jam of varnished broughams. Ladies rode chestnut ponies, veils shielding their faces from the sun. Cissie pressed her nose to the glass.

Hyde Park: it snagged on Bonnie like a hangnail. It was all lovely, wasn't it, the sweet lap dogs and the lawns not yet parched to hay? A pristine July day. But she clutched her gloves tighter, wringing them in her lap. They passed close by a lake. A boy in shorts was wading in past his knees, muck swilling up his thighs. She wanted to shout at him to be careful, that he could slip and drown, that anything might happen. The night at the Angler pressed in on her. Coarse red hair, the rough chin that pricked her neck, how she felt that every breath she sucked in had already passed through him.

Hyde Park. The big new terrace on the North side, Polygon Street. It's a glorious spot.

Perhaps he had walked this avenue or ridden along it on a fine horse. *I have a daughter around your age*, he had said, and she saw the way that Cissie nestled against her father, his arm around her shoulders.

'Stop,' she said suddenly.

'Why?' Aubrey asked, rapping the ceiling for her. 'Are you unwell?'

'I just want to walk.'

'I will accompany you,' he said, gathering his gloves and hat.

'Please,' she said, already fumbling for the door. 'I just want some air. I want to be alone.'

'But you can't possibly.' She saw his fight with propriety: his wife alone in Hyde Park. But it was not just that: she saw that he was worried about her. London was a nest of dangers for a woman as fine as her.

'Please,' she said again, the door opening. She scrambled out, her bonnet falling in front of her eyes. 'I won't be long. I will join Cissie at the hotel. I can look after myself.'

'Then take this for a cab.' He reached into his pocket. 'And a little left if you need it.' He handed her a guinea. She accepted it mutely. Her fingers shook.

'I won't be long,' she said again. 'Please, don't worry about me.'

Bonnie waved as the carriage disappeared, the wind rustling her hair. As she walked, the sun began to lower, a breeze cooling the afternoon. It was growing quieter, the swells packing up, the park beginning to drain away. She walked quickly, skirting the lake, footsteps hammering the path. The man was dead; no good could come of Bonnie picking at it. But she felt tugged by the same thread that drew her to Josephine: that desire to understand something of his life, something of what he had been as a person. If she could only see his house, she thought, then her imaginings might lodge themselves in reality. The sharp panic that beat through her in the middle of the night might ease. Boots on the stairs, men's rough hands and that bristled rope, tightening.

The path was pocked and full of puddles. She tried to lift her gown to avoid the dirt, but it was no good. Dust grimed the hem. Her sweat was beginning to dampen the fabric under her arms. The dress had been new. Annette would have to clean it, or perhaps it would fall to the two housemaids who were soon starting at the house. How carefully they would need to soak it in cold water, to scrub it with a horsehair brush.

The quick patter of feet behind her: children chasing a hoop. A man wheeling a gingerbread cart eyed her, turning as she passed him. It was best to keep her head down, to hurry only slightly. A piece of gravel had worked its way into her shoe but she limped on, uncertain how she would move the acres of petticoat and unlace her slipper. She neared the gate at the north end of the park, new houses stretching beyond it. Coaches raced past and she chose her moment carefully, darting across the street.

She would only look at the terrace, only see the house he had lived in. Nobody would recognize her, not dressed like this. Perhaps she would wait a little in case his daughter appeared. She needed to know if the girl was still stooped with grief or if her days had resumed something of their old rhythms. It was inconceivable to think how much Bonnie had shaped his daughter's life, how she had ripped a hole in the existence of a person she didn't know.

A flower-seller pointed her in the direction of Polygon Street. The ribbons of Bonnie's bonnet untangled and flapped against her cheek. She yanked them into such a tight knot that her breath shallowed. The street opened itself before her. She saw the house that must have been the gentleman's: the middle residence on the terrace, the pillars wider than any of the others. Tall black railings guarded it. Bonnie's footsteps stammered to a halt. She bit her thumbnail and the quick bled, the pain sharp.

The street was quiet. She stared at the windows of the gentleman's house. In the blue dusk, some shone yellow with candlelight. Was that the daughter's bedroom on the second floor with the narrow balcony? Perhaps, without her father's income to support them, they no longer lived there at all. Bonnie's hands moved to her pocket, the guinea hot in her fist.

A couple emerged from one of the smaller houses and stared at Bonnie. She pretended to be fussing with her dress. When they did not draw their eyes away, she began to walk slowly down the street. She neared the gentleman's house, her heart racketing. Candles were lit in the drawing room, the curtains not yet closed. If she stood on tiptoes, she could see a long gilt mirror, red wallpaper. A plump, grey-haired woman was sitting on a chair, head bowed over a book. Bonnie's heart thundered. His wife?

And then, the drawing room door swung open. Bonnie gripped the railings. She thought she was going to fall over. She could not believe it, did not want to believe it – Crawford, she thought; and his lies slit her open like a gutting knife.

Because there, striding into the room, was the gentleman she had killed.

Downpour

When they arrived back at Endellion the next day, the downpour was torrential, rain pounding the carriage roof. The drive was a river. Bonnie watched it silently, gripping her arms until the skin turned white. The house was fuzzy in the distance. Crawford would be inside. She welled up with so many things she wanted to say to him, so many ways she wanted to hurt him in turn, that her mind felt clouded. Rage stung her chest, filled every bite of her breath. Her crime unmade; a man brought to life. Should she have been relieved? *Murderess*; how the word had gummed to her like resin until she felt infected from the inside. All those nights she had been sure she would be caught and hanged, and Crawford had comforted her, his arms protecting her. He had found the position at Endellion for her, guarded her from harm, told her how she could make herself safer still by marrying Aubrey. She thought he had done it all because he loved her.

They walked into the dim hallway, and Rex stepped forward, taking their cloaks, playing the part of the dutiful footman. Bonnie removed her own and thrust it towards him. Annette was mopping the floor so ostentatiously that Bonnie knew she must have been compensating for some secret wrong. And then Bonnie saw an empty bottle rolled under the chaise, a shard of crystal gleaming on the tiles. So that was how it had been.

'Where's Crawford?' she asked Annette, trying to keep the tremor from her voice.

'In the library.'

She left Aubrey and Cissie in the entrance hall and hurried down the corridor. She pushed open the door. Crawford was there, sprawled on the sofa nearest the fire. He lowered the broadsheet, cast it across the room.

'Where's Aubrey?' he mouthed.

She closed the door behind her, watched as he stood and moved across to her, about to pull her into an embrace.

She flinched. 'Don't.'

'Don't what? What's happened?'

All the things she might have said; all the conversations she'd imagined between them; all the ways he would fall apart. And yet, she stood there and could find nothing to say. She needed to gather herself. She needed to sharpen her words, find a way to impale him like he had impaled her.

'My love,' Crawford began.

My love. She could not.

'Don't you *dare*,' she hissed.

'What?' He laughed, but he was uneasy. 'What the devil are you talking about? If you just—'

'Yesterday I saw the man I killed,' she interrupted. The vein in her temple felt tight, painful. 'A man you told me I had killed.'

He seemed to sag for a moment, a puppet with its strings cut, his lips a little parted. She could almost hear the pulse of his mind as he thought of a new silken line he might spin her, a way he might extract himself. She felt a cold sweep of power.

'You have nothing without me,' she said, raising her chin. 'I'm the mistress of this house. You're nobody. I could have you cast out.'

'Listen,' he said, taking a step closer, seizing her hand. She tried to writhe free but his fingers dug into her. There was real fear in his eyes. 'I love you. Don't forget that I love you. We can still have all this.'

She yanked her hand back with a sudden force.

'We will *never*—'

'Please—' he tried again.

The door clicked open. Bonnie drew back, but it was only Rex.

'Get out,' Crawford barked. 'Shoo.'

Rex's face darkened, the door closing behind him. Crawford had always liked to sharpen their hatred against each other, to pitch himself at the centre. His two little dogs, baying for his favour.

'Bonnie,' he tried again, but she pushed past him. In a few paces she had reached the door. Just before she slammed it behind her, she glanced back. Crawford's hands were by his sides, his palms held open, his shoulders wilted. She would not allow the stirrings of pity; she marched into the hallway. The light was dim and black, the rainclouds not yet blustered away.

'Bonnie.'

She jumped.

Aubrey was standing before her. 'What's wrong? You don't seem yourself.'

She shook her head, her cheeks flushed.

'It's nothing. It's—'

'Here. Let's take a walk,' he said, handing her one of his coats. It was far too big but she rolled up the sleeves. When they stepped outside, Bonnie was surprised to see that the rain had stopped, the grounds shining like a polished stone. She knew which direction they would walk. It was the same path they took every day, Zephyr trotting beside them. Down the lime avenue to the cemetery, through the back gate. Aubrey did not speak, did not try to coax her into sharing what she was not ready to impart. She wondered if he ever burned with questions or if he was content simply to know his presence was a comfort. He took her arm and a little of her anger began to ease.

The drains had worked, all the surface water gurgling away. They followed a narrow path, then a wider one, Bonnie walking fast, feet rapping the gravel. It was no longer possible to see across the whole cemetery: newly planted trees broke it into smaller pockets. Ahead of them was a pit dug into the ground that would become the catacombs. Labourers began to emerge from sheltering under tarpaulins, shaking the rain from their caps, gripping their spades and hammers. A racket of digging and hammering started up and it seemed somehow fitting that noise needed to be made, that the world was not simple or peaceful.

Bonnie stood above them, peering into the ground that fell away before her. The earth had been excavated, a ladder leading to a deep vaulted passageway. She clambered down it clumsily, slipping, righting herself.

'Miss—' one attempted. 'After the rain, you oughtn't—'

But she had already jumped down, filthy water spraying against her dress. She stepped inside. It was like standing in a giant sett, such a dark, subterranean place where just the barest light filtered down. Five layers of neat burial cells were already complete, each just wide enough to fit a coffin. There would be almost a thousand of these body holes, sealed with bricks or tablets of stone. How safe the dead would be, held tight by the four walls that fitted around them perfectly. Some, she knew, would be fixed with bells in case the occupants woke up and found themselves trapped.

'Bonnie,' Aubrey called, anxious. 'It isn't safe.'

She imagined crawling into one of these spaces, just lying down and falling asleep like a hibernating animal. All the things that would no longer matter. All the things she would not have to untangle. If she ignored Aubrey calling, would he drift away, forget about her? Would Crawford gradually peel himself away from the house, find other tricks and plots to satisfy him? He was done, surely: he knew he had lost her. But a part of her wondered if she was wrong, if somehow he would find a way to sink himself into the walls, until Endellion was *his*.

'Bonnie,' Aubrey called again, and she hurried back down the narrow corridor. He held out a hand and helped her up.

'Shall we go home?' he asked.

'Not yet.' She struck off down another path, faster now, her shoes scuffing the gravel, a buzzing in the back of her head. She should have shouted at Crawford. She should have made him fall to his knees and weep. She screwed shut her eyes, hurried on. Brick graves would be dug all around them. Some might reach twenty feet, whole families neatly stacked in order of their deaths, the generations turning over. What small betrayals would the dead once have nursed? What hatred, what resentments, what secrets, and some of them never dragged into the light?

Aubrey's footsteps slowed behind her and Bonnie didn't realize why at first. They were in the far corner of the cemetery, canes marking a perfect rectangle. It was the empty space that would become Josephine's mausoleum. It jolted her. Josephine and all the secrets she'd kept from him. *Deceit is unforgiveable*, Aubrey had said. Had he been thinking of Josephine or had he always felt that way? Perhaps another man might have been suspicious of Josephine before it came to her planned escape. Another man might have shouted the truth out of her, pried into her letters or possessions. If he had, would things have ended differently? Not in a furious argument the entire household had overheard and then with a woman drowned. For a moment, she considered telling Aubrey everything, cutting Crawford's sting out of him. The shining calipers, the calm way Crawford had twisted her to get her to marry Aubrey, his plans so carefully laid. But hadn't she wanted it too, been a part of it? And when Aubrey lowered his head over the empty burial plot, she knew she could not do it: she could not shatter the smooth glass of what they had.

The labourers had angled a plank over two tin buckets to make a bench and Bonnie sat on it, not caring that it was wet and mucky. Aubrey sat heavily beside her. His fingers danced a small, anxious tune on his arm.

'You haven't seemed yourself,' he said at last. 'Are you unhappy already? If you have regrets—'

'Regrets? No. No. How can you think such a thing?' She kissed his cheek and he leaned against her.

'Thank God.'

A blackbird sang into the silence.

Bonnie gestured at the canes marking the plot. 'I find myself thinking about her.'

'About – Josephine?'

Bonnie nodded. She looked at Aubrey, his clear blue eyes staring at the patch of earth. 'What happened to her?'

Aubrey winced, but she didn't soften the question. She had to know. She had to understand what he had done. If he was to blame.

'She drowned.'

'I know that. But *how*. What happened?'

Aubrey began to shred a twig in furious flakes, discarding it, picking up another. It cracked like a wishbone.

'Were you angry? The night you realized she would run away.'

She was a knife, pressing hard against the skin. She wanted to seize his lapels, shout, *Tell me. What did you do to her?*

'How did you know about that?' His brow crumpled. 'Who told you?'

'A house like Endellion keeps its secrets badly.'

He rubbed his forehead. 'It is – it is a memory that brings me great pain.'

'But you must have tried to stop her. When she said she was going to run away, you must have thought of the scandal—'

'She wasn't.'

'Wasn't what?'

'Going to run away. She changed her mind.' He exhaled slowly. 'By the time I realized what she had planned, she was already resolved on staying. She saw that what she had with me was better than a secret, sordid life. If she'd gone, she'd have had no standing, no real income.' Shreds of bark pattered through his fingers. 'I – I told her that she couldn't. Stay, I mean. That we would live separately. That I would give her an allowance and an apartment, but we couldn't live as a married couple any longer.'

Bonnie felt her shoulders drop. She flicked a piece of gravel with her shoe. 'And then?'

Aubrey stared at the canes marking the neat borders. 'There isn't much to say about what happened next. She was upset. She tried to make me reconsider. And then Cissie found her the next morning. Found her floating – Cissie who – no child should ever see such a thing. It torments me. How could a person undertake something that drastic, that irreversible? She must have been so unhappy. It was all my fault. If I'd handled it better, perhaps it would never have happened.'

'It wasn't your fault.' Bonnie rested her head on his shoulder. Her teeth were starting to chatter.

'Here,' he said, tucking his coat around her, and the last of her gave way to this kind, gentle man, so different from his brother. She believed him. He hadn't killed his wife, just as she hadn't killed the man at the Angler. It was just another piece of poison Crawford had whispered in her ear. Sometimes, she thought, there is no story. Sometimes, there is just a rumour stoked out of spite.

The Scullery

Another hot August passed, and Crawford did not leave. He was everywhere and nowhere: the smell of his pipe as she entered a room, a half-eaten biscuit on the sideboard. The cemetery kept time for her, a place where everything else fell away, and she thought only, *Crawford is still here.* She could not grasp what held him there, except his desire to be close to the house. All his plans were surely ruined.

In the time it took her to plant a row of hollies along the terrace walk and mulch them down with stable dung, Crawford did not leave.

In the time it took the horses, straining on ropes, eyes bloodshot, to pull the gargoyles up as high as the chapel corbels, Crawford did not leave.

He was there; he seemed baked into the walls themselves, his face watching her from every cameo in the hallway. That sly slide of eyes, the creak of a board.

And she was not the only one who wondered why he was still there. Aubrey broached Crawford's presence with her lightly, enquiring whether he might arrange a new residence for him, and she silenced him by pretending to feel wounded: Crawford was her *brother* and they could hardly be separated now. But the truth was that Bonnie was afraid of what Crawford might do if she untethered him wholly from the house. It was better to wait for him to leave of his own accord. Soon he would tire of it as he had abandoned the burial ground, the cemetery, all the women who had come before her.

It was easier to forget Crawford when, in September and October, the cemetery began to knit together. The cohesion was reassuring, as though Bonnie's life could be corralled in a similar way. The trees bedded themselves in. Raw foundations sprang into structures recalling real buildings: the avenue of detached mausolea with their own front doors, as though the dead would let themselves in and out at leisure. The chapel, unadorned stone inside, gaps where the windows would sit, the compartments taking shape. Nave, transept, apse.

'I think I prefer it this way,' Aubrey said, touching the unfinished stone. Portland, he had told her; resilient but easy to carve. 'Just a shadow of what it might be. Right now it's a ruin.' He looked around him. 'It might be perfect. Or it might not be. But that is the charm of something half-finished.'

And there were so many people to gather together, so many different things that Bonnie might think about instead of Crawford. Gravesmen were appointed, bodybearers. She helped familiarize the new sexton with his cemetery book. It contained a map of the plot, the order book and the register. Already, names were filling the pages. She ran her finger down the columns, each neatly filled in: name, abode, charges paid. And one column left blank. *Date of death*. The unknown, lingering alongside each carefully scripted name. Time, clicking its claws, waiting.

Richmond Road became a hub of small workshops. New trades set up at Cross Deep. Stone masons established dusty workshops, tall gravestones propped up outside. Granite, sandstone, marble. Blacksmiths flaunted their metal plaques, the chains and rails that could surround a grave, in the same style that might be used to fence in a municipal garden. A shop began selling mourning ware: black-edged handkerchiefs, jet hairpieces, black suits and gowns that might be rented with a day's notice. Faces peered in through the railings of the cemetery and Bonnie smiled back as she tidied the hydrangeas and andromedas, keen to see it through their eyes and make it as beautiful as she had originally imagined it. This, she thought, as she packed down the soil and watered in a new cypress, was her ground. Crawford could not touch this careful space that she and Aubrey had planned and built together.

But when Bonnie returned to the house at the end of the day, Crawford would crash back in. She heard his laughter echo through the rooms, a command barked at Rex. Her familiar unease came back: that there was something eluding her, just beyond her grasp. Even Cissie seemed infected with fretfulness, the girl shrinking into herself, shielding her scrap-book, tapping her feet in constant agitation.

'It's nearing winter,' Aubrey said. 'I hoped that the pattern might change this year. But she endured so much.'

At night, Bonnie barely slept, her ears pricked for any sounds. Too hot, too cold. The walls seemed to swell, spongy to the touch, pressing down on her like organs. When she did sink into the hinterland between sleep and waking, she imagined tiny footsteps scuttling behind her head, ears sprouting in the wainscoting.

One night in early November, Bonnie lay awake, just watching the darkness. Aubrey's arm was slung over her chest and she could have moved it, but she found she liked the weight of it, the way he curled around her. She felt the beginnings of her menses, a heaviness and bloat in her belly, and she stood up to line her drawers with linen. A disappointment settled on her, swiftly followed by annoyance at herself for being foolish enough to hope. Four months had passed like this. There was nothing living inside her, taking root: she felt like an empty house, stripped down to its bare walls.

Endellion creaked, a whispering running through it. She could have sworn she heard the clicking of a door. She pressed her ear to the wall. There was someone moving through the house. She stepped onto the landing. The air was silent, unstirred. The hallways had grown cluttered with new items that she had bought; a side-table, a vase, a seascape, and Endellion no longer felt like a museum in the process of being emptied and closed down. It was a task Cissie had helped her with, though she had guided the girl towards more modestly priced articles.

She listened: silence. Perhaps she had imagined the patter of footsteps on the stairs. She just needed to check that Crawford was safe in his quarters, and then she might sleep at last. She hurried down the broad staircase, down the narrower flight to the kitchen in the cellar. It was quiet, just the soughing of the trees outside the scullery window, the rattle of mice in the walls. She stopped at the silver room. Through one door, she could hear Rex snoring gently. Manton's old quarters were silent.

Bonnie waited, listened. The rucking of the trees seemed louder. She wanted to be back with Aubrey. Because where was Crawford? These winding hallways, these rooms buried behind rooms; all the whispers of the past. She hurried back into the kitchen. The knives were safe on their blocks, the pans gleaming overhead. Just as she was about to climb the stairs, she realized that the sound wasn't trees after all – it was coming from inside the house. It was more like – fabric rustling, the rhythmic gasp of breath.

The scullery door was open. And before Bonnie had even looked inside, she was sure that she had already seen it. Annette, Crawford; it was always going to be this way, wasn't it? Tears of shame and rage edged into Bonnie's eyes, but she blinked them back. *Fool*, she thought. *Fool*.

A muslin sheet was hanging up to dry, almost obscuring them. But Bonnie could see Crawford, his back to her. Annette's legs were wrapped around his hips as she was rammed back and forth, forced hard against the wall.

And as Bonnie backed away and fled upstairs, she fancied she had seen Annette's expression: her mouth like a hooked fish, her eyes half-shut in pleasure.

Scullery

The next morning seemed to have slipped loose of its runnels. It was one of those days when the air felt humid and damp, when clouds gusted furiously across the horizon. At breakfast, Aubrey dropped tea all over himself, scalding his chest. One of the mares had escaped from the stables overnight and was found on the banks of Eel Pie Island, wet and bewildered. When Aubrey and Bonnie walked to the cemetery, she found one of the chapel gargoyles smashed on the ground, pulverized except for a single stone tongue. And Cissie would not go to her lessons, would not leave her bedroom.

'I can't bear another winter of this,' Aubrey said, his breath silvering the air.

'Let me talk to her,' Bonnie replied, already turning and walking back to the house.

'She won't see you,' he called after her. 'It's useless.'

'Didn't I help last year?'

She would go to Cissie's room and talk to her plainly. The stories she read were simply that. *Stories.* They were not lessons on how to conduct herself, how to see the world through a prism of romance and tragedy.

But to her surprise, Bonnie found Aubrey was right. When she tried to push open the door, she met with resistance. There was something blocking it.

'Cissie?' she called. 'Cissie, it's only me. It's Bonnie.'

Silence; the clink of china.

'Cissie? It's Bonnie.'

But when Bonnie pressed her ear against the wood, she heard Cissie's voice, high, resolute. 'Do not let her in. I said, do not admit her!'

There was the drag of something heavy – a chair? A cabinet? – and then Annette inched open the door, a bowl of warm water in her arms. Bonnie stepped back.

You, Bonnie almost said, but she backed away, hurrying down the stairs before she caught the curl of triumph in the maid's smile, the words that trailed her. *Miss Cissie says she doesn't want to see you —*

Annette and Crawford. Annette allowed into Cissie's room when Bonnie was barred against it. *Annette*. Like a spider, spinning its careful silk, weaving her way into everyone's affections. She would find Crawford. He could not hide from her any longer. Something had to be done. The light was so dim, the lantern unlit, and Bonnie tripped down the final three steps of the staircase. Her ankle stung with pain, but she mastered it, wincing only a little. With each footstep, fury jabbed through her, but she still hurried through narrow arched doorways, flinging each open. The library branching off the parlour; the whole house stacked into accordioned folds as though it was keeping Crawford secret from her. Parlour, dining room, reading room, study, library.

She found Rex in the kitchen, picking at a fillet of trout. 'Where is he?' she demanded.

'Who?'

'Crawford.'

He thumbed in the direction of upstairs. The drawing room.

'He's not there.'

'He is.'

But she knew she had checked each room too cursorily. He could easily have been sitting in the corner, screened from view, chuckling over her search for him. He could have been waiting behind the door. Her fists tightened.

'You don't always have to be his dog, Rex,' she said. 'He'd kick you into the gutter if there was anything in it for him. He isn't your friend.'

'He ain't yours neither.'

'And that's it, isn't it? He'll treat you just like he treated me if you don't do his bidding.'

Rex didn't reply. He pulled off another flake of trout, crumbling it between his fingers. And as Bonnie took the stairs and walked down the hallway, she wondered if, for just a moment, Rex would be unsteadied by what she had said. If he might see the flicker of truth in it.

She pushed open the drawing room door. One sofa faced the window, looking out over the pasture and lime avenue, the walls of the cemetery in the distance. And sure enough, there was the top of Crawford's head. How often did he sit there, watching her and Aubrey walking to and from the cemetery, picking over every touch of their hands? Carefully, she walked over to him. She could be serene. It was the only way to match him. She took a breath.

'I've decided I'm going to tell him,' she said.

Did she mean it, or did she just want to jolt Crawford out of his composure? It worked: his eyelid quivered. 'You won't.'

You're like a girl made of glass, Bonnie. I can read everything about you, turn you in my fingers like a small crystal sphere.

He was wrong; she kept her gaze still, focused.

'And if you do, do you think he'll still love you? All those lies you told him. Those lies on lies on lies.'

'At least he'd know. At least I'd be honest.'

He laughed. 'Saint Bonnie.' He levered himself up, standing level with her. He reached out and rapped just above her left breast, hard on the ribs. 'You see, that's your biggest mistake. You're too soft, too easily won. You let it cloud matters. All the errors you've made, all the things you haven't noticed. It's because you're sentimental.'

Her chest was a small circle of pain where he had touched her. 'If I were sentimental, I'd do it. I'd do it to protect him.' She was already speaking in hypotheticals; she felt the threat emptying, losing its power.

'Protect him from what?'

There was something about the way he grinned at her; something that made her belly swing down towards the floor. She had spoken unthinkingly; but the answer to Crawford's question seemed to burst before her.

'From – from—' she hated that stammer – 'from you.'

'I wouldn't hurt a fly.'

They'd spent hours mapping out their imagined life together after she married Aubrey, and Crawford had always dismissed his presence. He was stripped clean from any of their fantasies. *You needn't worry about him*, he would say. And why should she have shadowed an idea with the inconvenience of a real person? But what if all along – she swallowed, her hands trembling. What if Crawford never intended him to be there at all? What if —

He reached out and tucked a strand of hair behind her ear. She did not flinch.

'You want this life, Bonnie Bee. You want to keep it. This – this—' he laughed scornfully, '*fairytale* I've built you. That's why you won't tell him.'

'But I built it.' *Careful*, she told herself; she could feel she was starting to slip, her fury stoked. She had to think of the way to undo him, the softest bit to prod. 'And it is a *fairytale*, as you call it. Because I love him.'

She saw it briefly: that quick twitch of pain, his mouth a little downturned. He gathered himself, his breath whispering against her cheek as he moved closer. 'But this is the thing. You can't stop what you've started. We both know you'll never tell him. You're on the merry-go-round. And you're going to lose.' He seized hold of her wrists, his face pressed close against hers. 'If you hadn't been such a damned sentimental fool, Bonnie, nothing would have come between us. We'd have had this house together. But if you don't watch yourself, you'll lose everything you've fought for, every bit of it.'

She would not ask him how. But her mind spun with questions.

'*I'll* lose it? Don't you see, it's you who mis-stepped. You pinned everything on me. You thought I'd still want you, even as you hid things from me, as you lied to me.' She tried to pull her hands free but it was no good. He had her locked in place. 'You didn't keep me close enough.'

His grip tightened. Once more, she wrenched her arms, reared away from him. He only gripped her harder, her wrist burning where he held her. 'Let me go,' she hissed. 'Let me go!'

She could not bear his smell, the heat of his breath. She twisted her hands, but he clung on, a smile at the edge of his mouth.

'You're caught, Bonnie Bee, don't you see? You're caught fast.'

'I saw you with her,' she spat back. 'I saw you, last night.'

He pulled her closer towards him, his arms wrapped tight around her. He pressed her against the wall, angled his knee between her legs.

'Let me *go*.'

'You didn't see a thing though, did you?'

'But I did.' She held her chin high. 'Sweet Annette, hammered against that wall—'

He flinched, smiled. 'You little whore,' he whispered. 'You only fucked him because I told you to fuck him.' He moved his hands down her sides, across her breasts, his fingers brushing her nipple. She bucked, writhed. If she screamed, what would he do? How would she explain it if Aubrey rushed in? 'You'll stay shut in with your *husband* at night, now, won't you? Be a good little whore. No wandering the house.'

A sound behind them; metal clattering. Crawford sprung back and Bonnie stumbled, catching herself on the edge of the sofa. Annette was standing in the doorway, a bucket upturned beside her. How long had she been there, watching? What had she heard?

'What – what is this?' Annette demanded, brown water seeping over the floorboards, her hand over her mouth. 'The two of you. That is – that is – disgusting. That is sinful!' She raised her finger at them. 'She's your *sister*.'

Annette began to back away, fumbling for the door handle, but Crawford crossed the room in four quick strides, caught her by the arm, yanked her forward. Annette let out a cry, tripped, and he dragged her across the floor.

'I'll tell Mr Moncrieff,' she wept. 'I knew there was something not right about you. I knew it. I'll tell him, I swear it. I'll tell him about all I've seen!' She turned to Bonnie. 'You think I didn't know about that nightgown? How you stole it from Mrs Moncrieff's bedroom. What other things did you take? The calipers, the brooch? I knew it wasn't Manton, I knew—'

'Tell the master?' Crawford asked, rattling her.

'Crawford!' Bonnie cried, throwing herself at him, but he batted her away. She knew that look in him, knew it like a scent: those times he had returned late, a cut on his lip, his eyebrow. Rex's thick rolled neck, the bruises that bloomed along Crawford's ribs. Had she ever truly understood what he did? She saw, too, the moment that Annette realized what Crawford was: the instant when her face changed from disgust to fear, as Crawford slammed her against the wall. The side table rattled, its porcelain figurines chiming.

'I'll tell him,' Annette said again, weaker now. 'I will.'

Crawford pressed his body against hers and she writhed like Bonnie had, his hand a pincer, digging into her jaw, her cheek. Bonnie stood there, helpless, her hands at her sides.

'You'll tell him nothing,' Crawford hissed, spittle glistening on Annette's cheeks.

Annette's chest shook with the beginnings of tears. It was scarcely a day since Crawford had kissed her, desired her. But she was lucky, in a way: how quickly her opinion of him had unclouded, how soon she had seen him for what he was. She would not waste years on him.

'I'll tell him,' she repeated, but whimpering now, only bearing a little of her old defiance. 'He needs to know what, what – *rot* is in this house. You don't scare me.'

'If you tell him,' Crawford said, his other hand tiptoeing up her chest, stroking her neck. 'If you tell him, I'll slit your throat.'

He thrust her away and she fell back in a heap, her skirts drenched with the brown water from her bucket.

'Annette,' Bonnie tried, reaching to help her up, but the maid cowered, her eyes wide with fear.

It must have been close to midnight when the fire started. Bonnie saw the auburn flicker against the ceiling and she sat upright, seizing hold of Aubrey. 'Fire,' she cried. 'There's a fire.'

Before they had even scrambled to their feet, she knew where the fire was: she knew it as they stumbled down the stairs and out into the grounds, boots unlaced, running, breath tight in her throat. And sure enough, as they turned down a serpentine path towards the river, the black smoke thickened, the sky orange ahead of them. She coughed, fumes cutting her throat and lungs, Aubrey hazy beside her. Lit by the red of the flames, Annette's cottage looked made of gingerbread, the thatch catching, burning stalks drifting into the sky.

'Bonnie! Wait!' Aubrey cried, but she did not think. She crashed forward, her boots pounding down the door, shouldering her way into the small room. Heat unlike anything she had ever known, as thick as a wall, batting her back. She tried to call Annette's name, but all she could do was cough. She stared about her: the bed, with its pink quilt, was empty, the covers cast aside. Annette was gone, fled. She felt the shape of someone behind her. Aubrey was crouched low, overwhelmed by coughing. She seized his hand, a searing pain as a cloud of sparks rained down on her. Out; they had to get out. She crawled, half-dragged herself back through the door and threw herself over the threshold, tumbling forward, the grass suddenly cold underneath her. Aubrey was there, holding her, and she tried to tell him she was fine, but her throat was empty.

'She's gone,' Bonnie croaked. 'She's gone.'

They would need to pump water from the pond. They had to extinguish the blaze and stop it spreading. In a moment, Bonnie would haul herself to her feet and they would do it together.

But as the seconds passed, she did not move. Her hands were singed from sparks, her thighs aching. She knew Rex and Crawford would be watching, hidden by the trees, entertained as a man at Vauxhall might spectate on a fireworks display. She could picture Crawford's slight smile, Rex with his hands tucked into his pockets. *Well done*, Crawford would tell him, Rex brimming with joy because he had pleased him. *Another rat smoked out.*

The roof crashed down, sparks flying. And Bonnie knew that this had nothing to do with Annette. The woman had been terrified, had likely already fled Endellion. No; this was Crawford flexing his muscles, his way of telling Bonnie: *see what I am capable of.*

She reached for Aubrey, pulled him closer to her. She could hear his heart through his shirt, its frantic pitter-patter as he regained his breath. Crawford would find a way to get Endellion. He wanted it with a need that terrified her. And if he couldn't have it, he would take a match to the house, and he wouldn't care who was trapped inside.

Part Six

Josephine

Dawn flushed the sky, and the flames in the cottage were finally extinguished. The roof was gone, black and tumbled in. The trees around it were only a little singed, their branches mercifully damp after a week of rain. Bonnie and Aubrey had worked through the night, some of the cemetery labourers roused by the stable boy, water pumped from the heart-shaped pond.

'You must rest,' Aubrey said as the last flames died back. His nightshirt was soaked and she could make out the ridge of muscle below his ribs. 'Try and sleep.'

She wanted to cleave herself to him and not let him out of her sight. But that was no way to do this. Bonnie's mind was a jar of water, carefully balanced. She could not let it slip. She thought of Crawford in the Angler as he played whist, how steady his hands would be, how he would regard his opponent silently, like a cat might eye its quarry, cards fanned out before him. Nothing in his manner changed.

Wait.

'Very well,' she said, but it felt like a string was tugging her back to Aubrey as she crossed the lawn to the house. She looked up at Endellion, half-expecting to see its sides crumbling like card, but it still stood there, crenelated, defiant. A face at the window: Cissie. Bonnie raised her hand in greeting but the girl ducked away.

She had to think like Crawford. He would gain nothing by acting now. He would wait, surely, for the cemetery to be finished: he would wait for the money that awaited them, for the scrutiny on Aubrey to pass. She had time, she told herself. Perhaps.

As she climbed the stairs to her room, she tried to slow the quiver of her heart. Carefully, she washed the stench of smoke from her hair, dabbed her burned hands with honey and bandaged them. And then, she took the stairs to the kitchens, found Crawford and Rex sitting at the table, a quiet joke stammering out as she entered. Rex flinched; Crawford only turned to look at her, enquiringly, searching her face for an acknowledgement of defeat. She stared back levelly. His eyes were so liquid, so dark, she could scarcely see the pupils. But there was so much he did not know. He could not see that her blistered knees were trembling, that she was biting the inside of her cheek so hard that she tasted iron. The pain in her hands was screaming.

'Annette has left our service,' she said calmly, her throat gravelly from the smoke. 'We already have two new maids joining us. I will see if they can begin sooner. I trust you will make them welcome.'

When she left, Crawford blocked her way. He glanced at her bandaged hands as though to remind her of what he had done. She lifted her chin.

'If I might pass.'

She watched him fidget. He moved aside, slowly.

Upstairs, she walked through the hallways. The new pieces of furniture that she had bought gleamed brightly. Hellebores that she had grown from bulbs nodded at her in their vases. She tightened her fists. She would remain mistress of Endellion.

The hardest part was not knowing. Sometimes she met Crawford on the stairs and he swept past her quickly, his eyes set on a distant point beyond her. Sometimes she saw him exercising the horses on the lawns, driving Boudicca up and down the woodland paths, racing far too fast. Always he was closed to her and she burned with the need to know what he was thinking, what he was planning.

As the weeks turned into months, the house seemed to fracture at its edges. Perhaps the cracks in the plasterwork had always been there, the roof leaking and causing the walls to flake. Perhaps Cissie would always have shrunk into herself as winter descended on the house and the date of her mother's death neared; perhaps Bonnie's agitation was a contagion, her bleeding fingernails marking her out as someone who could not be trusted. When Cissie refused to see her, Bonnie often stood outside the doorway and felt tears brimming. All of their intimacy, lanced out so cleanly. *Mama.* She had the sense that the girl could smell the stench of something fundamental rotting within her. Only Cissie could see the maggots working their way through her heart.

'Can't I go to her?' she asked Aubrey, again and again. How was she to protect Cissie if she wasn't allowed near her?

Each time he looked doubtful. 'It's the first year she's had another person in her mother's place. She will come back to you, I'm sure.'

But Cissie did not. She scarcely left her room. The new maids, Jane and Sara, brought her meals up to her, as well as a regimented list of drinks served every half hour. Chicken broth, custard, arrowroot, turtle soup, champagne and brandy. Cissie turned each of them away. Once, Bonnie heard the smash of a glass against the wall.

The cemetery should have brought her peace, but with each day, she felt herself hurtling towards an ending she could not grasp, a plan of Crawford's she could not make out. Time refused to stall. She patted in daffodil bulbs, up and down the main avenues. She found herself dreading the time they would sprout, each day the network of roots spreading further under her feet. The catacombs spawned into a thousand little boxes, wide stone steps leading down to a vaulted tunnel, finials cemented into place. Everywhere, there was construction, and it was all so ordered, all so *planned*. The sexton's lodge took form near the entrance, the yards and sheds already stocked with fresh bricks, sealing stones and shining new tools: spades and planks, barrows and hoes. Sometimes it seemed as though the cemetery was readying itself for them all, the brick graves yawning open, impatient.

And as the cemetery grew, her own body counted the months: the cruel splash of red that dampened her drawers. Did it shock her because it seemed so crude when everything else was so hidden from her? Or because of the loss in it, another thing she could not control? It was as though Bonnie was not moving forwards but simply waiting, her body part of the collusion. Make no change, stay still, like a fox in covert.

She bound her sadness tight to her: the women with swelling bellies she passed on the riverwalks, the children from Orleans House who sometimes played in the gardens. No swell to her front, a resolute flatness. The babies that she had not managed to will into being seemed to gather at the edge of her, just out of sight, and she told herself they were patiently waiting, that soon they would step forward and she would cradle them in her arms, inhale the sweet scent of them. But she thought too: what if they never came? What if this was all her life would ever be, everything petering out so soon?

Did Crawford watch her? Sometimes, she was sure she caught the flicker of a green jacket in the lime avenue as she walked down it, or smelled the faint trace of tobacco. Each time, Bonnie did not let her footsteps falter. She felt the glint of eyes everywhere: the glossy dart of a blackbird, the rustle of a hedgehog in the leaves, until even the red yew berries looked like tiny devilish eyes. Even if she did not see him, she sensed his impatience like a horse, stabled for days.

'Can you smell pipe smoke?' she asked Aubrey, one afternoon in March. In a month's time, the cemetery would be opened by the Lord Bishop of Winchester; the next day Aubrey would hold a dinner for the directors and share details of how the plot had progressed. Before then, he wanted to show Cissie her mother's finished mausoleum in the hope that it might snap her out of her misery, prove to her that Josephine had not been forgotten.

Aubrey shook his head.

'Oh,' she replied, her smile feeling pencilled on. 'I must have imagined it.'

Cissie walked on the other side of her father, her footsteps dragging. She did not look at Bonnie. Pimples bloomed across her cheek and she picked one as she walked.

'Isn't this a fine day?' Aubrey tried, forcing brightness into his voice. Bonnie glanced at his daughter, willing her to reply, to seize her hand and laugh like she had once done. Cissie's mouth twitched down at its edges. But it was something, at least, that Cissie had allowed Bonnie into her presence.

Bonnie did not know if it was a relief, as they walked further from Endellion, to realize she was not imagining the scent of pipe smoke. She saw it drift from the woodland fringing the lime avenue. Panic spread up her arms, across her chest. What did Crawford think when he saw the three of them? He had always been so opaque to her, had held himself at such a remove. The more she reached for him, the further he slipped away.

She was glad that Aubrey walked fast, Cissie too, towards the road to Richmond. Bonnie tried to resist the desire to glance behind her, to see if Crawford was following them. She kept her eyes ahead, Aubrey's tweed coat prickling her arm.

The cemetery gates were half-closed. A man was painting them a hard, shining black. The lodge that flanked the gates was almost complete: turreted to match the Gothic Endellion, a crenelated roof, arched windows. It looked like a fortress, a safe harbour, and Bonnie found herself holding her breath as she walked through the entrance to where pathways branched in each direction.

'This way. I want to show you the chapel, Cissie,' Aubrey said, leading them down the main avenue. The cypresses had bedded in well. He added with the same strained cheer as before, 'Bonnie planted these daffodils. Won't they be pretty, Cissie?'

Bonnie saw that they had already sprouted. The small green blades felt like a knifing in her chest. How fast time was seeping away from her; how little she could grasp.

The path rose, the chapel in view. Masonry dust filled the air. The spire was almost complete, just waiting for the iron-monger to weld lead to the tip. It was strange to see it so close to being finished, so *solid*. Everyone was moving, busy, filled with vitality, the veins thick in the labourers' wrists as they heaved a limestone font through the doorway. The glaziers' cheeks shone pink as they melted the bright windowpanes into place. Beside them, Bonnie saw the stained glass carefully stacked in hay: a fragment of a foot, a black-headed lamb, each piece gently outlined in lead, waiting for the sun to shine through it.

She pressed her hand to the cold stone.

'Just as you drew it,' she said to Aubrey.

And when his mouth failed to find a smile, she realized how he, too, had felt the strain of holding everything together. She rested her head against his shoulder. Something green flickered in the corner of her eye; it was likely just a branch, rucked by the wind. But still, she ducked quickly into the chapel, dust swirling about her. Aubrey coughed into his handkerchief. Marble tiles were being levered into place in a chequerboard pattern.

'It's a mechanical bier,' Aubrey explained, standing at the front of the church. 'It will be fitted with rollers so the coffins can be rotated after each ceremony.'

He talked on and she half-listened: the pews that were being carved in a workshop in Hampton to match those at Rouen Cathedral, the eagle lectern that was being cast in a foundry near Hounslow.

'You built all this, Papa,' Cissie said.

It was the first time that Bonnie had heard her speak in weeks.

'Well, I drew the plans—' He shook his head. 'But it was Bonnie's idea. We built it together.'

And it was true, Bonnie, thought. It had been both of them: this place was theirs.

I have lied to you —

The words were there and she could not speak them. They were there, trapped inside her, bucking against the bands that seemed to snap shut around her chest. If she half-closed her eyes, she could sweep away Crawford, sweep away Cissie's pain. They would go to Italy, Cissie had once said, and she had described it so enticingly: the heat baked into the stones, the scent of lemons, a violin being played in a distant square. And Aubrey, pointing, explaining, a fire in his voice: there, the fluted niches, the tapering ribs of the Basilica; there, the segmental arches of that bridge! And then the curtain might fall on them all, the story wound to its happy conclusion. Crawford gone; every mistake she had ever made, every lie she had ever told, unstitched, unravelled, simply undone.

But back outside in the daylight, Bonnie's eyes could not settle. She saw Crawford in every shifting shadow, fancied that she could still feel the jab of his finger against her ribcage. She pressed closer to Aubrey as they followed the winding pathway from the chapel to the far corner where Josephine's mausoleum was almost complete. It was constructed like a miniature chapel, columns flanking the arched entrance, pinnacles soaring upwards. Little statues were set in niches, the stone a fresh shade of cream.

Bonnie glanced at Cissie, expecting her to be moved, but she seemed largely unaffected by the sight. Aubrey shifted from foot to foot and Bonnie knew the effort it was taking him to stay silent, not to ask any questions. She picked a cyclamen, moved to hand it to Cissie. Cissie drew back as though scorched.

'No,' she said, dully. Then, louder, like a wound breaking open. 'No! Do not touch me!'

'I didn't mean to—' Bonnie tried, a lump rising in her throat. 'Please, Cissie—'

'Bonnie was just being thoughtful,' Aubrey interrupted, but his daughter squirmed away when he reached for her.

Cissie turned to them, her face wild. 'I will die like her,' she said. 'I will die just the same, and then you may lay flowers for me.'

'Cissie,' Aubrey said, his voice catching. 'My darling daughter, no—'

It was unbearable. Bonnie could not stay, not when her presence had done this. She excused herself, leaving Aubrey and his daughter alone at the tomb. And as she hurried through the back gate and took the narrow path across the pasture, she saw Crawford emerge from the woodland. He glanced back at her and smiled as though he intended her to see him. There was something on his back, long and slender. She half-ran after him, her pulse quickening, following where he had walked. She ducked into the kitchens after him.

The maids were there, flour dusting their arms. 'Oh, Mrs Moncrieff—' Jane began.

'We didn't expect you down here,' Sara said. 'Are you hungry?'

'Where did he go?' she asked, cutting across them.

'Where did who go?'

'Crawford.'

She had to know if she was mistaken. She had to *know*.

'He went directly to his quarters, madam, and then upstairs—'

'Thank you,' she said, crossing the silver room, pushing open Crawford's door. The hinges did not creak. It was gloomy, the curtains undrawn, a few clothes discarded on the floor. Bonnie stared around her, half expecting him to spring out from the shadows, to shout *Got you*.

She lowered herself to her knees, fumbling for the loose board where Crawford had stored the calipers, the brooch and trinkets. It lifted easily, silently. She moved her hand into the gap. She could see nothing, the dark black and velvety. Cobwebs snagged against the sweat on her hands. She touched something long and metallic.

Her heart pattered. She angled it out. Aubrey's double-barrelled shotgun.

She was sure Crawford had meant her to find it. He wanted her to be afraid, to understand what lay in wait for them, to feel the stirrings of his power. The impasse was over. A roiling sensation gripped her as though she might be sick. The gun was heavy, icy in her hands. She thought of Cissie, spinning wildly in the rain. Aubrey, his fingers ink-stained as he sketched out monuments and palaces; his quiet excitement as he had stood on that mound of earth, casting out his hands as he declared, *The chapel will sit here.*

And then, nothing. A gap, a silence where those people she loved had once been.

The Nursery

Bonnie knew Crawford would find her. His days of tiptoeing around were over. It did not surprise her, then, to enter the drawing room later that afternoon and find Crawford and Aubrey sitting on the sofas facing each other. Jane and Sara had laid out scones, the jam glistening in a china bowl.

'Ah, *sister*,' Crawford said. 'We were just talking about you. Would you care to join us?'

Dread rose in her throat like bile. 'I hope I didn't interrupt you.'

'Not at all,' Aubrey said, standing. 'Please, sit with us.'

'It's so rare I ever see your husband by himself these days. You seem to stick so closely to him.' Crawford took a bite of scone, crumbs falling from the corner of his mouth. 'He was just telling me about your plans for Italy. It sounds delightful.'

Bonnie felt like she was trapped underwater, bubbles rising from her lips. 'I shouldn't intrude,' she said, backing towards the door. 'Aubrey, how is Cissie? Perhaps we should see if she's recovered—'

'It occurred to me,' Crawford said, ignoring her and turning to Aubrey, 'that I've told you so little about my sister and what she was like as a child. Did I ever tell you the terrible tricks she'd play?'

There was a slight slur to his voice. He was drunk, Bonnie

realized: it was scarcely five o'clock. It was startling to see him so undone.

Aubrey shifted, scratching the back of his neck. He must have grasped something of the atmosphere, because he said, 'If Bonnie wouldn't like you to share stories—'

'Oh, but my sister is *very* accommodating.' Crawford stared at Bonnie. He did not blink. 'Tell him about the red-headed man, what you did to him. What a devil you were then! Won't you tell him?' He leaned forwards. 'I'm sure Aubrey would find it so entertaining.'

'I'm sure Bonnie will share what she wants to share,' Aubrey said, more firmly this time. Bonnie was surprised by the anger she found in his voice.

'Ah, but you see, with Bonnie you think she's a sweet angel,' Crawford said, matching the venom in Aubrey's tone. 'When I met her first of all, she—'

'Met her? But she's your sister,' Aubrey interrupted. 'You mean, when she was born?'

Crawford laughed, stabbing the butter knife at Aubrey, silver flashing blue. A pain tightened across Bonnie's scalp. She thought of the gun, nestled in the floorboards, its cold black barrels. 'Indeed she is. And we'll be burned in hell, then, for what we've—'

'Please forgive me,' Bonnie said, reaching for the door handle. 'I have an ache – in my head, just here.' She tapped the back of her skull.

The handle would not engage at first and she scrabbled for it, pulling harder. And then she was out of the room and safe in the hallway. The lantern flickered. She sank against the wall, her hand over her heart, her ribcage rising and falling. He would not have unmasked them both, surely? He meant only to unsteady her. But she knew that he would tell Aubrey in time:

just before the end, he would let her witness how much pain the truth would drive through her husband. She thought of the rats in the pit, boxed into that corner, the way the terrier tossed them in the air, teased them. The clean snap of its jaw.

'Mrs Moncrieff?' It was Rex, a tray of almond puffs in his hand, his voice mocking. 'Oh dear, Mrs Moncrieff, you look so unwell.'

They were everywhere: there was no peace. There never had been. Her siblings, all piled into the same bed like puppies, the cold weight of the rector's expectations, pressing her smaller and smaller. The way Crawford and Rex had devised test after test. And now, here they were, filling this house, dirtying the ottomans with their boots, steadily making it theirs. They were circling now; she knew they were, growing restless and scattering little crumbs to hint at what they intended. They would strip it to its bones. They would stop at nothing. How long did she have?

Bonnie took the stairs two at a time, her hand grazing the banister. She simply needed to *think*.

'Bonnie?'

She tried to smooth her dress, to rub the panic from her eyes, but Aubrey climbed the staircase after her. 'Whatever is the matter?'

'Nothing—'

He looked at her tenderly, his head on one side. 'I don't want to pry but—'

Her understanding was slow, curdling. He thought she was going to have a baby. She imagined it anchored within her. A soft anemone for a mouth. And then she pictured her insides like a slab of tripe: pale and bloodless, slippery.

'No,' she said, pushing him away. 'Forgive me – I – no. It is not that. I am not – with child.'

The fall of his face stunned her.

'I see,' he said. 'I apologize.'

So he had also been patiently waiting. She had not thought that men cared or pined for such things.

'It is just – it is my head. I want to lie down.'

'I'll have Jane fetch you mint tea.' His voice was tentative. 'I've noticed that you and your brother seem a little – distant. I think – I wonder – whether, now that the cemetery is nearly complete, he has anything of his own to employ him? In fact, I must admit I'm not sure what he has found to occupy him for these last months. Perhaps it might be time to find him a place of his own?'

It was all too much. She pushed open her door. 'Please, I just want to sleep.'

She climbed into bed fully dressed. Her bones felt leaden, the pain in her head as sharp as a spike. Aubrey bent to kiss her, and she ran her finger over the soft crease in the centre of his forehead, as gentle as the fold of a book.

'You and Cissie should leave for Italy in the morning. Please. Say you are going to Richmond and leave me here. I can follow and—'

'What are you talking about?' He almost laughed. 'Bonnie, this is madness. Leave *you*, and the cemetery so close to opening?' He kissed her cheek.

'Please,' she begged, almost crying. 'Please, if you love me, then leave.'

He reached for her hand, concerned now. 'You're frightening me, Bonnie. What's wrong?'

She shook her head, could not look at him.

'If you're too unwell for the directors' dinner tomorrow, I can write to them, tell them not to come.'

'Don't do that.'

'We can talk about this later,' he said. 'You must be tired. The strain of the cemetery – it has been excessive. I didn't think of the weight it would add on you too, and with Cissie so unwell—'

Bonnie sank back against the pillows. He did not understand, and how could he? How could she begin to explain about Crawford and Rex, how swiftly it had spiralled away from her? And now she was almost undone, her life narrowing and darkening to a small loose floorboard, a gun waiting there, biding its time. If she took it, he would know she had been in here, and his rage might undo them all. She could no more protect Aubrey and Cissie than she could bring down the sky.

If she told Aubrey everything, would he even believe her? Would she too be fed a carousel of beef teas and brandy and blended marrow? Doctors, dressed in raven black, bending over her, their cold fingers testing the pulse in her throat, assessing the shade of her tongue. *Malady of the brain*, they had agreed when Aubrey had at last summoned them to see Cissie. *It is a common affliction in a girl of her age.*

And so Bonnie let Aubrey tuck the covers around her, solicitous, as tight as though she'd been bandaged in, and she accepted the mint tea he brought her. The leaves had not been washed and there was a thin scum on the surface, of earth or scat. The sounds of a ballad drifted through the floor. Crawford singing to himself.

Knees up, Mother Brown
Under the table you must go
Ee-aye, Ee-aye, Ee-aye-oh
If I catch you bending
I'll saw your legs right off —

Aubrey glanced at the door and back at her, but he said nothing.

When he left, she stared at the ceiling, watching the light

shifting across it. She listened to the echoes of the house, the creak of its windows. A glass pane beat back and forth in the wind. Floorboards complained as Jane and Sara walked down the landing. She heard the swish of a broom, a mop being squeezed clean, the edge of their chatter.

Their talk washed over her. The preparations they would need to make for the directors' dinner the next day; the joints of beef they were marinating, all the potatoes they had peeled and soaked in water. Such matters had once concerned Bonnie too, but here she was, lying in bed and it wasn't even six o'clock. She shifted onto her side, closed her eyes. On it went. Laundry day next week, Jane said, and the mistress was due on her menses.

'Perhaps this month she will catch,' Sara said. 'And then we shan't have any stains to get out of any linens except our own.'

'It must be soon, surely. She's been married almost a year.'

Bonnie pulled the quilt over her head. All these people watching her. It grew hot and close quickly, but she remained still. Their talk died away. Just her breath. Just her own heart.

The mint tea cooled on the pot cupboard. The sun was beginning to dip. She hoped, even then, that she had misunderstood Crawford. Perhaps the gun was just a thing to own, not a weapon to fire. Because the more she thought about it, the more it snagged: what did he really seek to gain if they were all dead? The inheritance would not pass to him. And if he meant to hide their deaths and assume Aubrey's position, surely he could not succeed in that forever? Questions would be asked, suspicions nurtured. She needed to unsettle him, jar him into giving something away.

I was dropped here, last night, by a bird.

Except, he wasn't. Except, his past still trailed him, ate at him, provoked him. That long trudge along the towpath to school each morning, trying to keep his shoes clean of mud, each step pulling him away from his rotten barge, its damp tarpaulin. Endellion would have swung into view, its white flank beaming down at him each day, its views of the river uninterrupted by hedgerows or walling. That past life, she knew, was sealed off to everyone except her. How he had hated laying it bare; how strange he had been afterwards, drawn back into himself. Bonnie pushed off the covers. She reached for her shoes. She knew the way to trip him up. She would prise off his shell and leave him pink and raw and squirming.

Supper had not yet been served and she could hear Sara and Jane in the kitchens: the clank of pans, the hiss as onions hit hot oil. She took her cloak from the peg, slipped out of the front door. Out in the gardens, it was cold, silver light filtering through the trees. There was nothing wrong with what she was doing, but still she found herself taking the longer woodland path to the riverside where she would not be seen, breaking into a half-run. She passed the pond, glimmering in the early evening light. She quickened her pace, a stabbing in her ribs. A magpie careered out of her path. A hare sat on its hind legs and bounded away.

She followed the river upstream, past the grand houses that lined the Thames. Ragman's Castle, Orleans House, Strafford House, York House. A few labourers nodded at her as she passed.

'Mrs Moncrieff,' one said, tipping his hat, and she forgot for a moment that he was addressing her. She bent her head and broke into a run, the sun soon gone, the river turned grey.

She neared the barges beside Eel Pie Island. It was windy and they knocked against each other. A few of them were caved in and rotten, held together only by loops of rope. Patched tarpaulins stretched across each boat, as thin and tight as chicken skin. A few children sat around the hulls, throwing peeled sticks into the river. A mother nursed a baby as she flung chunks of bread into hot fat, the fire smoking across the Thames like mist.

This was where Crawford had lived, bone cold in winter, the tarpaulin rustling and creaking above his head. Occasionally, the sounds of Endellion must have drifted up to him. Concerts and parties, violins in the air. Crawford might have sat there, dipping his toes in the silty water, the moon sharpening itself like a knife. He would have gripped that secret like a precious stone. That is, until the day when he had taken the path to Endellion and hoped he would be acknowledged at last. How Mr Moncrieff's denial and rage would have soured his pride, his resentment curdling him from the inside. Shut out; kept apart. What could that do to a person? She remembered how he had stared at the house when he had walked across its entrance hall for the first time: the wonder, the fury on his face. Bonnie drew her shawl tighter around her arms. The more she tried to work her way into his mind, the more distant she felt from herself, the more afraid.

The woman with the baby looked up, her eyes raking over Bonnie's paisley shawl, her thick woollen dress. Her voice lifted. 'Can I help you, miss?'

'I'm looking for a woman who's lived on these barges for years. Who—'

'That'll be most of us,' the woman said, wincing as the child clamped hard on her nipple. 'Molly, no.'

'She knew a boy called Crawford and I hoped she might—'

'Mary Crawford? And her son Tommy?'

'No—' And then it occurred to Bonnie that Crawford might not have been his Christian name after all. 'Perhaps. Yes.'

The woman shielded her eyes, peering closer. 'What is it you want?'

'I – well. I wanted to know about him.'

The woman sucked on her teeth, her eyes narrowing. 'Know about him.'

There was no use lying; it had boxed Bonnie into enough corners. She gestured in the direction of her house. 'I live at Endellion. I recently married the master there. And I have reason to think that a – a wrong was committed against Crawford. I want to understand it and make amends if I need to.'

The woman dipped her head, her mouth puckering into a slight snarl. 'There's nothing to make amends for, I can tell you that much. And never a boy who deserved it less.'

'How so?'

The woman laughed. 'He was always so full of his little green jacket, his fine feather quill. Trotting back here. How we longed to tell him the truth, but we knew it would mean a boxing. Mary was a dragon, right enough.'

'The truth about what?' Bonnie asked.

'Little Lord Thomas we'd call him. All his damned airs.' She pursed her lips. 'None of us missed him when he left. Said he'd make a fine name for himself. And I hear he's been seen around these parts since. Hasn't come here, has he? Hasn't dirtied his shoes.'

'But what truth?' Bonnie repeated, trying to steer her back. 'About Endellion? About the old Mr Moncrieff?'

The woman shook her head. 'Oh, missy. No, no, no. Hoodwinked you as well as himself, I see.'

'Then tell me.' She reached into her pocket. 'I'll pay you for your trouble—'

'Keep your money,' the woman snapped.

Bonnie tried to find a new way in. 'Crawford – Tommy – but he was the old master's son?'

'Oh, when that idea was in his head, there was no dislodging it. Lord knows how it got there. But his mother said she'd never seen him so happy and she wouldn't take it away from him. She was always too soft on him.'

'What do you mean, idea?' Bonnie frowned. 'Are you saying he was never connected to Endellion?'

'Oh, his father was at Endellion all right.' The woman looked up at Bonnie, flashed her a smile. 'Borrowed money off the master, I do believe, for that boy's education. Worked his way up to butler in the end.'

'You mean – you mean Manton?'

'I never knew his name. But I'd have loved to have seen the look on Tommy's face if someone told him he was the bastard child of a servant. Lording himself above us all.'

Manton. That strange familiarity she hadn't quite been able to place. Crawford was Manton's son. Relief spread through her. There was none of Crawford's poison in Aubrey, no invisible knot linking the two men. Not brothers at all, then. Her heart quickened. Bonnie had the bait at last, the thing that might unravel him. As she bade goodnight to the woman, she found herself slipping into a run, her hair pounding against her back, her mouth cracking into a smile. How thoroughly Crawford scorned anyone below him, how he cleaved to his sense of thwarted grandeur. The truth, she knew, would not drive him away, his obsession with the house magically slackening. It was not as simple as that. No: but still, Bonnie had this information, a little card that she might lay down whenever she chose, a weight to knock him off balance when he did not expect it. Dew spangled her shoes. Crawford could not bear to be wrong or foolish. And after all this, he was simply the butler's son. All his ideals cut loose, undone.

Ruined

The carriages arrived just after six o'clock, huge and lacquered like a row of beetles. Only Mr Eland's was smaller, chipped and powder-blue, and Bonnie rushed to help him down the steps.

'My dear,' he said, handing her a small paper bag. 'I have a gift for you. A cutting of a rose I recently propagated, by crossing a Gallica with a Damask.'

A few months ago, Bonnie's thoughts would have been filled with where she might plant it, the right sunny spot. But now, she found herself smiling wanly as she accepted it, the gift already forgotten. 'Thank you,' she said, leading him into Endellion behind one of the MPs. In the hallway, two of Marble Hill's footmen took Mr Eland's coat and hat, and she saw how snidely they nudged each other as Rex dropped the MP's topper, a flush spreading up his throat.

She half expected Crawford to emerge, just so he could witness her discomfort and surprise. The Highgate man, showing himself at last. She watched the hallway for any sign of movement, listened for his footsteps on the boards. But there was only the eager tread of footmen, the hubbub from the dining room.

'You must see the mantelpiece in the dining room,' one of the MPs exclaimed to his wife, giving her a small shove forwards as they moved out of the hall. 'Didn't I tell you what a curious knick-knack this house is?' Bonnie recognized him from the hunt: the tall man who had tapped his nose when imparting a *grave confidence*. 'The irregularity of it all! The—' he cleared his throat, as though inviting applause – '*artinatural* quality. I believe it was Mr Moncrieff's first wife who designed it all. But oh—' He turned to Bonnie and Mr Eland where they stood behind him. 'I should not mention her.'

He watched Bonnie carefully, as though hoping to disarm her. She smiled at him. 'Do not stay silent on my account. Aubrey's first wife had a flair for theatre that I don't even try to imitate. She made this house extraordinary. I wish I'd met her.'

'How curious,' the MP murmured, and let out a squawk of a laugh.

Bonnie drifted away. She resisted the urge to wipe the lip of the claret jug. She could see grit gathering at the bottom. It should have been strained through a muslin hours ago. She touched the glass. Cold. Manton would have warmed it slightly on the hotplate.

Behind her, the smaller MP was delivering a nonsensical soliloquy on the cemetery, and Bonnie found it curious how he could turn a place that consumed her so utterly into something so tedious. *A meritorious scheme, where memory may echo back long-lost accents of departed worth, and where reason may preach her consolatory lesson of immortality —*

His wife looked both bored and faintly embarrassed.

Seats were taken for dinner, and Bonnie took the chair at the head of the table, opposite Aubrey. She ought to have drawn up the seating plans more selfishly, placed the tall MP at the far end of the table. His eyes lingered on her for too long. Mr Lyle, that was his name. The wine beat through her and she pushed away her glass, listening to what the men were discussing, many leaning over the women who had been placed between them.

'– Because you see, my wife is desperate for you to build us a folly,' Mr Lyle said.

'I believe it is *you* who desires one, actually,' his wife began, but he silenced her with a brief flap of his hand.

Plates were handed out by the Marble Hill footmen. A great slab of pork belly had been roasted until the crackling snapped like glass. Carrots, as neat as bullets, drowned in butter. Rex stood by the door, turning a gold button in his hand; once he moved towards the gravy boat, then thought better of it and returned to his position. His gaze slid to Aubrey, to Bonnie. When he stood nearer the candles, she noted a bruise on his chin; she wondered absently if he had been brawling.

'She's mad about ruins. I'm afraid to go away for an evening in case she has our whole house blown up for effect like Scotney Castle.' Mr Lyle added in a theatrical voice, *'For this is the age of oddities let loose!* And *you* must build us our next oddity.'

His wife grimaced.

'A folly?' Aubrey said. 'I was thinking, I might design a hospital next. I've enjoyed bringing practicality into my work.'

'Oh, but where's the profit in that! Cemeteries and follies, I tell you, are where treasure lies,' Mr Lyle continued, his knife sawing at the soft meat of the pork.

'But why follies?' Bonnie asked.

Mr Lyle looked at her like she was stupid. 'There is no *why*. They're called *follies*. Madnesses.'

'I know what folly means,' Bonnie said coolly. A quiet settled on the table. She forced warmth into her voice. 'I just wondered why you might want one.'

Mr Lyle spoke slowly, like he was addressing a child. 'Well, you see, my dear. It harks back to ages past. It gives a sense of history. A sense that something much greater was there before. It's why the cemetery appealed to me too: this *commemoration*. Well,' he laughed, 'that and the handsome profits.'

'But you're creating a history that is nothing but a lie,' Bonnie said, with a vehemence she did not expect. From the corner of her eye she saw a glance between Aubrey and Mr Eland: a small exchange of pleasure. They did not like this man either. She raised her voice. 'It is a commemoration that is commemorating nothing at all. Follies have always looked to me like the ruins of a conquered nation, not a hint of grandeur. They're all that an enemy has left behind after triumphing, after pillaging and looting. I've always thought they make a house look weak.'

Annette's cottage flashed into her mind: the blackened half-tumbled walls, the roof gone.

'But harking back to a forgotten past is important,' Mr Lyle said.

'Not if it's a sham. I don't understand it,' she said. Her gown prickled, too tight on the sleeves, too nipping at the waist. She would not touch the pork; she sliced a potato cleanly. 'This desire to dig it all up.'

'Ah,' Mr Eland said. 'But if you'd seen the creatures they've unearthed at Lyme Regis in the last ten years, the questions they pose for our own history, our own inheritance, you might reconsider. I saw them at the Royal Society, the earth stripped away from their bones. Great finned beasts with long-toothed mandibles.'

'You would leave them to sleep, I suppose,' Mr Lyle said. 'You would have us eat with flint knives and hunt mammoths.'

'You deliberately misunderstand me.' She watched him flinch and it pleased her. The whole table was turned towards her. She felt a swelling within herself, that she was equal to this, equal also to Crawford. 'Where history bears a relation to our present, the past, as Mr Eland says, is vital. But where it's just a *glorying*, a *fiction*, a folly, a place that serves neither history nor function—'

A tap on her shoulder. She turned around and Jane was there, twisting her apron. Her cheeks were red, her eyes small and darting. 'Jane? What is it?' Bonnie whispered. Jane shook her head, gestured to the door. Bonnie stood too suddenly, the chair almost tipping over, a footman catching it. At the door, Rex moved slowly out of her way, a slight smile on his lips.

'Please excuse me,' she said to the party, and Aubrey stood too but she touched his shoulder. 'I'll call for you if I need you.'

The door shut behind them. Jane turned to her, tears breaking down her cheeks.

'Good God, Jane, what's happened? What's he done?'

Jane shook her head, dabbing a handkerchief under her eyes. 'What's who done?'

'Tell me what's happened,' Bonnie insisted.

'Oh, madam. It's—' she suppressed a sob behind her hand. 'It's Miss Cissie. Oh, you must come.'

'Is she ill? Is she hurt?' Bonnie was already running, hurrying to the stairs, thundering up them. Cissie's words filtered back to her. *I will die like her* —

'Good God, tell me she isn't—'

'She's – she's feverish is all. She won't be calmed. We've tried everything. She says there's a serpent trapped inside her and all sorts of dreadful things. She's in a frightful state and oh – we didn't know what to do. She called for you—'

'For me? Not her father?'

'This is no place for a gentleman, madam.'

She thought of Cissie's wan, waxen face when they'd walked to the cemetery. The sicknesses that had blighted her, the bowls of vomit she had seen Jane and Sara carrying from her bedroom. She stopped suddenly, Jane piling into the back of her.

How hadn't she seen it before? She had been so wrapped up in Crawford, so fixed on him.

'We didn't think her menses had begun,' Jane said. 'If we'd known, then we'd have discovered it sooner—'

She'd heard Jane and Sara talking outside Bonnie's bedroom. *Perhaps this month she will catch, and then we shan't have any stains to get out of any linens except our own.* And all she'd been able to think about was her own grief, her own childlessness, rather than the conspicuous absence of Cissie in their discussion.

'Cissie,' she exclaimed, pushing open the door and running to her. The girl was lying in bed, her face red and puffy. 'Cissie, my sweet girl.'

Tears streamed down Cissie's cheeks into her hair, but she didn't turn away from Bonnie, didn't shield herself like before. She held out her arms like a child greets its mother, as though only Bonnie would be able to soothe her. And what could Bonnie do except stroke her hair and let her cry?

'Sweet girl,' she repeated, and then, her tears choking her. 'I'm sorry. I'm sorry.'

'Shall I fetch the doctor?' Jane asked, fidgeting in the doorway.

'What will become of this poor girl?' Sara started to weep, squeezing a flannel into a bowl of steaming water.

Bonnie turned to the two maids. 'There will be no theatrics here tonight. And you will send for nobody until I tell you. You will not even discuss this amongst yourselves. I will hear *nothing* spoken about this. Word will not leave this room. Am I understood?'

They nodded, mutely, Sara dabbing her eyes with her apron.

'But who—' Sara asked.

'I said, enough,' Bonnie spat, with a sudden burst of anger. Her hands trembled. 'There will be *no* speculation. Please, leave us in peace now.'

Monster, she thought. *Monster.* She knew who. That night in the scullery, the muslin half-veiling Crawford; how oblivious she had been. She had seen what she expected to see.

Cissie began to scratch at her legs, bunching the fabric of her nightgown in her fists. Bonnie reached for her hand and stilled it.

'What's wrong with me?' Cissie begged. 'I'm dying, aren't I? I'm going to die.'

'No. No.' She turned Cissie's face to hers, spoke to her gently. 'You aren't dying, do you hear me? You need to rest. And then I will tell you all I can. But you are in no state to hear it now.'

Bonnie tucked herself under the covers beside Cissie, held her as she snuffled and wept. 'This isn't your fault,' she whispered again and again, and it seemed to soothe the girl, seemed to help steady the staccato heave of her chest.

'I – I couldn't bear you,' Cissie said. 'Because you reminded me of him. But I didn't know who else to call for.'

'Cissie, he isn't – he isn't my brother.'

Cissie stared at her, uncomprehending.

Bonnie tried to keep her voice level. 'I think – Cissie. I think, and I didn't know this, or I didn't want to know it, but I think – we have to be very careful. I think he could hurt us.'

'Hurt us?'

'What he did to you was a terrible, terrible wrong.'

Cissie let out a gasp of a sob, then settled back against the cushions.

'You need to rest. You need to sleep.'

It took a while for Cissie's breathing to still. Eventually her eyelids closed and she drifted into a half-sleep, her limbs twitching from time to time. Bonnie laid cool flannels against Cissie's forehead, stilling her fingers as they raked her arms, her chest. The phrase bloomed: *with child*, and a brief, hard part of

Bonnie envied Cissie, despite all she had gone through. When, in a fit of restlessness, Cissie cast off the covers, Bonnie glimpsed the tight dome of her belly, small enough that her corset would have held it in. Bonnie pressed her own stomach. Flat. Empty.

She shook herself, dipped the flannel in water, dabbed Cissie's forehead once more. The girl frowned in her sleep but did not wake up. She was sure that Crawford would have heard this commotion through the walls; at the very least, Rex would have told him about her sudden absence from dinner. He would realize she knew what he had done. He would not risk everything unravelling now; he would stop at nothing to silence her.

Bonnie squeezed the flannel harder, emptying the last dregs of water into the bowl. Her fingernails whitened, her knuckles too. She picked up the cloth, hurled it against the wall, but the muted *whump* of it only made her angrier. If Cissie had not been there, she would have smashed the dressing table and gloried in the splintering of wood; she would have taken the mirrors and hurled them to the floor. She paced instead, up and down, the ball in her chest knotting tighter. She needed air, coolness, and she pushed open the sash window, breathed in the cold. The candle huffed out and she inhaled that sweet tendril of smoke, twisting into the air.

Everything began to knit together, falling into a grotesque pattern. How furious Crawford must have been when she defected to Aubrey, his plans undone in an instant because he had not kept her close enough. But then – Bonnie shut her eyes, tried to breathe steadily – the answer must have come to him.

Cissie.

Cissie; of course. Guileless, sweet Cissie who wanted nothing more than to be loved. That was how he would keep Endellion; it was only she and Aubrey who were expendable. Cissie was valuable. Cissie was their answer. If she and Aubrey were gone, all that mattered was the baby in Cissie's belly, the marriage Crawford would engineer. Could Cissie have told him about the inheritance passing to her? Might Annette have known, and Crawford could have prised it out of her?

Bonnie stared out into the blackness, at the trees that bickered. A commotion below; laughter. The directors were leaving, Rex helping them into their carriages, a coachman holding a lantern. Mr Lyle stumbled on the steps then fell into his chaise roaring with laughter.

Jane and Sara must have told Aubrey not to disturb them because she heard his footsteps in the hallway, pausing at Cissie's door, and then continuing to his bedroom. It was a cloudy night and the stars were obscured, the moon nothing more than a faint blanch. A black shape darted across the lawn. A fox, perhaps, or a stray dog.

Behind her, Cissie stirred and Bonnie shut the window, breathing against the glass. In a moment, she would turn and go to her.

'Who's there?' Cissie called out, pushing her covers down.

'It's me,' Bonnie said, hurrying to her. 'It's only me. Bonnie.' She lit a candle from the last of the coals, watched as the wick flared. She could do this, she told herself; she would tell Cissie what had happened to her.

'Cissie,' Bonnie said, sitting beside her. 'Sweet Cissie.' The girl rested her head on her lap. She was so small for seventeen, a little bird of a thing. In the candlelight her skin looked jaundiced.

'The snakes,' Cissie said at last. 'I cannot make them stop.'

'They are not snakes,' Bonnie said, more tenderly than she thought possible. She could feel her ears pinking, that familiar drumbeat in her skull. That she had to explain this to her; that anyone did. 'It is – it is a child.' She waited. 'There is a child inside you,' Bonnie repeated. 'A baby.'

'How—'

Bonnie gripped her hand. 'Crawford is a wicked man. He tricked you. He didn't act out of love but out of – of spite.' She leaned closer, urgent. 'You are not to blame, Cissie. This is his fault, not yours.'

'Lord Duggan—'

Bonnie shook her head. 'Lord Duggan isn't real, Cissie. Or at least he was only when he wrote to your mother.'

Cissie pulled her covers over her head, her voice high and sharp. 'You're wrong!'

'You're upset, I know you are. But this won't help you.'

'Look,' Cissie scrambled away, running across the room, levering open her desk. The scrap-book was inside. It had been months since Bonnie had seen her with it.

'You should rest,' Bonnie tried again. 'This won't help. You wrote the letters yourself. You know you did.'

'*Look.*'

The book cracked open. Bonnie leafed through the pages. She would indulge the girl. She wondered what letters Cissie might have written to herself about this, how she might excuse the horror she had experienced, this egregious wrong committed against her. There, at the start, were the letters to Josephine that Bonnie had already read; then the false letters in Cissie's slanting script.

'Please,' Bonnie said. She could not bear it. 'Let's put this dreadful book away—'

'There,' Cissie said. 'Look. *There.*'

Cissie turned the page. Bonnie paused. The letters here were in a different hand from Cissie's own. Bonnie's heartbeat thumped in her ears.

'Let me see this,' she said, angling the book away from Cissie. Her eyes raced over the page.

Dearest Mousekin,

I have found a way to come to you at last, after two years of hope and distant correspondence. You will be surprised to see I have been in your company for some time, waiting for the right moment to unmask myself. How lonely you must be after your father's new marriage! How bereft I am to see anybody assume the place that was rightfully your mother's, the woman I loved beyond all else, no matter how close and dear that new person might be to me. But in Josephine's place, I have watched you flourish. I know both she and your new mother would bless our union; how I hunger to call you my wife at last! Two lovers will entwine; we will do as husband does to wife. Do you not feel it too? Think how your Mama, an angel in heaven, would rejoice. Meet me, my darling. Meet me in the kitchen when it is late and I will show you what it means to be loved, held, cherished, as I often showed her.

Cissie lay face down on the bed. A heat rose in Bonnie's chest. The outrage of it; that Crawford would use Lord Duggan against Cissie like this. But Bonnie had led him to it, hadn't she? All those evenings he had prised information out of her, begging Bonnie to tell him what Cissie's letters had said. The way he had laughed, when really he had been storing every piece of knowledge she gave him, waiting until he could dangle the bait into Cissie's mouth.

'I did not understand what he meant,' Cissie wept. Her voice was muffled. 'I do not want to be loved at all if that is the way it is.'

'Oh, Cissie,' Bonnie said. Her throat ached, a sharp gouging pain. 'You did not understand. He committed a terrible wrong. The child—'

Cissie sat up suddenly, her face aghast. 'Child? The *child?*' she demanded, as though she had only just grasped what Bonnie had told her before. 'Ruined? Ruined? Is that what I am?'

Ruined. A caved-in castle, a fragment of a girl once whole. It was a word from her romances. 'It is – you are not—' Bonnie swallowed. 'We will find a way out of this, Cissie, I promise. It need not mark you at all.'

Bonnie thought the girl might rage. She thought she might start to cry. At the very least, she expected questions. But Cissie simply fell back against the pillows, twin flames from the candle dancing in her eyes.

'Cissie?' she asked. 'Cissie. What can I say?'

But Cissie looked at her with a face that was so blank, so empty, that it frightened her.

'Cissie?' she said again.

Nothing. And in time, Cissie fell asleep again, her breathing steadier than last time, her limbs still. Outside, an animal bayed.

Lines from the letter raced through Bonnie's head.

How bereft I am to see anybody assume the place that was rightfully your mother's, the woman I loved beyond all else, no matter how close and dear that new person might be to me.

She reached for the scrap-book, opened it quietly. She flicked between Lord Duggan's original letters to Josephine and the new letters to Cissie.

The writing was the same. Identical. That unusual flick of the *h*. Letters sent from Crawford to mother, then to daughter. Bonnie felt that she had never seen a person so cleanly, so coldly. How far back had Crawford's desire to hurt Aubrey stretched? All those nights when he disappeared from St Giles, he was coming here, to Josephine, gradually untethering her from the house, from her husband, from a life she might once have cherished. And when she drowned, that was when he had lighted on Bonnie.

WANTED. In a Gentleman's family, a short distance from Richmond, a single woman as LADY'S MAID for a young girl of sixteen years –

Bonnie had to stand to breathe more easily. For Crawford to turn to Cissie next; this gentle, sleeping girl, her lips a little parted. She thought of all the things that Josephine would protect her daughter from if she could. Bonnie was in her place now. She reached out a hand and stroked Cissie's cheek.

The rats, let loose in a pit as men leaned forward and jeered, the stale reek of ale filling the room. Their fear like the scent of iron. Trapped, nowhere left to go. Bonnie thought of how they flattened themselves in the corner, then raised themselves to their full height and lunged forward. All this time Bonnie had simply been waiting. But the cleverest rats, she knew, would strike first.

Knife

The kitchen was cold, the stove dark and ashen. The dough for the next morning's bread was rising through the night. Bonnie stepped on a puddle of spilled water and she slid forward, hand slapping the wood as she caught herself on the table. She waited. Nothing stirred.

Copper pans dangled from the ceiling, some big enough to bathe a baby in. Brass jelly moulds, a long salmon dish. The silver room and Rex and Crawford's quarters were only a few feet away. She had to be quiet. The knife block was empty. Her hands slipped on the cabinet drawer as she inched it open, slowly, trying to still the rattle of cutlery. She groped around. Impossible to see in the gloom. Her fingers settled on rolling pins and grape scissors, toasting forks and a whisk. She tried the next drawer, levered it out carefully.

The knives were inside, wrapped in cloth. She unbundled them. A boring knife, a cleaver, two paring knives, a filleting knife. In a separate box she found the long slim carving knife, the silk lining stained with old animal blood. Bonnie had watched Annette tuck a small gutting blade into the soft bellies of salmon and trout and rip through the flesh, wet guts tumbling into her hand. After, she would use the filleting knives to lever out the spines and ribs. Every so often, Manton used to sharpen the knives, each laid out on the table before him as he ground them against his soaked whetstone. 'There,' he would say, holding each blade to the light. 'Sharp enough to shave a man.'

Bonnie had been right to hire Jane and Sara: they too had diligently kept the knives whetted. The blades were a little brittle from so much sharpening, but when Bonnie pressed them against her finger, she saw the quick bloom of blood. Good, she thought. Good.

A thrill of power went through her as she placed the carving knife to the side and slid the other blades back into the drawer. She thought of Cissie, slammed against that cold wall, her legs gripped in Crawford's hands, and fury lit her up. All the hurt this knife could inflict, the strength she could wield.

She heard low dull murmurings and she fled across the flagstones, back upstairs, the knife pressed against her chest. Back in her bedroom, she wrapped the blade in a scarf and laid it at the bottom of her wardrobe. But she would not sleep in her own bed. One certainty filled her mind: she had to keep Aubrey close to her. She had to know he was safe. She thought of Crawford, erratic, unravelling. Drunk before five o'clock, the careful way Rex had watched her leave the dining room. She knew too much, and it was her and Aubrey they wanted. All of tomorrow, she would cleave to him.

He didn't wake up when she climbed into bed beside him. She placed a hand under his nose, his breath warm and steady. The relief of it. She tucked her knees under his, wrapped her arms tightly around his chest.

'What happened?' he whispered, stirring. 'Sara and Jane told me not to worry.'

'It was Cissie. She was upset. She's better now.'

He turned to her, kissed her on the mouth. 'It isn't only Cissie who's concerning me.'

'Me?'

'I think I should call a doctor, Bonnie. You – you haven't been yourself.'

'No,' she shook her head. 'Please. Please, Aubrey. I'm just tired. I'll be better, I promise.'

He sighed. 'Very well.'

She stared ahead in the blackness. This man she loved. The solidity of him.

'I will be fine,' Bonnie replied. 'And so will Cissie.'

Was it a lie? But then she remembered Cissie at Christmas, picking those burned raisins out of the flaming bowl, how she had barely flinched. Cissie had beaten them all. Cissie would recover, Bonnie thought. She would master herself.

In the morning, Bonnie woke to find the bed empty beside her. She sat up quickly, hurried to the window. It was late, the sun high. She had to find Aubrey; she had to be wherever he was. She bound a shawl around herself and hurried downstairs. Her nightgown snagged on the banister and she tugged it, tearing the fabric.

'Aubrey?' she called. The breakfast room was empty, bacon fat congealing on a plate. Odd that Sara hadn't cleared the table. She climbed upstairs again, the cameos eyeing her, the light dim without the lantern. Lighting it was usually Jane's first task of the day. Perhaps they were busy downstairs, cleaning up after the directors' dinner. Of course; that would be it. So why then, was the house so quiet? No sounds of singing or clanging from the kitchen.

Aubrey's study was empty, the door ajar. He would be at the cemetery, but it was strange that he hadn't waited for her. They usually went together each morning, and this was the day when the carpentry in the chapel would be finished, the final pews fitted, the scrolled panelling fixed to the wall. A fluttering set up in her chest. Where was he? She had to stay calm. She could not show her fear. It was a struggle not to break into a run as she worked her way through the house, opening doors, closing them. Cissie, at least, was still asleep, her face turned into her pillow.

Thoughts flashed through her mind: Aubrey, killed out in the open, the murder passed off as a shooting accident. Those mistakes happened, didn't they, a man mistaken for a fox through the trees, for a pheasant? Or colder, crueller: his throat slit, his body discarded. Surely they would not be so cavalier. Crawford was more careful than that.

She caught movement in the corner of the library and Bonnie almost screamed. Rex was sitting in the armchair. He clicked his knuckles and smiled.

'Where's Aubrey?' she asked, as calmly as she could. 'And Sara and Jane?'

'The master instructed them to take a day to visit their families,' he said breezily. 'Wasn't that kind?'

'Liar.'

The word, so cold and short, the hostility suddenly exposed between them.

'Aubrey had to travel to London on an urgent matter.'

'You're wrong. He'd have woken me. Where is he?'

Rex watched her. 'Crawford persuaded him not to.' He put on a simpering accent. 'Poor Bonnie's nerves have been so frayed lately.'

She was careful not to react. 'My nerves are not frayed.'

'Well. Your husband seemed concerned and decided to leave you to sleep when he received a letter from a director at Highgate. There are accusations of his graveyard imitating another too closely. It could ruin the cemetery, stop it opening.'

'What? How?'

'It's more than half a day's ride to Highgate. He'll be back tomorrow. He took a travelling case.'

Tomorrow. Bonnie's stomach turned over. Just her and Cissie in the house, alone with Rex and Crawford.

Rex stood, holding out his hands in helpless supplication. 'Poor Mrs Moncrieff, left all alone,' he said. He was so tall, so wide. He looked like a giant against the small pink chaise. She saw how he revelled in it. Crawford's dog, closing in. His eyes roamed over her: her nightgown, almost transparent. 'There's no need to look so afraid,' he said. '*Mrs Moncrieff.*'

'I'm not,' she replied, her voice steady. But she found herself backing out of the door, down the hallway. She let herself into Aubrey's study, scrabbled through the papers on his desk. Nothing; down the stairs, her feet cold on the wood. In the cloakroom, she found his coat on a peg. She searched the pockets, withdrew a crumpled letter.

Dear Sir, I write to you with urgent concerns —

Even though she'd expected it, the truth still pounded down on her. It was unmistakeable: there was the same looping *h* of Lord Duggan's, of *Crawford's* hand. Another forged letter.

She was alone. Her husband feared for her mind. She knew how they would make it look.

She tried to think calming thoughts: soil crumbling between her palms, the first unfurling of an orchid bud. She stumbled into the entrance hall, sunlight piercing her eyes. Rex had followed her. He gave her a small, knowing smile.

Brothers

Bonnie had to find Crawford. He was just a man, she told herself. Just one person. Because in her mind he had begun to sprawl, to press himself into every corner of her. And so too, did he seem to infest every cranny of Endellion. A tin of tobacco in the drawing room. His cravat in the library. A half-eaten pie in the kitchen. His hairs would be between the floorboards, his piss watering the flowers in the garden. He was everywhere and nowhere; she could neither escape nor find him. She had the sense he had just slipped out of every room she entered, creeping only a few paces ahead. If only she might come across him, then she could disarm him, unsettle him. The secret throbbed in her chest. *Manton.*

But the more he held himself away, the more she flinched at each shadow, each flutter of the sun against the wall. He was here, she thought: and yet, where was he? She opened boxes that he could not possibly have hidden in. She checked behind curtains, her fingers trembling. The absurdity only compounded her fear. Frayed nerves, wasn't that what Rex had called it? She blinked, her hands on a curtain that he would never be hiding behind. The jar of water, she told herself. The jar of water.

She had to steady herself.

When she heard Cissie's tread on the ceiling above, she could not bear it, and she hurried away from the sound, into the pantry. The dough intended for the morning had bubbled and spilled over the sides of the bowl. She was suddenly ravenous, her belly rumbling. She ripped a mouthful of bread from the stale loaf but it tasted sour and earthy: she spat it into her hand. Her breath gusted out in thick rasps.

Crawford's jacket was slung over a chair. She was sure it had not been there before. So he *had* been here. Even if he had not witnessed it, he would have heard her frenzy. Chests dragged open, doors slammed shut, her footsteps racing through the house. Had he sat in this kitchen and been entertained, amused? Tapping his fingers. Biding his time.

She needed air. She burst into the garden. Spring was almost here. Snowdrops and daffodils, the blue flash of hyacinths, already felled by their own weight and lying in the soil. A tendril of smoke lifted from beside the greenhouse. It was him. She was sure of it. A thorn caught her foot. She ought to have dressed properly at least, retained some semblance of normality. The grass creaked. Heart skittering, a sharpening pain, like someone had driven a skewer into her side. Her rage a vibration, deep within her.

He was just a man, she reminded herself, and when she rounded the corner and saw him, she found she was surprised by the truth of it. He was so *ordinary*. His dark hair, raked back from his forehead. His eyes, so black and shining, staring straight at her, as though he had expected her to find him there. He looked at her in that familiar way: appraising, admiring, and she wrapped the shawl tighter around her.

'Bonnie Bee,' he said, pulling his pipe from between his teeth. 'Have you missed me?'

It was an ugly echo of their first meeting at Endellion, as though time could simply slip backwards. She told herself she would not be disarmed, but she could think of no retort to make, no clean way to cut him down. An image rose, unbidden: how he had pushed her against the greenhouse table one night, nudged apart her legs, pressed himself into her. When he'd thrown back his head, his adam's apple had been so ridged and exposed. That small square in his throat.

He leaned closer to her but she snatched herself back.

'Don't you dare touch me.'

He smiled. 'That isn't very nice, Bonnie Bee.'

She had to master herself. She had to unnerve him too.

'Is that so, Lord Duggan?'

He looked at her for a flicker of a second.

'I know everything you've done, Crawford. You know I do.' She paused. 'But there are things that I know, and you don't.'

'And what things might they be?'

She glanced away, feigning boredom. 'Wouldn't you like me to tell you.'

'You're lying.'

'You can think that if you choose,' she replied. A sharp pain was splitting her skull but she forced herself to fold her arms, to let out a small laugh. The strength it took to lean closer to him, to allow herself to breathe in that familiar scent. Cloves, peppermint, pipe smoke. 'I know what a lonely little boy you were, how you wanted to feel special, important. How you wanted the man you thought was your brother to feel your pain, to have nothing just like you did. But more than that, you wanted the man you thought was your father to love you, and when he didn't, it broke your heart.'

He forced a laugh. 'How typically *Bonnie*. How very sentimental. It didn't break me.'

She spoke low, steadily. Her hands were hot, a line of sweat running down her back. 'I know how long you've plotted all this, how long you've wanted what Aubrey has. You seduced

Josephine because you wanted to steal her from Aubrey. But it didn't work. So you tricked me into coming here. At the beginning, your plans weren't as big as they are now. You just wanted to be close to the house, didn't you? You just wanted to disrupt it. But then you became greedy. What a fool you were, handing me to him on a plate. But I'm grateful to you, truly I am.'

He shrugged, but she caught a small flash of pain in his eye. 'Sometimes, your dogs run away and you can't stop them.'

It smarted: she couldn't deny it. But that was what he wanted. She kept talking, her voice rising higher and higher. 'And all those times at the Angler when you vanished for a few days, you were here. Trying to lure Josephine away. Trying to make Aubrey's life a misery. But she didn't want you in the end, did she? She decided not to leave Aubrey, and then she drowned. She was beyond your control, then. That must have hurt. That must have *stung*.'

Crawford watched her. 'You don't know anything.'

Bonnie did not speak. She felt the tingle of it, the pleasure of withholding. Composing herself.

Crawford raised his hand to his hair, tucked a single strand out of his eyes. The strength in his forearms, that familiar flex. She felt a shock of fear, steadied herself. Her knees would not stop trembling.

'You have it all wrong,' he said. 'You always do.'

She waited.

She could see he could not resist, his mouth breaking into a smile. A little boy's pride, showing off what he had done. 'You think she drowned? Just like you thought Aubrey killed her, because I told you to think that. Everyone's always telling you what to think and you just lap it up.' He narrowed his eyes and she knew a blow was coming. 'Of course Aubrey didn't kill her. He wouldn't crush a mouse. It was me, Bonnie. I did it.'

Bonnie couldn't help it. Her hand went to her mouth.

'When she said she wouldn't leave with me, I dragged her into the pond. Oh, she fought. She fought and fought and called out her daughter's name, but in the end, what chance did she have? I couldn't let him win. I left her floating there. How peaceful, if you hadn't known the misery of her last seconds. Her desperation. A woman doing away with herself. A woman her husband knew was distressed, upset. There are echoes here, aren't there? Your *frayed nerves.*'

Bonnie did her best to keep her gaze level. She swallowed. 'You couldn't let Aubrey win? But he was going to live separately from her. He didn't even want her. All that effort, taking away a person he didn't even cherish.' She continued, her voice tuneless. 'And then, of course, there was Cissie.'

'Cissie,' he echoed. He pulled back his shoulders. She scarcely needed to prompt him. He was enjoying unravelling it all. *Look how clever I've been.*

'Now that – *that* – was easy. Easier than I ever thought possible. She didn't even fight or scream. She was so *limp.*' He moved closer to Bonnie. 'And the best thing of all? She caught. I hooked her. All those months you've been waiting and hoping, and she caught in a single night.'

The look of triumph on his face, the ecstasy of it.

'My poor brother with his barren wife.'

Rage passed through her, simmering, red-hot. Bonnie smiled, an ugly grin that cracked her cheeks like china. 'He isn't your brother.'

Crawford laughed, shook his head.

'Didn't you know that?' Bonnie feigned disbelief. 'All this time, and you thought you were owed something. You thought you were important.'

She glimpsed the flicker of confusion on his face, quickly suppressed.

'Everyone else knew. They all laughed at you. They're still chuckling over it now, down on the barges. Little Lord Thomas and his grand ideas, the boy who thought he was a prince. And your poor mother, who couldn't bear to wreck her son's ideals.'

Crawford raised his finger, his breath meaty and close. 'You're lying—'

But Bonnie could not stop, not when she saw how she'd slipped her way under his skin.

'They were full of it on the barges. How we laughed about it!'

Crawford lunged for her, slamming her against a tree, his hand on her throat.

'And to think you drove away your own father,' Bonnie hissed. 'You weren't Tommy Moncrieff, but Tommy *Manton*.'

The blow took her by surprise, a ringing in her temples. Her head ricocheted against the bark. Her teeth; her jaw; she tried each in turn. Nothing broken, not yet. And it snapped her. A convulsion in her limbs. By God, she would *fight*. She hurled herself forward, biting, clawing, blood streaming from her nose and that cold, fast desire: to hurt, to maim, to win. Crawford seized her arms, pressed her back against the tree, but she raised her leg, kicked him hard in the thigh.

She should have known her victory would be short-lived; should have known that against a man of Crawford's bulk, she stood no chance at all. His hands gripped her throat, and the more she writhed, the tighter he held her. Her breathing stuttered, stopped. Blind, white panic. Behind them, the pond; Josephine had not known what Crawford was until it was too late. The sun beat down in splinters. Her head felt heavy, drenched, like swimming underwater too long and finding the surface was further than she thought. The more she kicked and struggled, the more distant the sky seemed to be; his hands, so tight. A blackness spread across her eyes.

This is it.

Aubrey; the gun; she bucked but her limbs were limp.

And then air, rushing, at last, enough to choke on. She slumped to the ground, felt the cold earth under her. Something hot on her chin. Blood. And Rex and Crawford locked together.

'Let me *go*,' Crawford bellowed as Rex shook him.

'You're forgetting yourself,' Rex hissed. 'How would you explain it? An *accident*, with Bonnie strangled, bruising on her throat, the girl watching at the window? This isn't what we agreed.'

The girl – Bonnie gripped her neck, took in a gasping lungful. The trees might have partly shielded them, but Cissie would have seen enough. She looked up and there was Cissie's pale face at the window, her mouth open in a silent shout.

Crawford threw Rex from him. 'You're my dog,' he sneered, nudging Rex with his boot. 'I'll whistle when I need you.'

And he was gone then; they were both gone. Just Bonnie and her fingers pinching her neck, as though coaxing herself to breathe, reminding herself that she was alive.

The Somnambulist

Even in the time it took Bonnie to rush across the lawn and up the stairs, Cissie had not moved from the window. Her forehead was pressed to the pane, the glass shivering. There was no candle lit, just the fire, casting orange patterns on her back.

'Cissie?' Bonnie whispered. Her voice came out a low, ugly croak. 'Cissie.'

Cissie turned and her face was waxen. She looked like a death mask, her eyes still and glassy.

'You see,' Bonnie said, stepping closer. 'You see a little of what I meant yesterday. When I told you that he is not my brother. I regret every day I have ever known him.'

The girl stood carefully, as though her limbs might snap if her movements were too sudden. Her hair was stuck to the snot on her cheek. 'There's – there's blood. Your lip. He was hurting you and I tried to shout but nobody heard—'

'I'm better now, aren't I?' Bonnie said with forced cheer. 'You mustn't worry—'

And then Cissie flung herself towards Bonnie, her arms around her waist. Her grip was so clawing and desperate that Bonnie almost felt herself tugged over: fingernails dug into her back, Cissie's face pressed hard against her shoulder. 'Oh, Cissie,' she said, and that last barrier between them gave way, the two of them, clasping each other.

'What will we do?' Cissie asked. 'What will we do?'

'Everything will be fine,' Bonnie said. 'It will be. We will make it so.'

But there was nowhere to hide. If only the house might sprout another turret, grow another room, and seal them inside.

'It's me they want,' Bonnie whispered. 'It isn't you. If I'm alone, then you'll be safe.' And she thought only *the knife*.

When Bonnie saw Crawford riding Boudicca in widening circles, she sneaked back to her own bedroom. Even when she drew the curtains, she could still hear the hooves hammering against the hard ground, the peal of the reins. Better to know where he was, she thought, but the sound seemed to grow louder and louder in her ears, that *c-rop c-rop c-rop* chiming with her own heartbeat.

In the mirror, her face was puffed, ghastly. Her left eye was nearly closed, dried blood on her chin. It stung when she dabbed it with cold water. She pulled Josephine's stool closer to the glass. In the half-light of the drawn shutters, Bonnie could almost believe she had become Josephine: that intensity in her eyes, the sharp jut of her chin. Crawford had killed her, left her floating on the surface of the pond. A string tugged them together: both duped by Crawford. But Bonnie knew him where Josephine had not had the chance: she had unsettled him, cut up his plans, and that might give her a small advantage.

As she sat there, there seemed something off in the air. Something like – *smoke*. Bonnie threw herself to her feet, the stool upended. When she turned the handle, she almost expected to find her door locked, the hallway outside already alight. But it opened easily. There was no furnace in the hall, no flames beating up the stairs. The scent was faint, as though Sara had just burned scones. She crossed the landing and it grew stronger, a small strand of smoke escaping from under Cissie's door.

She shouldered her way inside. The girl was hunched over the fireplace, something black and smoking on the hearthstone. Bonnie saw how painfully thin she had become, the stones of her spine sharply jointed.

'Cissie,' Bonnie said, hurrying to her. 'What are you burning? What is that?'

No answer. Cissie prodded the smouldering object with a poker. As Bonnie neared her, she saw that it was the scrap-book, charred and blackened, the edges of the pages glowing. Smoke poured from it. Bonnie seized the tongs, levered it back into the grate. It caught properly, flames eating it up.

'Cissie,' Bonnie said again, but the girl's face was pale and uncomprehending. 'Come, let's bring you to bed.'

Cissie allowed Bonnie to lift her up, the lace of her nightgown tight around her throat. It was like leading a somnambulist across the room.

'What's that?' Bonnie asked. A jewel of blood shone on the floorboards. There was another on the rug. 'Did you cut yourself?'

Still, Cissie said nothing. Her lips were pale and flaking.

'Cissie?'

There was a high *plink* sound like a raindrop chiming against hard earth. Bonnie glanced down and the girl's feet were wet with blood, a small rivulet running off her ankle.

'Oh,' Bonnie exclaimed. 'Oh, Cissie. No, no.'

'He ruined me,' she said, dully. 'He ruined me.' She touched her belly. 'It still writhes. It does, I feel it. I want to cut it out of me.'

'Lie down,' Bonnie said, a fluttering in her chest. She helped her to the bed. 'I need to see what you've done. Will you let me?'

Cissie nodded, lying back as Bonnie lifted the nightgown. Bonnie had expected to find the cuts inside her, a skewering with something long and sharp. But she saw that the soft hair between Cissie's legs was almost bloodless: instead, she had cut her inner thighs in crude, shallow slashes. How little this girl knew. She had used a knife, and the gouges were mercifully shallow.

'Oh, love,' Bonnie said, touching the girl's forehead. The bowl of water was still on Cissie's dressing table from the night before and Bonnie carried it over to her bed. Carefully, she dabbed a wet flannel over the cuts.

'It hurts,' Cissie wept, tears pouring down her cheeks. Her legs flinched with each sweep of the flannel. 'It hurts. It hurts so terribly,' Cissie wept, tears pouring down her cheeks. Her legs flinched with each sweep of the flannel. 'And the – the – baby is gone then? I have rid myself of it?' she asked, her voice rising with hope.

'The baby is—' Bonnie broke off, and Cissie must have read it on her face, because she fell back against the pillows, her body wracked with sobs.

'He has ruined me,' she said again and again, a pillow held over her mouth, and when she rose for air, a line of saliva linked her teeth to the cushion. 'He has ruined me!'

'You are not *ruined.*'

Helplessness swamped Bonnie. If only there was a way of cleanly lifting the child from Cissie, undoing what she never intended, never understood.

'In the morning, when your father returns, we will tell him what was done to you. He will see at once that it wasn't your fault.'

'And then I will die.'

This fixation on death, Bonnie thought: it followed no order.

'How can you think such a thing? Of course you won't.'

'You know nothing!' Cissie shouted it with such conviction that Bonnie flinched. 'When a heroine is ruined,' she said slowly, irritably, as though explaining a simple fact to a child, 'she dies. I will die just like Mama. He ruined her, and he has ruined me too.'

Bonnie could bear it no longer. She held Cissie by the shoulders, a sureness filling her. All those times Bonnie had changed her life, dusted herself off. The euphoria as she had fled her village in the donkey cart, face pressed against the hay; that moment she had slipped through the bars at Mrs Pennyweather's. 'Listen to me,' she said. 'You are not going to die or waste away. You are in charge of your own life. A heroine does not die because she's been ruined. A heroine changes her fortune. She finds another way out.'

Cissie stared at Bonnie. She blinked, slowly. And there was that look in Cissie that Bonnie recognized from Christmas and the burning bowl of raisins, from the afternoon they had spun around in that cold, driving rain. It was a gathering of herself, a tucking away of her pain. A colour flared in Cissie's cheeks. She gave the smallest of nods.

Sow

For the rest of the afternoon, Bonnie left Cissie alone in her room. It pained her to be apart from the girl, but it was Bonnie they wanted to be rid of; Cissie was now their golden prize. Before Bonnie had left, she had shown Cissie how to angle a chair against the door and the girl had nodded, white-lipped.

She would not stay in Josephine's bedroom, would not be in a place where they expected to find her. Bonnie went into the room only to find the knife, just where she had left it. The handle chilled her fingers. She would go to Aubrey's study. She crossed the landing and the hallway, keeping to the wall where the floorboard creak was quietest. And when the study door closed behind her, she was surprised by the sense of peace that filled her. Aubrey was here in the half-empty inkpot, in the sketch half completed, as though he was just about to bluster in the door and assume his seat at his desk.

But soon, this ease began to give way. Bonnie watched Crawford stabling Boudicca, then crossing the lawn back to the house. The kitchen door slammed. There were no footsteps on the stairs, no sound of muffled whispers. He and Rex would probably be sitting in the kitchen discussing how to make up for Crawford's lapse, how to engineer Bonnie's accident. Surely, they could not risk waiting for Aubrey to return and all she might tell him. Bonnie pressed her ear to the door.

The house creaked in the wind, curtains sucked against the glass and puffed away again. The knife shone, sharp enough to carve through gristle and rind. She sat there for what felt like hours, her neck burning from Crawford's hands, her back stiff. As the room darkened, she longed to light a candle, but then they would see the slant of light under the door. The house filled with tiny noises, each one more magnified than the last. Mice rattled in the walls. The floorboards ticked. Somewhere there was a crackling sound like a fire in a grate. A door must have been ajar because it swung back and forth in the breeze. All these sounds became Crawford or Rex on the stairs, making their way towards her. They would hear the pulse thrumming in her throat, surely. They would sense the sweat that rose from her. A gentle creak of wood; what was it? She sat more upright. A shout from downstairs and she almost cried out. What was happening? She scarcely breathed. Her hands tightened around the knife. The clock ticked on the mantelpiece. Ten minutes, fifteen. Still, they did not come.

And then, suddenly, in the distance, she heard the stable door slamming. She raced across the room, stared out the window. At first, she could see nothing in the dark. Just the door flapping on its hinges, cracking against the brickwork. And then; hoofbeats. She peered closer. A figure rode out, swallowed immediately by the darkness. Rex; could it have been him? She was sure he had been broad-backed, tall. Her knees began to shake. And if Rex was gone, then where was Crawford? He must still be downstairs. Still in the kitchen. Faintly, she wondered if this had all been part of the plan, if she was supposed to see Rex leave and feel emboldened, to creep downstairs where Crawford would be lying in wait. But she could not sit still any longer. It seemed as though her life had narrowed to a small, dark tunnel, and there was only one way to move forwards, only one way out.

When Bonnie was a girl, her father would slaughter a pig each autumn when the sow was fat from rootling all summer. As the days shortened, Bonnie would garland the sow's ears with daisies and tie a ribbon around her enormous waist. She would drag her father to the sty.

'How can you kill her when she looks as pretty as this?' she would ask.

And each time he would lower his head and say, 'It must be done, Bonnie. There's no other choice.'

'When?' she would beg. 'At least tell me when so I can say goodbye?' Her sisters would laugh at her for being sentimental, and each year he would shake his head and say he wasn't sure. But one morning just after the trees began unleaving, Bonnie would be woken by the pig's scream. She would run outside and find the pig, clamped and writhing between her father's thighs, a knife stuck in her throat as she was bled into a pan.

Bonnie's father always said that he did not know exactly when the time was right. It was not a thing he planned, but a decision he would simply make one morning the moment he woke up. *This is the time. I can delay it no longer.* And then, he said, he did not let himself pause or think. He was an arrow already set on its course.

The knife handle was slippery in her hand. Her only hope was surprise. She opened the study door carefully, took the stairs as quietly as she could. She registered only small beats around her: the cold pine steps under her feet, the warmer air from the kitchen. Everywhere, she anticipated him. Behind each door, crouched behind a table, ready to spring out and seize her. But the room was still, empty.

No time to stop. She checked the scullery, the pantry. Into the silver room. Just the need to see it done, to do it. Cissie; Josephine; Aubrey. All these people he had hurt or would hurt. If she paused she would quaver. There was only his quarters left, but would he really be waiting there, when Rex had left so recently? What if Rex had returned; what if it had been nothing but a ruse? She opened Crawford's door, crossed the room in two steps, her shoulder angled back. She held the knife high.

Was it the stuttering of breath that caught her by surprise, the wet suck of air? The sudden scent of the room, its hard iron edge? Something was out of joint. The sheets were dark, wet. Blood? She tried to gather the worn edges of her thoughts, tried to raise her hand again. But the knife clattered to the floor. She let out a cry, half whimper, half fury.

'Bonnie?'

His voice was frail, plaintive. He was not in the bed at all. She spun round, struggling to make out a shape in the corner.

'Bonnie,' he said again, but quietly, as though it was difficult to speak.

She scrabbled on the floor for the knife, gripped it again. This time her hand was shaking and she could scarcely hold it. 'I'll kill you,' she said. 'I'll – I'll kill you if you come near me.'

But her words felt clumsy, too big for her, like a little girl playing a silly game.

'You're too late for that.' Each word, dredged from deep within him, spoken with effort. A short rush of breath like a laugh. 'He's fled. Another dog's left me.'

So it was not a trick; so Rex was truly gone.

'But he—' he stopped, coughed. 'I – I – It—' A gurgle.

'Crawford,' she said, kneeling beside him, touching his cheek, raising his head upwards from its slump. More panicked now. 'Crawford.'

After all this, Rex had killed him; Rex, who had grown tired of being kicked. Bonnie had done nothing. She felt the slow seep of her own impotence, her rage building inside her once more, nowhere to go. To have this snatched away from her, this final squaring; it was not fair. She would have done it, she repeated to herself. She would have.

He turned his head to hers, his black eyes shining. 'You left me, Bonnie.' He spluttered. A liquid blackness fell from his lips. 'I was going to make you queen of this house. A palazzo. A talking parrot.' He leaned forwards, closer to her, close enough that he might kiss her.

Everything in her recoiled; a sour taste rose in her mouth. Her knees were warm from his blood, pooling on the floor, coal-black in the moonlight.

'You wanted it for yourself, not me,' she said. 'You always wanted everything for yourself.'

'I won't die, will I?' There was an odd pitch in his voice. He tried to raise himself but fell back. 'Tell – me – I – won't.'

'Oh, but you will. And nobody will remember you.'

A cry broke from him. Bonnie did not speak again. She would sit with him. She would sit and wait for him to die, to know that the last of him had faded away and he could not hurt anybody else. His breaths grew ragged and catching. Josephine, dragged under the water; Cissie, rammed against the wall of the kitchen. All the things he would still do, if he could.

And yet.

Before she knew it, she found herself making small hushing sounds as a mother might calm a baby.

Shhh, she said, *shh*, as he coughed and spluttered.

Shhh, she said again, and his breaths thinned until they stopped altogether, his head slumped forwards against his chest.

Catacombs

Bonnie stood in the kitchen, her hands pressed against the table, her head bowed. The shake in her legs would not subside. Crawford was dead. In the morning, Jane and Sara would return and find him blood-soaked, their distress echoing through the hallways. The house would be flung into panic, footsteps beating through Endellion, a hush descending. Men would be summoned, investigations begun. It would be clear, surely, where the finger pointed and if it wasn't, couldn't Bonnie guide it?

Rex.

Rex, who had fled in the night. Rex, who Crawford had failed to keep close to him, who had turned on him at last like a dog attacking its master. By the time Sara and Jane raised the cry, Rex would be long gone, lost in the warren of St Giles or another city altogether – stowed in a ship to Paris or Rome or Istanbul. He would go to ground.

It seemed so easy, all the corners tucked in. A man's death, so neatly explained. Bonnie's palms pressed down harder on the table. She could go to bed and forget what she had found; she need do nothing more. How much she wanted that. How much she craved it.

But she knew that no plan was watertight. Crawford of all people might have taught her that. His mistake had been to see people like faceless little pawns he might move about at will. And she knew, her jaw tightening, that Rex didn't have Crawford's steady mind, his nerve. Perhaps he would be seen on the road or at an inn. His size and heft made him distinctive. It would take just one passerby and he would be convicted, likely hanged. But it would not be a clean silencing. Rex did not care for her. He would have nothing left to gain and he would spill everything Bonnie had plotted and done, his words spreading like spores. And what of Annette, if she heard about Crawford's murder; what of Manton? Would they come forward, perhaps even implicate her, their resentment mounting after being cast out?

Bonnie pressed harder against the table. The pain was almost pleasing. No. It needed to be different.

It would be bright outside when Jane and Sara returned from visiting their families. They would light the stoves, heat a pan of hot milk for Cissie. Their gentle chatter would spread through the house. At some point, they might go to Crawford's quarters to turn down his bed.

They would find a clean room, the bedsheets missing, pale light at the window. His clothes would be gone too, the room stripped of anything familiar. 'What's this?' Sara might say. 'Has he left?' They would find Rex's narrow room empty too. Perhaps Jane would suddenly remember that she saw the stable door was open when they walked down the avenue.

And there it would be: a different story with different surmising. Men would not storm this house, picking through it like beetles in rotting wood. There'd be no murder, no hunt. Rex and Crawford would simply have slipped away into the dark. Easily rubbed out, forgotten. Bonnie's life would be her own, mistress of Endellion, wife of Aubrey Moncrieff.

Bonnie had hours until the sun lightened. The house was empty except for Cissie. It was just like when she first came to

Endellion. She knew how to remove the traces of a person. The dirt and grime that a human leaves behind: dropped hairs, the sweat ground into a sheet or shift. She simply had to wipe Crawford clean from the house, as though he had only sauntered away and clicked his fingers for a horse.

There was a barrow outside the kitchen that Jane used to gather vegetables from the garden. Bonnie heaved Crawford across the tiles. The lolling weight of him was shocking, her hands and gown soon slippery with blood. He left a dark trail behind him like a snail. She would come back and mop the floors later.

She hauled the body out through the kitchen door, lugging him into the barrow. Thank goodness there were no steps. Gravel snagged under the wheels until it was as difficult as pushing a sledge. Bonnie grunted, struggled. The sooner she was on the compacted earth of the avenue the better. Crawford's arms hung loose, his head nodding forwards, jolting with each step as though in silent agreement with what she was doing. It was not Crawford, Bonnie told herself; this husk where a person had once been. All his spirit emptied out, all the plots he had laid so carefully, simply gone. She gripped the arms of the barrow, pushed forwards with all her weight.

It grew easier at the lime trees, just a case of missing the potholes. Branches shivered in the wind, a light rain spitting against Bonnie's cheeks. The back gate to the cemetery was ajar. In the darkness, it was difficult to make out the gravel paths, the tall cypresses, but this was ground she knew, that she had planned.

Almost there; just a slight hill. The paths had never felt so long, so sprawling. The spire of the chapel shone in the rain. On she heaved him. Drizzle stung her cheeks, a dull throbbing pain in her arms and spine. These things she could bear. Soon this would be nothing but a memory, a thing done and closed off.

At last, there it was: the sunken entrance to the catacombs, its wide staircase, an angel carved into the stone above it. The entranceway gaped like a mouth, the gates not yet in place. She had no choice but to drag him down the steps, each soft thump running through her. Inside, the gallery stretched in both directions, the moon just visible through an iron grating. The apertures were small and square, as long as humans. Coffins would be slid onto these shelves like loaves in an oven.

Bonnie had thought she might be able to lift Crawford onto one of the higher shelves, but it was all she could do to heave him across the ground. She chose one of the furthest catacombs, angled his head inside. What now? The brickwork was rough and snagging; a body was not like a wooden coffin that would glide in easily. She tried to shimmy him in. It was no good. It was only when she lay on the ground, her hands on his legs, her own feet pressed against the wall opposite, that he juddered forward. She panted, breathless. A little more; a little more. It was enough, finally, if she folded his legs and made him fit.

Her body ached, a staccato quiver setting up behind her right eyelid. She wheeled the barrow to the yard – how light it was without a person inside! – and selected a sealing stone, hefting it in, lifting the barrow once more. Carefully, arms straining, a ticking in her neck, she carried it down the steps, along the corridor. It was almost done. The stone fitted into the aperture like the last piece of a puzzle.

She bumped the wheelbarrow back up the steps, noticing a trail of blood. On the pathways, it would sink into the dark gravel, but here the stone was so fresh. A few labourers' buckets were gathered by the entrance, half-full of rainwater, and she lifted them, sluicing the blood away, watching as it disappeared into the porous brick at the bottom of the steps. She sat down heavily. Her head slumped forward. She was so tired. Her back stung and ached. The scent of his blood seemed to have worked its way into her skin like oil.

In a moment, Bonnie would rise. She would let herself into the sexton's lodge and prise his leather-bound book from the wall. Cemetery map, order book, register. She would add a new name. Agnes Trimble, charges paid, the catacomb closed off. A concocted person, one that Crawford himself had invented. And then she would return to the house, scour the kitchen floor and Crawford's quarters. She would lift the loose floorboard and place Aubrey's gun back in its cabinet, and then she would clean the blood from her arms, her face, her hands. Her dress and Crawford's possessions and bedclothes would form a single bundle. She would take them to the river in a sack of stones. Soon he would be wiped out, traceless.

But for a little while, she would rest. She sat under the saplings that would arch and grow into great cypresses and yews and cedars, that would knot their roots beneath the bricks of these catacombs.

She had done it. Her heart sang in her chest. Rain dappled her skin. Endellion was in the distance. *Hers.* In the moment before Bonnie stood, she thought she caught the flicker of a white shape, flitting between the trees. It was nothing, she told herself. It was simply the wind, a fox. It was simply her imagination, not a ghost, not Josephine running across the grass, her spirit lifted at last.

Fled

The morning happened almost as Bonnie had planned it. Sara and Jane arrived early, the sound of singing and laughter filling the house. Bonnie waited upstairs, her hands never settling, lifting a bottle, replacing it. She opened cupboards, stared at the clothes blankly. She smeared ointment into her cheeks then rubbed it off. The bruise on her throat was like a necklace.

The only detail that diverged from Bonnie's plan was that Sara and Jane had taken the towpath from Richmond. The missing horse was undiscovered; so, too, did they leave Rex and Crawford's quarters unchecked. Aubrey would notice the open stable door when he returned, Bonnie thought, pacing the hallway. And then everything would finally begin to move forward, conclusions drawn, everything settled. At last, just after ten o'clock, she saw his carriage, and she waited in the entrance hall.

'An utter waste of time,' he said, pulling off his gloves. 'Can you believe it? The man denied ever writing a letter! And I was too late to return last night.' He took in Bonnie for the first time, his mouth falling open. 'Good God, what happened? Have you called the doctor? Your eyes are bloodshot—'

'I fell,' Bonnie said. 'I – I lost my balance on the stairs. It looks worse than it is.'

'Does it hurt?'

She ran her hand across his back. 'I think I stand a good chance of recovery. If you are especially doting.'

He kissed her. His lips were soft and full. 'I've missed you.' He drew back for a moment. 'Have you exercised the horses this morning?'

Bonnie forced herself to look puzzled. 'No?'

'Peculiar,' he said, reaching for his coat once more. 'The stable doors were open. I'll see that there's nothing out of place.'

She watched him go, heard the crump of his boots on the gravel as he rounded the building. Bonnie knitted her hands together. She would act composed, surprised. She would answer Aubrey as smoothly as Crawford would have done.

When Aubrey returned, Bonnie pretended to be busy lifting a vase from the sideboard.

'Boudicca's gone.'

Bonnie arranged her expression into surprise. The china clinked as she replaced the vase. 'Boudicca? How?'

'I don't know.'

'She must have escaped like last time.' Bonnie heard the creak in her voice like a bad Drury Lane actress.

'And saddled herself and unlocked the doors herself? No. The stable boy was adamant he shut her in properly this time. This is the work of thieves. Where the devil is Rex? I'll see if he's noticed anything amiss.'

Bonnie tried to look puzzled. It was all working. It was all fitting into place. 'But I haven't seen him all morning.'

'What? Not at all? What's he been doing? This is the final straw – you'd think the man had never set foot in a house like this before.'

'And Crawford hasn't risen either.'

Aubrey ran his hand over his chin. 'Sometimes he sleeps late.'

Bonnie cast down her eyes. 'I'm afraid to say – we quarrelled last night. I told him that it wasn't right for him to stay here any longer. He and Rex have grown so close lately. They – I'm afraid to say, I think they were very drunk last night.'

Aubrey nodded. 'I'll have a word with Rex about it. It isn't on. I'll see he isn't still in bed. And if Rex has left Sara and Jane to do his chores again—'

They took the steps together. The kitchen looked so ordinary in the daylight. Jane and Sara were folding a sheet. The ewer was on the table, the floors scrubbed and polished. Pristine, faultless. It was unbelievable to see it. Aubrey knocked on Crawford's door. No answer.

As the door creaked open and Aubrey peered inside, Bonnie half-expected Crawford still to be there, slumped against the wall, his joints stiff, that awful slack-jawed expression on his face. But the room was just as she'd left it: the bed stripped and waiting, the cupboards empty.

Aubrey turned to her. 'By God,' he said. 'I think they've gone. They've taken the horse and gone.'

Consecration

The morning of the cemetery consecration dawned bright, the lawns and woodlands steaming in the early spring sunshine. Bonnie leaned her forehead against the windowpane, half-listening to Jane chattering as she curled Cissie's hair. The shock of the condensation against her skin was a relief, her hands tight and clammy, sweat circles already gathering under her armpits.

'Italy will be as hot as an oven, will it not? And what fine places will you visit?' Jane asked, but Bonnie barely listened. She was not thinking about Rome at all. Out there, behind that tall wall, the cemetery waited, the new stones of the chapel and the mausoleum and the catacombs flashing in the sun. Soon they would walk down its paths and take their seats in the front pews of the chapel, investors and local clergy turning as they entered. All they had planned would be made real. The stained-glass windows would dapple their cheeks, the Bible gleaming on the lectern, the bier empty and waiting for its first body. Aubrey would present the Lord Bishop of Winchester with a petition and the plans of the cemetery, requesting consecration. Formalities, all of it, because of course the bishop would bow his head and submit. It would all be done, sealed, finished.

'I should think Papa will take us to the Caffè degli Inglesi,' Cissie said, frowning. 'Emmeline told me it makes sweet orange drinks and *everyone* is seen there. If we *can* be seen, that is. Or—'

'And then?' Jane prompted.

Cissie's voice was strained, nervous. 'And then Papa will tire us out with his endless prattle about Wyatt's designs for the Pantheon. And it will be a lark, won't it? It will all be just as we hoped?'

Bonnie felt a twinge just below her clavicle: these calm, glossy stories masking the turmoil beneath them. Cissie's belly would swell in Rome and after only a few weeks they would need to remove themselves to a quiet villa in the countryside where she might pass her final months undetected. There would be no stopping what had already begun.

'And Papa will – he will be just like himself again, won't he?'

Bonnie left the window, kissed Cissie's cheek. 'Of course. Your Papa just – he worries for you.'

Bonnie had told Aubrey the afternoon after he had returned from London and found Rex and Crawford had gone. She had stood at his study door and flung the words at him, frightened that if she waited, she wouldn't say anything. *Cissie is with child.* Four words, as sharp as the rattle of a gun. But Aubrey had not seemed to grasp what she meant at first, his pen hovering over the page.

'Cissie is a child?' he repeated simply, as though his ears had chosen what he wanted to hear. His lip trembled, a paleness in his cheek. 'That is what you said, wasn't it? Tell me, it's what you said—'

Bonnie went to him, clasped his hand. She expected fury, a trembling rage that would split the house in two. Papers thrown against the wall, proclamations. But of course, that was not Aubrey. He simply began to cry. Big, childish sobs that seemed dredged from within him, a sight far worse than anger. 'I – have

– failed – her,' he said, again and again. He looked up. 'Who? How?'

Bonnie broke then, tears edging from her eyes. For all she had been unable to prevent, for all the wickedness she had helped to nurture in this house. She had not understood; she had not known.

'Who?' he had demanded, but then he had sunk back. 'No,' he murmured. 'Pray God, no.' He let out a cry, burying his head in his hands.

'He is not my brother,' Bonnie whispered, an urgency in her voice. 'He is not. I would have killed him if I could have.'

The truth felt freeing, but she knew that Aubrey would think she meant she had severed the connection in her mind, that Crawford was as good as dead to her.

'Oh, but if you could see Cissie. She is very distressed,' Bonnie said, wiping her cheeks. 'She is not to blame. You must see that.'

Aubrey picked up his pen, pressed it against the page. Ink bloomed in a dark wet circle. 'Please. I want to be alone. I cannot see her yet, cannot face what was done to her. I know it's cowardly. But – please. I just – I can't.'

He had sealed himself in his study all day, Jane and Sara bringing him scones and a bowl of stew that he left cooling outside his door. Sometimes Bonnie let herself in but he did not even look up, his head bowed over furious sketches. When she drew closer, she saw that his hand was moving in ragged squares, but there was no ink in his pen. A day passed, another. Correspondence mounted. At last, Bonnie went in and rested her hand on his shoulder. 'Aubrey?' she said. 'Aubrey, we need to talk about what we will do.' She touched his fingers, stilling that endless motion.

'What we will do about what?'

'The – the child.'

He lowered his head. 'Her mother would never forgive me for what I have allowed to happen.'

'You aren't the only person who ought to have protected her, Aubrey. You shouldn't take this all on your shoulders. He was a wicked, wicked man. He deceived us all.'

Silence fell. He dropped his pen.

'I thought,' Bonnie began, quiet, cautious. 'I thought that we might go to Italy after the cemetery opens, as we planned. We could find a villa near Rome and stay there all summer, the three of us.'

He looked up at her. 'You mean—'

'We – we have wanted it, haven't we? A child. I know you have too. Nobody would suspect.'

He lowered his head, his fingers finding his pen again, his sketches resuming, the nib pressing so hard it tore through the paper. Bonnie left him, closing the door softly. That need, that ache, lodged itself like a splinter within her. To press a tiny, mewling baby to her chest, to quiet its cries. To lessen the harm that was done to Cissie, in whatever small way she could. She found Cissie waiting in the hallway, her face full of questions she dared not express. *What did he say? Did he agree?*

'He will, I think,' Bonnie said. 'He will, in time.'

Cissie's smile was tentative, a sudden gleam in her cheeks. And a brightness spread through Bonnie, as though the whole world was opening like a bud.

It was mid-afternoon when the ceremony finished, the bishop's prayers ringing through the chapel. *The foolish and the senseless alike perish and leave their wealth to others —*

Aubrey's leg hopped, his hands reaching for hers. Crawford

was gone, she thought. He was gone. But the afternoon was not over. Rain clouds massed and fell away as though the day also did not know what it was supposed to be. The congregation fidgeted, caught between restraint and pleasure. A cemetery was a sombre place but its completion was a triumph. So too was it a day of grief: a woman would be laid to rest, two and a half years after she had drowned.

They processed outside, silent except for the rustling of coats and gowns. Some of the labourers had brought their families, and Bonnie watched them milling around in their best Sunday clothes, pride beaming from them as they held out their fingers, mimed winches, pulleys. All the work they had done, all the hands that had made it possible.

The sun shone again; Bonnie shielded her eyes. The fresh stones of the chapel were blinding, so incongruous with the old Gothic design, as though the building had just been unpacked from a box. The sheen of the new was everywhere, in the crisply raked gravel, in the piercing white of the stones lining the pathways, the bevelling marks of the mason's chisel still clean and sharp. Even the grass was so green it looked painted. What would be here, Bonnie wondered, in a hundred, two hundred years' time? Aubrey's plans would be gathering dust in a library somewhere, her own planting ideas likely discarded decades before. Perhaps the cemetery would be overgrown, abandoned; and did it matter as long as it remained a place of beauty and remembrance?

Cissie took her arm. 'That MP smells like old vegetables,' she whispered, pointing at Mr Lyle. 'Quick, before he comes over.' They began to stroll through the grounds, a little girl chasing a hoop behind them. Soon Josephine's hearse would roll down the carriageway.

There were five snaking paths they might have taken, and

yet it felt almost inevitable that they walked the way they did, as though an invisible string was winching Bonnie back to what she had done. The catacombs loomed ahead of them: the stone circle, the wide steps to the locked gates.

Crawford was down those steps, tucked into one of the cells. Nobody had noticed that there was one stone pressed carefully into place. Probably they never would. When other bodies joined him there, it would cease to be remarkable. Three weeks had passed since that night. What happened to a person in that time? Beetles would be making a meal of him. His blood would have pooled purple in his back, his thighs.

Bonnie made to move away, but Cissie stayed still, staring down the steps.

'Come,' Bonnie said, gently, but Cissie didn't give any indication she had heard.

It was the quickest of glances, a brief incline of Cissie's head. Her eyes met Bonnie's for a fraction. But in that moment, the sky seemed to see-saw, the great blue bowl tipping itself over. Bonnie stood still, stiff.

The knife that Cissie had used to hurt herself. Bonnie tried to remember: had she taken it away? She recalled, too, the determination that had gripped the girl, her eyes narrowed after Bonnie had spoken to her. *A heroine changes her fortune.* Bonnie thought of the creaks that she had heard that night, sounds that she could not be sure were real or imagined. The ghost she thought she had seen in the cemetery: had it been Cissie, following her, understanding that her own crime was brushed away, taken care of?

A magpie chattered; the girl with the hoop had caught them up. Only a few seconds had passed since Cissie had smiled at Bonnie. Bonnie dared a glance. The girl's jaw was set. Another beat passed. Bonnie took a breath.

'Shall we walk?' she asked.

Cissie took her arm and the two women moved on.

It was a grand affair. Aubrey had spared no expense. Josephine's shining hearse would be the first to enter the gates, pulled by eight black horses, ostrich feathers fluttering in the breeze. The coachman idled his whip on the mares' backs, his face drawn in practised grief. The crowds fell silent. Hats were doffed. They followed the horses in silence, Cissie walking between Aubrey and Bonnie, the paths narrowing to the quiet corner at the back. The doors of the mausoleum were ajar, waiting to greet her. The peculiarly grand little house was just as Aubrey had drawn it all that time ago: fluted columns, twin pinnacles, and a cross adorned with carved artichoke flowers.

Aubrey stepped forward to help lift the coffin. It was as new as the cemetery itself, the wood gleaming, silver handles catching the sunlight. Her old coffin would have been discarded, chopped up and burned. The muscles at the back of Aubrey's neck tensed. Bonnie wanted to say something in comfort, but the moment drifted away, and the bishop cleared his throat.

More prayers were spoken, each a little vague and florid, but it did not matter, because what mattered was this: the doors of the mausoleum opening fully, the coffin being laid to rest inside. A burial befitting Josephine Moncrieff.

This great garden of sleep is sublime indeed, the sort of place I long to rest when I am called to join the choir invisible —

All these metaphors for death. Called home, passed away, a lily cut down. As though death was sedate, like sitting down for tea, not a man gasping as he lay on the floor, choking on his own blood. Not a woman, dragged beneath the surface of the water, fighting, clawing, held there. No: it was a restful end, lilies plaited in hair, cold hands folded in prayer. Death dressed up and made palatable.

At last it was done, and Aubrey took a step back and held Bonnie's arm.

'All of this, for her,' Bonnie whispered, and he looked at her and kissed her cheek.

Just before the doors were closed and locked, Cissie stepped forwards, clutching a bunch of lilies. Her steps were quiet, careful, and when she had laid them down, Aubrey held out his arms. The girl nestled into them, her eyes squeezed shut. Bonnie broke away, not wanting to intrude.

'It must be difficult,' Mr Lyle's wife whispered to Bonnie, 'knowing he loved another. That he still respects her like this.'

The woman waited, her head cocked, perhaps hoping a confidence might pass between them, a jealousy uttered. It surprised Bonnie that she was expected to feel this way. That she would ever have cause to doubt Aubrey's affection for her, or that she would ever feel anything except sadness for what had been taken from Josephine. 'No,' she said, watching the woman's mouth snap shut in disappointment. 'I couldn't be happier she has this at last.'

As the crowds dispersed, Bonnie linked her arm through Aubrey's. It was miraculous that they had raised a mark on a paper to this: a great mausoleum, a way of marking the importance of a person. And more than that: there was a whole cemetery waiting for other families to feel that same comfort mingling with their grief. They would all know that the person they loved was safe and undisturbed.

Above the cemetery wall, she could glimpse the top half of Endellion, white and shining in the sunshine. Its arched windows surveying the land, its turrets and crenelated roof holding firm. She raised her hand to it, a half salute.

'Good God.'

A gentleman was staring at Bonnie. She blinked, wondering if she had met him at the hunt, if he was someone she was supposed to recognize.

He laughed. 'You look – by God!' he said.

'She looks like what?' Aubrey asked, faintly amused.

Bonnie prickled at the way his small eyes roved over her, drinking her in. She could not explain why but a light panic began flickering in her chest.

'I could stake my life on it.'

'On what, sir?' Aubrey asked.

'You look just like a girl I once met,' he said. '*Met* – ha! Was robbed by. This girl, she led me a merry dance, and then a man she claimed was her brother set upon me.'

A cooling in Bonnie's belly, her heart percussive, quickening. She bit the inside of her cheek. She would make herself equal to this: she could be equal to any of them. She would not be undone at the last. She was about to speak when Aubrey took her by the arm and steered her away. Somehow, she managed to lift her feet and move on. Her insides felt weighted, a queasiness rising in her gut.

'What a piece of madness,' she said. Her laugh was brittle, almost hollow.

A peewit trilled above them. She stole a quick glance at Aubrey. He was staring straight ahead. A second flickered past. And then he smiled and squeezed her hand.

'What a piece of madness,' he agreed.

Author's Note

The cemetery at Endellion is entirely fictional, as is the house itself, which I have imagined on a site between Orleans House and Marble Hill House. However, the house is loosely based on the nearby Strawberry Hill House, Horace Walpole's mock-Gothic mansion.

Acknowledgements

I am very fortunate to work with three of the most exceptional women in the industry. My editor Sophie Jonathan: you are a gift. Your ability to see to the heart of a first draft is nothing short of extraordinary and it is a joy to collaborate with you. Camilla Elworthy: one of the best things about finishing a novel is knowing that we have several road trips ahead of us. You have been a real friend from the very start; thank you. And to my agent Maddy Milburn: I am so grateful for the day I entered the Caledonia Novel Award and met you through it.

A big thank you to Elle Gibbons for all of the brilliant marketing; and to Nicholas Blake, Daisy Dickeson, Mary Mount, Sara Lloyd and everyone else at Picador; and the team at Madeleine Milburn Literary Agency. I appreciate all you have done to support me and my books. The covers, marketing, copy edits, sales, admin, publicity, foreign rights and TV. It has been a real privilege to work with all of you.

To readers, bloggers and booksellers, for all you have done to support my books. A particular thank you to Simon Savidge for our walk in Abney Park Cemetery, back when I was pinning down the plot for this book.

Many friends kept me going during the difficult early drafts of this novel, in particular Lucy Clarke, Nayela Wickramasuriya, Phoebe Lee and Elizabeth Wignall. I have also cherished the encouragement and friendship of a group of writers with young children: thank you to Rachelle Atalla, Jessie Burton, Sophie Cameron, Imogen Hermes Gowar, Daisy Johnson, Hannah Kent, Kirsty Logan, Kiran Millwood Hargrave, Anbara Salam, Nell Stevens and Francine Toon.

Mum and Dad: parenting and writing hasn't always been an easy juggle and your support, both practical and emotional, has made it feel possible. I know how lucky I am. May my son always be returned to me in a sea of croissant crumbs, Dad; and covered in mud and river water, Mum. Thanks also to my siblings, Peter, Hector and Laura; and to my Aunty Dinah.

I began this novel in earnest when I was pregnant with my son. I am finishing it a week before my daughter is born. My wonderful babies: thank you for keeping me company during the creation of this book. And to my husband, J: I always promised that I'd dedicate this novel to you, and I hope you don't mind sharing it. Thank you for all you do for us.